I0760260

BORN OF FIRE

AN ELEMENTAL ORIGINS NOVEL: 5TH ANNIVERSARY EDITION

A.L. KNORR

Edited by

THERESA HULL

PROLOGUE

Nicodemo steadied the tripod and made a few last adjustments to the sound on the camera phone. He pressed play and then walked to the chair sitting in the line of focus. He sat down and scratched his head, ruffling his thin blond hair. Age had thinned his hair, thinned his power. But it hadn't thinned his determination or the strength of his love.

He still wasn't used to being on camera and felt self-conscious. He mused at the irony that he had committed many dangerous acts of questionable morality and a few for which he deserved eternal damnation, but stick him in front of a camera and his palms went all sweaty.

He cleared his throat and began to speak in Italian, his voice calm and warm. He reminded himself that more than likely, this video would never need to surface. It was a safeguard just in case... He pushed the rest of the thought aside. He didn't want to think of the 'in case.'

It took less than three minutes to record the final clip of the series. He leaned forward and stopped the recording. He watched the clip and gave a satisfied smile that although it was a first take, it was good enough. It didn't need to be perfect. He took a deep breath and hung his head for a moment. He closed his eyes and the movie screen of his mind filled with her loving face. His heart thudded painfully. He opened his eyes and shook the vision off.

He booted up his laptop and downloaded the video clip, encrypting it and putting it into a zip file with all the rest. He sent the file off to his lawyer with the simple subject line: *Last one. Thank you, again. Nic.*

A knock on the door of the small stone cell made him turn. The smooth, beardless face of Dante poked in. Nic remembered being Dante's age. The world had been full of possibilities, ripe for the taking. Now, Nic knew better.

"There you are," Dante said, speaking in Italian, their mother tongue. "You haven't chickened out, have you?"

Nicodemo allowed the teenager a smile. "No. Have you?"

Dante opened the door all the way and stepped in, excitement visible in his face and body. "No way." His eyes fell to the tripod and then to the laptop. "What are you doing? Recording your memoirs? You're going to be fine. I won't let anything happen to you."

Nicodemo ignored the question and powered down his computer. "You know your father would probably fire me, no pun intended, and lock you in your room forever if he knew what we were up to."

"By the time he finds out, it'll all be over and he'll be grateful. You'll be stronger than ever and you won't have to feel the pain ever again."

Nicodemo sighed. That was the theory of it. The risk he was taking would be worthwhile. But the pain... Would he be able to stand the pain? He turned his eyes on the boy. He was trusting his life to Dante. There was no one else he could ask, no one else who would let him risk his life like this.

Dante was very nearly dancing from foot to foot in anticipation. Nicodemo tried not to hold it against the kid that he was so excited to watch Nic endure hours of agony. Once it was all over, he was going to owe Dante big time for pulling him back from the fires of hell.

"Should we go over it one more time?" Nicodemo asked as he took the tripod apart and tucked it and the laptop into its leather case.

"Nic, we've been over it a dozen times already," Dante replied. "No one is home today; the villa is empty. It's the perfect time. Everything will be all right."

Nicodemo nodded and put the chair against the wall. He handed the laptop bag to Dante. "Put this in my suite, would you?"

"Of course." Dante took the case.

The two left the cell together, heading down the long dark hallway. The stone floor turned to earth and the ceilings lowered. They took three steps down into a cold, dank hallway which brought them to another darker, much more medieval cell. The wall outside the cell was lined with buckets of water. Nicodemo eyed them grimly.

The entry to the cell was so low they had to crouch to go through it. The metal door gave a grating scream as Nicodemo pushed it open and stepped through. He stood up inside the dark cell. It smelled like old urine and moldy earth. He looked at the tempered steel door.

Dante set the case against the wall outside the door, came through behind him and noticed him eyeballing the metal. "What? You don't think it will hold you?"

"Doesn't matter. I don't plan on fighting it."

He scanned the dingy cell. His eyes fell on a fluffy white pillow lying on the wooden platform which served as a bed. He picked it up and sniffed it. Lavender. He raised his eyebrows at Dante.

"What? I'm only thinking of you. It stinks in here." Dante shrugged.

Dante took Nicodemo by the shoulders, startling the older man. Dante fiercely kissed first his right cheek, then his left. "I'm proud of you." He took a stopwatch out of his pocket and showed it to Nic. "Sixteen hours, on the mark. I'll be back to check on you."

Nicodemo nodded. "Let's just get this over with."

PART ONE

ONE

I closed my eyes, leaned my head against the plane window, and let out a big sigh. We were airborne. It was the end of a week of hell and I couldn't be happier to leave my life behind.

"That sounded awfully serious coming from someone so young," said the lady beside me. "First time on a plane?"

I turned to look at my seat mate. The woman had super short gray hair and was peering at me from over her glasses. She had a book open on her lap. Her expression exuded maternal warmth.

"First time going trans-Atlantic. It's not the flight, though."

"No?"

"Careful, if you get me talking, I might not shut up." I turned back to the window, my warped reflection mirrored my movement. "I talk too much. Or so I'm told."

The lady was silent for a moment. "We've got a long flight ahead of us. Why are you headed to Venice?"

"I got an au pair position. Two little boys. I'll be there all summer."

"Well," she said, her eyebrows jacking up her face. "That sounds like the perfect experience for someone your age."

"Yeah, I'm super excited about it."

"Then why so glum?"

I chewed my lip. Shame heated my cheeks and to my dismay, tears pricked behind my eyelids. What was it about a kind stranger that made me want to dump out all my problems?

"I screwed up."

"How very human of you."

"But, I hate being a stereotype," I blurted.

"You're a stereotype?"

I tugged on the end of my fiery red ponytail. "I'm a redhead."

"And?"

"And, I have a temper. I'm a redhead, with a temper. Do you think that it's true? That red hair comes with a temper?"

"Well, they say stereotypes exist for a reason, that there's always a thread of truth in them. A hair, if you will." She waggled her eyebrows.

"Very punny."

"Thank you. But no, I think we've all got a temper somewhere under the surface. Maybe it's harder for some of us to control, but that just comes with practice. And breathing." She held up a manicured finger. "Breathing helps a lot." She closed her book and tucked it into the seat pocket in front of her. "What was this horrifying screw-up?"

I twisted my headphone cord around my thumb. "I have two brothers. R.J. and Jack. Normally, we get along pretty good. But Jack—the younger one—he was pushing my buttons all week. He broke the clasp on my luggage, dropped chocolate on the couch which I then sat in and stained my favorite jeans. Then he hid my passport and laughed while I tore my hair out looking for it for three days."

"How frustrating."

I nodded. "Seriously. So three nights ago, after dinner, Dad told Jack it was his turn to do the dishes, but he went to play video games instead. I didn't notice at first because I went to pack. But then I came into the kitchen and everything was still a mess. My mom had gone to bed with a headache and Dad was in the garage with R.J. I lost it. I was already so fed up that I just blew up." I paused, my heart pounding as I relived the moment.

"What did you do?"

"I barged into his room and..." I took a breath and put my hands to my cheeks. My face felt like it was burning up. My voice hitched. "I kicked his controller out of his hands and grabbed the back of his neck, pretty hard. I picked him up and shoved him toward the door, yelling at him to pull his weight." I stopped and closed my eyes against the awful memory of what came next.

The lady waited in silence.

"I didn't mean to..." I cleared my throat. "He slipped on some paper. His room is always such a disaster. He fell. I mean, we both fell. But he hit the doorjamb. The sound of it... the crack..." I shuddered.

"Was he okay?"

"He hit it with his face."

She grimaced.

"He bit through his bottom lip, chipped his front tooth, and got a black eye." I rubbed my face, trying to wipe away the memory. "There was a lot of blood. I thought I was going to be sick. Not from the blood, well maybe partly, but I just..."

"You felt horrible."

I nodded and looked out the window into the black nothing. "I still do. My parents hit the roof. They told me I had to cancel Venice."

"But, you're here. So what happened?"

I turned back to her kind face. "Jack. He can be a real brat, but he's also one of the most forgiving people I know. He knew I was sorry. I didn't eat for two days. He got my parents to change their minds. He even owned up to terrorizing me earlier in the week."

"Sounds like a good kid."

"Yeah, he is. Better than me."

"I'm sure that's not true."

"How good can I be if I can't rein in my temper and I end up hurting people?"

"Well, Jack forgives you. Sounds like your parents do, too. Why not forgive yourself. Wipe the slate clean, and use this summer to figure yourself out? You're an au pair, now. What a perfect opportunity to practice patience and control, right?"

"Right." In theory.

"Put the past behind you. Learn from it, and move forward. We all make mistakes. Resolve to be better."

My stomach clenched at the memory of Jack's bloody face. I crossed my arms and blew out a breath. "I will."

SIX-YEAR-OLD BOYS WERE NOT SUPPOSED to look like they were four. They were not supposed to have pain-filled eyes. They were not supposed to have dry, pale skin. They were not supposed to have thinning hair or bald patches, limp limbs and a protruding spine. They were not supposed to have purple smudges under their eyes. Isaia had all of these things. I'm no expert, but I knew enough to spot a sick kid when I see one, and Isaia was one sick kid.

My stomach had yet to settle fully and my eyes felt full of sand, but the jet-lag fell away as Isaia approached, carried like a toddler in his father's arms. My mind flashed back to the welcome letter I'd received about my host family and their sons. *Cristiano Baseggio, nine, a soccer fiend with a talent for mathematics. Isaia Baseggio, six, a sweet, shy kid with a fondness for bedtime stories and Lego.* Definitely no mention of illness. Why hadn't they told me that one of the kids in my care for the summer wasn't well?

My indignation went up in smoke when Isaia turned and his eyes caught mine. My breath hitched as our gazes locked. His eyes were black as coal and grabbed me as fiercely as two desperate fists at my collar.

Pietro's head bent toward Isaia and he kissed his son's patchy blond crown. The tender love the father expressed was heart-meltingly beautiful.

"Sweetheart, can you greet your au pair?" His mother, Elda, sat beside me on their couch. She had a soft accent, an even softer voice, and tired eyes.

Isaia—whose gaze had not unlocked from mine—held out a hand toward me. He leaned out of his father's arms. "Madonna," said Pietro, when he realized that his son was reaching for me.

As a reflex, I held out my arms and the boy leaned so far that Pietro had no choice but to hand him to me. My heart puddled as the tiny, warm frame settled into my lap. He put his head against my shoulder the way it had been against Pietro's, and his small hand touched my cheek before he tucked it under his chin.

My heart pounded. "Hello, Isaia," I said quietly, feeling anything but quiet inside. Questions flooded my brain, but for once they jammed up behind my teeth instead of leaping out of my mouth. Goosebumps swept my forearms. Isaia was hot and limp in my arms, like a warm sack of bones.

Elda and Pietro's faces were slack with shock. Elda had a palm on either side of her face, the whites of her eyes visible.

I looked from one to the other. "Does he do this with everyone?"

"On the contrary," said Elda. "He doesn't let anyone touch him aside from family." She spoke to Pietro in awed Italian and he sat down on the stool beside her and spoke back, sounding just as amazed.

Isaia looked up at me and the suffering in his black eyes clamped like a vise around my heart. My throat constricted. What was he suffering from? Why had he reached for me? A stranger. And what had this little guy done to me? I had never had an attachment to a child form so quickly before. Emotion roiled under the surface and I worked to swallow it down. I was probably just exhausted and jet-lagged, just overreacting. I realized Elda and Pietro were staring. The silence in the room felt crushing.

"I think we're going to get along just fine, don't you?" I asked Isaia.

Elda cleared her throat awkwardly and I looked up.

"Isaia doesn't speak," said Pietro.

"Oh!" I couldn't hide my surprise. He was mute? Another significant fact they'd left off the briefing. It occurred to me that I could complain to the placement agency about being misled. But as Isaia melted against me and as I looked from one embarrassed parent to another, I pushed the notion away.

"At least, not anymore," Pietro added.

Elda cast her eyes downward.

"He used to speak?" This was only getting stranger. "What happened?"

Pietro scratched his head. "We don't know. Doctors can't explain it. We've taken him to see three different specialists." He shrugged. "He has never been strong since birth but he used to speak perfectly well. Then one day," he snapped his fingers and made a dry pop. "He just stopped."

Elda kept her eyes on the floor. Was it me or her husband that she was avoiding eye contact with?

"When did that happen?" I put my hand against Isaia's back, feeling the hot, bumpy spine under my palm.

"He was three?" Pietro looked to his wife for confirmation.

"Three and a half," Elda answered. Her gaze flicked to mine but not to her husband's. I had the strangest sensation that she knew something about the boy's condition that her husband didn't know. I shoved the ridiculous thought aside. I only just arrived and I was already making assumptions about their family dynamics.

"The best thing for him," Elda continued as her brown eyes locked on mine, "is to make sure he drinks a lot of water. He's prone to rapid dehydration. I cannot impress this upon you enough. Otherwise, he's pretty low maintenance. More than you would expect from looking at him." Was her expression apologetic?

I nodded. "Alright. Lots of water. Got it."

Pietro looked at his watch. "We can discuss more later, but for now I have to drop both boys off at the school, and then get back to the office." He stood and called for Cristiano.

Thumping echoed from the hallway and a lithe, tanned boy appeared carrying a mini soccer ball. He spouted a lot of Italian at his father, who gave it back just as rapidly.

"Cristiano, come meet your au pair," said Elda.

Cristiano and I said hello. I couldn't help but smile at his broad grin stacked with dimples. His cow eyes were lined with a ridiculous thatch of eyelashes. His teeth were straight and gleamed like porcelain. Cristiano was beautiful, wiry, and full of energy. He had brown hair, brown eyes, and brown skin and reminded me of a chocolate chip cookie. He was the spitting image of his father, except Pietro's eyes were blue. Cristiano was a picture of health, and the complete opposite of his younger brother. Cristiano, I concluded, was probably responsible for the hurricane that had passed through their home. Their villa was big and beautiful. It was also a complete disaster. Toys were scattered everywhere: crayons, markers, toy cars, and soccer related paraphernalia covered every surface. There were enough toys for ten children, not just two.

"This is Saxony. You have to use your English when you talk to her, okay?" Elda said to Cristiano.

He nodded and gave me a little wave. "Hello." His voice penetrated every corner of the room and every movement he made was quick and twitchy. He dropped the soccer ball and kicked it down the hall. With one last look at me, he turned and went after it.

"Go get your backpack, please," Elda called after him. "Daddy takes you to school in ten minutes."

"School?" I asked. "They're not out for the summer?" I was mostly surprised that Isaia was going anywhere but to bed.

"Just a few more days," she said. "They're in private school. It runs on a different schedule from the public system."

"Andiamo," said Pietro to Isaia, holding a hand out.

For the first time since he'd settled in my lap, Isaia stirred and climbed down. Again I was startled by his tiny stature. He looked me full in the face. My heart thudded. His eyes were so... haunted. He crossed the room and took his father's hand.

I was able to observe Isaia and his brother side by side. The two boys next to one another barely looked related. Cristiano patted Isaia on the top of his head in an absent-minded way as he spoke with his father. Elda got up and said goodbye to her boys. She kissed them both, then knelt and spoke to Isaia in a reassuring tone. He nodded soberly. Just before the boys disappeared down the stairs, Isaia looked back at me a last time. The sunlight slanting through the window reflected his right eye and I thought that it glowed red, just for a fraction of a second. I blinked. Surely just a trick of the light.

When the boys were gone, Elda turned to me. "You're probably exhausted."

"A little." In fact, I wanted nothing more than to lie down on the carpet under our feet.

"I'll show you to your apartment."

Their guest apartment was tiny but charming and included my own little kitchen and a view over the canal. Elda and I agreed to go over the schedule and the boys' needs later that evening. She said goodbye and left me to myself.

I fished my phone out of my purse and collapsed on the bed. I pounded out a text to my three best friends; Akiko Susumu, Targa MacAuley, and Georjayna Sutherland.

Landed! Met the fam. I've already learned that streets are called Calle, and Venice is supposed to be hot as a deuce this summer. How're you guys?

I closed my phone and set it on the bedside table. Their responses would come in scattered on the wind. My besties and I were spread across 8 time zones for the summer. I closed my eyes and sighed with exhaustion and happiness. I tried to nap but it was a long time coming. Isaia's eyes, those obsidian orbs, refused to fade from my mind.

TWO

"I think you must be some kind of wizard," said Elda early one morning later into my first week when she saw that the living room, kitchen, and dining area were clean. "I forgot what my floors looked like."

"Thank you, but the real trick will be to teach Cristiano to put his things away for himself." I put her espresso cup under the nozzle of their machine and set it to make her a shot.

Elda and I often had a few minutes where we passed company in the kitchen before she left and before the boys were up and dressed.

"Yes, if you can accomplish that you are a magician for sure," she said, bending to fasten the buckles on her red leather shoes.

"You always have such amazing shoes," I said. "Where do you get them?"

"Ah, welcome to Italy, the land of beautiful footwear. I will have to show you my favorite shops sometime. Of course, the best ones are in Milan, but we have some nice ones here in Venezia, too."

Elda and I chatted until she had to leave, and then I began to make lunch for Cristiano. Today, Isaia had no classes or camps, so we would spend the day together. It was my last working day before the weekend. I was debating what to do with Isaia, since it would be just the two of us. I could think of a million things, but I didn't know if they'd be interesting to a kid, or if he'd have the energy for much.

"Buongiorno." I smiled as Pietro entered the kitchen carrying Isaia. I put his espresso on the island where he could reach it.

He took the cup and thanked me.

"Good morning, Isaia," I said. I still wasn't used to the grip he made on me with his eyes. Even though he couldn't or wouldn't speak, I assumed that he understood most of what I said. In the few days that I had passed as the boy's au pair, I came to think that Isaia understood a lot more of the English language than his older brother did.

Isaia reached for me. Pietro handed the boy over, now accustomed to our morning routine. Isaia's warm body settled against me. I kissed the top of his head, feeling the heat radiating from him with my lips. I didn't think he had a fever, but somehow, he always seemed right on the edge. Elda had explained that his normal was actually a touch high, and he'd been like that since birth.

"I meant to ask Elda before she left, is it okay if I take Isaia to see a glass-blowing demonstration on Murano later today? Elda passed on a gift card for a private demo that she doesn't have time to use. It will expire next week. I thought he might enjoy it. I know I would, too."

"That's a beautiful idea," Pietro said. "Please do." He fished in his wallet and pulled out a business card, handing it to me. "Call Giovanni for a ride. Don't bother with the water buses, and don't pay him," he added, raising a finger. "I have an agreement with him."

"Grazie! How kind."

Pietro and Cristiano said goodbye and I turned to Isaia. "It's just you and me, little man. Are you hungry?"

He shook his head.

"Would you like to go to Murano today?" I asked.

He gave a small shrug, and then seemed to think better of it and nodded.

"Okay, but we have some hours to spend before. I'll clean up the kitchen, and you can go play."

He nodded and meandered slowly down the hallway toward his room. I frowned after him. The boy seemed to have no energy whatsoever. Cristiano was unstoppable from morning until night when he crashed hard in a skinny, sweaty mess. I had never once seen Isaia run or kick a ball or do anything more strenuous than play with Lego or color. I wondered for the millionth time why he was so lethargic and what had made him stop speaking.

I had done a few hours of research one evening, finding medical websites that talked about children losing their speech after a traumatic event. Many had recovered their powers of speech after therapy, but Pietro and Elda both said that Isaia had never been through a traumatic event, not even so much as a painful visit to the dentist. He'd lived a sheltered and protected life. He'd never been an energetic kid, even in the womb.

My phone dinged as I was tidying the kitchen.

Targa: *Finally arrived in Poland! Remind me never to let my mother on a plane. Like ever.*

Me: *Whyzat? She okay?*

It surprised me that Targa's mom, Mira, might have airsickness. She seemed like the strongest, most impervious woman I'd ever met. She intimidated the hell out of me.

Targa: *Can't handle the altitude, I guess. Check it out...*

She sent through a photo of the front of a huge mansion with a bazillion windows and crawling with ivy. My eyes bugged.

Me: *That's where you're living for the summer!?*

Targa: *Crazy, right? It's crammed full of mermaid and seascape artwork from top to bottom, too. This rich Polish dude is some kind of collector.*

Me: *Have you met him yet? What's he like?*

Targa: *Not yet. Tonight at dinner. Gonna nap now. Latr Gatr.*

Me: *Have you heard from Akiko or Georjayna?*

Targa: Negatory. Don't expect to hear much from Akiko, remember? Georjie is probably in the air right now.

Me: *K.*

I frowned. My best friend Akiko had warned us at our goodbye dinner that she was going to be mostly MIA. Her grandfather was sending her to a remote mountain village in Japan for the summer. I still hadn't met her grandfather. She had somehow always dodged introducing us and I had finally stopped asking.

It was obvious she didn't want us to meet. Either way, I didn't like the guy on principle. When he says 'jump,' Akiko answers 'how high?' Besides, who sends a seventeen-year-old girl into a foreign wilderness to spend a whole summer with people she doesn't know? I shook off my annoyance and finished cleaning up the kitchen, then went to Isaia's room and peeked in. He was sitting on the floor in his bedroom, his back propped against his dresser. He had a book open on his lap. He looked up and held the book out to me.

"You want to read together?" I asked, coming into his room.

He moved to the child sized sofa under his window. I sat down next to him and he crawled under my arm and curled up against my side. My entire body was instantly warmer.

"You want me to read out loud?"

He nodded.

I looked at the cover to see it was called 'La Fenice', The Phoenix. On the cover was an illustration of a beautiful bird of red flames, rising from gray ashes.

"This is a cool story, kiddo, but I can't read it to you. It's in Italian, and I promised your parents that I would speak to you only in English. Do you have any English stories?"

He looked thoughtful, then he left the room and I heard him push Cristiano's door open. A moment later he reappeared with another book. It was a collection of fairy tales from all over the world. I opened it to the first story, but Isaia shook his head and took the book back.

"What, you don't like that one?"

He flipped through and handed it back to me, open to the story he wanted.

"The Firebird, a Slavic Fairy-tale," I began. "Boy, you sure like your fiery bird stories, don't you?"

He sighed and settled under my arm.

I began to read slowly, enunciating each word. By the time the young Prince Ivan saw the glowing bird in the orchard, Isaia was asleep. I closed the book and debated waking him but I was loath to move him. I looked down at his pale head, the thin blue veins threading down the sides of his face, his wispy blond lashes delicate against his cheeks. My heart swelled. His breathing was slow, and seemed just a little bit labored. His warm, boneless body lulled me into a thoughtless stupor. I barely registered my cheek touching the top of his head as my eyelids, suddenly as heavy as wet canvas, drifted shut.

AFTER OUR NAP, I prepared a bag for our afternoon outing. I put two apples, a small bottle of water, and sunscreen into my purse. Isaia watched all of this silently. I caught his curious gaze as I was putting a travel-sized bottle of aloe vera lotion into my purse. "Pale girls like me know all the tricks," I winked at him and dangled the little bottle. "Aloe is fabulous on sunburn, and ghosts like us can't be too careful."

His bottom lip hung open, bemused.

Isaia and I stepped out of the house just as the taxi was pulling up at their private dock. A tall, slender man in a striped shirt smiled at me from behind the wheel and doffed his captain's hat. "Ciao!" he said, a wide grin splitting his face. "I'm Giovanni.

Benvenuti a Venezia, Saxony. Have you enjoyed your first week in Venice?" He moored the boat and held out a hand to Isaia. "Giorno, Isaia."

"Very well, thanks," I said, "Although this is my first venture out as a tourist. I have been getting to know these little rascals."

I stepped into the boat and put a hand on Isaia's head. I realized when my hand touched his blond hair that I'd forgotten to put a hat on him. I rifled in my bag and pulled out my cotton fedora. I placed it on Isaia's head as we pulled away from the dock. I kicked myself for forgetting and shaded my own face with my hand.

We passed under a small arched bridge and into the sun. Tourists snapped photos of the pretty teak boat as we passed beneath them. Laundry hung outside many of the windows and wisteria and ivy crawled over wooden trellises. Algae covered steps disappeared into the murky water. Elda had explained that a long time ago, families used the canals for bathing, swimming, and doing laundry, but now it was illegal to swim in the canals.

"So, you want to visit Murano today?" asked Giovanni.

"Yes, we have tickets for a private glass blowing demo," I explained.

Isaia moved closer to me on the seat and put his little hand in mine, leaning against my shoulder.

Giovanni stared at the boy for a moment, his mouth slightly agape. "I've known the Baseggio family a long time," he said seriously. "I've never seen Isaia take to anyone like that. At least, not since he stopped talking."

The Adriatic opened before us, the horizon was dotted with islands. We increased speed as we crossed the expanse of water toward Murano. I looked down at Isaia, and smiled to see him close his eyes as the breeze cooled him.

"That's what Pietro and Elda say, too. Do you remember what Isaia was like when he could speak?" I raised my voice over the wind.

"Certo, certo," he said, nodding. "I've known both the boys since they were born." He slowed the boat as we approached Murano. Colorful buildings rose up before us. "It happened like that." He snapped his fingers. "One day he was chattering away, and the next day..." He sliced his hand laterally through the air.

"Was he always petite for his age?"

"Oh, yes," Giovanni nodded. "He has always been small and weak, let's say."

I had the urge to clap my hands over Isaia's ears, realizing with regret that it wasn't good for him to hear us talk about him in this way. I looked down at him but he was looking out at the ocean.

"Sorry buddy," I said under my breath and put an arm around his skinny shoulders.

Giovanni steered us into a docking station at Murano. The dock itself was a dead end but it opened into a walkway filled with strolling tourists. A tall stone fountain in the shape of a lion's head graced the edge of the dock. Giovanni and I agreed on a time for him to pick us up, then he backed the taxi out of the dock and waved as he drove away.

"How are you doing, buddy?" I put a hand to Isaia's cheek. He felt warm, and no wonder, the sun was intense. But though I was sweating, he felt warm and dry.

"Here, take a drink." I twisted the cap off the water bottle and gave it to him. He gulped greedily and handed it back empty. "Whoa. Note to self. Bigger bottle next time."

I adjusted his hat and took his hand. We walked by shops filled with every kind of colored glass creation imaginable. Chandeliers, vases, animals, wineglasses and tumblers, jewelry, picture frames, and dinnerware. The items that could be made out of glass seemed endless.

We found the location of the demo. Their window display held the most elaborate pieces of glasswork that we'd seen so far. I pulled on the red glass door handle only to discover the entrance was locked. I frowned and pulled out the ticket, double checking the time. It was correct. I pressed the button on the small brass panel beside the door.

"Prego," said a pleasant male voice, trilling the 'r'.

"Buongiorno, I have tickets to a private glass blowing demonstration. Are we at the right place?"

"Ah, si, si. Please, come in. I'll be with you in a moment," the voice answered.

The buzzer sounded. I opened the door and held it for Isaia. A blast of air-conditioning swept over us and we both sighed. The front room was empty of people, so we contented ourselves by looking at the glasswork on display. The room was lined with mirrors. I made a silly face at Isaia when I caught him looking at me in the mirror and was rewarded with the tiniest smile.

A few moments later, the owner of the voice appeared from behind the cash desk. He and I blinked at each other and our smiles stretched simultaneously. Cute. Very cute. His hazel eyes looked warmly down at me from the platform behind the till, and then at Isaia. He had short curly black hair which was receding slightly, even though I doubted he was much over twenty. His broad shoulders seem to fill the room and his dimples made my heart trip.

"Buongiorno," I said, grinning stupidly.

He smiled back even broader. A warm feeling seeped through my stomach.

"You're American?"

"Is my accent that bad?" I snapped my fingers in a 'gosh darn it' gesture. "I'm actually Canadian."

"Ah, Canadian. Wonderful, and no your accent was perfect." We exchanged a firm, hot handshake. He must have been working in front of the oven because his hand was far warmer than it should be.

"I'm Rafaele Dimaro. Welcome to our little shop. You must be..." he referred to a paper that had been taped to the counter, "Elda Bassegio?"

"No, I'm Saxony, her au pair. She gave me her ticket since she wouldn't be able to use it in time. Is that okay?"

"Of course. And who is this?" He looked down at Isaia, who'd been standing solemnly at my side.

"This is Isaia." I took the hat off his head and frowned at the purple smudges beneath his eyes. I could have sworn they weren't there a minute ago.

"Welcome Saxony and Isaia," said Rafaele, putting his hands together. "Are you ready for a private demonstration of the ancient art of glass blowing? A secret that was protected for thousands of years?" He waved his fingers mystically.

Isaia stared.

"We're ready, right?" I took Isaia's hand and he looked up at me and nodded. I noted with pleasure that there was some interest on his face. Finally, something that animated him, even if it was slight.

"Then please follow me," said Rafaele. He swept an arm across his face like a magician behind a cape.

Isaia's mouth lifted at the corners.

I was not prepared for how stifling the workshop was. A blast of hot air blew my hair back. My eyes went dry and my upper lip felt suddenly damp. No wonder Rafaele's hands were so warm. A short hallway lined with shelves full of glasswork led to a workspace. Two ovens yawned from a stone wall. Tools littered a metal table and seats lined the workspace at a safe distance from the heat. A red glow emanated from one oven, while the other was dark and cold. Metal blowing rods leaned against the wall in a line.

"Prego." Rafaele gestured to the seats.

Isaia and I each took a chair in the front row.

"Before we begin, I'll explain a little about the history of..." The door chimed, and Rafaele broke off. "Oh accidenti. Excuse me, I've forgotten to lock the front door. I will help the visitors quickly and then return. Forgive me."

He left in a rush, and Isaia and I waited. I fanned myself with my hat. As the minutes passed, Isaia grew restless. He was staring into the fiery oven when I heard him inhale. It was a raspy, wheezing sound.

"Isaia?"

He turned and looked at me. His coal black eyes were filled with a pain that hadn't been there a few moments before. My heart skipped a beat.

"What is it, honey?" I crouched in front of him. "Isaia?"

He put his hands on my shoulders to brace himself. The same red glow I'd seen on the first day rose in his eyes. The hair on the back of my neck stood up. The glow was there and then gone, like a flicker, only this time there was no sunlight coming in from anywhere.

I gasped. I had not imagined it. I put my hands to the sides of his face, fear curdling in my guts. He was burning up, and his breathing grew more labored. I put my lips against his forehead. He was beyond feverish. Elda had explained that he sometimes gets sudden fevers, but she'd never impressed upon me their ferocity. Or was this one extra bad?

Peering into his eyes, I watched for the strange glow to reappear. I put my hands to the sides of his ribs. I almost snatched my hands back from his belly, he was nearly hot enough to burn me. His torso was even hotter than his forehead. He inhaled again, wheezing. He lifted up his t-shirt and displayed his skinny white belly. Our faces lit up from underneath, throwing strange shadows across us. A red glow lit his belly from the inside, as though he'd swallowed a piece of hot coal. The dark shadows of his ribs stood out through his skin. I thought I could even see his heart flicker darkly in his chest.

"I-Isaia," I stuttered, but I had no words. I put a hand against the shelf to steady myself. The world spun. I squinted my eyes shut against the vertigo and hoped that I was imagining things.

I opened my eyes. The glow was still there.

The sound of voices came again from the other room. The door chime went off.

I took a steadying breath. "I have to get you home. Right now."

I pushed his shirt down. The glow was still faintly visible through the fabric. What kind of illness was this? What could make a kid glow from the inside out and make him so hot that he should be dead by now?

Rafaele entered the workshop. "I apologize about that... whoa!" He nearly stumbled over us. I stood up and stepped in front of Isaia to hide the glow.

"Is everything okay?" His smile had disappeared and his brows knit together with concern.

"No, I'm sorry." I took one of Isaia's hands but kept him a little behind me. Isaia put his head down, as though he was ashamed. His breath whistled in his chest. "Isaia is suddenly not feeling well. I have to take him home."

"Of course, of course. I'm so sorry." Rafaele stumbled to get out of the way. He followed us through to the shop, all the while asking if there was anything he could do to help.

I dug for my phone and texted Giovanni to come back, it was an emergency. My phone dinged immediately and he said he'd meet us in ten minutes. I breathed thanks that he wasn't far away.

"Is there something I can do?" Rafaele asked again.

"Do you have water?" I asked, mentally cursing myself. Elda had warned me to keep him hydrated. But he'd had water not that long ago. Was it not enough? Had I been neglectful? Had I brought this on? Guilt burned in my throat.

"Yes, absolutely." He bent over behind the till and opened a small fridge. "This place gets so hot, we'd be crazy not to." He handed me a cold bottle of water.

"Thank you." I opened it and handed it to Isaia. He began to drink. He winced as though swallowing too much. "Not so fast, darling," I told him.

I assured Rafaele that Isaia would be okay, but I knew that worry was etched all over my face. My lips trembled. Isaia was most certainly not okay, and he was in my care. Why wouldn't Elda have prepared me better? Was it possible this had never happened before?

"Signorina, please," Rafaele implored as I opened the door. "Leave me your number. I will worry. Text me later that everything is okay. Please?" His request was so sincere and sweet that it gave me pause. If I were him, I'd want to know that everything turned out okay, too. I gave him my number.

I picked Isaia up and strode in the direction of the dock. Each breath he took whistled faintly. We arrived at the dock and I set Isaia down and called Elda. I felt as though I couldn't draw enough breath. Was this what a panic attack felt like? *Pull yourself together, Saxony.*

"Saxony?" Elda's soft voice made me sigh with relief.

I tried not to sound completely panicked. "Elda, are you able to meet us at home? It's Isaia, he's got a fever."

"Where are you?" She was sharp and all business.

"On Murano. We went to the glass-blowing demo but left early because Isaia..." I paused, the image of his glowing belly swam before me. "Got really hot. Giovanni is on his way to pick us up."

"I'm on my way home now. Get him some cold water, as quick as you can. And if you have something you can make wet, put it on his head to cool him down."

"Yes, okay. See you, soon." The phone went dead.

I squatted in front if Isaia and watched him drink. I reached into the lion's head fountain and pressed my wet hand against Isaia's forehead. Through all of this he barely took his eyes off me. It was easy to see that he was in pain, but he was so calm that I couldn't help but think that this had happened to him before and he knew it was going to pass.

I looked around to make sure we were alone. "May I?" I took the hem of his t-shirt. He nodded and I lifted it. The glow was still there, but not nearly as bright as before. I smoothed his shirt down and locked eyes with him. The red glow was nowhere to be seen. I stood up and watched for Giovanni's boat. My heart clattered. What kind of disease makes your torso and eyes glow from the inside out?

THREE

The boat ride back was notably tense. Giovanni raced us home as quickly as he dared while I tried to figure out how to tell Elda and Pietro what I had seen. I barely noticed as the boat juddered across the waves. I kept an arm tight around Isaia, who had lain in my lap as soon as we'd gotten into the boat. The glow... I couldn't shake it. It had been real, hadn't it?

We returned to an empty house. I put Isaia into bed and left the covers off. After laying a cool washcloth over his forehead, I took the digital thermometer from the first aid kit in their bathroom. While the thermometer did its work, I fetched a glass of water and a glass of ice and set them on his bedside table. After switching his ceiling fan on, I sat beside him and waited, watching his narrow chest rise and fall. He watched me through half-lidded, unfocused eyes. I flipped the washcloth over, startled by how warm it felt. Time to refresh it. When I returned from the bathroom faucet, I took the thermometer from his mouth. The thermometer gave Celsius only, so even though I could read 72 degrees, I didn't know what it meant. I was accustomed to reading body temps in Fahrenheit. I used my phone to convert the number. When I saw the conversion, I almost dropped my phone. My hands trembled.

"I think this thermometer is broken," I joked nervously to Isaia. "According to this, you're almost hot enough to bake muffins."

I put the broken thermometer on the bedside table. If the temperature were right, he would be dead by now. I looked up what to do for a fever on my phone. "Run a lukewarm bath," I read aloud. I dashed into the bathroom and cranked on the faucets. My hands shook and I thought that I might be sick. I looked at the toilet, trying to decide if my breakfast was actually going to come up or not. I bent and took a few swallows of water from the tap. I went back to get Isaia as the water filled the tub, taking a moment to watch for the glow. His eyes were glassy but without any hint of red. There was no tantrum, no childlike thrashing, and not a peep of sound. He lay there limply.

"Up we go, buddy. Time for a little bath, okay? This should make you feel better." He wheezed as I carried him to the bathroom. I grit my teeth at the sound, and nausea passed over me again. Was he dying? Where was Elda? What was taking her so long?

I sat on the toilet and held him on my knee. I pulled off his shirt, looking with grim satisfaction to see that the glow was now gone. I got his jean shorts off and lowered him into the water in his underpants. Grabbing a stuffed bath toy, I put it under his head to make him comfortable. "Is that okay?"

He gave the smallest nod and the awful sound of him sucking in breath seemed a little better.

Rapid footsteps pounded on the stairs.

"We're in the bathroom," I yelled, and my limbs felt weak with relief.

She burst into the bathroom. "Mama is here." Elda knelt at the tub, her hand going to his forehead. She shot me a grateful look. "Brava, Saxony."

I couldn't bring myself to smile at her praise. My heart had finally stopped lurching out of my chest, but my mind had not slowed in the slightest. What was going on with this kid?

We got him out of the tub and into a pair of pajamas. I watched her sit at his bedside and go through all of the maternal motions that I had been through already; putting a hand on his forehead, placing the cool washcloth on his head, and taking his temperature for a third time. He endured all of it without protest. The thermometer now reported only slightly above normal, but I narrowed my eyes at the thing. I must have read it wrong. Or maybe I'd messed up the conversion?

I explained to Elda that he'd gotten sick at the demo. I stuttered and stalled, trying to figure out how to tell her about the glow. I would sound crazy. Was I crazy? I had already started to doubt what I had seen.

Elda listened quietly. I couldn't tell what she was thinking. Three times I opened my mouth to say something about the glow, and three times the words got stuck in my throat. Isaia watched me struggle with the story the entire time. I'd never felt so conflicted before. Would she think I was lying? Making something up for drama? I didn't know her well enough yet. If she had seen the glow before, she would have told me about it, wouldn't she?

I choked out the story, leaving out the most critical part. I was hoping she might give me some kind of opening that would make me feel better about telling her that her son looked like he was on fire from the inside, but she gave me no such confidence.

"Poor thing, I can see that it's really upset you," Elda said when I had finished stumbling through it. "Don't worry too much, Saxony. This kind of thing is normal for Isaia. I told you that he sometimes gets fevers, and that they pass within a day. You did everything right, and I'm grateful."

We left Isaia to sleep. I found myself wishing that I had thought of taking a photo or a recording of the glow of his belly and his eyes. If it happened again, that's what I would do. Then I would have proof.

Elda was watching me. "You're really shaken, aren't you?"

The way she said it made me think that she had never before seen the glow. My anxiety must have looked like an overreaction to her.

"Sure, I was... I am worried about him," I replied. "How hot does he get, normally?"

She paused, just for a moment. "The usual. Maybe 38.5, 39." She blinked rapidly a couple of times.

She's lying.

I pushed the thought away violently. Of course she wasn't lying. She was his mother. She loved him, and she would arm me—his au pair—with all the knowledge I needed to care for him. That's how it worked when the health of a child was involved. Right?

I went up to my apartment in a troubled daze. Just as I closed the door behind me, my phone chirped. It was a text from Rafaele.

Everything is okay?

I smiled in spite of my worries. It was thoughtful of him to follow up. I texted back.

Me: *He is okay. He had a fever but it's already gone down. Thanks for asking.*

Rafaele: *Of course. Poor little guy. Maybe we can finish the demonstration another time. I'll give you a rain check. They say rain check in Canada?*

Me: *Yes, they do. And thank you, Rafaele.*

Rafaele: *Welcome. And call me Raf.*

Me: *Okay, but if you call me Sax, I'll kill you.*

There was a pause. I hoped he was laughing at my joke.

Raf: *Understood. *Smile**

I rubbed my hands over my eyes. Not even my first week in and already there was some crazy drama, as well as a cute boy. I had something to write home about now. But if I told my friends about Isaia, there was no way they'd believe me. I was already the drama queen in our group. When I was younger, I'd tended to exaggerate, and that bad habit had come back to bite me in the ass. Now I felt like I had to earn my credibility again. I couldn't do that by telling crazy stories about a little boy whose eyes and stomach glowed red.

I began to research glowing eyes and glowing skin on the internet. I got a whole load of links to graphic design websites, fantasy stories, movies and tv shows with demonic and angelic characters, and vampire fan sites. Nothing remotely medical or helpful surfaced.

I turned off my phone and stared at nothing. All I could see was Isaia's glowing belly, the shadows of his ribs lining his skin. I shuddered. How was I going to talk to Elda and Pietro about what I'd seen without sounding like a crazy person?

I WOKE the morning of my first day off feeling groggy and troubled. A day enjoying Venice would be the perfect distraction. I tucked my map and phone into my purse, determined not to use them unless absolutely necessary. I knew where we were in general, and which direction I had to go to find Piazza San Marco.

Once outside, I began to walk. As I got closer, the calle became choked with tourists and my pace slowed considerably. I passed a cute cafe that looked like it had once been a car from a vintage train. The semi-circular window displayed crisp looking salads, mozzarella balls, toasted bruschetta, deep fried frutta di mare, and a host of brioche and pastries. I stepped out of the river of tourists and slipped through the narrow doorway.

"Prego," said the frizzy-haired waitress behind the counter.

"Uno cappuccino, per favore," I stumbled through the words. Nearly every Italian working in Venice spoke English, but I wanted to at least try to pick up some of the language.

"Si, due minuti."

The waitress brought my coffee and I squeezed myself into a table. Pulling out my phone, looked for a second time at the photos that Targa and Georjayna had texted. Targa had sent through a collection of images of the mansion on the Baltic, a couple of selfies in front of artwork, and one of a handsome young man gazing up at a sculpture of a knight. It was obvious she'd taken it without him realizing it. He looked like a naval officer; short blond hair, lean and fit, naval jacket, and fine bones in his face. I wondered if Targa was finally feeling chemistry with this guy, Antoni. As far as I knew, she'd never had a genuine crush.

I scrolled over to Georjayna's images. These were of breathtakingly gorgeous gardens and a Victorian house. But again, I was more interested in the shot she'd sent of her adopted cousin. She'd snapped it from across the lawn. He was carrying a bunch of broken window frames. I zoomed in and shook my head. He was drop dead gorgeous. Too bad he wasn't very friendly.

"Tutto bene?" the waitress asked, startling me. Clearly, it was time to leave the table for someone else to enjoy.

"Si, grazie." I dropped my phone into my bag. "Which way to the Basilica?" It had to be close.

"To the right and to the right again. You are only a few steps away," she answered.

After thanking her, I rejoined the crush of people on the street. Less than two minutes later, I stepped out into the iconic Piazza San Marco. My breath caught in my throat and vertigo swept over me. Thousands of white pillars lined the square. The piazza was heaving with people; taking photos, selling trinkets, standing in queues. The Basilica loomed over it all with four gorgeous white horses that looked as though they might gallop right off the roof. An orchestra played across the square and I crossed to them, dodging children and pigeon poo. Moving slowly through the crowd toward the ocean, I reached the sea. The view took my breath away. I took out my phone and snapped a bunch of photos. I walked, enjoying the view of the canal even though it was crowded with gondolas, water busses, and boats. As I was leaning with my elbows on the thick railing and watching a gondola float underneath the bridge, a feminine voice addressed me.

I turned to see a young woman with short brown hair. She had a few coins in her hand and a pleading look on her face. She spoke rapidly in Italian.

"Non parle Italiano," I said.

"Ah, you're American."

"Canadian."

"Bellissima," she said. "Please, I don't normally do this, but, do you have eighty cents?"

I appraised her. Clean clothes, a fresh haircut, deftly applied makeup. Her blue eyeliner outlined her green eyes perfectly. Her ballet flats looked brand new. She was definitely not indigent. It was strange that she was asking me for only eighty cents.

"I might," I said. "Are you okay?"

"I am, I just lost my wallet," she explained. "I think I know where I left it, but I have a job interview close to Piazzale Roma and I don't have time to go back. I have to catch the next waterbus or I will lose my chance." She pointed to the waterbus as it pulled up to the dock. The sign said she had only a few minutes before it left and that it was indeed destined for Piazzale Roma.

"That really sucks." I reached into my pocket and pulled out a euro. "Good luck with your job interview, I hope you make it."

"Oh, thank you! Grazie mille!" she cried, taking the coin. "What is your name?"

"Saxony. What's yours?"

"Federica, but Fed to my friends. A very pleasure to meet you, however short our meeting. You are very nice." She held out her hand and we shook. She walked quickly toward the waterbus. Turning back, she called, "If I get the job it will be thanks to you! Come visit me at the Gelateria Artigianale, close to the CO-OP beside Piazzale Roma." She waved.

I waved back. "I will."

She disappeared into the crowd and I continued on my way, wondering if I might have made myself a friend. As I walked in the direction of home, the greenery increased. Wisteria dripped over the tops of balconies and roses blossomed behind spindles of stone. I held up my phone to take a photo when a text flashed on my screen.

Raf: *Ciao Saxony. How is Isaia today?*

Me: Ciao Raf. Much better. You are sweet to inquire.

Raf: *Bene. Glad to hear it. What are you doing?*

Me: *Playing tourist. You?*

Raf: *Working. But I have another question for you.*

Me: *Tell me.*

Raf: *I have tickets to a presentation on the history of glass blowing tomorrow afternoon. Would you like to join me? I thought you might like it.*

It took me precisely half a second to make the decision and I smiled as I typed. If I hadn't been so distracted thinking about Isaia, I might have been daydreaming about Raf's dimples.

Me: *Absolutely. A che ora?*

Raf: *So, you are learning some Italian after all?*

Me: *Si, pochino.*

Raf: *How about 16:40 at the Bridge of Sighs. You know it?*

Me: Surprisingly, I do.

I had passed it ten minutes earlier. It was called the Bridge of Sighs because criminals being escorted to their prison cells had to pass under it on their way to jail. They would sigh because they knew they were caught and the sound would echo under the bridge.

Raf: Good. See you then.

I grinned. I had a date with a cute Italian man. Which, let's be honest, was one of the reasons I'd wanted to come to Italy in the first place.

FOUR

The next day, I walked the Jewish Ghetto because Pietro had told me that the best food in Venice could be found there. I sampled several kinds of bruschetta; gorgonzola, pomodorini and basil, speck and pecorino. The flavors melted in my mouth. My mom loved to cook so I bought a little book containing only recipes for bruschetta as a gift for her. I passed tiny restaurants with outdoor tables jammed with laughing tourists. Gondolas moored at the edges of the canal held people relaxing against pillows while enjoying glasses of wine and plates of food.

By the time I circled back to Piazzale Roma to see if I could find the Gelateria that Federica had named, it was already mid-afternoon. Soon I would have to make my way to the Bridge of Sighs to meet Raf.

Gelateria Artigianale was easy to find. A lineup of people snaked down the street from its doorway. I stood on tiptoe to look over the crowd but the girl working was not Federica. Either Fed didn't get the job, or she had but she wasn't working at the moment. I turned back toward the waterbus station and ran smack into her. Both of us cried out in surprise.

"It's you!" she said, holding a hand over her heart.

"It's you too!" I replied, laughing.

"You came to find me. You are so sweet, Saxony." Her brown eyes sparkled.

"Did you get the job?"

"I did, you are amazing to follow up and ask. Today is my first day, obviously. My shift starts in ten minutes, but I'm early. I'm always scared I'll be late when I have to go anywhere in Venice during the summer." She held up a purple wallet and shook it. "Let me buy you a coffee. We can celebrate."

"You got your wallet back!" We stepped into the cool of the cafe next door.

"Yes, it was still at the enoteca, just where I left it. I called to ask them to hold it for me until I could get back there this morning. What a relief."

We chatted while we waited for our coffees and then found a vacant table.

"How long will you be in Venezia?"

"Actually, I'll be here all summer. I'm an au pair for a family who lives in the Cannaregio borough."

"Oh, beautiful! I can introduce you to some of my friends. There is a festival in a couple of weeks called Festa del Redentore. Have you heard of it?"

"No, is that the one with all the masks?" I asked, visions of a long beaked face coming to mind.

"No, that is Carnivale. That one happens in February. This one is in July and was originally to celebrate the end of the black plague. By now it's mostly an excuse to have a party. It's a lot of fun. You must come," she begged, putting a hand on my forearm.

"Absolutely." It sounded like the perfect opportunity to meet a lot of people all at once. I wished her luck for her first day. We exchanged numbers and said goodbye.

During the boat ride to the Piazza San Marco, my mind went to Akiko, the only one of my friends I hadn't heard from since I arrived in Venice. I pulled out my phone, readying a text, but put it away again. She said she'd be remote, and that she'd write when she could. I pushed the anxiety about her away. I had to trust that her grandfather knew what he was doing... which was easier said than done.

I arrived at the Bridge of Sighs a few minutes early so I took the opportunity to take photos of the Doge's Palace. The Turkish window frames, pink and white marble, and curved arches made it hard to look at anything else. I stood at the top of the bridge and craned my neck at the delicate florets over each window.

"Hi! You're actually on time," said a deep voice, sounding surprised.

I turned to see Raf coming up the steps. "Why? Are Italian girls never on time?"

"Almost never. At least, in my experience. I think they want to show you who is going to wear the pants right from the start or something."

"Hey, I'm a pant-wearer, too. I wear all sorts of bottoms."

He laughed. "I'll remember that. Are you ready to have your mind expanded, pant-wearer?"

"Absolutely. Where is this mind-expanding meeting?"

"It's in the courtyard of the Doge's Palace. Which is pretty cool because they don't do a lot of these types of things in there, and when they do, it's hard to get tickets."

I followed him past a long lineup of people to an entrance with a red carpet. "Well, look at you go with your VIP perks."

He grinned. "Our studio has an agreement with the association who puts these on." He handed two tickets to the lady at the entrance and winked at me while she scanned them. We walked under a long archway to a beautiful courtyard. Rows of chairs faced a white stone wall. We found our seats and settled in. I loved these sorts of things, as long as they weren't too long. I'd never been great at sitting for long stretches of time.

"So, glass-blowing," I prompted as we waited. Raf turned his hazel eyes on me. "Is this your destiny?"

"I don't have a choice in the matter," he said. "Our studio has been in the family for close to two hundred years. If I had wanted to do something else, I think I would have given my father a stroke. I'm already a little more than a quarter of the way through my apprenticeship."

"How long does it take to become a master glass-blower?"

"Twenty years. It's not the easiest art form."

"Holy crap! That's twice as long as a doctor."

"Yeah, it's a long time," his gaze went to the front and I followed it to see a woman in a white pantsuit step up behind the podium. The white stone wall behind her lit up with a projection of an antique map of Venice. The title 'Glass Blowers of Venice, an Ancient Secret' overlaid the map.

"Looks like we're about to begin," Raf said, rubbing his hands together and looking gleeful.

"Dude, you're way too excited about this. Don't you know all this stuff already?"

His cheeks colored. "I do, but it never gets old."

"Well that's good, because it sounds like you're going to be married to it for the rest of your life."

I was rewarded with a spectacular smile.

The woman introduced herself and began by explaining that while the art of making glass is older than Christ, the island of Murano had been home to the masters of glass-blowing since the 15th century. Artisans were often lured by kings and queens of other countries to teach their craftsmen the secrets of mirror making and the art of coloring glass.

"In the early days," she said, flipping the slide to show a list of dates:

Dorsoduro: 899

The Great Fire: 1105

The Rialto Fire: 1516

The Arsenale Fire: 1569

Santa Chiara: 1574

"...the glass blowers were located on the main island of Venezia. But there were many fires that nearly destroyed the city. Only the worst of them are listed here. After the Rialto fire of 1516, straw roofs were banned and the glass blowers, along with their dangerous ovens, were moved to the island of Murano to prevent further catastrophes."

The image of a Y-shaped chimney popped up on the screen. I recognized the shape as I'd seen many of them throughout the city.

She went on. "In fact, Venice was so troubled by fire that these unique chimney designs were invented here." She used a pointer to highlight the Y-shape at the top of the chimney. "Notice the inverted flu at the top, which is designed to catch and prevent the spread of sparks on the wind. They also contribute to the city's unique skyline."

A hand appeared in the air in front of us.

"Yes?"

"But Venice is surrounded by water and constructed mostly of stone. How could there so many devastating fires?" the woman asked.

"Great question." She flipped through the slides until she landed on an illustration. A cross section of a Venetian building had been cut away to reveal the interior layers of the walls. "Because Venice is built on a lagoon, the building materials they used had to be very light in order to minimize sinking. The stone on the outside is really a facade. You can see from this illustration that inside the narrow stone layer is actually brick, which is lighter but also more flammable than stone. They also burned straw and wood for heat, and used wood in their construction and for their furniture. Combined with cloth hangings, tapestries, and candles, fire was a very real threat for the people of Venice."

She went on to detail the history of glass-making as it evolved after the artisans were moved to Murano. She flipped through many beautiful images of chandeliers and drinking vessels, plates, sculptures and figurines, each more intricate than the last. I began to shift in my seat at the forty-five minute mark.

Raf leaned toward me. "She's almost finished. You okay?"

I nodded and made an effort to stay still.

When it was over, Raf walked me home and we chatted about what we'd learned. He described in better detail how the powdered metal oxides are added to the glass to color it. By the time I got home, my glass-blowing curiosity had been satisfied, aside from actually seeing it done. We stopped outside my door, and I wondered what to do with my hands.

"Thanks for inviting me. I learned a lot."

"You're welcome. I'm glad you came," he said quietly. He looked down at me through half closed eyes.

Little butterflies fluttered around my heart. I cleared my throat. "What are you doing for Festa del Redentore? A friend asked me to join her party for the fireworks. Do you want to come?"

"A friend? You've made friends already?"

"By accident. A girl named Federica asked me for change yesterday. She invited me to join her and her friends for the festival."

"Federica Arnago?" He raised his eyebrows.

"Uh... I don't know, I didn't ask her last name."

"Short girl. Cute, with short brown hair? Green eyes?"

"That sounds like her, yeah. You know her?"

"If it's who I think it is, we went to school together. How funny that you met her."

"So, will you come?"

"Thanks for asking, but I actually have to go to Milan for two weeks. We have a shop there and my father has asked me to look after it while the manager takes a holiday. It'll be the first time I'll miss Festa del Redentore." He took my hand and bent down and kissed my cheek tenderly, just beside my mouth.

I kissed his cheek back, his stubble tickling my lips. A warm feeling spread through me and I smiled at him when he pulled back.

"May I call you again when I am back?" he asked.

"I'd like that," I said. "Are all Italian guys as polite and gentlemanly as you? Because you know we Canadians don't have that stereotype of you at all."

"Oh, really? What do Canadians think Italians are like?"

"Forward. Passionate. Maybe a little pushy." I smiled and cocked an eyebrow. "Mama's boys."

He laughed. "Well you're right about two of those things. We are mama's boys, and we are passionate. But we're raised to be gentlemen." He kissed my cheek again. "Buonanotte, bella ragazza."

"Buonanotte." I didn't intend for it to come out as a whisper, but I seemed to have lost my voice.

FIVE

"Saxony!"

I turned toward the sound of my name, scanning the crowd for Fed. Every soul in Italy had turned up on the streets and docks of Venezia for the festival. The sun had already disappeared below the horizon but it was still hot and humid. My summer dress stuck to me. The air hung with clouds of cigarette smoke. The only saving grace of the night was a lazy breeze that lifted the damp curls away from my forehead. I had put the considerable bulk of my hair on top of my head to keep it off my neck.

Boats and gondolas choked St. Mark's Basin. Rows of them had been fastened together, and bobbed in the water. People picked their way along the linked boats, using them as a bridge. Partiers danced on larger boats further out and pulsing beats floated across the water, mixing badly with the rock music pumping from the speaker outside the cafe where I had agreed to meet Fed.

"Saxony!"

I saw a slender pink palm wave from behind an old man in a fedora. Fed appeared, her face glowing with sweat and excitement. She wove her way through the crowd like a dancer. She kissed first my right cheek then my left. I threw my arms around her neck and gave her a squeeze.

"Oh," she said with delight. She laughed and flapped her hands uselessly against my back.

"That's how Canadians say hello." I released her. "You Italians have mastered the kiss, but you need to learn how to hug."

She took my hand. "Perfect, I'll introduce to you some people you can teach. My friends are over there." She pointed into the middle of the canal and pulled on my hand. "Did you wear your bathing suit?"

"Yes. Under my dress."

"Perfect."

"Do they speak English? Your friends, I mean," I asked as I stumbled through the crowd after her. "Because if they don't we're not going to get very far. Hey, this wasn't here yesterday!"

We'd hit a wide bridge floating on the tops of black barrels.

"Yes, they put it up every year just for this festival," she explained. "It links Venezia to Giudecca." She pointed to the island across the water. Fairy lights twinkled along the rooftops of buildings on the far side. "And to answer your question, some of my friends speak English and some don't."

I followed her along the bridge, avoiding slobbering dogs, baby carriages, and crowds of smokers who'd decided to stop in the middle of the bridge and make everyone go around them. Everyone was talking and laughing and sweating. Fed began counting names off on her fingers. "Dante, Jacopo, Karim..." She listed off a few more names. "They're are all fluent."

"All boys?"

We arrived at a short dock.

"Yes, then there's me, Sara, and maybe Rosaria if she decides to come. But the girls don't speak hardly any English. Watch your step here."

She took my hand and helped me into an empty gondola. We began to pick our way across the sea of bobbing boats. Every vessel was decorated with balloons, garlands, and flowers.

"Karim doesn't sound like an Italian name." My sandal hooked a paddle, and I nearly tripped.

"Careful. It's not. Karim is from an Egyptian family, but he's a Canadian, too. Biggest guy you'll ever meet in your life. A teddy bear, though."

"People don't care that we're using their boats as lily pads?" We stepped past open coolers full of beer, piles of purses and bags, abandoned shoes, and water bottles.

"No, this is all part of the fun. Scusi!" She smiled at three girls eating bruschetta from a wooden platter and drinking wine. They smiled back and spoke to us in Italian. Fed answered and the three girls laughed. One of them blew us a kiss as we stepped into the next boat.

"When the fireworks start, all of these boats will be full," Fed continued.

We stepped into a gondola where two teenage girls and a boy lounged on pillows. The boy got to his feet. He looked about thirteen. He had a cigarette in one hand and held out his other hand to help us cross. He winked and smiled at me, asking something in Italian.

"Mi dispiace," I apologized. "Non parle Italiano."

"Ah," he said with obvious pleasure. "You are American?"

"Canadian, actually." I put my arms out, steadying myself in the rocking gondola.

"Ah." He nodded and took a drag of his cigarette. He blew two streams of smoke from his nostrils. "You are very pretty. Come find us later."

I turned to Fed and saw that she was laughing. I made a face as I turned my back to the boy and stepped out of the gondola. "What is he, twelve? They start young here, don't they."

"Get used to it." She stepped down into a wobbly canoe filled with crushed plastic bottles, paper food wrappers, and empty beer bottles. "Local garbage bin. Watch your step."

"Gross." I wrinkled my nose at the smell of stale beer.

We stepped into the next boat, which was full of people smoking and drinking. One of them got up to let us pass.

"So basically," I said, resuming our conversation, "I can talk to you, and a few of the boys. The rest have no English?"

"Well, they all have a little bit. We take it in school. But if they have no reason to practice, then it's easy to forget. You'll find that the best ones by far are myself, of course." She paused to take a little bow. "Then Karim, and Dante. Dante is crazy smart. He speaks German, Spanish, and French, too."

"Holy crap. Let me guess, he's funny, cute, and taken, too."

"Yes, yes and no," she laughed. "He's single. Lots of girls like Dante. *Lots.*"

"But not you?"

“Ha! No way. I've known Dante since I was born. Plus, he's..." She paused, and I strained to hear what she said.

"Sorry, what did you say?"

She turned back to me. "He's kind of... dangerous."

As we continued making our way across the boats, I pictured a dark, mysterious rock-star type. Maybe peppered with tattoos. I was about to say how intriguing she was making him sound when she waved her arms and shouted at a motor boat drifting in open water.

“There they are,” she said to me.

Her friends waved and shouted. Dance music floated across the water toward us.

"I don’t think we can make that jump," I joked as I looked across the dark water.

Fed grinned. "Unless you really want to swim, they'll come and pick us up. We'll be able to watch the fireworks away from the crowd. It's awesome, you'll love it."

"Whose boat is that?"

A nervous flutter had begun in my tummy.

"Dante's."

The dangerous one.

The sleek motorboat turned its nose toward us and floated stealthily across the water, making all other boats look like they were put together with popsicle sticks and glue. The music switched to a hip-hop remix of *Sexual Healing* by Marvin Gaye. Two girls in the seats at the front of the boat squealed and got up to dance, reaching beckoning hands towards Fed. They were both slender and tanned. The blond one wore a bikini top and a short skirt and the other wore a tiny, skin-tight dress. They were both ridiculously beautiful. Hood ornaments. I pushed the thought away in shame. I didn't know these girls.

The motorboat slowly began to turn, like a sleepy sea monster. It drew alongside us and Fed grabbed the edge. The music was turned down. Two of Fed's friends waited to help us board. A blond man dressed in a white fedora, slender as a straw, and a big man with a fierce black beard and topknot. I thought he must be Karim until I saw another man who dwarfed all. He was bald and was holding a water bottle in his paw of a hand. He looked deep in conversation with the driver.

Fed boarded first, and then me.

"You must be Saxony?" the slim blond man asked, holding out a hand. "I'm Jacopo."

"Yeah, that's me." I took his hand and he pulled me close to him and kissed my right cheek, then my left.

"Piacere," I said.

"Nice to meet you, too. Take a seat."

I sat as the boat drifted away from the boat jam. We sliced through the water like a predatory fish. Jacopo sat down beside me, a half-full beer bottle in his hand.

Fed already had a plastic cup of some pink liquid in her hand. "Everyone, this is Saxony."

Her friends lifted their drinks toward me, except for the driver, who had his back to us.

I grinned. "Ciao, y'all."

"Something to drink?" Jacopo asked. He lifted a seat cover and exposed a cooler. "We have beer, or Stefania can make you a spritz, or one of these iced tea things..." He pulled one up and peered at it. He looked older than the rest of Fed's friends, deeply tanned with visible lines across his forehead.

"That iced tea thing sounds great, grazie." I took the cold can from him.

"Fed says you're Canadian?" he asked, his voice rising as the dance music was turned up a notch. The other men in the rear of the boat listened for my answer, too.

"Yes, from Eastern Canada. I'm here for the summer. You're from Venice, I assume?" I opened the can and took a sip. It was sweet and definitely alcoholic.

He laughed. "No, not very many of us are from Venice. I'm from Napoli. Marco here is Roman." He nodded toward his friend. "I moved here for a work a few years ago. I manage two hotels here in Venezia and one in Verona."

I blinked. Fed's friends were not high school kids. "Wow, that sounds busy. How did you get into that line of work?"

As I listened, I scanned the view of Venice from the boat. Street lamps lined the walkway in front of the square, sending their light across the water in wavy lines. The crowd covered every surface of the island, including roofs. People shrank to the size of ants as we left the island behind. The boat slowed in a patch of open water. The driver turned off the engine and the vibration stopped. He was the only one who hadn't greeted me yet, or even looked at me. He must be Dante. I studied his back, curiously.

He was not overly tall but he was wide at the shoulder and slender at the hips. He wore a pastel pink polo shirt with yellow and white horizontal stripes, powder-blue cotton shorts, and white leather flip-flops. I thought that maybe Fed was a little overzealous by referring to him as 'dangerous.' With all that pastel, he looked like cotton candy.

As Jacopo told me about his career in the hospitality industry, I couldn't tear my eyes from Dante. He moved gracefully to the beat of the music. One tanned arm reached down and plucked a plastic cup from a cup holder. I caught a glimpse of a tattoo on the outer edge of his left wrist but it was so small I couldn't tell what it was. Finally, he turned and looked me full in the face.

I no longer heard a word Jacopo was saying.

Dante was not cotton candy.

EVERYTHING about him said that he knew who he was and what he wanted out of life. I had the sense he'd been born with that look. When he'd turned, he didn't look anywhere else, he knew exactly where I was sitting and his eyes found mine and held them.

A tiny vibration began in me. It wasn't that he was so good-looking, although he did have nice features. It was his expression. I wasn't sure I could look away even if I wanted to. His almond shaped, dark brown eyes were slightly upturned at the outer corners, giving him a mischievous look. A smile played about his lips. In his expression was a challenge, like he was daring me to look away. Let him challenge. I wouldn't drop my eyes first even if the boat caught fire. I lifted my chin just a little and he cracked a lopsided smile. I relaxed.

He crossed the short space between us and Jacopo moved over to make room. Dante sat beside me and threw an arm over the back of the seat behind me as though he'd known me his whole life. I shifted to face him.

"Who are you?" he asked, cocking his head to the side.

"I'm Saxony. Who are you?" I cocked my head to mimic him. On the outside I was all sass, but my heart was pounding like the drum of a warship.

"Yeah, but who *are* you?" he repeated, lifting his hand from behind me, he took a stray curl between his thumb and forefinger. A whirlwind of butterflies took off in my stomach. He hadn't touched my skin, but somehow, he sent a message to everyone on the boat that I was the only one who mattered. I was conscious of the looks we were getting, but I was too captured by him to care.

I opened my mouth to respond, but he continued, "Look at this hair."

His eyes finally left mine to roam the mass of curls on the top of my head. He put a hand into his pocket, lifting his hips to reach his fingers inside. He pulled something out but it was hidden in his palm. I had no time to react as he snapped open the butterfly knife and lifted it to my hair. I gasped as he cut something, quick as a snake.

My hair fell down around my face and shoulders. I half expected a hank of curls to go tumbling onto the floor of the boat, and I touched my head to make sure. "Did you just cut my hair?"

"Only the elastic. This is much better." He snapped the butterfly knife closed and put it back in his pocket. He leaned back to admire his handiwork. He fluffed my curls with one hand, setting them as though he was a practiced hairdresser.

My mouth hung half open in shock before I snapped it shut and narrowed my eyes. What would I have done if he had actually cut a few locks? Jack's face flashed before my eyes for a moment and I took a breath.

"You're very, very lucky," I said, punctuating every word.

From the corner of my eye, I saw Jacopo look over at the sound of my voice.

"Oh, she's proud of her hair," laughed Dante.

I stiffened. Was he mocking me? Then he stopped laughing and a look of admiration came over his face.

"She should be." His finger touched my cheekbone. He leaned in close and lowered his voice, "She is very, very beautiful."

He said it like he really meant it.

My shock at his boldness dissolved. "He is very, very silver-tongued."

"Silver-tongued," he repeated. "I like this term. Can I use it?" He leaned back with a crooked smile and didn't wait for an answer. "We should spend some time together. I think you're a girl good with words, no? I like words. I like to collect them. I don't know so many of these phrases in English. Teach me more." He looked at me with anticipation.

Dante and I talked and laughed as though we were the only two people on the boat. He was unlike anyone I had ever met and I was fascinated. My blood hummed as I finished my iced tea. At some point, another drink appeared in my hand, dripping and cold.

"Are you originally from Venice?" I asked, thinking about what Jacopo had said, that very few of them were actually Venetian.

"I am. Fed and I are the only native Venetians on this boat. I know everyone there is to know in Venezia. My family has been here literally for hundreds of years."

"That's a lot of history. Do you have a massive family tree hanging on the wall in your foyer?"

I didn't know my own family's history beyond my father's great grandparents. They had emigrated from Ireland during the Great Famine and felt compelled to anglicize their name from Ó Cainghe to Cagney. My mother's side? They could have been horse thieves for all I knew.

He barked a laugh. "All over my father's house. We have library shelves dedicated to our history. My ancestors were one of the patrician families that founded the Great Council; their form of government. Venezia was a very rich and relatively peaceful republic for six hundred years, thanks in part, to my family."

"What about The Doge?" I asked. "He had a pretty snazzy palace, all that pink and white marble. You sure you're not related?" I teased, tugging on the hem of his bubble-gum pink sleeve.

"There were a few Doges in my family," he grinned, his tilted eyes sparkled.

"Didn't he have any power?"

"Early on, yes. It was an autocracy. But by the twelfth century, The Doge was mostly a ceremonial position, and one that families fought to get and keep. It was a bought and paid for title and didn't have much in the way of real power." His eyes gleamed. "It's the men behind the scenes who were the ones with the real power."

BOOM!

I jumped.

Pop! Pop!

The bright red explosion flowering in the sky and the crackling of a multitude of spinning white flowers announced the fireworks. Conversations stopped. When Dante put an arm around me and pulled me close, it seemed like the most natural thing in the world to tilt my head back against his arm. The sky filled with color and light. The beautiful explosions echoed the fireworks going off in my stomach as Dante tilted his head toward mine and our temples touched. I closed my eyes for a brief moment as a wave of dizziness passed through me. Sighing deeply, I let my neck relax. My head felt heavy.

Dante turned and kissed my sweaty temple, and then turned back to the fireworks. I looked over at him, admiring the long eyelashes against his cheek and the play of colored light over the bones of his face. He turned and looked at me. His gaze dropped to my mouth and in a moment of panic I turned my face back up to the fireworks. I liked him, and I was definitely fuzzy from the alcohol, but I hadn't had so much that I was about to kiss someone I'd just met. Especially in front of a bunch of his friends. He turned his face away.

When the fireworks concluded, Dante got up and yelled, "Who wants to get wet?"

The girls cheered. The guys nodded, wiping sweat from their shining brows. The breeze had died and it was even hotter now than it had been during the day. Dante started the boat and steered us smoothly toward open water.

"Aren't we going the wrong way?" I asked Jacopo, but it was Karim who answered.

"To reach the Venice beach we have to go between Lido and Le Vignole." He gestured with an enormous hand toward the dark water between two islands. He really was the largest human I'd ever seen. A solid mountain of meat, mostly muscle. His bald head shone with sweat.

"Hello, giant man." I held out my hand. He swallowed it in his baseball mitt of a hand.

"Hello, tiny woman." His voice was so deep I couldn't help but picture tectonic plates rubbing against each other under the earth's crust. I'd never been called tiny before. I'm not as tall as Georjayna, but at 5'7" and curvaceous, I'm not remotely petite. I dwarfed Targa and Akiko. Now I knew how they felt.

"Fed tells me you're Canadian?"

"I am," he said, nodding. "I was born in Egypt, but raised in Calgary." He was gigantic but he had a baby face, wide inquiring eyes, and a gentle expression.

"How is it that you find yourself in Venice?" I asked, savouring the breeze as the boat went faster. My loose curls whipped about. They'd be hell to pick out later.

"It's a good place to start my life over," he said. "I did some stupid shit back home that got me into trouble. I did some time, destroyed some lives, now I'm here. A fresh start, y'know. I work for Dante's father now." He leaned in and said, "I don't normally keep company with Dante's guys, but he wanted me along, so..." He shrugged and took a swig from his water bottle.

"Is that so?" I kept my voice casual but I swallowed. What did this guy do? Was he dangerous? I made a note to ask Fed for more details. "Where did you do this stupid shit, exactly?"

My mother would have told me to mind my own business, but my mother wasn't here.

"Calgary," he answered. "I did time in Drumheller Penitentiary. Ever been to Drumheller?"

I shook my head. "No, my family did a trip to Banff once but we never made it that far east of the mountains. What did you do time for?"

"Only what I got caught for," he said with a lopsided smile.

"Stop scaring her, Karim," Dante said from the wheel. "She's not going to want to hang out with us if she finds out we're a bunch of criminals. Besides, you're sorry. Aren't you?"

"Yeah, I am actually." Karim looked me in the eye and nodded so sincerely that I thought he might actually mean it.

We drifted perpendicular to a long beach full of lights. Small explosions of firecrackers filled the sky and the sounds of music and partiers drifted across the water.

"This is Lido," said Karim. "There," he said to Dante, pointing to a group of partiers near a large tent. Drum and bass music grew louder as we approached. Dante stopped before we got too close and pressed a button. A whirring sound vibrated through the boat as he put down anchor.

There were two splashes and the boat lurched sideways as a couple of the girls dove into the water from the nose. Fed was pulling off her shirt. "Saxony, are you coming?"

"Absolutely." I stood and unzipped my dress. I stepped out of it and then held it for a moment. Were we going to party in nothing but wet bathing suits?

"Here." As though reading my thoughts, Dante held out a waterproof bag. "Put your dress in here. I'll carry it to shore for you."

"Thanks! Good thinking. Are you always this prepared?" I dropped my dress into the bag.

He winked at me and my face grew hot. Lucky for me it was dark and no one could see my blush.

Dante pulled off his polo, exposing a rippled stomach. I flushed again.

More splashes as Jacopo and Marco dove into the water. The backs of their heads glistened, seals swimming toward the beach.

I dove in headfirst and my blood instantly cooled. Dante swam beside me until our feet found the sand. He took my hand as we walked out of the water, enveloping my fingers in his as naturally as though we'd been dating for months. I looked at him in surprise, but he kept his face forward. Eyes watched us approach and people shouted greetings.

Fed was talking to someone I didn't know, but as they were chatting, she scanned the beach. When she spotted me, she gave a nod. It might have been my imagination but I thought she look a little stressed. If she was surprised to see Dante holding my hand, she didn't show it.

Dante and I approached the fire together. Two men sat with their backs to us and turned as Dante spoke. They scrambled to stand.

"Prego," one of them said, gesturing to his chair.

"No, grazie," I said, my face hot.

But Dante put a hand on my hip and guided me into a seat.

"I'll put this here," he said as he set the bag with our clothing in it against my chair. "Get dressed whenever you feel like it,"

"Thanks, Dante." I smiled up at him. *Points.* A flash of Raf's face filled my mind. So far, Italian boys were turning out to be kind and thoughtful.

Dante sat down beside me and a girl in a red bikini opened a cooler and handed him a beer. She pointed at me and asked Dante what I wanted in Italian. I opened my mouth to respond, but Dante answered. She handed him a bottle filled with orange liquid.

"Try this, you'll like it," Dante said.

"What is it?" I took the cold bottle and looked at the label, holding it in the light of the fire.

"Aperol spritz. It's a Venetian drink. You'll be in love with all things Venetian by the end of the summer." He took a swig from his own bottle without taking his eyes from mine.

I opened the bottle and took a sip. It was sweet with a bitter aftertaste. I took another swig, promising myself this would be my last drink. "Is there a washroom nearby?"

"Just go in the sea," he said, pointing the neck of his beer bottle toward the water.

I balked and my mind went blank with embarrassment.

"I'll show you," Federica said as she walked up to the fire. "I have to go, too."

"Grazie." I got up to follow her.

She walked ahead of me and I strode to catch up, but there were so many people on the beach that I almost lost her in the crowd. We approached the speakers and the bass thumped in my chest. A line of girls in bikinis and tiny dresses stood waiting for the outdoor toilets.

Fed stopped at the queue and turned to face me. It wasn't just my instinct before—she did look stressed. Her lips were pressed tightly together, the corners downturned.

"You okay, Fed?"

"I didn't know he'd take to you so much," she said. "I didn't think he even liked redheads."

I blinked. She'd said she didn't like Dante, but this sounded like jealousy.

"I just..." She shifted her feet. "Never mind." She shook her head and blew out a frustrated breath. Just then, one of the washrooms became available and she went to take it, leaving me bemused.

When I came out of the toilet, Fed was already back at the fire. I was making a beeline for her when a warm hand ran down my arm and clasped my fingers. Dante pulled me around to face him, and suddenly we were nose to nose. His almond shaped eyes sparkled down at me. Pleasure blossomed in my stomach like a rose.

"Dance with me," he whispered against my ear, his accent rich and warm.

Thoughts of Fed vanished as he pulled me toward the dance floor. The music enveloped us as Dante's arms wrapped around my waist and he pulled me against him. His soft lips brushed the curve of my ear and I shivered with pleasure. Closing my eyes, I melted against him, letting the music sweep me away.

SIX

I woke as my phone chirped. I cracked open an eye. Bright sunlight streamed in through the lace curtains on my window and dappled across my bed. I was sweating, so I threw off the single sheet, clawing at it with my legs. It was going to be even hotter today than it was yesterday. Yawning, I put a palm to my temple. A dull thud throbbed there that matched my heartbeat. How much had I had to drink last night? I reached for the glass of water on my bedside table and guzzled the entire thing before picking up my phone. The screen told me it was almost eleven. I squinted at the blurry text message beneath the time.

Fed: *Buongiorno. How do you feel this morning?*

I rubbed my eyes and refocused so I could tap out a response: *Someone made frittata with my brains. How do you feel?*

Fed: *Just sleepy. Glad it's Sunday. Have fun last night?*

Me: *I had a great time, thanks for taking me.*

She didn't answer for a few minutes. And then finally, *You are welcome.*

Another text showed on my screen-not from Fed, but Elda.

Elda: *Are you up? I need a favor. I'm sorry, I know it's your day off but I have an emergency at work. Cristiano is at a friend's house but could you watch Isaia? Just for a few hours?*

I groaned. My head flopped back on my pillow. As much as I loved Isaia, the last thing I felt like doing was babysitting. I couldn't refuse just because I was hungover.

Of course. Be down in 15?

Elda: *Thank you so much! I'll make it up to you, I promise.*

I nodded grimly and got out of bed. The mirror caught my eye, and I grimaced. Mascara had left smudgy rings under my eyes, and my hair was a bushy disaster. I hadn't showered after swimming last night and I could feel the salt on my skin and in my hair.

I got into the shower and scrubbed myself clean and washed my hair thoroughly. I picked the tangles out of my wet curls, and then twisted my hair into a bun at the nape of my neck. Instantly, short spirals sprang out on my forehead and around my ears. My mom always said that my hair was a reflection of my spirit. If that was the case, then I was rebellious and uncontrollable.

I wrinkled my nose as I threw the dress I had been wearing the night before into my laundry basket, putting on a clean summer dress. I went downstairs.

Elda sat on the marble step at the door, buckling up the straps on her shoes. Her brow was deeply furrowed.

"Everything okay?" I asked.

"One of my employees missed an important deadline. If I don't do some damage control, we could lose an account that is almost half our business." She shook her head. "It's really my fault for relying so heavily on one vendor, but they're a big chain that we can't say no to. I'm not sure how long I'll be gone but I'll call you later. Isaia is playing in his room. Take him for gelato or something, he loves it. I left some money on the counter."

She apologized multiple times and was still saying sorry when she finally shut the door.

I found Isaia in his room doodling in a sketchbook. He had a glass of water and ice sitting on the floor beside him.

"Hi sweetheart. Looks like you and I get to hang out for a few hours." I sat down beside him and kissed the top of his head. "What are you drawing?"

He turned the page toward me. It was covered with doodles of fireballs, all the same shape.

"Wow, Isaia. Very nice." I was about to comment on the irony of his penchant for all things fiery, but I thought better of it. "Guess what? Your mom said we could go for gelato. What do you say?"

He smiled and nodded, which was the best reaction I was bound to get. I slathered us both in sunscreen and found us each a sun hat. I filled a large bottle with water and tucked it into my purse. We stepped out of the air-conditioned comfort of the Baseggio's home and into the stifling heat of an Italian summer day.

I used my phone to search for the nearest gelato shop and

entered the address into my GPS. I took Isaia's hand and we walked silently, keeping to the shade. Thoughts of Dante made my stomach flutter, and I let myself relive the events of the night before. I barely registered that the streets were mostly empty. I could feel Dante's warm hands at my waist, his breath against my neck. I couldn't help but smile as I remembered him cutting my hair elastic, and his tilted eyes as my curls fell down around my shoulder. He was bold, that was for sure. Maybe a little too bold. But our chemistry... it was so compelling. I could forgive someone a lot because of chemistry like that.

The GPS directed us through an open courtyard. We crossed the little piazza, stepped into a narrow calle, and walked toward the sunlight at the far end. As we approached the end of the corridor, the sound of breaking glass shattered my daydream. A screech of twisting metal echoed through the calle. I winced, the sound offending my eardrums.

"What was that?" I looked down at Isaia as he looked up at me, his black eyes wide. I peeked around.

Two men disappeared around a corner in a hurry. A flash of a bright green t-shirt with two yellow stripes across the back. Broken glass scattered across the stones in front of a tabacchi shop.

The metal security shutter had been warped and jammed up in its tracks. A desperate voice called out in Italian. Isaia and I clutched each other's hands as we approached the tabacchi. We bent to look under the twisted shutter. The shop floor was a mess of smashed goods and broken glass. I gasped and my heart jumped. Behind the counter, an elderly man lay on the floor. I could only see his head and one arm. Sweat poured down his face and his eyes were squeezed shut in pain. He had a nasty looking cut on his cheek.

I looked around, readying a yell for help, but the piazza was empty.

"Hang on, I'll help you. Te aiuto, te aiuto," I said, hoping he could understand my horrible Italian. He opened his eyes. Blood dripped across the bridge of his nose and onto the floor. I swallowed down a wave of nausea.

Isaia tugged on my hand. He pointed up. A thin stream of smoke crept from the open door at the back of the shop, behind the man lying on the floor. Fire.

My stomach clenched. I pulled out my phone, nearly dropping it as my fingers trembled. I looked up 'Venezia polizia.' Three stations popped up, but all of them were off the island, two in Mestre and one in Marghera. I hit dial for the closest one. The long dash of the Italian ring tone sounded in my ear and a male voice answered.

"Ciao, uh..." I stuttered. "Is there someone who speaks English?"

The voice asked a question.

"I'm sorry, non parle Italiano. Parle Inglese?"

The voice answered, sounding annoyed. This was getting us nowhere. I shook my head in frustration. I spoke slowly. "If you can understand me, there has been a break in, in Venice. There is an injured man. We are..." I looked around at the walls, scanning for a sign, "...at Calle Angelo. In Venezia."

The voice responded, "Sei al Calle Angelo? Calle Angelo?"

"Si, si," I said, relieved. "Calle Angelo, aiuta me. There's a man in trouble. Un uomo in pericoloso. There might be a fire, too. Uh... fuoco, fuoco."

"Aspetta li," grated the voice. He asked for my 'numero di telefono,' which I gave him. After agreeing to wait, I hung up the phone.

Anxiety twisted in my stomach. What if the men who had done this returned? How long would it take for the police to get here? I peered into the shop to see that the stream of smoke from the back room had grown thicker.

I squatted in front of Isaia. "I need you to wait while I help the man get out." I spotted a cluster of benches in the center of the piazza and led Isaia to one directly across from the tabbachi. "Sit here, on the bench, okay?"

He nodded, his obsidian eyes wide and unblinking.

"It's okay. I'm here." I touched his cheek. "I'm not going far. Just wait for me here, where I can see you." I kissed his head and hurried across the piazza.

I ducked under the broken shutter and crunched over broken glass and a mess of water bottles, packaged food, and candy. I knelt in front of the man. He cradled a bloodied hand against his stomach. He must have fought with the men who had broken into his shop.

He looked at me from under bushy gray eyebrows and my heart squeezed with empathy. Blood ran from his cheek where he'd been cut and pooled on the floor. A wave of dizziness washed over me and I gripped the counter. He pushed himself awkwardly up to an elbow and I helped him to sit up. I opened a package of handkerchiefs. While I pressed one against the cut on his cheek, my hand trembled and I tried to focus on something other than the blood.

"Thank you," he said slowly, his voice thick.

Anger boiled in my blood and I reminded myself to tell the police about the green t-shirt with the yellow stripes. Maybe they could catch the guys today if they acted fast enough.

Glass crunched behind me and I looked to see Isaia walk under the shutter. His face was pale. The smudges under his eyes had returned and his little chest rose and fell with shallow breaths.

"No, sweetie, stay outside please," I said, pointing at the bench. "I'll be with you right away, okay?"

He shook his head and took another step toward me, grabbing his elbows. He didn't want to be alone, and no wonder. I wanted to take him in my arms, but I also wanted to get the old man out of the shop as soon as possible.

The smell of smoke hit my nose. I craned my neck, peering into the back room. Metal shelves piled high with boxes filled the storage space. But aside from a single shaft of sunlight coming from a small window near the ceiling, the room was dark. So where was the smoke coming from?

BANG! BANG!

A scream ripped from my mouth and my heart exploded into a gallop. It sounded like gunfire. Two flashes of bright light illuminated the rear of the shop and my vision peppered with spots.

"Firework, firework," croaked the old man, and resumed trying to stand.

Isaia began to cry. It was the first time I'd heard him make any noise. His little hands clutched against his mouth, a dry heave rasped through his fingers as his shoulders shook.

"It was fireworks, Isaia." I scrambled to my feet, gulping in air to slow my frantic heart. "Just fireworks. You're okay." My voice quavered. "We need to get out. Go back to the bench, Isaia. We'll be right out, okay?" I took a deep breath then gave a sharp cough as my lungs took in smoke.

I put my hands under the man's armpits. I grunted and heaved him upward none too gently. He and I groaned as one. Just as he got his feet under him...

POP!! POP!!! KSSSSSSSSSS. BANG BANG BANG!

We both ducked our heads at the succession of screaming crackles and popping bursts. My ears rang, and the strobe effect of the fireworks flashing through the shop stole my vision for seconds at a time.

BOOM!

A blast of hot air from an explosion that was too powerful to be fireworks sent me sprawling across broken goods. I cried out as the man fell on my calves and something sharp cut into my knee. A fiery line of pain sliced across my left palm. The walls shook and dust fell from the ceiling.

"Isaia!" I screamed.

Dust and dirt fell in my eyes. I rubbed at them desperately, my mouth dry with fear. All efforts to pretend I was in control had fled. Isaia couldn't respond, and the answering silence froze my blood in my veins. I was faintly aware of a warm flickering light behind me, and a growing heat.

A high pitched metallic scream. A bang so sharp I winced and covered my ears. The shop went from mostly light to mostly dark as the security shutter slammed shut.

SEVEN

Crackling flames of a healthy fire licked from the open doorway of the back room. The man let out of a stream of raspy Italian and reached for a cell phone sitting on the countertop. Heat poured from the storage room in waves. Whatever was burning, it included chemicals and plastics. Dizziness washed over me as I sucked in a toxic breath. I rubbed at my eyes, blinking the dirt from them.

I stumbled to my feet. My left palm stung and felt wet and sticky. I put an arm around the man and pulled him as hard as I dared, away from the fire and toward the shutter. I was terrified there would be another explosion. Sweat sprang out all over my body as the temperature inside the shop doubled, and adrenalin flooded my body. My legs shook.

A soft dull thud. The crunching of plastic. I turned to the sound and nearly choked on my tongue.

Isaia had collapsed.

"Isaia!" It came out a whisper. My lips trembled.

I let go of the man and stumbled across the shop. I tripped and recovered. My ankles rolled over the mess on the floor. I dropped beside him. "Isaia? Isaia, can you hear me?"

In the wavering firelight, his eyes gleamed. I could have wept with relief. He was conscious, but his little chest was heaving.

"Isaia, what's wrong?" I put a hand to his forehead and immediately snatched it back, cursing. His forehead was so dry and hot that I couldn't touch him. *Not again!* I looked at the man. He held his cell phone to his ear.

I leapt to my feet and peeked through the tiny holes in the shutter. Putting my lips to one of the small holes that dotted the metal, I yelled, "Fire! Fuoco!"

I looked back. The flames licked higher, and black smoke billowed up across the ceiling. I rattled the shutter and tried to lift it, but there was nothing to grab. The warped metal had jammed in the runners and was locked down.

A man appeared on the other side of the shutter. I almost collapsed with relief.

"Oh thank God. Please help us, can you lift this shutter?"

My heart soared when he answered in English. "Are you okay? Who else is inside?"

"A small boy and an elderly man with a broken wrist or hand. They both need medical attention, right away. Can you lift this shutter? I can't move it from the inside. There's a fire in here. Something in the storage room exploded. I'm worried something else will go off."

The man yelled at someone else I couldn't see, and I heard the words 'vigile del fuoco.' The shutter began to rattle and I heard grunting.

I looked down at Isaia and my heart stopped. His belly was glowing through his t-shirt. I dropped to my knees beside him. I took his hand but snatched it back, gasping as his heat burned me again. He looked down at his own tummy and back up at me, his expression urgent, his black eyes terrified and filled with pain.

"Isaia..." I fought to keep the panic from my voice and failed miserably.

The glow increased. It spread wide across his abdomen and I could see it easily through his t-shirt.

Behind me, the old man babbled in Italian but then he paused and muttered, "Madonna."

Isaia squeezed his eyes shut, wincing. Panic flapped wickedly like a bird in my heart. I forgot the growing fire in the back room as I watched the glow in his stomach increase in size. It moved up into his chest and he made a choking sound. Helplessness and panic crashed like fighting rams in my chest. I looked around and grabbed a bottle of water from a pile on the floor. I fumbled with the cap and held the bottle to his lips and tilted it.

He spluttered and coughed, seemingly unable to swallow. He opened his eyes and they glowed red like two embers. He coughed violently, and the glow in his chest split in two and began to crawl. One half moved out to his right shoulder and the other to his left. My fingers clenched and unclenched helplessly. My hand flew to my mouth in horror and I fought not to hyperventilate. The crackle of flames, the stench of burning plastic, and the yelling voices on the other side of the shutter all faded into the background.

The two glows in Isaia's shoulders traveled down each arm, flickering as they went. He wheezed heavily. The red in his eyes turned yellow, then white.

"Why can't you drink?" I cried. I poured a little water over his lips but it just ran down his face, sizzling.

Isaia's elbows lit up like two torches, the glow traveled down his forearms. His arms were white hot at the center and a bright glowing red on the outer edges. His eyes rolled back in his head.

I squinted against the light. The white-hot glow traveled into his hands and stopped in his palms. His body began to shake.

"Isaia," I whimpered. I had never felt so utterly helpless. "What's happening to you?"

His eyes closed, but the light penetrated his thin eyelids, giving them a pink glow. He turned his palms up, the centers of each hand as bright as stars and each finger glowing red. His hands shook.

Then he opened his eyes again and something changed, ever so subtly. The white began to fade slowly from his eyes. They refocused on me, as though he had passed out and came too again. The muscles on the sides of his jaw clenched. He looked me in the eyes and I gasped in shock at what I saw there. His focus faded in and out.

He was dying. I could see death creeping up on him as surely as I could hear my own heartbeat pounding in my ears.

Before I could register anything, he turned his palms toward me and slammed them flat against my stomach. A scream caught in my throat. All that escaped was a wisp of breath, like a sigh. I did not feel heat against my stomach, but a sharp cold feeling, like dry ice. I coughed, and a wisp of smoke drifted from my mouth. I knelt there, unable to react. Isaia's eyes still held mine, his eyelids drifted down, the light dimmed, dimmed. My eyes dropped, they were all I could move. The white-hot glow traveled through his hands and into the bowl of my pelvis as it passed through my skin and into my organs.

It was then that I felt the heat.

The scream that had been trapped in my throat ripped out of me.

There was a flash of apology from Isaia's eyes. He took his hands away and fell back into the mess of broken goods.

I collapsed with my forehead to the ground. The glow was now in my own belly. I gagged. First only smoke and bile came up, and then I retched and lost my breakfast. I spat and struggled for breath. I retched again and flaming embers spewed out. I sucked in air and coughed hard. An ember the size of a pebble came up to my tongue. I spat it sideways, away from Isaia, and watched with horror as it skipped across the floor like it had been shot from a gun, leaving a smoking black gouge. It lodged in the stone wall. I blinked, unable to register what I saw. The ember flickered and cooled to black. Surely, it hadn't come from me? Not possible.

My stomach and throat burned like I had swallowed a cupful of magma. Recovering the power of my limbs, I fumbled for water and found the bottle on the ground. My guts screamed for something cold and wet. I opened my throat and downed the whole bottle. The liquid sizzled as I swallowed it down, instantly soothing my seared insides.

I dropped the bottle, panting. My eyes felt hot and hard. I looked down at Isaia. He coughed, but he actually looked much better. He pushed himself up into sitting, and looked up at me. His eyes traveled from my eyes to my belly and back up again, blinking and wide.

I looked down. The glow was gone, but the fire was there—I could feel it. It was banked and waiting.

"Isaia!" I croaked. I didn't recognize my own voice. It was rough. Scratchy. Burnt. "Isaia." I put a hand on his forehead. He was damp and much cooler. It was the first time I had ever seen him sweat. "What have you done to me, Isaia?" I whispered.

His eyes were full of urgency. He tried to get up. He coughed again. A violent cough behind me brought me to myself. I remembered where we were. We were still in danger.

Another screaming firecracker went off behind us and I pushed Isaia down. Smoke rolled across the ceiling. It filled the space over our heads and slowly drifted down toward us. Voices yelled outside and the shutter rattled. The metal screamed and the shutter moved a half inch. Light streamed in through the crack at the bottom.

Isaia coughed and then pointed repeatedly and urgently at the flames. I knew instantly what he was trying to tell me. It was plain on his face and plain in the knowledge that I had only moments ago acquired.

The knowledge of fire.

It was sitting in my guts and talking to me. I had been inducted. I understood now why it had been making him sick—he was far too frail for what I now carried. What he had wasn't an illness, it was power. The pain of it was there, but I was strong enough to bear it. I was strong enough to wield it, strong enough to take on the flames now growing out of control and licking from the back room and into the shop.

Isaia coughed harder. The elderly man moved toward the shutter, coughing all the while. He and Isaia put their faces down low, close to the holes in the shutter to inhale clean air. They both had their backs to me now.

"Fuoco! Fuoco!" Shouts could be heard outside.

But I was in here, and I could do something. I looked at the flames and felt... affection. I stood and crossed quickly to the back room. I sucked smoke into my lungs, but it didn't bother me anymore. It tickled across my skin, soft and warm.

The shutter screeched again, but it was a distant sound. I raised my hands to the flames. They flickered toward me in response. A choice: should I call it forward and absorb it, or push it back and snuff it? The fire inside me had power over the fire outside of me. It felt not unlike trying to calm a bucking horse or a panicked dog.

Using my hands to coach the flames, I stroked them back and back, toward the back room from which they'd come. Whatever magic Isaia had given me, I could see it in the wavering heat that streamed from my fingertips. The flames had been fed by oxygen through the window in the back of the shop. But though there was plenty of air to feed this fire, it was now dying instead. *Because of me.*

As the fire dwindled, blackened shelves and smoldering boxes were revealed in its wake. The flames licked through the doorway. They curled like fingertips clawing for purchase on the smoking doorjamb. The fingers disappeared and I followed them, pushing the fire back.

I stepped through the doorway. Shadows of shelving and boxes appeared and disappeared in my vision, all of it lined with glowing embers. The sound of crackling flames had become a kind of music in my ears. The curling smoke made a stream in the air as it was sucked out the rear window.

The last of the flames flickered and went out. I lowered my hands. I felt as though I'd just woken from a dream. Goosebumps swept across my skin at the power I held.

I watched currents of smoke curl and drift. Dying embers highlighted the edges of the ruined contents of the room. Charred boxes lined the shelves like rows of lumpy headstones. Unrecognizable items smoldered and jutted from holes in boxes like broken bones poking up through blackened skin.

Voices called and I turned. Light streamed in through the front door of the shop. It lit up the mess on the floor and illuminated the smoke. The shutter juddered and jarred as it was shoved upward the rest of the way, filling the air with a horrible sound. I winced and covered my ears.

I squeezed my eyes shut as vertigo swept over me. Had it all been a dream? As though in answer, the fire inside me flickered and danced underneath my ribcage. There was nothing dreamy about the heat residing in me now. I opened my eyes, thinking of Isaia.

He looked back at me, his little chest heaving with coughs, but his eyes void of pain for the first time since I'd met him. He actually smiled, coughed again, and then beckoned me with his hand.

"I'm coming," I croaked.

The man looked over his shoulder. He took Isaia's hand and gestured to me with a jerk of his head. He cradled his injured hand against his chest.

I crossed the shop in a few quick strides, my feet crunching on broken glass. The stinging of my left palm and my knee reminded me that I was still human. My ankles ached from having been twisted earlier.

I took Isaia's other hand, and as hands reached to steady us, we ducked under the shutter and stepped out into the sunlight.

EIGHT

Less than an hour later, I sat on a park bench under the trees with Isaia cuddled on my lap. He coughed occasionally, but seemed otherwise relaxed. The emergency personnel hadn't allowed us to leave in spite of my pleas to take Isaia home. Caution tape had sprung up in a wide berth around the tabacchi, and a crowd had gathered to watch the uniformed police and firemen going in and out of the shop and talking with each other, taking notes.

My phone chirped and I pulled it out and blinked at it, feeling dazed.

Fed: *Ciao Bella. I'm off tomorrow eve. Meet me?*

I stared at the message, not really comprehending it. I couldn't even bring Federica's face to my mind right now. I tucked my phone away without responding.

When we'd finally escaped the shop, a medic had pulled the man aside to where a gurney had been erected. Isaia and I had been taken into an ambulance boat in a nearby canal. Medics fussed over us, checked our vitals, and listened to our lungs. They cleaned and bandaged my hand and knee. My ankles had been twisted, but not sprained. They'd iced and wrapped them.

Isaia showed more fascination for the ambulance boat than distress from the ordeal. He had suffered some smoke inhalation but the medics said that otherwise, he was unharmed. He was to rest, and he would cough for a few days but it should clear up on its own. If anything else arose, I was to bring him to the hospital.

While my hand was bandaged, I had numbly given an account of what happened to an English-speaking police officer. I told them about the man in the green sweater. I left out everything about Isaia passing his fire to me. I thought the officer had bought my story that the flames had gone out on their own. Isaia and I had been released from the ambulance and told to wait until we were dismissed to go home.

I watched from the park bench, moths fluttering in my stomach, as the man told his version of the story to another officer. His cheek had been bandaged. He gestured toward me, and his voice rose and fell with emphasis.

The officer shot several glances in my direction. When he was finished taking the man's statement, he made a beeline for me. I shrank down against the bench, holding Isaia tighter. The fluttering moths morphed into panicked bats flapping against my ribcage.

The officer looked down at me, his dark eyes serious. "I'm Officer Zambelli. I am told you are a hero," he said in a thick accent.

I shook my head emphatically. "No, no, definitely not."

"If what Signor Fantelli told me is true, you are. You were the first person on the scene after the break-in and assault, and you called for help. After the shutter collapsed, you put out the fire. Is all that true?"

I shook my head. "The fire went out on its own."

Maybe the old guy hadn't said anything about the white light that passed from Isaia to me. I shot him a grateful look. He was just staring at me, watching while the officer and I talked.

"You didn't put it out? He seems to think you did."

"No. The flames just went out," I croaked weakly.

"Signor Fantelli says the storage room had fireworks inventory and benzene lighters. All three of you are very lucky to have survived. It's very strange. A small window in the rear was wide open. That fire should not have gone out on its own." He studied my face, his gaze unwavering.

"Thank God it did," I rasped. "May I take Isaia home now? He's been awfully frightened. We both have."

We looked down at Isaia, sitting on the bench beside me. He dangled his legs and watched the action. He looked up at us. He was covered in soot and looked like a street urchin, but he was as happy as I'd ever seen him.

"A few more minutes, signorina," Officer Zambelli said. He reached into his breast pocket and pulled out a business card. "Please take this. If you happen to remember anything else, call me."

I took the card and watched as he joined his colleagues. They spoke to one another and sent more glances our way than I was comfortable with. I pulled Isaia onto my lap again, more for my comfort than for his, and prayed for Elda to arrive. I had called her immediately after stepping out of the tabacchi. My hoarse voice had probably done more to freak her out than my actual words. I'd tried to downplay the level of danger we'd been in, but she'd interrupted, saying she was on her way.

A younger version of the elderly man had appeared at his side. The younger man wore a business suit and tie. They spoke, and the younger Fantelli looked my way. I dropped my lips to Isaia's head and closed my eyes, taking deep breaths.

A moment later, "Excuse me. What's your name, Miss?" His voice was softly accented.

I looked up to see the younger Fantelli standing at my elbow. The elder stood behind him, peering at me. I set Isaia on the bench and stood up, feeling a little dizzy. I was very distracted by the new and mostly unpleasant sensation of fire inside my pelvis.

"Saxony," I croaked, and managed a smile for him. "How is your... father?"

"My Uncle, actually. He has a broken bone in his wrist, but he'll be okay. We want to say thank you for what you did." He held out his hand and I took it. He shook it warmly in a two-handed clasp. He pulled me forward and kissed my right cheek, then my left. His eyes were lined with moisture. "Really, I don't know what would have happened if you hadn't been there. We are so much grateful."

I blushed. "It's nothing. Anyone would have done it."

"No, they wouldn't."

Signor Fantelli stepped closer. He took my hand in his good one, kissed my right cheek, then my left, then my right again.

"Grazie. Grazie voi. Grazie mille. Bella angelo." Tears glistened in his eyes as well.

I swallowed my own tears back at the look on his face. My emotions were already riding close to the surface.

"Prego," I rasped.

Elda appeared on the other side of the piazza, her eyes scanning the space frantically. I waved at her. She began to run, and the sound of her heels on the stone echoed across the courtyard. She was halted by an officer and the two exchanged words. He looked over at us and let her go.

"What were you thinking?" Elda hissed as she took Isaia in her arms. She was visibly shaking. Her chin wobbled and her eyes flashed.

I took an involuntary step back, stung. Rationally, I understood her fear, but after everything we had just been through, my self-control was already stretched thin. My face flushed with heat. My body tightened up and I closed my eyes and visualized Jack. I took a deep breath.

The two Fantelli men stared at Elda, wide-eyed. The sweetness of our interaction had been swallowed up by awkwardness and embarrassment.

Elda ignored them. "You entered the scene of a crime?" she cried, her voice sharp. "For all you knew the... the... the criminals could still have been inside, and you thought it was a good idea to take my son in there?"

She wrapped her arms around Isaia and squeezed him so hard, he squirmed.

I opened my mouth but I was too stunned for words. She was right, actually. I had exposed Isaia to danger. My vision wavered, like I was looking at her from across the top of a bonfire.

"This girl is a hero, signora," said the younger Fantelli, his voice soft. "She may have saved my uncle's life."

"She may have," said Elda, rounding on him. "But it could have been at the expense of my son."

Mr. Fantelli took a step back at the venom in her voice and put up his palms. He looked at me with pity-filled eyes and put an arm around his uncle. Fantelli senior was staring at Elda, his brow wrinkled. He pulled away from his nephew and let out a stream of angry Italian at her. He gestured emphatically toward me and then toward the burnt out tabacchi shop, clearly defending me.

Elda spouted angry Italian back at him, her voice growing louder. Spectators began to look our direction. An officer started to walk our way.

My focus passed back and forth between Elda and the elderly man. My mind whirled. I needed them to stop fighting. Black spots appeared in my vision and their voices blurred together. I reached a hand out for something to hold on to, but there was nothing. My hand patted the air uselessly. The world turned sideways. Everything went black.

VOICES ARGUED. My head throbbed. My vision swam as I opened my eyes, so I squeezed them shut again.

"Miss? Can you hear me?"

I forced my eyes open. "I can hear you."

"How many fingers am I holding up?"

I looked at the medic's gloved hand. "Quattro. Do I get double points for answering in Italian?"

She smiled and took my pulse, then listened to my heart with a stethoscope.

I tried to lift my head.

"Stay down, please. You fainted. We'll take you to hospital soon, but emergency is backed up so it'll be a wait."

My heart began to pound along with my head. The last thing I wanted was to go to the hospital. Anxiety swamped my stomach at the very thought of it. "That won't be necessary. I'm feeling much better. I'm just tired. I didn't sleep last night," I lied. "I hate hospitals, so taking me there will only stress me out further. Please, just send me home to rest."

The medic frowned and spoke to a nearby colleague. I understood the words for 'delay' and 'four hours.' It sounded like if they sent me to hospital I would just be sitting around a waiting room for a long time.

"Really, I'm okay." I sat up slowly and she didn't prevent me. "May I have some water, please?"

Someone handed me a bottle of cold water and I drank it. I smiled at the medic. "See? Just a fainting spell. I have low blood pressure. Sometimes it happens."

She didn't look happy, but Elda, who was carrying Isaia, spoke to her in Italian and the medic finally agreed to let me go. We were released from the courtyard and as soon as we were out of view of everyone, I leaned against the calle wall. Shock made my legs weak.

"Saxony?" It seemed Elda had passed over the worst of her anger.

"I just have a headache," I rasped. "I'm okay."

The fire flickered in my belly, reminding me of its presence.

"Your voice sounds terrible." She put a hand to my head. Her eyebrows shot up. "You're feverish. Can you make it home? Maybe we should go to hospital after all? We need to call your parents."

"I will," I said. "The hospital is not necessary, though. I just need to rest."

My head pounded and thoughts of my bed beckoned. I walked toward home. Elda and Isaia followed. If Elda was still upset, I couldn't tell. I couldn't pay attention to anything other than putting one foot after the other.

Once we'd arrived home, Elda forced me to lie on her bed where she could keep an eye on me. I collapsed, not caring which bed I was in, and fell into a deep, dreamless sleep.

IT WAS the fire that woke me, licking at the insides of my ribcage. I winced. My mouth and eyes felt hot and dry. I sat up on my elbow and took a drink from the glass of water on the bedside table. Instantly, it took the edge off the pain. I spotted the digital thermometer sitting there and frowned. I brought it to my ear and pressed the button. When it beeped, I watched the screen.

85.

I no longer thought the thermometer was broken. I really was that hot. Any normal person would be dead by now.

There was a knock on the door and Elda poked her head in. "Saxony?" she whispered.

"I'm awake."

"How do you feel?" She approached the bed.

"You know that saying death warmed over?" I gave a rough, dry laugh and pushed myself upright.

"No, what does it mean?"

"Never mind. I'm okay." I wasn't, but I wasn't going to admit that. "How is Isaia?" I dropped my legs over the side of the bed.

"He's—" She paused, her brows creased. "It's strange, but he's really cold. It's the first time I've seen him be cold in his whole life."

This made some kind of sense. After all, the fire that had been giving him fevers had now taken up residence inside me.

"Is he in his room?"

Elda nodded.

I got up, passing her as I went to the door. My vision still wavered and I walked on unsteady legs. She followed me down the hallway and into Isaia's room. I opened the door to see a little lump in Isaia's bed, huddling under thick blankets normally reserved for winter.

"Isaia?" I said softly, approaching his bed.

A little hand pushed the blankets away from his face and his black eyes peeked out.

"Are you cold, buddy?" I sat on the side of his bed. I took his hand and gasped. His fingers were little popsicles.

I looked up at Elda with alarm. She crossed her arms, her brows drawn tight.

I was burning up while he was nearly hypothermic. I pulled his blanket back.

"Scootch over, little dude."

He wriggled sideways and I lay down beside him and pulled his narrow back up against my stomach. He was in full flannel pajamas but his entire body was rigid with cold. His icy frame felt delicious against my roasting torso. I wrapped my arms around him, pressing my fire against his back.

Elda sat on the side of his bed and we stayed like that for a long time. Isaia slowly began to relax. At some point, Elda got up and left. I dozed in and out of consciousness. Every time I came to, my head felt a little clearer. Isaia warmed up as I cooled down. He jarred me fully awake when he began to squirm.

"Feeling better? I know I am." I didn't feel like jumping up and down, but the worst seemed over.

Isaia crawled over me and left the room. I sat up as well, my face cracking with an enormous yawn.

Elda appeared in the doorway, holding Isaia. Her expression was unreadable.

"I guess I'll go upstairs, now," I said, feeling awkward.

"Saxony," she said, quietly. Relief was etched into her face. "Thank you. I'll look after the boys tomorrow. You just rest. Okay?"

I nodded. "Okay, thanks."

I gave Isaia's fingers a little tug and smiled at him.

He smiled back.

My body felt light with relief. Isaia was okay, and Elda wasn't angry anymore. But I needed time to think. Would I ever be normal again?

NINE

I sat on the little couch in my apartment, holding my cell in my hand. I looked down at it without seeing it as I mentally prepared to call my parents. It would be early morning in Saltford, so there would be just enough time to catch them before they went to work. I took a drink of water from the glass on the side table and dialed.

My mom answered, sounding gleeful. "Hi, sweet pea! What a treat. How's our world traveler?"

"Hi Mom," I rasped. "I'm good, how are you?"

There was a sharp intake of breath. "What happened? Are you sick? You sound terrible!"

"I sound worse than I am. It's just a little chest cold."

Why had I said that? I had fully intended to tell them about the incident at the tabacchi, so why had I lied? I already knew the answer. They wouldn't believe me anyway. And it was not the kind of story one could tell over the phone. It would send them into panic mode, they might even get on a plane, or worse, make me get on a plane. Emotions tumbled around inside me. The fire now living inside me had given me a shock, but it also fed me with strength. I didn't want to run home to my parents.

"Oh, poor baby. Is Elda taking care of you? You know it's not good for you, going in and out of air-conditioning all the time."

"I know, Mom. Yes, Elda is looking after me. I just wanted to let you know. I'll be fine." I closed my eyes and prayed that the roughness of my voice would eventually go away. "Is Dad there?"

"Yes, just a second. I'll put you on speakerphone, okay?" There was a click and the sound changed.

"Hi pumpkin."

I smiled at his loving tone. Tears welled in my eyes. "Hi Dad."

"You don't sound so good. What's up?"

"Just a bit of a sore throat and a cold. I'll be all right. How are you? How are the boys? How's Jack?"

"Oh, you know us. Nothing much changes. RJ and Jack are both fine. Jack got his tooth fixed yesterday. Looks good as new. How are the boys you're looking after? Good kids?"

I closed my eyes and breathed a word of thanks for such solid parents. We all knew I had done wrong before I left home. They knew I felt bad enough. Without rubbing my face in it, the implication hanging in the air was subtle but present. Were the kids testing me?

"They're really good kids. I lucked out."

"That's good. Happy to hear it."

Dad told me about the car RJ had bought and the work he was doing on the engine.

"How's the weather been in Venice?" he asked.

"Hot."

"Yeah, I can only imagine. It's been hot here, too. So listen, we have to run but call us again later, okay? Just to let us know how you're doing?"

"Sure, Dad."

"Can you find some bee propolis there, for your throat?" Mom asked.

"I'll look. Okay, love you guys. Have a good day at work."

We said goodbye. I sat there in silence, feeling the fire crackling in my insides. Why hadn't I told them about the tabbachi shop incident? I didn't want them to worry, but I very rarely lied to my parents. *You don't trust yourself, Saxony.*

I blinked at this sudden thought and realized it was right. I so rarely kept things to myself that if I had started talking I wouldn't know where to stop and before I could help it, everything would come spilling out. My parents would panic. They might even get on a plane and escort me home. My summer in Italy would be over before it had really begun. Yes, it was best to avoid the whole subject altogether.

But you'll have to face them sometime. They know you.

Overwhelmed, I crawled into bed and pulled the sheet over my head.

THREE FULL DAYS PASSED. When I had shown up in the kitchen looking dazed and distracted, Elda insisted that I take several more days to rest. My voice still sounded burnt out. The flames caused me some discomfort, but they wouldn't kill me. There was a strength to be sourced from this fire; I just wasn't entirely sure how to find it.

I'd barely seen anyone in three days. I hadn't wanted to, which was very unlike me. I'd made excuses to Fed when she'd texted, inviting me to hang out. Dante hadn't written, and I had barely noticed, which was also unlike me. If it wasn't for the fire, my stomach might be tied in knots for a different reason—I'd be wondering why he hadn't texted, worrying whether he really liked me or if I'd just imagined it.

My lips twisted in a sardonic smile. The fire had robbed me of the anxieties of a normal teenage girl with a crush.

I went into the bathroom, flicked the light on beside the mirror, and looked myself in the face. It was still the same face, but it had changed somehow. My eyes. They were still green, but now they had the same strange reflective quality that I'd noticed in Isaia.

I splashed cool water into my face, filled one hand, and drank. My other palm was still bandaged. The cool water eased my pain a little. With water, the heat inside me seemed easier to bank, easier to control. I looked up at myself again, my face dripping. Anxiety fluttered in my chest as the same questions surfaced that had been haunting me for three days. My eyes flashed red, like an animal caught in headlights, and I staggered back from the sink, startled. My face crumpled. Who was I now? Or what?

I swallowed my tears and took a few deep breaths. I needed to talk to someone. But who? None of my friends would believe me, and how could I explain it even if I'd wanted to? I had already picked up my phone multiple times, preparing to set up a video call with the girls, only to put it down again. Every time I started to reach out, something stronger held me back.

I drank more water, filled a glass, and took it to bed with me despite the fact that it was only seven p.m. I flopped onto my bed and sighed with frustration. The fire licked up inside my ribcage. My limbs had an unexplained energy, like they needed to move. I tried to ignore the feeling, closed my eyes, and waited for sleep.

My phone vibrated. I rolled over to check it. It was a text from Dante—the first one since the night of the Festival.

Ciao Bella

I smiled, and wrote back. *Ciao Bello.*

Dante: *Fed tells me you're sick?*

Me: *Just a bit of fever and a cough, is all.*

Dante: *Poor baby. Maybe I can come by? Cheer you up?*

I chewed my lip. I didn't know Dante that well, so I didn't feel comfortable having him at the house. But maybe it was time to stop playing hermit. I needed to get outside. Enough moping. It would be nice to think about something else for a change. Or someone else, rather. I smiled in remembrance of the dance party on the beach, Dante's hands pulling me close.

Me: *I'm feeling better. Just a little cooped up. How about we go for a drink? I'd love something cold.*

Dante: *Beautiful. Where?*

I thought again. I didn't want to go far, in case I felt bad and had to come home. There was a juice and smoothie bar not far from the Baseggio's villa.

Me: *Puro?*

Dante: *I know it. Love that place. Can you go now?*

Me: *Half hour?*

Dante: *Perfetto. Look forward to see you.*

I changed out of the jogging shorts and t-shirt I was wearing and into a white sleeveless blouse with a lace inset at the neck, shorts, and a pair of sandals. I left the house early so I could walk slowly. The evening was warm and the sun had only recently gone down, leaving the sky pink. A light breeze cooled my damp scalp.

Dante was sitting on the edge of a stone fountain not far from Puro, texting. He looked up and gave me a heart-stopping grin. I couldn't help but smile back. I wondered if he'd be able to tell there was something different about me. My stomach gave a nervous flutter.

Dante tucked his phone away and got up. He took both my hands and kissed each of my cheeks tenderly, his tilted brown eyes devouring my face.

"You most definitely do not look sick." He took my chin gently between his fingers.

"Thank you," I rasped.

"Whoa." His smile faded. "You look beautiful, but you sound rough. Poor thing." He made a sound of empathy and put an arm around my shoulders and squeezed. "Let me buy you a juice?"

I nodded, melting at his tenderness. I chose peach and strawberry juice and they topped the concoction with mint leaves. Dante ordered an orange juice and we took our drinks back to the fountain to sit down.

"You didn't text me," Dante said, looking impressed. "All girls text me relentlessly after meeting me."

"Wow, you're not cocky at all, are you." I canted my head at him. "I guess I'm not all girls." In truth, I probably would have texted him if my life hadn't been thrown into turmoil. But I wasn't about to tell him that.

"It's clear you're not." He nudged my shoulder with his and took a sip of his orange juice.

"So, everybody survived the Festa? All of your friends?"

He nodded, smiling. "But most of those guys aren't really friends."

"They aren't?" I was surprised. They'd seemed pretty chummy to me. Why else would they be hanging out on a boat together during a holiday?

"Most of them are... potential employees, let's say. What is the word in English? Recruits? Is that right?"

"You party with potential employees? What kind of work are they applying for? Who can drink the most and not drown?"

He laughed, his almond eyes crinkling. "I like to see what people are like in real life. When they're relaxed and off the clock, you know."

"What is that you do, exactly?"

"I have interests in a few businesses in Venezia, mostly in tourism, but some in private security." He got a faraway look in his eyes. "I'd really like to take over my father's business one day. If I can ever get him to see my worth." He muttered this last almost under his breath. I was about to ask him to expand when he snapped back to focus. He pulled a knee up and turned to face me, leaning in closer. "But I don't want to talk about them, I want to talk about you. What's your story?"

I took a sip of my juice, suddenly nervous under his scrutiny. "I'm pretty boring. Just a small-town Canadian kid looking for adventure in beautiful Italy."

"Tell me about your family." Dante finished his juice and set the cup down. "Sisters or brothers? Only child? Parents together?" He brushed my hair back over my shoulder, his fingertips grazing my neck. "Boyfriend?"

I shivered and the fire inside me flickered. Chemistry crackled between us, the kind that Georjayna and I were always going on about.

"Two brothers, garden-variety parents." I turned to face him, my voice fading to a smoky whisper. "No boyfriend."

"Hmmmm." He made a noise deep in his throat. "Are you taking applicants for the job?"

I bit my straw between my teeth, smiling at him over my cup. I took a sip and then said, "I might be. Must be fiercely intelligent, devastatingly funny, and kind to baby animals. Italian heritage will be considered a plus."

He smiled and leaned closer. "I passed kindergarten and had a pet turtle once, does that count?"

I gave a dry laugh, air whistling through my throat. His eyes crinkled at me. His lips were heading for mine. I had the sudden and ridiculous thought that Elda and Pietro were somewhere nearby, watching.

"I'll just pop these in the trash." I grabbed his cup and dodged his kiss at the same time.

He hung his head comically and I laughed again. I finally felt good for the first time since Isaia gave me the fire. Flirting with Dante made me feel like a normal teenage girl again. I batted my eyes at him over my shoulder and let my hips sway as I walked to the recycling bins.

He groaned and yelled, "You're killing me."

I laughed, feeling his eyes on me.

Two men stood near the bins, smoking cigarettes. One of them jerked his chin toward me. The other turned to look. They both blew two jets of smoke out of their nostrils at the exact same time. An image of two bulls getting ready to charge rose unbidden to my mind and my mouth twitched with humor. One of them said something to me in Italian. I didn't understand what he said, but the suggestive look on his face gave me some idea of his meaning.

Down, boys.

Dante's voice behind me made me jump. How had he gotten here so fast? He put an arm around my waist while he spoke to them, his voice soft but with an edge.

They exchanged more words, ratcheting the conversation into unfriendly. One of the guys flicked his cigarette at Dante's feet. I stepped back instinctively, but Dante didn't move. His arm tightened around me, holding me still. My head began to throb as the heat of the fire inside me intensified. My eyes felt dry and gummy. We had been having such a nice time. Why did they have to ruin our evening?

A tense moment of silence passed before Dante spoke again. The two men shared a look, their eyes wide. They uttered what were most certainly apologies and turned to walk away.

"What did you say?" I watched the two slink away.

The taller one threw a resentful look over his shoulder.

"It's nothing you need to worry about." He kissed my temple and squeezed my waist.

"No, really. I'd like to know."

"Sometimes I need to make my ...dominio a little more clearly," he said as we began to walk.

"Dominio?" I echoed, my eyes narrowed as I tried to make sense of his sentence. I put my fingers to my temples. The headache was getting worse. My eyes were growing hot. I had a flutter of panic. What if my eyes did the glowing thing?

"Baby, are you okay?" Dante stopped and stood in front of me. He took my face tenderly in his hands.

"I think I should go home," I said, closing my eyes.

"Still not feeling good, huh? Okay, I'll walk you."

"It's okay. Thank you, but really, I'm fine."

"Don't be stubborn, I'll take you."

"No, no. I insist. I'm alright. I'll just go straight home to bed, anyway. There's no need and it's not far." I said this firmly. I needed to be alone.

He didn't answer at first.

"Okay, have it your way, bella," he said finally. He kissed my cheeks. "Text me when you get home, okay?"

"I will. Goodnight. Thank you for the juice." I gave his hand a squeeze and turned toward home.

I had been a bit rude, I knew. But the throbbing in my head and the plummeting of my mood were overwhelming. Did I feel so badly now because of the confrontation? I couldn't be sure. For once I was thankful that I didn't understand Italian.

I felt Dante's eyes on my back until I turned the corner.

TEN

It was the middle of another sleepless night when I finally gave in to the anxious energy building up in my body. If I didn't do something expel it, it would drive me mad.

In irritation, I rolled out of bed. I pulled on a pair of shorts and a tank top. After tucking my house key and phone into my back pocket, I slipped out into the dark streets of residential Venice. I was grateful that the Baseggio's lived in a relatively quiet area of the city. The air was heavy and humid. Faint laughter could be heard coming from a nearby courtyard. I jogged toward a park that had a small beach. The water promised cool relief.

Jogging seemed to unleash more energy. I began to sprint, my legs and arms pumping like pistons. The cuts on my left palm and my right knee stung as blood pounded through my body. I ignored the pain. I'd never been athletic, but in this moment, I knew what it felt like to be an athlete. Power surged through me, fueling me. I felt like I was flying. Villas, shops, and courtyards sped by. I bounced off walls, planted a foot, and ricocheted around corners. My ankles felt as strong as they'd ever been. My hair flew back, my scalp cooled by the breeze. As I approached the water, I slowed enough to kick off my running shoes and drop my phone and my key inside one shoe. I ran to the water and dove in, moaning at the delicious feeling as it cooled my feverish skin.

I surfaced and took a deep breath, then sank to my chin. My wet hair floated like seaweed around me. It should have been peaceful, but that sense of unspent energy still plagued me.

Following my instincts, I called the fire to life and watched as it became visible through my shirt. Stones, sand and seaweed lit up around me, and fish darted away. The pain was there too, as always, but I was getting used to it. I began to experiment, drawing the fire up toward my chest and heart. The sensation of intense heat accompanied the glow wherever it went. I sent the fire down my right arm and into my hand and fingertips, still underwater. Shadows thrown by the stones on the ocean floor moved along with the light. I shoved my hand out in front of me, palm facing out into the ocean. The white and red glow shot out my palm, and a ball of light separated itself from me.

Did I just shoot a fireball?

I half-laughed, half-sobbed. A fireball. *I shot fire out of my hand.*

I watched, still in awe, as the water above my hand bubbled furiously for a second and then died. My arm and hand throbbed with heat, a sort of pleasure-pain. I let go of the glow in my right hand and it felt like it travelled back into my torso of its own volition.

Did the fire work both ways? Would it come out of my injured hand? I held my left hand up in front of my face. The sodden bandage dripped. Dark blood stained the bandage in a crescent moon shape. I wiggled my fingers, and the cut stung as salt water penetrated it. Taking a deep breath, I drew the fire into my left palm.

The bandage steamed, then dried up and curled at the edges. I hissed as the cut on my hand stung and burned more intensely, but some instinct inside told me not to quit. I gave it a little more heat. The bandage burst into flames. I stared in wonder as bits of ash dropped into the water and the bandage burned away. The pain from the wound stopped instantly.

I let the glow go back to my torso while I inspected my left hand. The gash across the outer edge of my hand was completely sealed. The white crescent moon scar looked four years old instead of four days. Smooth pink skin lined either side of the scar, as though the skin had melted.

My mouth dropped open as I realized what this meant: I could heal cuts by cauterizing them *from the inside.* I focused on the cut on my knee, sending the glow down my leg. I repeated the exercise, concentrating the heat around my knee and noticed the exact moment when the pain of the cut disappeared. I let the fire go back to my ribcage. Calling the fire to one of my hands, I lifted my leg up and used the fire as a light to look at my knee. A white scar crossed my kneecap.

My ears perked when I heard my phone vibrate from the beach. Who would be texting me at this hour? The light from the fire disappeared and the ocean around me fell into darkness. I left the water and picked up my phone to see a message from Dante.

If you don't let me see you soon I'll go crazy. You're torturing me.

My stomach gave a little flutter of pleasure that had nothing to do with the fire.

Me: *What are you doing up?*

Dante: *I'm dying for want of you.*

Me: *Very funny.*

Dante: *You're up too. Miss me?*

Me: *Maybe.*

Dante: *You're awake, and I'm awake. Let's be awake together. What are you doing?*

Me: *Swimming.*

Dante: *?*

Me: *Seriously. You know the little beach at the gardens on the west end?*

Dante: *Of course I know it, this is my town. You're there? Now?*

Me: **nods**

Dante: *Don't. Move.*

I put my phone into my shoe and went back into the water. I floated on my back, admired the stars, and waited for my company.

DANTE'S SILHOUETTE picked its way through the trees and across the grass. My feet found the stones beneath me and I stood. I began to make my way to the beach but stopped when Dante kicked off his shoes, dropped the bag he'd been carrying, and walked into the water in his clothes.

I smiled as he waded to me. He kissed both my cheeks, his hands on my waist. Smelling the bittersweet scent of aperol on his breath, I wondered how many spritzes he'd had.

"Hello," he said, his voice low.

He swept me up like I was a little kid. My arms slipped around his neck as he walked deeper into the water, until we were both neck deep and nose to nose.

"Are you feeling better yet?"

"I am, thanks." My heart hammered inside my ribcage.

"You don't sound better," he said. "You still sound like you've been smoking cigars your whole life. But don't worry, I like it. It's sexy."

"Oh good," I rasped. My mouth twisted in a sarcastic smile. "That's all I had in mind when I got sick. That Dante should find me sexy."

"Good, then we're going to get along just fine." He smiled, his eyes crinkling at the corners. "Why haven't you kissed me yet?"

I blinked at his directness. "Why haven't *you* kissed *me*?"

I knew full well that we'd had more than one opportunity and I'd always been the one to turn away.

"Because, I," he began, his eyes dropping to my mouth, "am a gentleman."

He moved his lips to a bare inch from mine, and waited there.

My stomach quivered. I moved my face forward just a fraction.

He jerked his head back. "Wait, are you contagious? Not that I wouldn't mind having a voice like yours."

I rasped a laugh. "No, I'm not contagious."

"Good." He brought his lips close again and waited for me to close the distance between us.

I did, anticipating a sweet, soft first kiss. But the moment I put my lips to his, he completely overtook me, the intimacy of the kiss startling me deeply. My joints flushed with pleasure and weakness. My thinking fuzzed out. I became fully acquainted with the term 'stealing' a kiss. I had been kissed before. A few times. But none had so completely taken my breath away. His hand found the back of my head and held my face to his. We finally broke and I opened my eyes, dazed.

"That... " I began, taking a deep breath, "was not very gentlemanly."

A wicked smile crossed his face. "You're right. Let me try again."

His lips touched mine once more. This time it was the soft, delicate kiss that I had been expecting the first time. It was sweet, demure, even pious. He pulled away, watching me through half-closed eyes.

A beat passed.

"The first one was better," I said, grinning.

He laughed and hugged me close, then brushed my wet hair away from my face. I caught a flash of the little tattoo on the side of his wrist, just below the wrist bone.

"What's that?" I asked, trying to get a better look.

"What? Oh, this?" He turned the outside of his wrist to face us. "It's a magus mark. Not a real one, of course. It's just a tattoo."

He held still so I could look at it. Colored in with black ink, the tattoo was no larger than a pea. Its shape was clear, though—a flame. Or a fireball. It was rounded at the bottom and sharp on top, little flames licked toward his pinkie finger. Something about it was familiar.

"What's a magus mark?" I rubbed my thumb over the tattoo, feeling its softly raised edges.

"Well, I could tell you..." he said, leaning in for another kiss, "but then I'd have to kill you."

He captured my lips and took my breath away again. I was grateful that he was holding me up because I wasn't sure my legs could keep me upright. But the magus mark was on my mind now, and I pulled away.

"Please?" I batted my eyelashes and trailed a finger down his cheek. "I won't tell anyone."

He laughed. "You really are a Bond girl." He kissed the tip of my nose. "What do I get in return?"

He waggled his eyebrows suggestively.

"How about..." I twined my arms around his neck and pulled out my best doll voice. "How about the satisfaction of knowing that you've shared something special in order to foster trust and a feeling of closeness in the early stages of dating?"

The combination of baby voice and smoky voice sounded adorable, which was exactly what I'd been shooting for.

He laughed again. "I'll tell you, just because I like you and you sound so much cute. But we have to get out of the water, I'm freezing."

Only now did I notice the gooseflesh on his arms.

"Dante!" I put my feet down and pulled him toward the beach. "You idiot. Why didn't you say something?"

He shivered as the night air swept over us. I didn't feel cold at all, I felt great. But he was completely stiff. He wrapped his arms around himself.

"I was just trying to be tough and manly." He laughed through a tight jaw. "How can you stand the water? It's freezing tonight."

He picked up the bag he'd brought, pulled out two towels, and handed one to me.

"You thought of bringing towels? You are far more prepared than any boy should be."

I dried the water from my skin, but then I wrapped my towel around him and rubbed his shoulders to generate heat. He kept the towel around himself and I followed him to a nearby park bench. We sat side by side, admiring the view of the stars reflecting on the water and the lights of Lido in the distance.

"I knew a guy named Nicodemo who could do amazing things with fire," Dante began.

Immediately, I became still. I could hardly breathe.

"What kinds of things?"

"You wouldn't believe me if I told you." He lifted the towel to his head and scrubbed his wet hair.

"Try me." The banked fire in my belly flared to life in anticipation of the story.

This was information that I needed. My heart thudded. Warmth flowed through me and for once it was more pleasure than pain.

"I was never supposed to know. I found out by accident one day when I overheard him and my dad talking in our living room. Nicodemo worked for us, but he and my dad were close. Nicodemo was family."

"So... what? He was like a fire-breather or something?"

He gave a wry laugh. "No, it went way beyond that." He turned to me and lowered his voice. "He could create it. Control it. What is the word for," he gestured toward himself with his hands. "Absorb it, that's the word. I know it sounds crazy. I would never have believed it myself if I hadn't seen it with my own eyes."

He faced the sea again, his eyes getting a faraway look. He wasn't worried about whether I believed him or not. I wished I could just tell someone my crazy story and not be scared of them not believing me.

"I never knew such power existed," he continued. "I was only about ten but I became obsessed with gaining this ability for myself. Every time Nicodemo had meetings with my dad, I would wait for an opportunity to catch him alone and ask him to teach me."

"And did he?"

He gave a half-laugh. "No, of course not. He couldn't. He showed me a mark that he had, like this one." He raised his wrist to show me the tattoo again. "Only his was natural, like a birthmark. He said only a real fire magus had the ability to control and create fire.

It was genetic, so it couldn't be taught. Biggest disappointment of my young life," he said with a trace of bitterness. "Anyway, I saved up my allowance and got the tattoo. My father just about killed me. At the time, I just wanted to look cool, but it's served as a reminder that no matter how much money you have, you can never have everything that you want. So that's it, now you know."

He put his arm over my head and around my shoulders.

I was about to ask him more about Nicodemo when my phone vibrated from inside my shoe. I reached down and looked at the screen.

"Oh, crap!" I said, standing up. Elda had called me twice and texted four times since Dante had arrived. I had been so engaged in our little make-out session that I hadn't heard my phone go off.

First: *Where are you? I knocked on your door but you didn't answer.*

Then: *Isaia is asking for you!*

Then: *I don't think you understand, he's ASKING for you!!!*

Finally: *Saxony! Please call!*

Guilt flooded me.

"What's wrong?" Dante stood and put an arm around my shoulders and looked down at my screen, his eyes scanning the texts. "Is that the lady you work for? At this hour? What is she, your mother?"

"I have to go, Dante. I'm so sorry." It was the second time I'd be leaving him rather rudely, but it couldn't be helped. I bent to pull on my shoes. The word 'ASKING' vibrated at the front of my mind. Had Isaia actually spoken?

Dante wrapped his arms around me, impeding my efforts to put on my second shoe. "You don't have to go. This is your time off. It's the middle of the night."

"You don't understand." I managed to pull on my second shoe in spite of Dante's arms around me. I stood and turned toward him, my hands on his chest. "Isaia, he hasn't spoken in..."

Dante interrupted me, his hands ran down my arms and curled around my wrists. "No, you don't understand. This is your opportunity to show her your boundaries, or she'll always think you're at her beck and call. I know people, trust me."

"What?" I was so surprised at his lack of understanding that I didn't know what to say. "I have to go."

I turned and took a step. Dante's fingers clamped down on my wrists like a pair of handcuffs. He jerked me back toward him. The fire in my belly flared up in anger. Why was he doing this?

We came nose to nose.

"You're not listening," he said in a dangerous voice. His eyes narrowed and his jaw popped.

"Dante, what's wrong with you?" My own eyes narrowed, and I felt the telltale flush in my face—my temper, rearing its ugly head. The fire was one thing, but now I was getting really mad.

I couldn't keep the threat from my voice. "Let me go. Now."

It was the wrong thing to say to him. His face darkened. "Why is it that just when you have the opportunity to get the upper hand, you flush it down the toilet? Don't be stupid, now listen to me. Dante has something to teach you."

His hands tightened, the bones in my wrists creaked painfully.

"Dante, you're hurting me," I rasped. "Let go, please."

Fear had begun to rise in me, along with the crackling flames readying themselves to leap to my defense. He let go of my wrists but only to put his hands on either side of my face, squeezing and locking me still like a bug with a pin through it.

Who did he think he was? This was not okay.

"I'm only doing this because I care," he said, but the anger in his voice was thinly veiled. Somehow, I had really pissed him off.

"Dante," I said, my voice sounding much harder than I felt. "Let. Go."

My eyes began to feel warm. I squeezed them shut.

My phone vibrated again. To me, it was akin to Isaia calling out for help. I couldn't ignore it. The fire roared to life, feeding on my fear, anger, and desperation to go to Isaia. A glow came up between our faces, lighting us both up from under our chins.

Dante blinked in shock. "What the hell?"

I couldn't have stopped it even if I had wanted to, the fire-fueled anger was more powerful than I was.

"I said let go!"

As I yelled the word 'go,' the heat flew upward, broke in two, shot up the side of my neck and stopped in my ears, just under Dante's crushing hands.

Dante yelled in pain and surprise and jerked his hands away from the sides of my head. He looked down at his hands, both of them quaking violently, the fingers open and stiff with pain. Two semicircular burns were seared into his palms and fingers exactly where he'd been holding the outer edges of my ears. He panted, and yelled again. Spittle appeared on his lower lip.

My anger dissipated. Panic and regret swept me and my voice shook.

"Dante, I..." A wave of nausea overtook me as I looked at the nasty red burns.

My phone vibrated again.

To my absolute shock, Dante looked at me and a laugh filled with pain ripped out of his throat. The hair on the back of my neck stood on end.

"You," he said, panting. "You're a magus. You're what I've been looking for."

I backed away. "I'm so sorry, Dante. I have to go!"

After taking one last look at the horrible burns on his hands, I turned and sprinted.

I RAN at top speed through the quiet midnight streets, my footfalls echoing off brick and stone, coming back to my ears a hundred times over. My wet hair slapped sharply against my back, feeling like a whipping. *How fitting. I deserve a flagellation.*

The fire inside pulsed with every intake of oxygen. All my anger at Dante was gone. Jack's face, his black eye, his split lip...

it all flashed in my memory. I had enough reason to know that what I had done to Jack was not the same as what I had done to Dante. What Dante had done bordered on assault and I was fully in the right to protect myself. Still, my temper had gotten the better of me. Again. And this time, the consequences were even higher. I never had a fire living in my torso before.

The only thing that kept me from bursting into tears was the pumping of my arms and legs. I missed my family and I wanted to talk to my friends. Regret that I had come to Venice in the first place washed over me for the first time and I nearly stumbled under the weight of it. I didn't want this power Isaia had pushed into me. It hurt me, and it had made me hurt Dante. It would have killed Isaia. I hadn't asked for this. I wouldn't have taken it even if it had been offered to me, if I had known what it really meant. I wished more than anything that I was hanging out in Georjayna's back yard with my best friends, laughing around a bonfire, not pounding through empty streets in the dark, leaving behind a man I'd kissed, and then hurt.

Once I reached the house, I unlocked the door with shaking hands. I bound up the stairs two at a time and went straight to Isaia's room. My heart hammered and I paused to calm my ragged breath. Sighing deeply, I gave a quiet tap on the door and then opened it.

"Oh, thank God," Elda cried. She got up from the side of Isaia's bed and hugged me before quickly letting me go. "Why are you wet?"

"I couldn't sleep and decided to go for a swim."

"In your clothes?"

"I'm sorry you couldn't reach me. I had my phone on vibrate and didn't hear it. Is he okay?"

"It's the most amazing thing," Elda said, forgetting my wet clothing. Her voice quavered. Her eyes were bright with excitement, and she grabbed my upper arms. "He spoke. He said your name. I don't know why your name was the first word he's spoken in almost three years but I don't care. He spoke!" A tear spilled down her cheek and she brushed it away, her movement full of nervous energy.

"That's amazing!" Joy filled my heart and all of the self-pity and homesickness evaporated as I approached the bed. "Hey buddy."

Isaia turned his face toward me. His eyes opened, two shining orbs.

"Saxony," he said in a small voice.

I gasped and covered my mouth with my hands, shocked at the sound of his voice. It was scorched out and smoky, just like mine. I choked back a happy sob and smiled at him.

"Look who's talking." I sat on the side of his bed. "What's the matter, sweetheart? Were you asking for me?"

Isaia crawled out from under his sheets and into my lap before wrapping his arms around my neck.

"Hang on a sec, buddy. I'm a bit wet." I pulled on the sheet and wrapped it around him before I hugged him close, like a warm little sausage.

He began to say something in Italian but then remembered who he was talking to and started again.

"I had a bad dream," he rasped.

Elda and I shared a look.

"But you're okay, right?" I said. "You know that now. It was just a dream."

He nodded.

Elda sat beside us. She put a hand on his head. "What did you dream about, love?"

We wanted to keep him talking, but Isaia turned his face away from Elda and didn't answer. Her face crumpled. She was bursting with emotions, I could see it. Joy at the return of her son's recovered speech, pain that he was favoring me, and the need to help him.

"You don't want to tell us?" I asked.

He shook his head. "I only want to tell you."

It must have something to do with the fire. But whatever it was, it was still just a dream. "Your mom loves you, Isaia. She wants to help you feel better."

"You made me feel better," he said, his voice muffled against my chest. "You took it away."

Elda's brows drew together in with confusion and worry. "Took what?" she mouthed.

I deferred to Isaia. "Can you tell us what happened in your dream?"

He pulled away from me, sniffing. His voice cracked. "In my dream, you didn't... you didn't take it. I was... getting dead." A fat tear rolled down his cheek.

My heart pounded. He'd dreamed about dying from the fire. "But, you know you're safe now, right? You're not going to die."

He nodded. "Sì."

I glanced at Elda. She stared at me, her face pale. Her neck worked as she swallowed. In her face, I could see the truth. She knew. She'd always known about Isaia's fire.

I rocked Isaia until he began to drift off. Elda left and returned with a dry bedsheet and a light knee-length bathrobe. She handed the bathrobe to me and I pulled it on over my wet clothes as Elda tucked Isaia into bed. I followed Elda into the kitchen. Her shoulders were slumped. Her eyes were puffy from crying and her short hair, usually perfect, was a mess. She couldn't look me in the eye. She was processing, and I could practically see the gears turning in her head.

"You look exhausted. Want some tea?" I gestured to a stool.

She wiped her bangs away from her forehead and nodded, giving me a tense smile. "Thank you."

I was trying to think of a way to get her to talk about Isaia's fire. I filled the kettle and turned it on, then pulled down two mugs.

"Chamomile? Peppermint?"

"Chamomile, please. After tonight I think I'm going to need something calming."

I looked at her plainly. "May I ask you something?"

She looked me in the eye for the first time since we'd left Isaia's room. Fear was written in her features.

"Okay," she said, slowly.

"Did you ever call a doctor about his fevers?" I tried to keep accusation out of my tone, but it was difficult. "I don't understand how such a loving mother wouldn't call a doctor when her child's fever goes way past the danger point, especially when it happens regularly."

She sighed. "No doctor knows how to help him. What he's got..."

"What?"

She propped her elbows on the counter and covered her forehead with her hand. Her chin wobbled. Dropping her hand, she looked me in the eyes, her own shining with tears. "What he's got will eventually kill him. He knows it, and I know it, and now he's having nightmares about it. What they have to do with you, I'm still trying to figure out."

I put down the box of tea. "Does Pietro know?"

She shook her head. "Oh God," she said, taking a juddering breath. She wiped at her eyes.

"Elda, it won't," I said.

She looked up at me. Anguish contorted her features. "It won't what?"

"It won't kill him."

"How do you know that?" she nearly wailed. She lowered her voice and whispered fiercely, "You don't know that."

"I do." I lifted my hands. My palms glowed white hot, my fingertips glowed red. "Because he gave it to me."

PART TWO

ELEVEN

Elda gasped and her hand clamped over her mouth. The light of my palms reflected in her face and glowed in her pupils, like the flashbulb of a powerful camera. She looked from my hands to my face and back again. Pulling her hand from her mouth, she whispered in a strangled voice, "When? How?"

"I'll tell you everything," I said. "But you need to talk first. Because you knew about this. Whatever it is, you knew that Isaia had a fire inside him. And now I have it. Your son won't die, which is wonderful. But now I have to figure out a way to live with this." I lit a blue flame in my palm. "I can barely control it, and it hurts, Elda." I needed her to understand what it was costing me. "It hurts every minute of every day."

She sniffed and grabbed a tissue from the box on the island. She blew her nose and dabbed at her eyes. She said something behind the tissue but it came out in a tight breath of air and I couldn't make it out.

"Pardon?" I lowered my hand and snuffed the flame. The heat traveled up my arms, converged in my spine and dropped into my belly.

She cleared her throat. "I know," she said. "I know it hurts."

"How do you know?"

"I know because he told me. He explained everything to me, after I got pregnant. And I know because I have watched it torture my son since the day of his birth."

"He?"

"Nicodemo."

I gave a start of surprise. His name, twice in the same night from two different sets of lips. "Why did he have to explain it to you after you got pregnant? Why wasn't Pietro there, too?"

"Because Pietro isn't Isaia's father," she whispered. Her eyes darted down the hallway.

Understanding finally dawned. "Nicodemo is Isaia's father? And Pietro doesn't know?"

"That's right." She balled the tissue up in her hand. "I've never told anyone. I was never intending to tell a soul. But, well..." She waved a hand toward me. "I didn't expect this and neither did you, I'll wager."

I gave a humorless laugh. "You can say that again."

The kettle was boiling. I shut it off and poured two mugs of tea.

Elda came around the island and pulled me into a hug, surprising me. "I'm so sorry, Saxony. I lost my temper with you.

I accused you of putting my son in danger. I was so angry and scared, and none of it was your fault. I know that."

She pulled back and looked at me, her eyes shining.

"Thank you. I needed to hear all that," I said softly. I handed her the mug of tea. "I need to know everything, Elda. I know it's your private business and I'll keep your secret, but it involves me now. I didn't ask for this, but I sure need some help figuring out what to do with it."

An image of pushing the fire into Dante's belly the way Isaia had pushed it into mine came unbidden to my mind. If he wanted it so badly, maybe I could give it to him, although I still didn't know how Isaia had managed to do it without killing me. I shoved the idea away. I needed to know more. Dante had behaved like a real jerk tonight. What would this kind of power do in the wrong hands?

Elda nodded. "Let's move into the living room."

I followed her to the couch under the window and we set our mugs on the coffee table. I tucked my feet up under me on the couch.

She took a breath and let it out slowly. "Seven years ago, Pietro and I went through a really hard time. I was just starting my business and it was a financial struggle. We had to dig into our savings further than we anticipated and because of that, Pietro worked even harder than he does now."

I gaped. "I don't even see how that is possible. He works twelve-hour days and flies to London every week. I've barely seen the man since I got here."

She nodded. "Yes, he works a lot now too, but back then it was even worse. Now, Pietro's work is going well, he doesn't have to work this hard. He does it because he wants to do it while he's young so we can retire early. In spite of how it looks to you, it's actually a lot better than it was. Back then, he had a huge client out of Dubai. He was gone for up to six weeks at a time."

"So you were lonely."

"I was, but that is no excuse. And it's more complicated than that. During one of these long stretches where I was alone, Cristiano was kidnapped."

I lost the grip on my tea and splashed hot liquid onto my bare leg. I swore under my breath and put the mug on the coaster, drying my leg with the corner of the bathrobe. The hot tea should have burned me, but it didn't.

"Are you okay?" she asked.

"I'm fine, sorry. You just startled me. Please go on. Cristiano was kidnapped? Um, holy crap."

"Yes, it was terrifying. Someone had snatched him from the schoolyard. He wasn't even in school yet, he was too little. He was just playing in the yard. He was taken right out from under my nose. I was there with a bunch of other moms and distracted by all the gossip." She shuddered at the memory. "I was so stupid."

"What did you do?"

"I went to a powerful man for help. A powerful man, but not really a good man."

"Why didn't you go to the police?"

She gave me a look of reproach, a look that said it was naive of me not to know better. "Going to Enzo Barberini *is* going to the polizia."

"Oh." I chewed my lip. "Did you tell Pietro?"

She shook her head. "Pietro would never have agreed to go to Enzo but I knew it was my best chance to get Cristiano back. Nothing happens in Venice that Enzo doesn't know about. I went that very same day, immediately, without even thinking about alternatives. In my mind, there weren't any."

"You must have been a basket-case."

She laughed. "Basket-case? It's a kind of slang?"

"I guess." I smiled. "Then what happened?"

"A couple of hours after I got home, there was a knock at my door. It was Nicodemo, and he was carrying Cristiano. Cristiano was unharmed, just asleep. I was so grateful and relieved, all I could do was cry like a baby. Nicodemo wouldn't tell me who took him or how he'd been retrieved, but I do know that the bodies of two men were recovered from a marina in Chioggia the following week, both of them had their throats burned out."

"My God." My stomach churned.

"I didn't associate Nicodemo with those bodies. At the time, I didn't know what he was. I assumed that Nic was just a delivery man. He was gentle and sweet and really good with Cristiano."

"He came back again after that?"

"Yes, he came to check on us. At first, he was just being kind. He knew that Pietro was out of town. I think he knew that I needed someone strong to lean on, and he could fill that need. And then, well, we fell in love."

Silence.

"And you got pregnant?"

She nodded.

"So what about the fire stuff?"

"I didn't know that Nicodemo was a magus until after I got pregnant. If it wasn't for Isaia, I never would have found out. Nic and I ended our affair before Pietro got back, but by then it was too late. When I told Nic I was pregnant, he was anguished. He said that he'd never planned on having kids. He was angry with me and himself for not being more careful. Then he showed me what he was. If I had been frightened before, I was really terrified then. He explained that he was a fire magus, a sort of supernatural being. He called the fire a curse. It was why he'd never wanted to father a child. He said that the ability either made you stronger, or it killed you. If a magus made it past childhood, it meant that they'd survive. But he warned me that if my baby inherited the curse, and if he or she was weak..." She swallowed. "They wouldn't live very long."

A lot of questions crowded together in my brain, fighting to be the first asked. "Nicodemo, he worked for Enzo?"

"That's right. Enzo paid him well in exchange for his services."

"I'm guessing Enzo didn't help you out of the goodness of his heart?" I was starting to wise up to the ways of life here.

"You got it, absolutely. I offered him shares in my company as payment but he didn't want that. He said that he'd hold the favor in check until he'd decided what he wanted. I'm still waiting. Every time there's a knock on the door I'm sure it's going to be one of Enzo's men, ready to tell me what he wants."

A horrible thought sprang up. "Does Enzo know that Isaia is Nicodemo's son?"

"I don't know. I'd like to think Nic never told anyone, but who can say what happens behind closed doors."

"This Enzo guy, does he have kids?" I already knew the answer, but I needed to learn whatever Elda could tell me.

"Why do you ask?" Elda set her mug on the coffee table and gave me a suspicious look.

"I might have met one."

Elda shook her head at me, a warning on her face. "Stay away from that family, Saxony. I mean it. I'm not your mother and I know you're a smart girl, but trust me. A young woman like you would be catnip for Enzo's son."

"What do you mean, catnip?"

She began to count the reasons off on her fingers. "You're young, beautiful, a foreigner, an English-speaking native. You're fresh blood for that family. Someone who hasn't been tainted by their rivals. Gone are the days of marrying for alliances. Nowadays, these powerful families want foreign blood. Enzo only has one son; Dante. Is that who you met?"

I nodded. "That's him."

"Don't see him again if you can help it," Elda said. "And whatever you do, he must never ever find out that you're a magus. Never."

Too late.

"I NEED TO MEET HIM," I said.

"Who? Enzo? No way, are you crazy?" Elda shook her head emphatically.

"No, Nicodemo. I need to talk to him."

Her face fell. "You can't. He's dead. The day he died was the day Isaia stopped talking."

"That's why Isaia stopped talking?" My jaw dropped.

She nodded. "Nic and Isaia never met. When we split, we promised it would be for good. No contact. Nicodemo wanted me to abort." Her voice broke. "But I could never do that. I have never told Isaia where he came from. I haven't wanted to upset him unnecessarily. The pain is the worst for him when he's emotional. Somehow, they were connected, though, because Isaia was never the same after the day Nic died."

My hopes for first-hand information crashed to floor as this puzzle piece fell into place. "I'm sorry to hear that. What happened?"

"I don't know. I received a package in the mail containing legal documents. A letter from a lawyer explained that the package was only to be mailed if Nicodemo had passed away and that I was to consider its delivery as official notice of his death. The package contained a will. Nicodemo left all of his worldly goods to Isaia. I never found out what happened to him but I'm sure that it happened while he was doing a job for Enzo. Enzo always gave Nic the most dangerous work because he was the most powerful man in his employ. I have wanted to go to Enzo or the lawyer and ask what happened but I've been too afraid. I don't really want to remind Enzo that I exist. And I think it might be better to let the dead rest anyway."

I wasn't sure if I agreed with her. "What did Nicodemo tell you about being a magus? He must have given you some knowledge that would help you understand what Isaia had to deal with?" My eyelids were beginning to feel heavy and I stifled a yawn.

"Yes, I've been getting to that part. One of the first things he told me was to keep Isaia well-hydrated, that it helps with the pain. Also, if you're dehydrated, the fire gets difficult to control. Think of dry tissues like dry grass. It can rip around inside you like a wildfire."

"Great," I said with an eye roll. "But I'm not so much interested in learning how to control it as I am of getting rid of it all together. Did he explain how that might be possible?"

She looked at me with pity. "There are only two ways to get rid of it: it will go out when you die, or you can give it away without killing the other person when you're dying. The fire wants to live. It knows when its host is dying and only at that time will it jump ship without killing the receiver. Otherwise, I'm afraid you're stuck with it for the rest of your life."

I digested this. The fire sitting in my belly flickered. *Get used to me. I'm here for good.* I thought back to the moment when Isaia had pushed it into me. Isaia must have known he was dying, it was the only way he would have been able to do what he did. Would he have still given it to me if we hadn't been trapped in a building that was on fire? He must have known that once he passed it to me, I would be able to stop the fire from killing all three of us.

"How and when did Isaia give it to you?" Elda asked.

"When we were trapped inside the tabacchi shop." I looked at her. "What you say makes sense because he really was dying. You could have lost your son that day."

Her mouth wavered. She put her mug on the table and reached for a tissue. Covering her face, she began to cry. Her body shook with heaving sobs. I moved over and put an arm around her.

"He's going to live," I reminded her.

She nodded, swallowing her sobs. "Thanks to you." She blew her nose and crumpled up her tissue. "Also, you and Isaia might have single-handedly saved Venice, or at least a portion of it. It might not seem like it, but this place is extremely flammable."

"I know," I said, and thought of the presentation I'd been to with Raf. He'd be back from Milan next week.

Elda got up and retrieved her purse from the island. She rummaged in it and pulled out her phone.

"There was a USB stick in the package that we received. I downloaded the files onto my phone and encrypted them. I keep the stick in a lock box at the bank," she said as she scrolled through her apps. She opened one and punched in a code. "I didn't think I'd ever be showing them to anyone. I almost deleted them already because it stresses me out that I even have them. But now I'm glad I kept them." She pulled up a video and handed me her phone. "Nic recorded these for Isaia."

My heart leaped with hope. The still on the screen displayed a blond man with thinning hair and a closely trimmed beard. He had a small silver hoop in his ear and his eyes were black, just like Isaia's. I could see Isaia in the set of his mouth and jaw.

I hit play and the man started talking.

"Ciao Isaia, e Nicodemo. Se stai guardando questo, allora la tua mamma ti ha detto..."

I hit pause and looked at Elda. "You've got to be kidding me."

She put up a hand. "Don't worry, I'll translate everything for you."

"Well, thank goodness."

She was staring at me.

"What?"

"Don't do that thing with your eyes, it makes me a basket-case."

I couldn't help but laugh at how she'd used her new slang, but I didn't know what she meant. "What thing?"

"The red, when they glow red. Don't do that."

"Oh, sorry." I hadn't realized my eyes had glowed. "I hope there's a clip for that because I don't know when I'm doing it."

"There is."

"Okay, well, let's start at the beginning?"

She hit play and we watched the first video together. I understood almost nothing, but when Nicodemo lifted his arm and showed a small mark on the outside of his wrist to the camera, I recognized it. It was the same shape and in the same place as

Dante's tattoo. I suddenly remembered where I'd seen it before; Isaia had been doodling the shape over and over in his sketchbook.

The clip finished and Elda turned to me. "Nicodemo is introducing himself to Isaia, basically saying that I would have told him by now that he's Isaia's father and so on, and also that we know now that Isaia is a magus. He explains that all magi have this mark somewhere on their bodies. They aren't necessarily born with it so you don't know right away if a child has the fire, but eventually it comes out. Have you seen a mark by the way?"

I held up my wrists for her to see, but she shook her head. "It's not always in the same place. It can appear anywhere. Isaia's is on the back of his right leg, high up almost on his bum."

"Oh, then no. I haven't seen a mark, but I haven't looked either."

"Well, I'm sure one will appear soon."

"What else did he say?"

"He explained what I already told you, about always staying hydrated," she said, yawning. "That's it for this one."

She selected the next clip and pressed play. She watched for a moment and then nodded. "This is the one about the eyes." She watched the rest of it. I watched over her shoulder as Nicodemo made gestures with his fingers and pointed to his own eyes.

"He explains that one of the most difficult things to master is the red glow. If you're not careful, when you're angry, upset, or excited, the fire will show through your pupils. He said that the secret to controlling the glow is to master your emotions. This is one of the reasons that I deliberately kept Isaia's life quieter than Cristiano's. Thank God Pietro has never noticed it, or if he has he must think it's a trick of the light. He said that to keep the glow dim, when you get emotional, to breathe deeply and speak slowly. He recommends starting a meditation practice and to always think before you speak."

"Fantastic," I said. "That is so not my strong suit."

"It gets easier. Eventually, you'll learn to recognize the feeling of the glow, and you'll be able to control it. It's just difficult at first."

We both gave face-splitting yawns and then laughed at each other's watery eyes.

"Shall we resume again, tomorrow?" I suggested. I was dying to know more, but I was rapidly losing focus.

She nodded. "If you're sure."

I yawned again. My jaw cracked. "I'm sure."

"Okay. I'm going to check on Isaia. It's..." she looked at her watch. "Three thirty."

We dropped the mugs off in the kitchen sink and I followed her to Isaia's room. As soon as we stepped into his room, we saw that he was sleeping deeply, giving off soft little snores.

"I can't believe he spoke," she whispered, stroking his hair back.

"He's healing, Elda," I whispered.

We grinned at each other in the dark.

Her smile faltered. "I'm not sure how I'm going to explain it to Pietro. After all, his first word was your name."

"I don't think that has to be weird," I said. "He's been spending a lot of time with me, and you guys saw from the start that he likes me. I don't think he'll question it."

She nodded. "I hope you're right."

We left the room and she closed the door. I was headed to the stairs when she said my name. I turned back.

"Thank you. I know you didn't have a choice, but you gave me my son back. You saved his life." She looked at me from down the hall, her hand on her bedroom door. Even at a distance I could feel her gratitude.

My throat closed up and I didn't trust my voice. I nodded and we went our separate ways.

By the time I got to my room, I felt utterly exhausted. I looked at my phone to see that Dante had texted shortly after I had run away from him.

We need to talk.

Frowning, I shut my phone off.

TWELVE

I stepped into the shower, turning the water to cool. It was only mid-morning but the day was already stifling and heavy. Surely this was going to be the hottest day since I'd arrived. I imagined I could hear the water sizzle as it hit my body, evaporating instantly. I felt like there was a bonfire raging inside of me, but outwardly nothing looked any different. The heat outside made the fire inside even more uncomfortable. I'd had three frozen fruit slushes for breakfast in an effort to cool down.

It had been over a week since Isaia had begun to speak and he'd steadily improved with every day that passed. When Pietro came home from London, he'd been overjoyed when Isaia actually ran to greet him. Elda and I had shared a happy look at Pietro's pleasure, though it was loaded with the secret we both carried.

Isaia had begun to play a bit of soccer with Cristiano, even if it was only for a few minutes at a time. This morning, I'd delivered them both to swimming lessons, grateful that they'd be in a pool today, instead of running around under the unforgiving sun.

Dante had called and texted me multiple times each day, asking to meet. I ignored all of his attempts to communicate and was thankful that I'd never told him where I lived or which family I was working for.

My phone chirped and I frowned, suspecting that it was him. I poked my head out of the shower to check my phone. Pleasure washed through me when I saw that it was Raf.

I'm back from Milan. Can a guy entice you to meet up for cold drink in Giardini later today?

Me: *You said the magic words. What time? I have to pick the boys up in two hours.*

Raf: *For me, before is better than after. I have to work tonight. Can you do in a half hour?*

Me: **thumbs up**

I cranked the water to cold and stood under it for as long as possible. Slamming off the shower, I thought I might soon resort to ice baths. After I toweled off, I ran a pick through my wet tangle of curls and left it to air dry. I pulled on a bright turquoise summer dress and jammed my feet into my flip-flops. My wide-brimmed hat would keep the sun off my pale face. The moment I stepped into the street, I could feel waves of heat coming off the stones. The air was still and stagnant, but as I walked toward Giardini and hit the calle along the ocean, the breeze picked up. I entered the large park behind a waterfront restaurant. Kids played while parents sipped iced drinks and wilted on park benches.

I took the opportunity to punch out a few texts to my friends. It was mid-summer already and we still hadn't heard a peep from

Akiko. Targa had reported a "friends only" status with the cute fighter-pilot-looking dude. I hoped he got promoted to something more than friends soon, for her sake. Targa was in desperate need of an authentic crush. She was so unenthusiastic about romance of any kind that I sometimes wondered if she was born libido-less, and if that wasn't a word then I'd submit it to Oxford's Dictionary with Targa's photo as the definition.

Georjie had admitted to spending more time gardening than on her laptop and I sputtered a disbelieving, "What!?" Picturing her with dirt under her fingernails and her hair under a kerchief sent me into paroxysms of glee. Her adopted cousin, Jasher, who had started out as 'friendly as a nest of vipers,' now had a 'cautiously optimistic' forecast. My mouth tweaked a smile. At least things were moving in the right direction. I told them that I'd demoted one pretty Italian boy to the bottom of the heap - 'anal discharge' was the term I'd coined, and I chuckled at Georjie's 'puke' emoticon in response to my graphic insult. Then I told them the other pretty Italian boy was now tagged with 'promise.'

I chose a bench in the shade near the fountain where Raf and I had agreed to meet. I tucked my phone away, took off my hat, and enjoyed the breeze moving through my damp hair. Kicking off my flip flops, I spread my toes, letting the air cool my sweaty feet. A spot of dirt smudged the middle toe of my left foot. Strange, I'd only just showered, and bent to rub it away, but it didn't disappear. I pulled my left foot up and set my heel on the bench so I could take a closer look.

There it was. The mark. It was even tinier than Nicodemo's, and brown like a mole. It was rounded on one side and had curls of flames on the other.

My magus mark.

I swallowed but my throat had gone dry. Somehow, that little mark at the base of my middle toe made the whole thing real. So, it was done. I was a magus. I shouldn't have been surprised because the pain was my constant companion, but the mark... I ran my thumb over the little flame-shaped mole, feeling breathless.

"Thirsty?" asked a warm voice.

I looked up to see Raf smiling down at me, two beautiful dimples accenting his cheeks. He looked even better than I remembered, with sparkling eyes and hair curling in the humidity. His broad shoulders blocked out the sun while he held out a cold bottle of lemon soda.

"You read my mind." I grinned and stood.

He leaned down and kissed my cheeks, putting a hand against my lower back. I put my arms around his neck and pulled him into a hug. Instantly there was a thin wall of heat between us.

"I like this greeting," he said, squeezing me. "Even in hot weather. I can't figure out why Italians haven't adopted it yet."

He put the cold soda against my shoulder, probably expecting me to squeal, but the chill made me sigh with pleasure. We parted and I took the soda. One sip, and already my parched throat felt better. We sat on the bench together.

"Welcome back," I said. "How was Milan?"

"It was boring. All work and no play, and no pretty Canadian girls to keep me company. What have you been up to while I was away? Did you enjoy Festa del Redentore?" He turned his shoulders toward me and put an arm up on the back of the bench.

"It was amazing. Fed introduced me to a bunch of her friends and we watched the fireworks from a boat. Then we went to a beach party on Lido and had a bonfire and a dance."

"Oh, really? I hope you didn't meet anyone too interesting," he joked.

I was trying to decide how to respond to this when a voice behind us said, "Yes, Saxony. Did you meet anyone *interesting*?"

Raf and I turned as Dante crossed the grass toward us. My heart leaped into my throat. His hands were jammed in his pockets and he strolled as though he didn't have a care in the world. The almond eyes I'd once found so sexy were glued to my face. Why had I never noticed the hard glint before?

I looked at Raf and he looked from Dante to me.

"I guess you did," Raf said quietly. The pleasure was gone from his face and in its place was concern. I didn't sense any jealousy, at least not from Raf, but he stiffened. It was only noticeable because we were sitting so close together.

"You've been ignoring me," Dante said, just as quietly as Raf had spoken.

There was no threat in his voice. He made the statement casually, like a comment on the weather. My eyes flashed down to his hands but they were still in his pockets. I wondered what shape they were in. He circled the bench and stopped in front of us. For the first time, he looked at Raf. I knew then that the two men knew each other. Of course they did. Hadn't Dante said that he knew everyone?

"Do you mind?" Dante said to Raf. His eyes shifted back to me. "We have something to discuss."

"I'm a little busy right now," I said, annoyed. "Why don't we talk tomorrow?"

"You and I both know that won't happen. So I need to insist," Dante said, again with no threat in his voice, or even impatience. He said it with the quiet confidence that he was going to get his way, at one point or another.

"I'm not going anywhere." Raf's arm closed around my shoulders. "The lady doesn't want to talk to you, Dante."

I felt a burst of anger come off Dante, like the heat of a little solar flare, but it died almost as quickly as I'd felt it.

"You two know each other?" I asked.

"Unfortunately," Dante and Raf both said at the exact same time. They were boring holes into each other with their eyes. Dante took his hands out of his pockets and cracked his knuckles. If the movement caused him pain, he didn't show it.

Raf stood up.

"Whoa, whoa," I said. Visions of the two of them bloodying each other up popped into my head. "I'll talk to you, Dante. But this will be the last time."

Both of them looked at me, Raf with surprise and Dante with grim satisfaction.

"Saxony—" Raf began.

"I'll be okay." I smiled at him. The fire crackling in my torso confirmed it. Dante couldn't hurt me and he knew it. That was the only upside to what had happened between us the last time

I'd seen him. "I'm really sorry we got interrupted like this," I said, shooting daggers at Dante with my eyes. "I'll call you when we're done, okay?"

Raf frowned. Finally, he nodded stiffly. "If that's what you want."

Without looking at Dante, he bent and kissed my cheek. I yearned to call him back, to start over, to go back in time and plan to meet somewhere else so Dante wouldn't run into us. Too late, though. Raf walked away, turning to look back a couple of times before disappearing down the path.

"That was rude," I said as Dante sat down beside me. I tried to keep my voice as neutral as his had been this whole time, but the man was a master of hiding his emotions and I wasn't.

"Oh, Saxony." He sat back and threw an arm over the back of the bench the way Raf had. He brushed my curls over my shoulder and put a hand on the side of my neck.

I stiffened. "What do you want?"

"I don't want to be rude, but you've been ignoring me for a week. It's making me crazy, baby."

I took his hand from my neck and opened his palm to look at it. My breath caught in my throat as I saw the half-ring of blisters across his fingers in the shape of my ear. I took the other one and saw the matching burn. Emotions pelted me. He'd been an ass, but I'd let the fire get the better of me. I looked up at him, regret heavy on my face in spite of myself. He looked at me without a trace of anger or accusation. When he saw my expression, his own face melted with sympathy.

"Aw, baby. I deserved it, and I'm sorry." He put his hands on either side of my face. Though he did it tenderly, the fire licked up my spine, cautious. He brought his forehead to mine for a moment, then pulled back and looked at me. He stroked my hair back from my face. "I'm fine. I know when I'm wrong."

His apology was so sweet and sincere, that I felt like an even bigger villain over what I'd done to his hands. But I was still upset with him, and Elda's words haunted me.

Stay away from that family.

Dante bent his head toward mine, my heart began to pound. The fire in my belly flared higher. I pulled my face back, but he ignored the sign of rejection. He leaned in and kissed the corner of my mouth softly, like the touch of a feather. I stiffened, unsure of what to do. I wanted to end all this in a mature and friendly way if possible, I definitely didn't want to make him an enemy. My heart pounded and my mind raced. How did one disentangle themselves from a relationship with someone unpredictable without making things worse?

This kiss scared me more than anything he'd done before. I had expected an argument, angry shouting, abuse—not tenderness. What was his game? Then another thought shoved the others aside like a rude fat man shoving through a crowd. It was a thought I barely recognized as mine:

You're a fire magus. Untouchable. Powerful. He can't hurt you.

I felt a surge of confidence in myself. With a hand to his chest, I pushed him back. When I stood up, he stood with me, his hands going to either side of my face, arresting me with gentle fingertips.

He looked deeply and searchingly into my eyes. "Yes," he whispered fiercely. "It's real. You're for real."

As his brown eyes shifted back and forth from my left eye to my right, I remembered what Elda said about the glow. I closed my eyes, cursing inwardly and searching for a way to turn off the red light. It was then that I could feel it, like a burning line of fuel. It traveled from my guts, up my spine, through my neck and through the thin stems of my eyes. I took a deep breath, kept my eyes closed. Mastering my emotions was supposed to be the secret.

"No," he said. "You never have to hide your power from me. Don't you realize?"

I opened my eyes and the look of adoration and desire on his face was so intense it made me gasp.

He bent even closer to whisper, "I've been searching for you my whole life."

MY SKIN CRAWLED and I stepped back. Dante seemed really unstable now. He knew what I was, and even though I had power in my control, I understood that he could use this knowledge against me.

"I need to think," I said.

I felt like I was in over my head and the only thing that kept me from running away from him was the fire and the power that came along with it. It gave me a feeling of security that I'd never had before. I thought of the turn of events that had put me into this position, and a spark of rage went flying up from my pelvis. It spiraled through me and then went out like an ember from a bonfire. I had a moment of fear at the intensity of that spark, thankful that it disappeared as quickly as it had come.

"You don't need to think," Dante was saying. "You just need to trust me. No one knows what you are better than I do. I'll take care of you. We'll be unstoppable together. I'll give you everything, and you..." He broke off, naked hunger and ambition lit his face. "You'll be my everything. My *Inferno*."

Dante's Inferno.

It was too much. I burst out laughing.

His face contorted with frustration. "You're failing to grasp what this can mean for you, Saxony. You'll be a queen in Venezia, and at the rate my family's territory was increasing when we had Nicodemo, you'll be a queen of Italy within a decade."

He was talking faster, his accent thicker because of his excitement and earnestness.

The laughter died in my throat.

"Our rivals thought things equalized when Nic died. We'll show them how wrong they are. They will not be expecting you. Neither will my father." He took a step closer, reached for my hands. "It's too beautiful. It's... what do they call it in English? Poetic justice."

My stomach clenched as he grasped my fingertips. He wanted what he wanted, whatever the cost.

"Dante, what are you talking about? I can't... I'm not going to help you take over Italy." I fought and failed to keep the incredulity out of my voice.

He blinked at me like he hadn't heard me properly. "Of course you are. Surely you can feel it, too. We are meant for each other. This is destiny."

"I don't know what you think *destiny* looks like but you're sadly mistaken, this is *accident*. A week ago I wasn't a magus, I was just a regular girl."

He looked like I'd slapped him. "What do you mean? That's not possible."

"It is possible," I continued. "I wasn't born this way—it was forced upon me. I didn't ask for it and I wouldn't wish it on my worst enemy."

When he grabbed my upper arms, his fingers dug into my flesh. His eyes narrowed. "Saxony, don't bullshit me. We don't have time for this garbage."

Anger flared. I pushed his hands off.

"It's not garbage," I seethed. "It's what happened. You remember the day my voice changed? It's never been the same since. That's when it happened. I wasn't sick. Now, if you'll excuse me, we're done here."

"We're done when I say we're done, and I say we're not done." He grabbed my arms once again.

I looked down at his hand on my bicep and back up at his face pointedly, letting my expression do the talking. *How dare you threaten a magus. Again.* I knew what he was doing. He'd been so angry at me for responding to Elda's requests—he'd wanted me to manipulate her by ignoring her. I could see now how Dante worked people. He was trying to jockey into place as my dominant.

Screw that.

I glared at him.

Fear flashed across his face, just for a second. He released me and held his hands up. "Sorry, I'm sorry. Just..." he sat on the bench. "Please let's sit and talk like adults. We can figure this out." He patted the bench beside him, and then held out a hand.

My confidence boosted, I seized my chance. "Dante, no amount of talking is going to change my mind. I'm not going to help you take over Italy."

His eyes flashed with anger again, but it evaporated as quickly as it had appeared.

"Okay, okay," he said, holding his hands up in a gesture of surrender. "Then just tell me what you meant by it being forced on you. I didn't think that was possible. At least, Nicodemo never told me that could happen."

I sighed. "I can't explain it to you, Dante. I'm collateral damage in all of this madness. I just have to figure out how to live with it."

"But don't you see, I can help you with that." He stood again, since I still hadn't sat.

"How?"

"Nic was part of my family for a long time. I know what a magus can do, I'll teach you. I can make it so that you never have to be afraid of your power, and so that you can use it to help people."

I scoffed. "Help people? Is that what you call what your family does?" The fire was crackling merrily in me now, melting my caution away.

His face hardened. "Careful. You don't know anything about my family, not yet." Then he smiled and said, "But you will, I'll tell you everything. You'll be my partner, my closest confidante. You'll have access to all of the resources at my family's disposal."

"Stop talking like that. I'm not interested. I know enough about the Barberini family—"

"What do you know?" he interrupted me.

I had already said too much. I turned away. "I have to go, Dante. I have somewhere I need to be." I made a show of checking my watch. I did have to pick up the boys from the pool, but I still had forty minutes.

"Who have you been talking to?"

"No one," I said, cursing myself. "Your family is infamous, you know that."

His eyes narrowed.

"Goodbye, Dante. Don't contact me again." I hadn't taken more than three steps when he grabbed me by the arm and spun me around. Rage blinded me but before I could react—

BAM!

A tightly coiled fist slammed into my stomach. Fireworks popped in front of my eyes. All the air whooshed out of me in one sickening, forced exhale. I dropped to my knees, my face an inch from the ground.

Breathe, Saxony. Breathe.

It felt as though the walls of my lungs were stuck to each other. My stomach churned and I thought I might throw up. Even as I was fighting for breath, the fire roared to life inside me, flooding my limbs with fury. I wanted to get up, to defend myself, but I couldn't breathe, couldn't move. Finally, my lungs unstuck. I sucked in a painful breath. I coughed, and a spray of embers littered the grass. My eyes cleared and Dante's shoes came into focus. Adidas. White, with three black stripes. Just standing there. One shoe moved to snuff the embers I had spewed, one by one.

Hands jacked me up by my armpits. I coughed again, but this time only smoke curled from my lips. I sucked in more oxygen, starved for it. With every gulp of air, the fire inside me licked higher, hotter. His body telegraphed another punch—the fingers curling, the fist drawing back, the shoulders turning.

My eyes widened. Nope.

The fire shot to my right shoulder and elbow and exploded in my joints. I sent my fist into Dante's face with the force of a cannon. I heard Dante's nose break as his head snapped sideways. He flew off his feet and landed hard in a heap several feet away.

I covered my mouth, in shock at the power of my own punch. The feeling of breaking bone against my knuckles made me feel queasy. A wave of nausea washed over me again as I crouched beside him. I'd knocked him out.

"You idiot!" I said, unsure whether I was addressing myself or him. Exactly how hard had I hit him? I reached for his neck to feel his pulse.

Before I could touch him, his eyelids fluttered. His upper lip was split and blood poured from his nose. To my horror, he began to laugh. It was a horrible wet sound. He groaned in the midst of his laughter and struggled to sit up. He wiped his nose with his hand but it was still pouring blood, staining his teeth and making him look like a Halloween mask. He finally looked on the outside the way he was on the inside.

"You're so stupid, Dante. I have a temper at the best of times." I watched him crawl to a nearby fountain so he could wash his face. "Why did you hit me?"

My stomach still ached. Only the fact that I had retaliated had dampened my rage.

"All fire magi are hot-tempered. I knew you'd do something, but I didn't think you'd internalize," he said, and spat a gob of blood. He dipped his mouth and nose in the cold water. He rinsed and spat again and then put his hands to either side of his nose, feeling the break.

He had my attention. "Internalize? What are you talking about? I don't know about you but a right hook to the face is not 'internalizing'."

He barked in pain as he snapped his own nose sideways.

"What did you just do?"

"What, do you think this was my first broken nose?" He stood up. The flow of blood had become a trickle. He grinned at me with bloody teeth.

I shuddered. "I need to get off this crazy train."

The only reason I wasn't running away was because he'd piqued my curiosity. "What do you mean by internalize? And if you hit me again, so help me..." I threatened. I could feel the glow in my eyes come out and I let it.

"Madonna. You're a thing of beauty when you do that." He spat again and wiped a hand across his face, leaving a streak of blood. "Internalizing is something that only mature fire magi can do. Usually. It means you used the power of the fire but you didn't show it. See? You don't even know how much potential you have."

"I don't get it."

"Young magi can't help but show their fire when they use it. It manifests as a glow that can be seen through the skin, or comes out as flames or sparks. But a mature magus can prevent this obvious show of power. It's a skill they have to develop to maintain anonymity. The way Nicodemo explained it was that he could direct the fire to places in his body and sort of... " he paused. "What's the word? Detonate it? So that it would explode behind a kick or a punch, like gunpowder. That way a magus can use her power without tipping people off that she's supernatural." He cocked an eyebrow. "Hai capito?"

He swiped an arm across his face, wiping away the remainder of the blood, and then spat another red gob off to the side.

I did capito. I capito'd perfectly. What he described was exactly what I had felt. The fire had detonated in my shoulder and elbow, making me throw a punch like a two-hundred-pound hockey player instead of a one-hundred-and-forty-pound girl. My hand was still throbbing from the pain of the impact. It was a wonder I hadn't broken every bone in my hand. I didn't know what to say. Dante really did have some knowledge, but somehow, I wasn't really feeling a 'thank you.'

"You didn't have to hit me," I said, bitterly.

"Yes, I did." All trace of malice and anger was gone. He thought he'd gotten through to me. "And I'm sorry," he said, his eyes softening.

I'd heard it before, *and* he'd been about to hit me a second time. I wasn't going to fall for his silver tongue again. Maybe he did know some things that could help me, but I didn't need to ask him because Elda was going to help me. If I took Dante's help I was going to owe him, and that was the last thing I wanted.

"Save it," I said. "I'm finished with this insanity. I'm walking away now and if you jump me, I'll internalize you right into the hospital."

"Don't be such a stubborn redhead, Saxony. You know I'm the only one who can help you."

I turned my back and walked away.

He raised his voice. "Do you know what happens to a fire magus who doesn't know what she's doing?"

I kept walking.

"She burns to death," he called. "From the inside out!"

THIRTEEN

My phone chirped just as the boys and I arrived home.

"We're home!" I called up the stairs.

"We're home!" Isaia repeated, and ran to the second floor after Cristiano.

I smiled every time I heard the sound of his perfect little voice. He no longer had any trace of the rasp that I had. I heard Elda greet her boys upstairs and I took my phone out of my purse and checked it as I kicked off my shoes. It was Raf.

Everything okay?

I smiled at his thoughtfulness. He was probably worried. My guts ached in response to his question, reminding me that I'd been punched today for the first time in my life. The fire flickered as I remembered, but I wasn't about to tell Raf what had happened between Dante and me; I didn't think Raf would react well. I also didn't feel as bad as I thought I should feel after taking a hard punch to the gut.

Me: *I'm okay, thanks for checking. I'm sorry about that.*

Raf: *That's okay. You can make it up to me. :)*

Me: *How about tomorrow night? I'm free after nine.*

Raf: *Sure, Giardini again or somewhere else?*

Me: *Why don't we just go for a walk? Maybe get some gelato.*

Raf: *Sold. Let me know where to meet you.*

Me: *Will do.*

I tucked my phone away and ran up the stairs to help Elda fix dinner. Tonight she was going to teach me how to make a Neapolitan ragù and steamed mussels for prima piatti. Once the boys had finished telling Elda in great detail about their day, they went down to the courtyard garden to play.

"I've been meaning to ask you," said Elda as she was clipping the stringy bits from the mussels. She paused with the scissors. "Did you want to come to Gallipoli with us? You never told me and we're leaving in less than a week. If you do, then I'll pack some extra bedsheets."

I blinked in momentary shock at how fast the time had gone. I hadn't forgotten that they'd be leaving, but I had lost track of time.

"Not that we'll need anything more than sheets," she continued. "Even those might be too hot. It's been above 35 all week in Puglia and it's supposed to climb."

"Davvero?" I said, using a new Italian word I'd picked up which simply meant 'really.' "That answers it then—that is way too hot for me." I had barely been able to handle the Venice temperatures, so there was no way I was going to go where it was even hotter.

Understanding dawned on her face. "Oh, I see. Hot weather makes it... hurt more?" She put down the scissors and tossed the mussels under running water. She peered into my simmering pot of red wine sauce and prosciutto. "Good, you can add the tomatoes now."

"Yes, it really does. Unfortunately." I added the skinned tomatoes and sauce and stirred. "So, on to the most important stuff. Please tell me you've had a chance to watch all the clips? Cuz I'm dying here."

I blinked for a second at my own words. I had meant it figuratively but Dante's last words rang in my ears and I hoped that I hadn't just said something prophetic.

"I have actually seen them before. I watched them a few years ago in case there was anything that would help Isaia. But I have to tell you, now that I've watched them again I remembered that I was disappointed the first time I saw them, too. I really thought there'd be more information. Kind of makes me wonder if I missed downloading some files somehow."

"Hit me with what you got anyway," I said. I peeked into the pot and felt rather pleased with the sauce I had made. I took out the casserole dish and put it on the counter, ready to layer with gnocchi, sauce and cheese.

"Hit you?" Elda repeated, looking confused.

"Sorry, I mean go ahead and tell me what you know."

"Ah. Allora, first, he explained that those born with the fire are either killed by it, or made stronger by it. The saying what doesn't kill you makes you stronger is literal for a fire magus. It was clear that Isaia was going to die from it, but as long as you're smart, you won't."

"Comforting," I murmured. "What does 'smart' mean?"

"Most importantly, and I already told you this but I have to emphasize it because Nic talked about it more in other clips, you must stay hydrated. He talked about the stages of dehydration for a magus, and Saxony"—she gave me an emphatic look —"it's serious."

"It's serious for everyone," I said. "People can only go three days without water. After that they're pretty much toast."

"Yes, but you have a smaller window than that. Much smaller."

The hair on my arms stood up. "How small?"

"You have about 16 hours before you die. Even that might be pushing it."

Less than a day. It wasn't a nice thought. But as long as I drank a lot, it should never be a problem. I resolved to carry a water bottle with me from now on.

Elda was studying my face intently.

"What?"

"Are you okay?"

"Yeah, I am. Just... processing." I stirred the tomatoes.

She was still staring.

"What?" I repeated, my hands wide.

She shook her head. "I know that you wouldn't have chosen this for yourself, Saxony. But..."

"But?"

"But, you're an amazing creature," she blurted. "I know there's pain, but from what Nic says, that gets easier to manage. The power that you have, you're basically a superhero. I kind of wish I was a magus. It always made me so afraid, because of what Isaia was going to have to deal with..." she looked like she wanted to say more, but she paused.

"But now that I have to deal with it instead of your little boy, you're all about the fireballs, is that it?" I said, sardonically.

She cracked a smile. "You make me sound like a horrible person. And I am sorry for your pain, if I could take it away, I would. But, you're strong, Saxony. You can handle this. It's kind of... a gift. Don't you think?"

"You try carrying a campfire around in your belly for a few hours and then ask me that again," I said, as I poured the steaming tomato sauce over the gnocchi. In spite of my sarcasm, I did understand what she was trying to say. I had a lot of power at my disposal, if I could just learn how to use it properly. "Let's focus. What else did he say?"

"Okay, so with the dehydration, he said there is sort of a steady progression of pain and an increasing lack of control over the fire. But after six, eight hours or so the fire begins to dry up and burn your tissues until..."

"Can we skip to the next part? I think I got the whole being roasted alive concept."

"Sorry, I thought you wanted every last word. Then, he talked about something called externalization. Externalizing means the fire will show through your body as a light, or it comes out in the form of flames, sparks, or smoke. He said the first step for a magus is to learn how to control the externalization of the fire. In the early years, he said there is always a fight for control. The fire is wild and you have to tame it, and this is more of an emotional exercise than a physical one."

I nodded—it made sense to me now that I've had to deal with it for several weeks. It was always harder to control when my emotions were running high. I layered the cheese over the gnocchi and put the casserole dish into the oven. "I think I understand that, too. So far, this is nothing new."

"Then, as you might guess, he also talked about internalizing it. Which just means that people on the outside can't see the fire. He said it is critical for a magus to reach this point for their own safety. The world is not really aware of the existence of fire magi, only a few select humans know about you. So, except for people you trust with your life, you need to keep your ability a secret."

"Kind of obvious, thanks Nic," I said. "Go on."

"Internalizing means that you can control the fire well enough to use it within your body to give you strength and speed when you need it. Sort of like..." she paused, thinking. "I'm trying to translate it with the right word..."

"Detonating it?"

"Si, perfetto; detonation." She put a pot on the stove and lit the burner. She dumped a piece of butter in to melt. "He said that the simplest way to learn this is to make one detonation at a time and in one part of the body at a time. For practice, he suggested detonating it in your shoulder when you skip a stone out to sea. But he explained that eventually you'll be able to detonate the fire in multiple places at once and with rapid succession. For this he said to start by running and detonating in your hips, to practice alternating quickly back and forth and to increase your running speed."

Okay, so that bit was new and interesting.

Elda continued, "He said that one of the best things he did to learn how to control his fire was take a martial arts class. He started just learning the movements, eventually adding detonations in his joints and soon he was able to detonate with every single movement. You can imagine how powerful you would become if you were to master this."

"I can, but I sure hope I don't need to have to use it that way. If I do, then it means I've got enemies," I said.

It sucked enough to butt heads with Dante; I didn't want to make a habit out of it.

"Everyone has enemies, Saxony," Elda said as she stirred chopped onion and herbs into the sizzling butter. "You are young, but give it time."

"So cynical. You sell blush for Pete's sake—what kind of enemies do you have?"

"Not the kind that need to be beaten up, thank goodness. But retail is a bloodbath, metaphorically speaking." She poured some water and then white wine into the pot and added the steaming basket.

I had to laugh. "That sounds a bit ridiculous, but okay."

She smiled and went on. "That was it about the fire itself."

It wasn't much to go on, but I felt a bit better armed than before.

"He said that he doesn't know a lot about the history of the fire magi, where they originated or how many there are. There were rumoured to be scrolls about the fire magi in the library at Alexandria, but those were supposedly destroyed. Poor guy was raised in an orphanage with no one to teach him about himself. The nuns who raised him told him that when his father dropped him off as an infant, they saw a strange birthmark on the side of his father's face, like a tiny flame."

"His dad left him at an orphanage, even though he was probably a fire magus? That's cold."

"His father told the nuns that Nic wouldn't live very long and then vanished. So I guess his dad thought he was doomed," explained Elda as she poured the mussels in the steaming basket to cook.

"I'm going to bet it was a bit of shock to the ladies when his eyes started glowing red and fire spouted from his fingertips."

Elda smirked. "Yeah, I wish I'd asked him more about how he managed to survive childhood in an orphanage run by nuns."

"By the way, my mark showed up," I said as I took plates down to set the table.

"Davvero?" Her eyes scanned my body anywhere that I had skin showing. "Dové?"

"Here." I lifted my bare foot and showed her the tiny flame shaped mole on the third toe of my left foot. She bent to look at it.

"Bella," she said, with wonder in her voice. "I wonder if Isaia's will disappear now that he doesn't carry the fire anymore?"

"I've no idea. Watch it and see." I took the plates to the table. Pietro would be home tonight and it would be one of the few times all of us would eat together. My mouth watered at the smells that filled the kitchen.

Cristiano and Isaia came running down the hall, giggling at whatever game they'd been playing. Isaia ran into me and wrapped his arms around my legs. He looked up at me, black eyes shining. I smiled down at him and put a hand on his head. Then he went running back down the hall after his brother, both of them thumping like elephants. Elda yelled after them to wash up for dinner.

I took a cup from the cupboard and poured some water from the fridge. I took a sip, set it on the counter and peeked into the oven through the glass door. The gnocchi bubbled nicely and saliva filled my mouth. I could feel the heat radiating from the glass door of the oven. Without thinking, I opened the oven door and reached in. I picked up the casserole dish. *One hundred and sixty three degrees.* The fire had given me the ability to read temperature. My mouth twitched, impressed in spite of myself.

"Saxony!"

I turned, holding the bubbling ragù. She stood there, her eyes wide, a bottle of wine in one hand and a glass in the other. She blinked a few times and then her face softened. "It doesn't burn you, does it?"

I shook my head. "I can feel the temperature, every degree, but..."

I set the dish down on the marble countertop and showed her my palms. The skin was pink, healthy, and un-singed.

I SPOTTED Raf before he spotted me. He stood in front of the gelato shop where we'd agreed to meet, in line behind a woman with three kids crowding around her legs. One was crying and the other two screamed the way kids do when they're trying out their voices. I grimaced at the pitch the little girl could hit. The woman juggled her purse, a wallet, and an ice cream cone.

Raf stepped in and took a cone from the man behind the counter. He handed it to the screaming girl, who instantly shut up. Then he took the other cone being offered while the woman paid. Raf handed it to the little boy, who looked like he was about to have a full-on meltdown. The child took the cone and stuffed it into his face instead. I smiled at the gratitude on the mother's face. She dropped her wallet into her purse, picked up the littlest kid and the family shuffled off to find a table.

"Aren't you a gentleman," I said.

He turned and smiled.

"Ciao Saxony. Come stai?" He kissed both my cheeks, his hand at my waist.

I kissed his cheeks back. "Sto bene, anche?" I said, telling him I was well and asking him how he is in return.

"Bene, bene. I'm glad to see you're in one piece. Which flavor would you like?" He pointed to the display of brightly colored gelato. I chose stracciatella and bacio, a kind of chocolate with hazelnut in it that tasted a lot like the chocolate hedgehogs I could get back home. I took a single serving wet nap from a bowl on the counter in anticipation of a mess. Raf ordered mint in a cup for himself and paid. We strolled toward an empty park bench with our gelato.

"Glad to see I'm in one piece?" I licked the bacio flavor and the sweet nutty flavor melted on my tongue. Gelato had been a brilliant idea. The cool ice cream pooled in my belly, soothing the heat.

"At the risk of sounding jealous, Dante isn't exactly the best choice of company. Of all the people in Venezia, I can't believe you met him."

"You're *not* jealous?" I teased. "Just a little bit?"

A dimple appeared in his cheek. "I tried jealousy once, but it didn't work. Just concerned. May I ask what he wanted with you? I'm sorry to sound nosy, but I can't help but worry that you don't know what you're getting into with him."

He sounded so serious. I sighed. If we had to talk about Dante, then we might as well get it over with.

"What do you know about him?" I caught a drip of stracciatella before it went over my fingers.

"I know a lot, actually. I went to school with Dante. We're the same age. We were close at one time, almost like brothers."

Raf dipped into his gelato with a tiny spoon and I regretted not choosing a cup. The weather was too warm and my gelato was melting too fast for me to keep up.

"What happened?" I spun my ice cream against my tongue to catch all of the drips.

"It's kind of a long story, but I'll give you the short version. Dante and I became friends the day we met, which was the first day of first grade. We had a lot in common. We played soccer together, had the same classes, and we both liked the same video games. In winter, we'd play in his basement for hours. I even got kind of attached to his dad, Enzo."

"You know Enzo?" My ears perked at the name of the man who had yet to collect a debt from Elda.

"I did. Enzo really took a shine to me, but I didn't know why until I got older."

"Why?"

"He saw me as the son that Dante wasn't. Dante has always had a mean streak."

"Enzo didn't like that?" I would have thought that a mean streak would be a prerequisite for the son of a crime boss.

Raf shook his head. "I know. It's counterintuitive. But, no. Over the years, Dante got jealous of how much his dad liked me. Enzo treated me like a son. You have to understand that Dante lives and dies by his father's approval. In Enzo's eyes, he was never good enough. The rift between them only grew as Dante got older. Enzo is a powerful man in Venezia, and I'm sure his authority extends well beyond the Veneto region by now."

"I don't have the impression he got that power by following the law." I crunched into my cone.

"No, you're right. But you might be surprised at what a paradox the guy is." Raf lowered his voice a fraction, and I suppressed the urge to look over my shoulder. "I mean yes, he's not exactly a law-abiding citizen. But he does operate by a kind of moral code. He's out for himself and his family, but he's also out for Venezia. I've seen him do some really generous things: donating a lot of money to charity, helping families in need. Compassion is a strategy that can help get him what he wants, buy the goodwill of the people and all that. But other times, I know he resorts to violence to get stuff done. He's got a lot of guys working for him. Long arms, you know?"

"Sounds like the Godfather." I laughed. Then I actually did look over my shoulder. All this talk was so strange. I'd seen mafia movies. I got the gist of how it worked, but it had always seemed like fiction to me.

Raf smiled. "Pretty much. The sad part is that Dante really looks up to his dad. He's desperate to follow in his footsteps. But Dante goes about it all wrong, and he's a tyrant. I don't know where Enzo went wrong raising him, but if Dante ever takes control of the Barberini fortune, I'll leave the region."

"Do you think Enzo knows that his son would make a bad... what do you call it... don? Is that the right term?"

Raf laughed. "You could just say boss, and I don't know. I haven't spent time with that family since I was twelve or so. I would guess so, though." He lowered his voice again. "They're a crime family, and I'm sure Enzo has a good idea of the kind of person he wants taking over one day." He finished the last of his gelato and tossed the cup and spoon into the recycling containers behind the park bench. He put an arm over the back of the chair and faced me. "Anyway, enough about the Barberinis. I just thought you should be aware."

"Thanks, I appreciate the concern." I popped the last of my cone into my mouth, wiping my hands with the wet nap, I then tossed it in the trash. "When you were spending time with Dante, did you ever meet a guy named Nicodemo?"

Raf's eyebrows shot up. "How do you know about Nic?"

"Dante mentioned him. Did you know him?"

Raf nodded. "I met him. I got a good feeling from him. Warm, you know?"

My mouth twitched at his accidental pun...or did Raf know what Nic was?

"I didn't have much to do with him," he continued. "He was one of Enzo's best men. He was always gone for some reason or another."

"Did..." I tried to think about how to ask what I wanted to know. "Was there something different about him?

Raf looked puzzled. "What do you mean?"

It was clear from his vacant expression that Raf didn't know that Nic was a fire magus.

"Nothing, just curious," I back-pedaled. "Do you know what happened to Nic?"

"No idea. The only Barberini I associate with these days is Fed. She told me he passed away but couldn't tell me the specifics. It's a mystery."

I froze. "Fed is a Barberini?"

"Yeah, she's Dante's cousin. You didn't know?"

"No. But that puts a few things into perspective." Fed had never been jealous after all. She really had been concerned about me getting close to Dante. Why hadn't she told me they were family? I wondered why she'd introduced me to him in the first place if she knew he was so dangerous. I pushed the question away. She never could have foreseen his attraction to me, or my becoming a magus. It wasn't her fault.

"Shall we walk?" Raf stood and held out his hand.

I stood and slid my hand into his. His warm fingers engulfed mine and the fire inside me crackled happily in response, which gave me pause. Sometimes it felt like it was part of me, and other times it felt like it was a parasite observing my life from the inside.

As we walked toward the sea, Raf lifted my hand to his lips and kissed the backs of my fingers. Then he looked down at me and smiled, tucking my hand into the crook of his elbow. We strolled together and enjoyed the cool air coming in off the water. It licked across my damp brow and lifted my curls. We talked about the differences between the Canadian and Italian school systems, what our families were like, and our ambitions for the future. Neither of us broached the subject of me leaving, or that this relationship was almost certainly temporary. If he didn't bring it up, I wouldn't either. *Live in the moment, Saxony. Just enjoy him.*

When we arrived at my door, it was nearly midnight. I turned to face him. A street light lit up the canal and cast us both in a soft yellow glow.

"So," I began, clearing my throat. "Elda and Pietro are leaving for Puglia for a few weeks. I'll have the place to myself. How about a movie night? For some reason, I feel like watching *The Godfather*. Can't imagine why."

He grinned. "That's one of my favorite movies."

He stepped closer. I tilted my face up to his.

"I would like that," he said quietly.

I closed my eyes as he bent to kiss me, softly at first. When he felt me press closer and twine my arms around his neck, the kiss deepened. The fire roared to life in my belly, licking up my spine. Its liquid heat spread through and curled around me. I wrapped my fingers around the back of Raf's neck and up into his hair, savoring the sweetness of the kiss. He tasted like mint gelato. When I felt the heat travel up my neck and warm my cheeks and eyes, my heart fluttered with panic. What if I opened my eyes and they were glowing? He'd freak out.

I kept my eyes shut as my mind raced. I slowly brought the kiss to a close and then dropped my face down toward our feet. I tucked my head under his chin and against his chest so he couldn't see my eyes. He kissed the top of my head and brushed my curls away from my cheek and behind my ear. Thank God he didn't seem to notice anything strange. I took slow, deep breaths to calm my racing heart and temper the flame. My cheeks and eyes cooled and when I was certain that my eyes weren't glowing like a rabid dog's, I stepped back and looked up at him.

"Thank you for a lovely night," I said.

He pressed a warm stubbly cheek against mine. "Until our movie night, then."

He waited as I unlocked the door. As soon as I was inside, door closed behind me, I leaned against the foyer wall and chewed my lip. If my eyes glowed whenever I was excited, what would happen when there was more than just a kiss going on? I covered my face with my hands, imagining Raf yelling with terror as a demon-eyed me glared up at him in the middle of a make-out session.

I groaned.

What kind of guy would want to be with a girl who was—let's face it—a freak of nature?

FOURTEEN

The days leading up to the Baseggio's departure were full of activity. I did loads of laundry and cleaned the house from top to bottom... and both of the boys were home full-time. Whenever Elda was home we took care of the boys together, but she often worked late as she prepared her business for her absence. Isaia gained energy like a locomotive going downhill, and Cristiano was so happy to have someone who could keep up with him that the boys were like little whirlwinds wherever they went. I barely had time to chat with Raf at all and fell into bed exhausted every evening. Dante continued to text, begging to talk. I ignored him. I also promised myself I'd reach out to Fed as soon as the Baseggio's left on their vacation. I didn't see Pietro until the night before the family left. I was helping Isaia get ready for bed when I heard his voice in the kitchen speaking to Elda.

"Looks like your dad made it after all," I said to Isaia.

I pulled his sleep shirt down over his head and let him go. Isaia ran into the kitchen for a hug and kiss from his dad. I followed him, smiling as I watched the two snuggle. I was reminded every time I saw the blond, ebony-eyed boy and the dark-haired, blue-eyed father together that Pietro was not Isaia's biological father. Pietro would never find out if Elda had anything to say about it. I wondered whether it had ever crossed Pietro's mind. Probably not, because Isaia looked more like Elda anyway. It was just the black eyes and the set of the mouth and jaw that didn't seem to fit anywhere between the two parents.

"Buonasera, Saxony," said Pietro from over Isaia's head. His mouth was tight and he had dark smudges under his eyes.

"Buonasera Pietro, nice to see you." I didn't like the look of the deep lines between his brows.

He kissed Isaia and sent him to bed. Isaia came to me for a hug and a kiss, too.

"I'll be in to read you a story," I told him. "Get into bed, okay?"

"Okay." He scampered down the hall, way too energetic to sleep. I didn't have the heart to tell him to slow down. The kid had been slow his whole life. Let him enjoy running for a change.

I turned to Pietro. "Everything okay?"

"One of my clients had a break-in last night. It's been a very long day." He handed Elda a plastic lunch container. She put it in the dishwasher. I realized that she looked even more stressed than Pietro did.

"That's awful. Was anything stolen? Are you allowed to say which client?"

He shook his head. "I can't say. And yes, some small items were stolen, but overall it could have been a lot worse."

Pietro and Elda conversed in Italian while I boiled water for tea. It felt like they needed some privacy. When there was a break in the conversation, I said, "I'll say buona notte and arrivederci tonight then. It sounds like you two need to talk."

"Thanks for all your help this week, Saxony. You've been a Godsend." Elda kissed my cheeks and giving me a hug goodnight.

"Buona notte, Saxony. We'll miss you in Puglia," said Pietro.

"Text me when you arrive safely, okay?"

They nodded, but it was obvious they were both distracted. I left them to their conversation, poking my head into Isaia's room. He was on the floor with books spread out in front of him. He looked up and smiled when I came in.

"Did you choose a story?" I scanned the books, noting the fairy tale book with the firebird story. I watched as he deliberated and finally reached for a story with dinosaurs on the cover. I smiled.

"Into bed with you, maestro."

We snuggled together and I read the story to him, feeling him relax and grow sleepy.

I closed the book. "I won't see you in the morning, Isaia. You're going to get up really early and you'll be gone before I wake up."

"Why can't you come?" he asked, blinking up at me, tilting his head back against my shoulder.

"I think it's better if I stay here. But I'll be here when you get back."

"But why?"

I thought for a moment. If anyone could understand my reason, it would be this little boy. "It's really hot in Gallipoli right now, Isaia. As much as I would like to see the south of Italy, I'm afraid it would be uncomfortable for me."

He nodded before I was even finished. "Too hot," he said, his dark eyes serious.

"Yes. So give me a hug and a kiss goodnight and I'll see you in a couple of weeks, okay?"

"Okay." He put his arms around me.

"I love you, kiddo."

"Love you, too."

My throat constricted as I watched him snuggle down into his sheets. I went to the door and looked back to see he was still watching me, his black eyes gleaming in the dark, eyelids at half-mast. I blew him a kiss and then closed the door.

Pietro and Elda were still deep in conversation as I slipped down the hall. Whatever had happened, I hoped it wouldn't ruin their holiday. They were leaving at five in the morning to catch a flight to Gallipoli and Elda had kindly told me to sleep in. So that's what I did.

When I rolled over and checked the clock the next morning, it was almost nine.

When I got out of the shower and checked my phone, I saw that a text from Raf had come in.

So you're a free woman now? How about that movie date?

I smiled. He didn't waste any time.

Me: *Come over Saturday night? Pietro and Elda told me we could use their theatre room.*

Raf: *Brava! What time?*

Me: *Why don't you come at seven and we can make dinner together and then watch after?*

Raf: *thumbs up* *What can I bring?*

Me: *I got it. No worries.*

Raf: *okay, a presto!*

I smiled at the butterflies that fluttered under my ribcage at the thought of a cuddly evening with Raf. I squelched the anxiety about my eye-glow that threatened to surface.

I walked to the Eurospar and took my time before buying groceries. I picked up stamps, charged up my phone, took a nap, and lazed outside of a cafe with a book. I read for half an hour before I felt the urge to talk to someone, so I texted Fed. A surge of guilt moved through me because I had neglected her, and I was embarrassed that I'd assumed she was jealous of Dante and me.

Ciao Bella, join me for a coffee?

Fed: *Where have you been? It's been ages! Are you hanging out with Dante a lot?*

I paused. I had to assume Dante didn't tell her what had transpired between us since Festa del Redentore.

Me: *Not so much anymore.*

Fed: *What happened? Never mind, save it so you can tell me in person. Can't wait! Have to work. Come visit me at work if you want. I'll give you a free gelato. :)*

Me: *Mmmmm! Sweet! What time are you finished?*

Fed: *Six. Ciao!*

I closed my phone but jumped when it rang. It was Elda. They must have arrived in Puglia.

I accepted her call with a grin. "Hi, how was your flight?"

"Saxony?" Her voice sounded weird. Urgent, yet like she was trying to be quiet.

I lost my grin. "Yeah, what's up? Everything okay?"

"We're here. But I had to call you because...wait a second..."

A door shut in the background.

"Are you okay? What's going on?"

"I could get into huge trouble for telling you this because of Pietro's confidentiality clause, but...well it's more important that you know what's going on. I don't have a lot of time so I'll have to be quick. Are you listening?"

"Of course, you've got me on pins and needles, tell me for Pete's sake."

"Pietro's client, they are a bank. One of the biggest in Venezia actually."

"Is this about the break-in?"

"Shhh!" She shushed me and I jerked my head back in surprise, Elda had never shushed me. "Are you alone? Maybe just listen, don't say anything."

"You're freaking me out. Can I say that?"

"Sorry, I don't think you need to freak out, just listen. The break-in that Pietro was talking about was at this bank. Only one thing was stolen, which is so crazy that it has to be a statement."

"What do you mean?"

"The stick, Saxony. The hard drive with Nic's videos on them. They were stolen from my lockbox. They were the *only* thing that was stolen. All the originals are gone. Now do you get it?"

Her words sank in. The fire flickered in my belly, but my skin felt ice-cold. Nic's videos were stolen? My mind immediately jumped to Dante. But how could he have pulled that off?

"He's coming for Isaia soon, I know it."

"What? Who?"

"Enzo. He's going to call my debt and take my little boy." Her voice broke and my heart broke to hear the fear saturating her voice.

"Breathe, Elda. That's not going to happen. He can't take a boy from his parents."

"You don't know, Saxony. He can." She breathed into the phone, and the sound of a heavy wind shooshed into my ear.

"He's not going to want Isaia—he's not a magus." Even as I said the words, the smoke in my mind began to clear away from the problem.

Elda said the words as the thought formed in my mind. "Enzo won't know that, and by the time he does they could have already taken him."

I closed my eyes. She was right, but I wasn't going to feed her fear. "If he does come for Isaia, which I doubt he will, then just tell him that he didn't inherit the fire. Tell him that Nic made the videos just to be prepared."

"You think he'll believe that?" She sounded incredulous. "I have to go; the boys are asking for me. Pietro doesn't know any of this. He doesn't even know that I was the owner of the lockbox. He's not the lawyer assigned to the case, one of his partners is. You can imagine..." She stopped herself. "I'm so sorry you've been dragged into all of this, Saxony. I just thought you should know. Be careful, okay? If someone comes knocking on our door, don't answer it."

I opened my mouth to say something comforting, but the line went dead. I set my phone on the table. I chewed my lip and stared without seeing. Enzo didn't know it yet, but Isaia would not be of interest to him anymore.

Isaia wouldn't, but I would.

I STEPPED out from under the grocery store's awning and into the sun carrying two bags of groceries. Blinking in the light, I set the bags down and put my sunglasses on. As I walked toward home, I replayed the conversation I'd had with Elda over and over in my head, heard the fear in her voice. Would Enzo really do such a thing? I now had more appreciation for the sheltered life my parents had given me. I was raised listening to classical and gospel music and taught not to swear.

At some point, we all have to grow up and enter the real world. But if the real world had scary guys like Enzo lurking in the shadows and holding a debt over your head, I wasn't so sure I wanted to grow up anymore.

A flash of bright green caught my eye and I looked up to see the back of a man wearing a green t-shirt with two yellow stripes across the back just before he disappeared around a corner. I gasped and my heart rattled against my ribs. It was the man from the tabacchi shop fire. I took off after him, my grocery bags swinging wildly against my legs. I turned the corner of the calle just before he disappeared at the far end.

"Aspetta, per favore!" I called, asking him to wait.

His head reappeared. I jogged up the calle up to him. He had a smile of curiosity on his face.

"Parle inglese?" I slowed to a walk.

"Pochino." His chest bounced as he huffed the word. "What happened?"

"You broke into a tabacchi shop a few weeks ago," I blurted.

His pleasant expression melted to scorn.

"Bah!" He flapped his hands at me once and turned away.

I dropped the groceries and grabbed his arm. The fire ripped upward into my chest.

"I saw you." I narrowed my eyes at him. My face flushed with heat and my eyes burned—I could feel that they were glowing red.

His expression went from annoyed to terrified. He yelled something in Italian, yanked his arm from my grasp, and fled. I tore after him. The fire licked downward, giving fuel to my legs. I caught him easily, hooking his ankle with my foot. He sprawled onto the stones, crying out and rolling over onto his back and elbows. He crawled backward and held a palm out at me, babbling a Catholic prayer. I stood over him, fists coiled.

"You could have killed three people," I hissed, my eyes alight. "One of them was a little boy."

I should have tried to temper the fire, but it felt so satisfying to make him afraid. I closed the distance between us as he crawled backward.

"No, no, no," he intoned. "There was no kids."

"That would have made it okay?" I cried, my voice echoing through the calle. He'd just admitted his crime to me.

"Hey!" a strong male voice shouted behind me.

I turned to see two men at the end of the alley. They yelled something in Italian. Concerned strangers looking to prevent an altercation? They began to walk toward us with intention. As they approached, their eyes widened as they saw my face.

"Madonna," whispered one to the other and put a hand on his friend's elbow.

I cursed inwardly.

A handful of pebbles pelted my side and skittered across the stones. The man in the green sweater scrambled to his feet. He dusted a hand on his pant leg, braced his other palm on the ground and exploded away from me like an Olympic sprinter. The pebbles didn't hurt, but they made me even angrier. I took off after him. The other men must have decided to stay out of things after all, because no one followed. We raced down the narrow calle. He elbowed his way through a crowd, and people cried out angrily as he jostled and shoved at them.

"Sorry! Scusa, scusa," I yelled as I followed the path he'd cut. I put my hands up like blinders around my eyes in a futile attempt to hide the glow heating up my eyeballs. This was not good.

Stop, Saxony.

But I couldn't. The culprit was within my grasp. A conversation ensued; two voices combating each other in my brain.

What are you going do when you catch him?

I'm... Well, I'm going to...

What? Burn him?

No.

Why don't you just let the police handle this?

Because I'm here now!

Are you turning vigilante? The fire is making you reckless. Just stop.

The banter stopped when the man disappeared into a door up ahead. A metallic bang echoed through the calle. A second later I was there with my fingers around the bars of a gate. A flash of terrified eyes. The inner door slammed. He was out of my reach. My chest heaved. Hot anger licked through me. I'd nearly had him.

What were you going to do with him, Saxony? Beat him up? Burn his t-shirt?

I slammed my hands against the gate. Startled pedestrians backed away from me. I rested my head on my hands for a moment, coaxing the heat from my eyes. Taking my phone from my back pocket, I snapped a photo of the door and the address. My teeth ground together in my head as I walked away. I had to fight not to turn back and apply fire to the gate.

As I got farther and farther from my quarry, the heat evolved. It licked up the back of my neck and curled around the front of my throat, warming me like I had taken a shot of moonshine. It spread down into my belly and thighs, wrapped around my waist, and crackled up my back. It turned liquid and rolled down my calves like lava. Under my heels. Across the arches of my feet. Into each toe. It spiraled around my forearms and energized every finger, fed into every fingernail. It sizzled under the surface of my skin.

I had lost him. The fire was not happy, and neither was I.

My limbs continued to load up with power, fueled by my anger. I was as tightly strung as a guitar wire. I arrived at the corner where I'd set down my grocery bags. They weren't there. I slammed a hand against the nearest wall, drawing a few curious glances. What had I expected? That no one would pick up two bags of fresh food left to rot in the sun? My face flushed, my eyes felt hot. I patted the top of my head and found my sunglasses, then dropped them into place over my eyes.

I suddenly wished desperately that I was alone. The need to expel the energy I now had coursing through me increased with every angry thought, every breath. My limbs began to twitch. It felt like I had taken in too much caffeine. I looked around for an escape. *The sea.*

I zig zagged my way through the calle toward the water. Energy coiled in my limbs like so many venomous snakes ready to strike. Running would help. I broke into a sprint, winding my way through a crowd; avoiding baby carriages, dogs on leashes, people taking selfies. A busker played violin in the corner of the courtyard and a semi-circle had formed around him. Music echoed off the stone walls of a church and filled the courtyard with Bach. I passed out of the touristy area and ran over narrow bridges and down shadowed calle. Blue sky. Ocean. I passed the park where I had broken Dante's nose.

The running only made me feel more energized, more powerful. I was an explosive about to go off. I couldn't wait for privacy anymore. The water here would have to do. A gap under a bridge ahead yawned darkly, offering privacy. I took a moment to stash my shoes, phone, and wallet under a bush. Then I took a running leap off the sidewalk and into the water, feet first. A sizzling sound filled my eardrums.

I swam underneath the bridge and then sank until my feet hit rocks. I opened my eyes, and the world was a dark blur. I aimed my palms toward the open ocean and released a string of fireballs. Poof. Poof. Poof. The sound was a series of muffled explosions. The water lit up around me, flashing with every shot. Relief was palpable with each release until the need to expel the fire was gone.

I pushed off the bottom and surfaced, gasping. I peeked out from under the bridge and saw people walking by, taking no notice of the strange girl drifting in the shadows. It was illegal to swim in the canals, so I had to get out fast. A few people glanced at the oddball girl swimming in the polluted waters in her clothes, but no one said anything to me, not even to ask if I was okay. I swam to the nearest set of stairs and climbed out of the sea, slipping on the mossy steps.

Once on the top step, I caught my breath, relieved that the need to blow something up was over. It was the first time I really felt like the fire was controlling me.

"I guess you won that one," I said.

The heat crackled low, demure. It had been satisfied.

Shame filled me at the recklessness I had given in to. I wondered if this was how recovering addicts felt when they backslid. I put my face in my hands, fighting back tears. This couldn't be how fire magi functioned, could it? At the beck and call of the energy inside?

I can't live like this.

FIFTEEN

As soon as I got home, I called Officer Zambelli. Dispatchers redirected me twice, but finally I reached him.

"Prego," came the familiar voice.

"Yes, Officer Zambelli. It's Saxony Cagney, the Canadian..."

"I remember you," he said. "Tell me."

"I know where you can find one of the men responsible for the fire."

"Tell me," he repeated.

Leaving out all magus activity, I told him what happened. My cheeks burned as I recounted how I had chased Green Shirt through a crowd. It sounded even more foolish when I said it out loud.

"You ran after him?" he interrupted me.

"I did. I know it was stupid."

"Very." He made a *tsk* sound. "Don't ever do anything like that again. I know you're the hero type, but you can't take the law into your own hands like that."

The fire flickered at his words and several retorts came to mind but I clamped my lips against them. Instead, I demurely apologized and promised I would never do such a thing again. Moving quickly past the topic of my stupidity, I gave him the address and told him that I'd be willing to ID the man if I had to. I reminded him that I was leaving Italy at the end of the summer. He thanked me for calling and told me he'd probably have to call me back.

The moment I hung up, my phone chirped in rapid succession.

Targa sent through an image of beautifully dressed people waltzing in a ballroom, with the caption: *My mom's wind-up party is like a fairy-tale.*

It really did look like a fairy tale. Huge chandeliers with what looked like real candles hung over a large space filled with gowns and tuxedos. Jealousy clenched at my gut. Targa was having an amazing summer. While, I... well, I wasn't even sure I was human anymore. I tapped out a response: *Holy crap, Targa. Why wasn't I invited?*

Georjayna: *What are you wearing? Send a pic of you and your mom.*

A few minutes later an image came through of Targa and her gorgeous mother, Mira. Mira was barely smiling but the two of them looked stunning. Mira wore a dark green column dress, not a stitch of makeup and her hair swept up. Targa wore a simple black dress with a shawl. She looked even more like her mother than she had when she left. I zoomed in. Her skin seemed luminescent, and her eyes an even brighter blue than I was used to. Maybe she'd put a filter over the image.

Georjayna: *Aaaaaaawwwwwww! You guys look amazing.*

Me: *Bella ragazza!*

I'd have to see with my own eyes if Targa actually did look different when we all got back.

My phone went quiet for a while, but about ten minutes later it vibrated again.

Akiko: *Hi guys. Nice pix, Targa.*

I whooped and nearly dropped my phone. It felt so good to see her name on my phone again. I couldn't help but tease her: *Who is this?!*

Then the texts came fast and furious.

Georjayna: *SHE LIVES*

Akiko: *Very funny.*

Targa: *Everything ok? We've been wondering when we'd hear from you.*

Akiko: *All ok. Gotta run. Sorry, I only have a few seconds.*

"No! No! No!" I wailed. My fingers flew on the keyboard: *Wait!*

Targa: *What are you doing? Intelligence work for a secret agency in Japan or something?*

I waited, holding my breath. But my phone had gone quiet. She was already gone. It chirped once and I inhaled sharply. But it was just Georjayna. Apparently, she was feeling the same way I was: *Bollocks.*

I dropped my head back and groaned. A desire to go home and get back to my life, back to my friends swept over me. Targa had cryptically reported that her 'libido-lessness' was no longer a problem but wouldn't disclose more information. Georjie had said, in her refined and understated way, that she and Jasher had become 'close.' I could have screamed in frustration with them both. I was dying to get the real stories, in the flesh. And no one had been more mysterious than Akiko. I wasn't sure whether I was going to strangle her or hug her when I saw her next.

But how could I go back to my regular life? And my relationships with my friends? I'd wager that none of them were going through anything so life-changing as me.

But you can't tell them. You can't tell anyone.

I have to tell someone or I'll explode!

I blew air out between pursed lips. These inner arguments were exhausting.

My phone chirped again.

Fed: *Meet me at my place tonight at 630? I'll make pizza and we can catch up properly.* She'd attached a GPS link with a little pin in it. I zoomed in on the address. It was in a very ritzy borough. Curiosity to see her place tugged at me.

Me: *Absolutely. I really want to catch up with you.*

Another text came in. From Dante.

I always get what I want, Saxony. Remember that.

I stared at the words on the screen and ground my teeth. I made a fist and then flexed my hand. A ball of white flame flared up in my palm and crackled as it died away.

I FOLLOWED my GPS to the address Fed had texted me. The villas in this borough seemed to grow larger and more beautiful the deeper I went. I crossed the final courtyard and approached a metal door labeled with her address. After pressing the buzzer, I waited.

"Hey, Saxony. Come on in," Fed's voice came.

Another buzzing noise unlocked the door. I pushed it open and stepped into a small but beautiful courtyard garden. A large in-ground swimming pool filled with sparkling teal water was surrounded by a white marble terrace and deck chairs. The marble patio led to the rear of the villa where a large table and chairs enough for eight people sat. Empty glasses still containing ice cubes peppered the table top as though a party had recently ended. Strange.

The weirdest feeling swept over me.

Get out, Saxony. Now.

I blinked at the paranoid voice.

Don't be ridiculous. Fed is your friend.

The other voice flew in like a vulture.

He always gets what he wants. Remember?

The fire crackled low.

Dante's voice made me jump. "Well look what the cat dragged in. I've always loved that saying. Come have a drink with us?"

He stepped out of the open patio door and onto the marble terrace. He was followed by all of the men from the boat except for Karim. They spread out on the patio and each took a seat. Jacopo carried a jug of spritz and began to fill the glasses. They all looked at me expectantly, even pleasantly. There was one empty chair.

Jacopo turned it toward me and patted it, inviting me to sit. "Nice to see you again, Saxony. It's great that you're thinking about joining the business, too. Dante says you have some special skills." His expression was friendly and open. I scanned the faces around the table. They all had the same open expression, all except Dante, who looked smug.

"Where's Fed?"

"She's inside. You can go on in and say hello if you want. We'll wait for you." Dante jerked his head toward the open door.

I approached the men slowly. They'd begun to look away from me now and speak with each other in Italian. A few of them laughed, their conversation appearing no different from any other conversation happening at a table of friends having a few drinks. Only Dante watched me as I stepped in through the open patio door.

The villa was just as beautiful inside as it was out. A large clean kitchen was the first thing I saw. This place looked old on the outside but it had been updated on the inside.

"Fed?" I scanned the kitchen and living room area where a TV was tuned in to a rowing competition. There was no reply. I looked behind me, but no one had followed me in.

"Federica?" I called, louder this time.

"Up here!" I heard her voice from an upper level. She sounded... resigned.

Following her voice, I went through the kitchen and poked my head around a corner. I ascended a wide set of stairs. At the top of the stairs was a loft scattered with couches. Well-stocked library shelves lined the walls. Fed was seated on a sofa with her legs pulled up and her arms wrapped around her shins. Her eyes were puffy. As she looked at me, her face projected abject misery.

"I'm really sorry, Saxony," she said, her voice wavering.

"What's going on?" I sat beside her.

"He's locked the gate and the front doors. You won't be able to get out. Not without burning your way out and exposing yourself to everyone here, anyway, and I highly recommend you don't do that."

"He told you what I am?" The heat in my belly cranked up a notch.

She nodded and rubbed her eyes. "Only this morning. I had no idea until I casually mentioned I was hoping to see you later today. He forced me to lure you here so he could trap you. I should never have taken you on the boat the night of the festival. This is all my fault."

"You didn't know what was going to happen. Did he tell you that I only recently acquired this, um, condition?"

"Yes. That's what sent him off. He was absolutely stunned about that. He showed me a video clip that Nic recorded before he died, talking about how the power can be transferred. I know Dante told you who that is. Well, apparently, Nic had a son."

I took this in, putting the pieces together. "I'm guessing Dante or Enzo has an arm inside one of the big banks?"

She huffed a humorless laugh. "Try all of them."

"How did Dante know where to look?"

"He saw Elda's name on your phone and did the math."

I swore, softly. I had been sloppy. The night that Dante and I had gone swimming, he'd gotten an eyeful of Elda's texts.

"How did he know she had anything in a lockbox?"

Fed gave me a look of pity. "Dante knew that Nic had recorded messages to someone. He was there. It didn't take much to figure it out."

I put my face in my hands and groaned. I could feel the sympathy pouring off Fed, but I also felt a lot of fear. I looked up. "What's he got over on you? Why did you help him?"

She shook her head and lowered her voice. "You don't know what he can do to me, Saxony. He could destroy my life if he wanted to. He's that malicious. You're a lot stronger than me, and a lot stronger than Dante. You'll figure out a way out of this. But if I had said no to Dante, it's game over for me. I'll never get into the university I want, and he can redirect my inheritance. He can make things go bad for me."

"Who is running the show here, Dante or Enzo?"

"Dante's got his own resources, Saxony." She lowered her voice to a whisper, her hands strangling each other in her anxiety. "None of the guys down there knew Nic. They don't even know what a magus is. Don't let them know what you are or there will be big trouble for you."

I shook my head. "Unbelievable. What benefit does Dante hope to get from exposing me to his friends?"

Regret soured in my mouth. How could I have ever been attracted to him? Now that I knew him for who he was he had transformed from attractive to repulsive, from intriguing to evil, from charming to narcissistic.

A creak echoed from the stairs and Fed froze in fear, her eyes wide. She took a book from the shelf beside her and plucked a pencil from a drawer nearby. She scribbled furiously on a page in the book. She showed it to me, saying in a normal tone of voice, "It's probably better if you go along with him. Or at least listen to what he has to say."

Her scrawl was difficult to make out. I squinted at it.

They're not his friends. They're recruits. The more witnesses there are to your abilities, the more he has against you. Leverage. He'll impress them by showing them a supernatural and make you think you need his protection, all at the same time. Dante doesn't think I have the guts to warn you. He asked me to convince you to show the fire, that it is for your benefit. Please, don't give me away.

I'd seen enough.

"Let's go," I said, standing.

"Where?"

"I'm going to get us out of here."

She ripped out the page she'd written on, put it in her pocket, and returned the book to the shelf. "This is not how I thought my day would go. Try not to burn down the house, okay?"

I didn't answer. *That depends on Dante.* The fire was licking along my spine and down my arms, warming my fingertips. She followed me downstairs and outside. When we stepped out onto the patio, the men stopped talking.

"I'm glad you're back," Dante said, standing. If he'd been hovering at the bottom of the stairs, he hid it well. He held a hand out to me. "I was just telling the guys you'll give them a demonstration of your power."

"Power?" I said, fixing my face with confusion. I took Fed by the hand. "Really not sure what you're talking about, Dante, but Fed and I were just leaving." I pulled her past the table and across the patio toward the rear gate. "Excuse us, guys. Have a nice night."

"Come on, Saxony." Dante said, following us. "She's a little shy about how amazing she is," he said to the table of guys who were watching with interest. Some of them chuckled, but they still looked at ease, sipping their drinks, enjoying the evening.

Stepping in front of me, Dante took my hand from Fed and pulled me around to face the table. "Just a small demonstration? You don't have to do much. Just a little candle flame, that's all."

"What are you going on about?" I said, my eyes on Dante, my face a mask of bewilderment. My mother never called me a little actress for nothing.

Some of the men at the table shared confused looks of their own.

Dante frowned. "You don't need to pretend, Saxony. They all know what you are."

"Do you know what he's talking about?" I asked Fed.

I regretted it the moment I saw her face. I had just put her in an impossible position. I had asked her to side with me against Dante and a bunch of guys he was trying to build trust with. If she did, she'd have an enemy for life. Fed crossed her arms and gave a slight shrug, which could have been interpreted in a lot of different ways.

I turned back to Dante. "I'd like to go home now."

The words had barely escaped my lips when a coiled fist hit me in the gut. The air whooshed out of me and I bent over. He hadn't hit me really hard, just enough to tell me he meant business—and enough to light the fire.

From the men at the table, there was nothing but breathless silence. If they were shocked that he'd just hit a girl in front of them, they didn't express it outwardly. I was more surprised than hurt, and I knew instantly what he was trying to do.

Oh, crap. The heat of the fire intensified and began to spiral through my arms.

"Come on, Dante, you don't have to do that," Fed said. I felt her hand on my back.

"Go inside, Fed. This doesn't concern you." Dante's voice was calm; he probably thought he had this demonstration in the bag.

From my view of the ground, I saw her feet walk past me slowly, back toward the house.

I took a few steadying breaths. I closed my eyes and gathered my thoughts. I tasted fear on the back of my tongue. It wasn't fear of Dante, though, it was fear of the fire. Fear of my own lack of control, fear of my own temper.

The boys were undoubtedly watching me with rapt attention. I tried to bring tears to my eyes, but they were too dry. I stood slowly, my face fixed with fear.

"Why are you doing this Dante?" I whimpered. "What did I ever do to you? I told you I'll never go out with you again. Why can't you just accept that?"

"Ha! That's rich," laughed one of the men. Then he spoke in Italian to the men sitting at the table. A few of them laughed, but others remained silent.

"Come on, Saxony." Dante bent close to my ear. "Just a little show. That's all we want to see. Preferably without too much violence."

A battle raged inside me. It was me versus the fire. I swallowed and turned to the men at the table, moving my hand to my stomach. They didn't need to know that Dante's punch hadn't really hurt. "This is the kind of guy you want to work for? A coward who hits women?"

Crack. My head snapped to the side when Dante hit my right cheek with his open hand. My body spun sideways and I went down on one knee. My vision turned red, peppered with white stars. That one hurt. The flames leaped and boiled in my torso, their power building. My limbs began to quiver.

I didn't know how long I'd be able to stay in control. The back yard was completely silent after that hit. I remained crouched, my face turned away from the men, my eyes closed. I should have cried out to add drama but it had so caught me by surprise that I hadn't made a sound. I took deep, steadying breaths. I pushed the men watching the show out of my mind, and Dante too. I went inside to where the heat was.

I need you to stay hidden. Work with me on this one, okay?

In response, the flames fueled my limbs with more energy. Nothing would have satisfied me more than to fire a fist into Dante's face.

"Let it out, sweetheart." Dante's voice came from behind me. "You know you want to."

I fixed my face with a tearful expression, even though I had no water in my eyes. I pulled the heat away from my face like it was an elastic band. The line of heat strained at the base of my skull, wanting me to release it, to light my pupils up. But if I did that, I was so screwed.

"Let me go," I whimpered. I hated the sound of my own voice; weak, petulant. It felt so wrong when I had so much power at my disposal. I looked up at Dante, and put my hand out. "Please stop, I don't know what you want."

Dante made a sound of disgust. "Quit the act, Saxony. Don't make me hit you again."

I stole a glance at the table of men. None of them looked sure about what was going on. Two of them whispered something to each other, their faces uncertain.

Dante drew back his foot and I braced for what was coming. I closed my eyes, wrapped myself around the fire, and clenched every muscle. When his foot caught me in the throat and I flew back, I almost didn't feel it. There was more pain from the explosion that went off inside me than in my neck. It felt as though every muscle fiber had a line of fire running through it. I couldn't draw air. I gave a strangled cough and choked in my effort to breathe. The force of the kick rolled me onto my stomach and I lay still except for my choked gasps. I had lost my hold on the elastic and the heat snapped into my eyes. They were hard and hot and if I faced Dante, everyone would see them lit like embers.

A couple of the men spoke quickly in Italian. I didn't understand what they were saying but they sounded upset. They must have been addressing Dante because he spoke back to them in Italian, and then he switched to English and addressed me.

"Can't you, Saxony? Can't you stop it?" he said. "You're powerful enough to stop me a thousand times over. This is just an act. Another couple of well-placed punches and you'll explode like a firework."

After this speech, he let out a stream of Italian toward the men, but he sounded forced.

Keeping my eyes shut, I let out a choked moan and curled into the fetal position. My body began to shake. The power was building in my limbs. How much longer could I keep it inside? My mind raced, trying to dream up a way out but I couldn't think straight. It was all I could do to stay curled in a ball, my body boiling with heat and power.

It's a test. It's a test. If you can't control it now, you never will.

I repeated this mantra. I pulled my legs toward my torso and wrapped my arms over my face. The quaking increased. My teeth began to chatter. Whimpers escaped me in my effort to stay in a ball. I took deep slow breaths, it seemed like the only thing I could control.

Chair legs scraped against stone. Angry voices. I opened my eyes a crack and peeked out from under my arm. The two men who had been whispering to each other earlier stood up. They spoke to Dante and gestured toward me, sounding upset. Dante began to argue with them as they turned and stepped into the house. A few faces turned toward me, and another guy got up and took a few steps my way. I clenched my eyes tightly shut again. Dante spoke more, urgency rising in his voice. He drew close to me. A hand hooked under my elbow and tried to pry my arms away from my body.

"You're being ridiculous," Dante hissed at me. "Just show them your eyes. Then it will all be over."

I couldn't help it. The fire detonated in my shoulder and my elbow shot backward, catching Dante somewhere soft. It must have been his gut because I heard a whoosh of air and then a gagging sound.

A handful of voices rose all at once, shouting over each other. Some sounded like they were actually cheering me on. I heard my name said a few times. Others sounded angry. I kept my eyes shut and pulled my elbow in, cursing inwardly. The gagging sound ceased and was followed by a pained laugh.

"That's it," Dante wheezed. "Now just do that again, only this time externalize it. Show them what you're made of."

Sounds of Dante nearby, climbing to his feet. His voice, uttering a bunch of surprised Italian. Some of the other guys, yelling at him. They sounded like they were moving away. I kept my eyes closed and my quaking limbs coiled inward. I was desperate to see what was going on. The voices sounded more distant now.

My legs and arms no longer felt like normal flesh and bone. They felt like long coiled springs of hot energy. It was all I could do not to let them explode outward and send fireballs everywhere. I braced myself for the next attack, but the next time I heard Dante's voice, it was coming from inside the house.

I cracked an eye and was shocked to see that I was now alone in the back yard. That was sudden. Voices came from the house. Angry voices. Dante yelled. Other voices yelled back.

Slowly, stiffly, I lifted my head. I watched the patio door, expecting Dante to come through it at any moment, holding a baseball bat or a knife or something really nasty. But it was Fed who stepped through the door. She rushed over to me.

"My God, your eyes," she said, coming to her knees beside me. She put a hand on my back. I half expected her to jerk her palm back in pain from the heat of my body. "Are you okay? The guys are at the front door, fighting." She sounded amazed. "What you did, it worked. But you better get out of here, fast. Dante will be back any second. You look terrifying."

I tried to move but my spine felt locked, even my jaw felt like hot stone. The boiling heat needed an escape and I was afraid to force movement, in case I went off like a bomb. I tried to tell Fed to stand back but the words came out through clenched teeth.

"What?" She bent her ear close to me.

"Shtnd bck," I ground out from between locked molars.

She got up and backed away. "Where should I go? What are you going to do?" She panicked, running through the garden and inside the villa.

I eyeballed the pool. It was the only place I could go. Keeping my limbs locked in, I rolled my body across the stones. I must have looked ridiculous. Just as I was teetering at the edge of the pool, Dante reappeared in the doorway.

I tipped into the pool with a splash, opened my body out toward the pool bottom and released all the energy I had been keeping inside. Two bright flashes of light and: *Crack! Crack!* Two loud, sharp sounds filled the water. My body instantly relaxed, all tremors and locked joints released. I found the bottom of the pool with my feet and stood up, surfacing. I rolled my head and water streamed from my face and hair. My neck throbbed and the right side of my face felt tender to the touch, but otherwise, I felt normal again.

I looked around for Dante and Fed. Fed poked her head out of the doorway. Dante was slowly getting to his feet. The patio doors had exploded and he was covered in glass.

A draining sound gurgled beneath my feet. A large crack had opened down the middle of the pool bottom. Water seeped into the ground.

Fed stepped out of the doorway, her hand over her mouth, her eyes round.

Dante got to his feet, brushing glass out of his hair. He looked at me and his eyes changed somehow. Resolved. Bitter. He looked from me to the pool, and back again.

"That was really stupid," he said.

SIXTEEN

I waded to the steps and walked up out of the pool, wiping my face. "Seems like I'm always in wet clothes lately," I muttered, squeezing out my hair while I eyed Dante.

Glass shards tinkled across the stone patio as he brushed them out of his hair and off his clothes. "We have a lot to talk about."

"Well, I'm not paying for the damage. You know full well whose fault it is."

"I'm not talking about the pool." He took a few steps toward me.

"You really want to do this, Dante? Face off with a magus?" I felt my eyes get hot.

"You're not a real magus, Saxony."

"No?" The husky sound of my voice contradicted him. I wasn't sure what he was getting at. I canted my head, my eyes glowing.

He took a few more steps, nearer to Fed, but ignoring her. "What if I told you there was a way you could go back to being a normal teenager?"

As he passed in front of Fed, her eyes focused on Dante's lower back and they widened. Her gaze darted to my face, full of urgency.

"I know there is, Dante." I said, trying to work out what Fed was trying to say without alerting Dante. "But not for me. The fire is making me strong, not weak. I've got it for life. I thought you might have figured that out by now."

I scanned his body. Dante's hands were at his sides. I took a step back. My skin crawled with a dry, prickly heat.

"Come on, Fed. Let's get out of here."

Dante whirled, his movements so fast they were a blur. He reached a hand behind his back. Fed screamed as Dante locked a forearm around her neck. I didn't even have time to react, I was so taken by surprise. I had been expecting an attack on me, not on Fed. A clicking snap. A flash of light. A sound like a jet.

He had a small blowtorch, the kind used to make creme brûlée, right next to Fed's face. She cried out and tried to squirm away from the heat.

"Dante," I began. Sparks flew up my windpipe, pitting holes in my throat. I spat them off to the side. "What are you doing?"

He had truly lost his mind. The acid of regret burned my heart. Why hadn't I gotten her out of here while I had a chance? We should have started running the moment I'd left the pool. The fire had made me arrogant.

Dante looked at me from behind Fed, his mouth, which I had once found so alluring, now cruel and twisted.

"I'll start with her hair," he said, his voice little more than a whisper. "And then we'll see what happens to an eye when we flambé it just a little bit."

Fed whimpered and breathed heavily through her nose as she fought panic.

"I'm not going to let that happen, Fed," I said.

How? Saxony, you're in way over your head.

"That's right, you're not," said Dante. "You're going to walk in front of me, into the house. I'll tell you where to go. Move." He moved the flame a fraction closer to Fed's face and she cried out and turned her head away. Her cheek was flushed with red. Beads of sweat had sprung out on her forehead.

I walked toward the door where they stood, my eyes as hot and hard as they'd ever been. I bore into Dante's face with my eyes as I passed them. Too bad I couldn't actually shoot lasers from my eyes. What was the whole point of the red glow if it couldn't help me in a situation like this? Just to give me away? What kind of stupid ability was this? Bitter thoughts pounded me as broken glass crunched under my feet. I stepped across the threshold of busted patio doors and into the kitchen.

"To your right, down the hall. Slowly. If I see even a wisp of smoke, Fed's face will never look the same, and you'll be the one to blame."

I slowed my steps, took deep breaths, and squeezed my eyes shut in frustration. "Where are we going?"

I heard he and Fed as they shuffled together after me down the hall. The very air that Fed drew sounded laced with fear.

"If you only trusted me, we could have avoided all of this. Keep moving." He directed me through the house and out into another small courtyard.

Across the courtyard was a much older villa. It looked ancient, in fact. The crumbling stone exterior was pitted with holes, the window ledges worn and cracked. Rusty bars with arrowhead tips covered the window openings. The whole building looked haunted.

As we walked across the stone courtyard to the door of the old villa, I noted that the heat inside me had changed. It felt soft and molten, and it oozed rather than flickered. Why? I had the strangest feeling that it knew something I didn't know. My forearms prickled as fear came over me in waves.

Inside, a dozen desks filled a large stone room. Sunlight streamed in through two windows. The place had the feel of an old military office. Each desk had a computer and all the necessities for work. Whatever this place was, it was fully functioning.

My mind skittered for options but I felt too scared to act on any of my ideas, discarding them as quickly as they came up. Should I refuse to move? The propane in the blowtorch would eventually run out but he wouldn't let that happen before he burnt her. Hurl fire at his head? I would risk burning Federica. With my ability to control fire, could I snuff the flame of the blowtorch? I didn't have enough control. Again, I would risk burning Fed.

"Interesting that you chose a blowtorch for your weapon, Dante." I sounded a lot calmer than I felt. My heart was thudding so loud it almost drowned out my words. "That way you could just blame me for burning your cousin."

"Through the door on the right. Down the stairs."

I put a hand on the metal handle of a short, wide wooden door. It swung open and cool, dank air drifted up. I looked down the dungeon stairs. "You're kidding, right?"

"Do I look like I'm kidding?"

I turned to look at the two faces behind me, reflected in the light of the torch. Fed's face shone with sweat. Dante's face was almost serene.

I took a deep breath. "Can you please just turn that thing off and we can talk like adults?"

"It's too late for that, Saxony. You've had plenty of chances. Quit stalling." He moved the torch closer to Fed's hair and touched the flame to a few strands. She cried out as they crackled and sparked. Smoke wisped up from her head.

"Stop! Stop, I'm going."

I began to descend.

THE FIRST THING I became aware of as we descended was the sound of dripping water. Droplets landed hollowly and echoed off the stone. The gloom was heavy and I fought the urge to light up a hand, just so I could see better. Dante would most certainly hurt Fed if I did.

"Left."

I turned. Faint nausea curled in my stomach. The floor turned from stone to earth as we passed under the building. The ceilings were so low I had to tilt my head to the side. We went down an earthen floor hallway and came to three crumbling steps leading even deeper.

"Now what?" I said, my voice filled with acid. A million nasty names and swearwords festered behind my lips. *Don't make things worse.*

"In there." He jerked his chin toward a small metal door.

I looked at the small square door of the cell in front of me. I swallowed. An awful scenario began to rise in my mind. He was going to lock me in there?

"Don't worry. You'll be fine, Saxony."

Liar.

He moved the blowtorch a little closer to Fed's face and she made a strangled sound.

"Hurry up," he said. "My arm is getting tired. If you're not inside that room in three seconds, I'll blister her ear."

I gulped, ducked my head under the lintel and stepped through. The metal door slammed shut behind me and the sound of the blowtorch ended. I stepped back from the door and tripped as my foot hit a crumbling step. I staggered and half fell backward. Three little steps led up to the floor of the room. I was standing in a small divot in front of the door. I bent and looked through the little window in the metal door.

Dante's face appeared in the grate. "I'll be back in a little while."

"Fed?" I rasped. "Are you okay?" Fingers of fear curled through me, making my legs feel weak.

"I'm okay," she said. "Saxony. Don't give in—"

"Move, Fed," Dante snapped, cutting her off. Their soft footsteps moved rapidly down the hall.

"Dante?" I yelled, hoarsely. The name echoed bluntly. I listened as their footsteps pounded on the stairs in the distance, then all fell quiet.

My mind felt fuzzy, disjointed. This couldn't be real. Was I really locked in an ancient cell somewhere under Venice? Molten lava rolled and swelled through me, searing and baking my insides. I put my fingers through the small grate. I screamed Dante's name as loud as I could.

No answer. No sound at all. I gulped air and the fire surged wickedly under my ribs.

I turned to look around. There was a foul taste in my mouth and the air smelled like old urine and moldy basement. A wooden platform was built into the wall. A bed? High ceilings. The only window was high up in the wall opposite the door. It was far too high for me to peek out of and there was nothing under it to stand on.

The cell was not dissimilar to the ones that I had seen when I had toured the doge's palace. A low square of concrete in the corner with a round hole in the top would have served as a toilet. My eyes were drawn to a painting on the wall, a large circular image filled in with black and white squares. A game? A smaller version of the same had been drawn on other places on the wall.

I had a sudden thought and patted myself down. My heart

skipped with excitement as I pulled out my phone with shaking hands and turned it on.

My stomach dropped at the small text in top left corner: *No service*. Of course there was no service down here. How far underground was I? Twenty feet? And surrounded by earth and rock.

I'm a fire magus, I thought. *I can get out of here, can't I?*

Heat the bars up and kick them out, or send a fireball through the stone wall. Outrage roiled under the surface and I fought to keep it at bay so I could think. When I spotted a pillow on the wooden platform, I was immediately intrigued. It seemed such an odd thing for a dungeon. I picked it up, feeling that it was damp but white and clean. I sniffed it. There was a faint scent. Lavender? My lips twisted at the irony of this single item of luxury in such a place. How nice of him to want my head to be comfortable.

I tossed the pillow back on the bed and went to the door. Stepping into the hollow, I grabbed the handle and pulled. The door had a narrow slash of a window with bars across it and a slot with a little sliding door covering it. Must have been for food. I peered through the bars but could barely make out anything in the gloom. I yelled Dante's name again. Sparks flew from my lips, and pain flecked my bottom lip.

The only answer was dripping water.

I began to pace. Anger made my heart pound and heat flush through me at rhythmic intervals. I tried to swallow but my throat and mouth were dry. I needed a drink. The heat increased a notch. My eyes wandered to other things written in the walls and went to take a closer look. There were names and words written on the walls and in some cases scraped into them. The words were in Latin, or vulgar, I couldn't tell the difference.

I went back to the door and yelled Dante's name repeatedly. My voice rasped and whistled, a little weaker, a little drier each time.

I gasped when I heard footsteps. "Finally," I said, trying to keep the anger out of my voice and failing. "You've taken this way too far."

His face appeared in the window. "Hello Saxony, have you cooled off?"

"Have you?" I shot back.

He tilted his head side to side as if to say, 'So, so.'

"Dante, what are you doing? Let me go."

"Of course. On two conditions," he said. "One, and by far the most desirable of the two options, is that you agree to stay with me. Join my family, remain by my side as my inferno. Help me recruit, work for and with me. Help me earn my father's business and I can make you happy, I can give you everything you want."

"What do you know about what I want?"

"Girls are not complicated," he said, as though explaining something to a child. "They want compliments, to be treated like a princess, given gifts, be told they're beautiful, and to live a life of luxury and love. They need adoration, and a man to lean on."

I sputtered a humorless laugh but stopped abruptly when a burning pain sliced through my chest. "What's behind door number two?"

He shook his head and made a tsk sound. "You won't like it. Door number two isn't fun, not for you."

I waited. My skin crawled with the feet of a million fire-ants as I watched his face.

"Door number two means we wait until you dehydrate. When you're close to death, you'll pass the fire to me in exchange for a drink of water. You might live. You might not. It's sad if you choose this path." He put a tanned hand to his chest, oozing false sympathy. "But I can promise you I would take great care of the fire."

"You're a madman. Let me out of here and I won't destroy this cell and everything above it. You know you can't keep me in here." My voice was full of false bravado. I was not at all convinced that I was powerful enough to break out before I burned myself to death.

"I can, actually. This door is nearly a foot thick, these bars are tempered steel. You might be able to make them glow, you might even be able to warp them if you're really strong. But long before that happens, the fire inside you will roast you from the inside. The more you use it, the faster you'll cook. You've already been without water for a couple of hours... probably more."

My heart pulsed hotly, every beat rushing in my ears. "You can't make me give you the fire, Dante. If I'm going to die anyway why would I willingly put such power into the hands of a sociopath like you? Not even if you continue to threaten Fed would I give it to you."

"I would never hurt my own cousin, Saxony," he said, giving me a look full of pity. "Family is everything to me. To Fed, too, that's why she was willing to help me out."

"You lie," I hissed.

"Do I?"

"So?" I ground out through a locked jaw. "That's even more reason why I'll never give you the fire. I'd rather die."

"You will. The pain of the burning will be more than enough, but just in case I've underestimated you, I have two men landing in Gallipoli. A word from me and one of your little boys can disappear. It wouldn't be the first time."

The molten lava erupted and hot teeth bit into every nerve. My eyes grew so hot I thought I could hear them sizzle.

"You wouldn't." I wheezed.

He laughed. "I would. Those men are there. You underestimate me because you're such a good little girl."

I had nothing left. No cards to play. My mind galloped desperately for something I could use, anything.

Dante lives and dies by his father's approval.

"Does your father know what you're doing, you evil little snake?" I watched his face for a tell. My vision blurred and refocused as my eyes pulsed with heat.

He paused, just for a fraction of a second. What did that mean?

"My father *taught* me what I'm doing, Saxony. He's the master at getting what he wants." He stood, and his face disappeared from view.

The hesitation was the only thing that made me think that what he'd said about his father was just bravado. His face appeared again as he bent over, his head almost upside down.

"And how would you keep me here in Italy if I agreed to join your little crew of miscreants and crooks? I could just be lying to get you to let me out," I said.

He shrugged. "The same way I can make you give me your fire, I can make sure you never leave my side. But join my family and you won't want to leave anyway, I can promise you that. Life with me, you'd love it." He winked. "Don't make me rid the world of a beautiful treasure such as you." His voice was soft, like he was speaking to a lover.

I glared at him, feeling the red glow intensifying. Blinking, I palmed my eyes, wincing at the sharp pain.

"Hurts, doesn't it?" Dante said. "I'll let you think things over. Pain is very persuasive."

His face disappeared and the sound of his footsteps died away.

SEVENTEEN

At first, the heat increased only incrementally. Then I began to feel like I had a bad fever. My head pounded and I felt dizzy, and all of my joints ached. If I didn't move, the pain was significantly less. So I lay on the bed. The scent of lavender from the pillow covered the smell of old pee as my head warmed the fabric.

I thought about Fed, the only other person who knew I was down here. I wondered what she was doing. Was she trying to escape Dante? Was she laughing with him at the stupid girl they'd managed to lock into a cell?

I pushed away the hope that Fed would act on my behalf. She'd already shown she wasn't hero material. If I had any chance of getting out of here, I was better to try sooner rather than later, because the pain was only going to get worse.

I clenched my teeth and got up, my vision blurred. My joints had stiffened and I moved toward the cell door like an old woman in need of a walker.

The coolness of the metal door was a blessing against my palm, but soon the metal heated under my influence. I took a deep breath and sent the fire into my hand and into the metal. A rod of molten lava shot down my arm. An anguished cry escaped my mouth, but I didn't stop the heat. The entire cell lit up from the light of my hand. Slowly, the door began to turn pink, and then red. The red light concentrated around my hand and seeped outward. It moved far too slowly for my liking, and the burning sensation in my arm intensified. I couldn't bear it. I screamed and yanked my hand away, panting. I should have been sweating, but my forehead was as dry as the desert and hotter than black pavement on a summer day.

I stepped back. Winding up like a baseball pitcher, I threw a fireball at the door as hard as I could. A bright white streak hissed through the cell and hit the door. It made a dry thump. Sparks sprayed outward. A cry ripped from my lips and I bent over in pain. The fire had ripped through my arm like a ripcord made of barbed wire. My throat was so hoarse and hot now that my cry was little more than a dry squeak.

My fireball had made a small dent. Could I do it again? And again? The thought of that pain over and over made my knees buckle. There was no way. If I was hydrated, I could do it easily... but I was so dry. So dry. My throat and mouth were parched, my tongue felt three times its normal size. I sat on the stone, leaned back on my hands and let my chin loll on my chest. A moan vibrated through me as the fire spread across my ribs.

I lay on my side on the cool stone and became still. How long before Dante would return? How much time did I have to try and break out of here? How long had I even been in here?

I had to keep trying. Neither of Dante's offers was an option for me. I didn't know if he was lying about having sent men down to Gallipoli, but I couldn't afford to take the chance.

My mind kept going to Enzo. The unknown patriarch. My gut told me that he didn't know what his son was up to. Maybe, if he knew what I was, he might make me a job offer, too. But I thought that if I turned him down he wouldn't try and force me to stay by threatening someone innocent that I cared about. It was so clumsy. So ugly. Dante was a blunt instrument, with none of his father's strategic thinking, not to mention any of the morality that Raf had spoken of. I promised myself that if I got out of this alive, I would pay a visit to Enzo. It was the only way to hit Dante where it hurt. Enzo was the only person Dante feared. True, Raf hadn't spent time with the family in years. Things could have changed. But right now it was the only shot I had, if I didn't die first.

I gritted my teeth and got to my feet. I coughed, and embers spewed from my mouth. I threw another fireball, but this one went out weak and sloppy. Misdirected, it hit the doorframe. A silent scream raked my throat. This one had literally burnt me. I brought my hand in front of my face, shaking. The ends of my fingertips were black and smoking. I retched at the smell of burnt flesh. When in the ocean, calling the fire had been healing. But here, without water, it would destroy me.

My knees gave and I fell sideways into the toilet. I gagged. The fire sucked up my esophagus and into my throat. Smoke wisped from my mouth, and I thought I could smell burnt hair. I cradled my burnt hand against my chest.

I tried to call Dante's name, but I had no voice anymore. Smoke drifted from my mouth. I drooped sideways against the wall. An involuntary dry whimper came from me as the flames raced through my torso, searing every nerve and all my tissues wherever they went. Then all went sweetly dark.

THE ACHE in my neck tugged me to consciousness. I opened my eyes and pushed myself off the wall. I wheezed, the sound breathy and parched. A wisp of smoke drifted from my mouth, then up and in front of my eyes. Moving like I was in a vat of mud, I crawled on my elbows to the door. Did I have one last try in me?

I peered up at the door, my vision blurry and blackened at the edges. The dent I had made was right behind the door handle. Could I make one more dent? Right at the latch point? I rolled onto my back, threw my right hand back, and mustered everything I had. My jaw locked as I slammed a fire ball at the door handle. There was a hiss, a crack, and a flash of light. My back arched in agony and my vision went completely black. I heard the clank of something iron hitting the dirt floor. I turned my face toward the door, but my vision wouldn't clear. My head locked into place and I went completely still. I wasn't sure if I could move anymore, but I was too wrecked to try. Pain and heat were all I knew.

I no longer cared about anything except ending the agony. When Dante came, I would tell him that I'd marry him for a drink of water. I would light fire to the Vatican, throw enough fireballs at the tower of Pisa to make it fall over, bring down the Basilica in a fiery explosion of marble horses. Whatever he wanted he could have. I'd sign in blood just to make the burning stop.

I was incapable of intentional sound; not a word, not a whimper. The world was nothing but heat and flame. My blood bubbled and thickened in my veins. My heart felt half its normal size, sizzling as it shrank and dried out. Every shallow breath fanned the burning fire inside me and every exhale was thick smoke. It drifted from my mouth and jetted from my nostrils. Smoke gathered along the ceiling in a haze. I wondered if I might actually self-combust and burst into flames at the end. I thought of my parents. My eyes tingled, too dry for tears. In my mind's eye, I was a smoking black relic, a prop from a mummy movie.

Footsteps echoed. I was in too much pain to feel much in the way of relief, but at least the end was near. I heard a metal key inserted into the lock, but the door squeaked open without the sound of turning bolts.

"Oh Dio," whispered a voice.

'Door' and 'open' were the only two words I could make out in a string of noise. Who was that? More fierce whispers. Whoever they were, they were whispering in Italian and I could have sworn that one of them was a woman. I strained to recognize her. Mom? Delirium and false hope twined through my melting brain like a cancer. My burned ears could no longer detect familiar markers in speech. The voices could belong to anyone.

A masculine face appeared in the tiny opening at the end of the tunnel my vision had become, wavering and blurry. I thought I heard my name, saw his lips move. I struggled to place him. His features drifted in and out of focus. Raf? His words were garbled, echoey. A hand went under my neck and waist but they were snatched back quickly. A cry of pain and surprise. More words I couldn't understand.

The next face that appeared was feminine. Her features swam, but I knew this face. It seemed to take forever, but my brain finally registered. Fed. She disappeared from sight.

Footsteps left the cell. I wanted to scream after them, but I was beyond all sound. Urgent whispering echoed down the hall, then all went silent. I lost track of time. It hadn't been real. Just when I was sure I'd been hallucinating their presence, footsteps entered the room again. My body spasmed in shock as ice cold water splashed over my form, but I had never felt anything more delicious.

A sizzling sound. Steam filled the air. A wet hand lifted my head, held a bucket to my mouth. I couldn't swallow, but I was able to open my throat and let the water pour down into my stomach, sizzling like an angry rattler as it went. It was so delicious that it almost hurt. A few moments later, another bucket of water was thrown over me.

"Saxony? Can you hear me?"

I understood words again. My mouth moved like a fish gasping on the deck of a boat, but no sound came.

Raf let loose a stream of angry Italian and put a hand on my forehead. Though he winced at the heat, I must have cooled enough because in one swift movement he slid an arm under my shoulders and another under my knees, picking me up off the floor. I was crushed against his chest like a limp sausage. My head lolled back. He bounced me to lift my head against his shoulder, and the jarring movement sent flames roaring through my torso. I wheezed in pain.

"We're going to get you out of here. Don't worry Saxony. I've got you," Raf whispered. He said more words in Italian to Fed, sounding outraged and disbelieving.

I let my eyes close as he carried me out of the cell. He had to duck awkwardly to get us through the small door, and the movement gave me vertigo. I passed in and out of consciousness as he carried me, the whole thing feeling like a dream. Every once in a while, I heard Italian, first Raf's voice, then Fed's. Then I felt fresh air on my skin. Fed held a bottle to my lips and cool water filled my parched mouth. My singed tissues soaked the liquid up greedily. I imagined my insides looked like burnt hamburger.

Raf carried me through dark streets. The two of them stopped talking until we entered a dark alley, then Fed said something in a half whisper. Raf responded and there was a jingle of keys. A door being unlocked. We entered a dark space. Raf walked forward in the dark. I gave a hoarse wheeze when I had a humorous thought of us tripping over something lying on the floor, a child's wheeled toy or a pile of Lego. But Raf glided along silently, like a ghost, until we came to a set of stairs. He bounced me again, getting a better grip, before ascending the stairs. I was pleased to feel that the bounce was merely a sharp shooting pain instead of an excruciating snake of fire through my body. The water was doing its work.

Just when it felt like we had been climbing forever, I saw a flash of brunette hair as Fed slipped by us and opened a door. A beautifully frescoed ceiling yawned in my vision. I was laid tenderly on a soft bed. I tried very hard to ask how Fed had escaped, but my power of speech hadn't returned. Raf murmured reassurances.

A wisp of smoke came drifting out of my mouth and curled gracefully in the air over my face.

Raf stopped talking mid-sentence, his eyes focused on the smoke, watching it curl. He blew gently and the smoke drifted sideways.

"Madonna," he whispered, watching the smoke disperse, his face a mix of amazement and horror.

I was given another drink and a cool towel was placed on my head. Raf sat on the side of the bed and gave me sips of water every few minutes. I recovered enough control to move my hand clumsily. My hand slapped against his forearm and I tried to touch him. The only way I could say thank you. I succeeded in a hoarse moan, sounding like a ghost haunting an empty hallway. Raf covered my hand and squeezed it gently.

"What the hell did he do to you?" he asked, softly. His cool hand touched the side of my face.

Again I tried to answer and failed, a thin wisp of smoke crept upward from each nostril.

"Never mind. Don't worry. Rest now. We'll talk when you're better." His soft brown eyes belied an edge of outrage.

I had never felt anything more delicious than his cool hand on my face. I turned my hand toward it and closed my eyes.

EIGHTEEN

A creaking sound awakened me. My eyelids drifted open. Where was I?

Sunlight streamed through a thin crack of a tall curtain. Two matching antique chairs upholstered in gold and black velvet stood either side of the window. Further down the wall was a majestic fireplace of yellow stone. Above the fireplace was a tall portrait of a man in sixteenth century garb with a hunting dog curled at his feet. The face was dark, intense, and goosebumps rose on my skin when I looked at his black eyes.

He can see me.

I shook off the creepy feeling and pulled myself up to my elbow, testing for fire. There was no burning anymore, but my entire body was tender, like I'd been beaten with a meat mallet from the inside. I groaned as I sat up. Hearing another creak, I realized that it was the sound of a door out in the hallway opening and closing. I shifted myself up against the upholstered headboard. It was remarkably comfortable. Whoever had constructed the bed had built the headboard so it could be used like a chair back.

"I think that's the most brilliant thing I have ever seen," I croaked as I ran a hand along the velvet upholstery. At least I had a voice again.

I put a hand up to my throat and swallowed with some pain. Looking to the night table beside me, I found a glass pitcher and cup with water. I poured myself a glassful with a shaking hand and took a sip, swallowing slowly. I paused as I felt the liquid pool in my belly. Something was different. There was no fire. I looked down in shock at my own torso, as though expecting to see through myself. I closed my eyes. There was no heat. I jerked upright and winced at the ache in every organ, every muscle. I set the glass on the table, nearly missing it in my distraction. I put a hand to my belly, trying to feel for the fire. Nothing.

I whimpered. My hand came up to cover my mouth as my eyes prickled with tears. Goosebumps swept over my skin. Never before had I felt such a clash of emotion. Was I happy that the fire was gone? Was I upset? Did I miss it? Where had it gone? I hadn't given it to someone else, had I?

My memory came back to me, clearing up like clouds drifting away from a mountain scene, the details of trees and rocks coming into focus. I remembered Dante, his ultimatums. I remembered the cell with nothing but a lavender scented pillow for comfort and a stinking five-hundred-year-old toilet, Dante's threat to bring me close to death and then force me to give him the fire. And I would have done it, too. All of it played across the technicolor screen of my mind, snapping into clarity.

I thought of his threats against Isaia. With thoughts of him, the fire inside that I thought was gone exploded to life. I hadn't lost it after all, but something had changed. The fire was hotter than ever, yet there was no pain. There was a beautiful sensation of heat radiating from my heart. It no longer felt like a beast waiting for me to make a wrong move.

I lifted my shirt to look at my abdomen. The glow appeared, obediently. I let the glow spread, watched it travel down my legs, up to my shoulders and out through my arms to my hands. My entire body was now alight.

"Whoa."

I looked up. My light filled the room, threw sharp shadows of the posts of the bed and the chairs along the wall. I looked up at the portrait of the man, my light illuminating him and his dog so brightly that every color popped. I held my hand up in front of my face and looked at my glowing fingers.

I heard the creak of the door in the hallway and as quickly as flicking a light switch, I extinguished the light. The room fell into shadow. I waited, but no one came in. As the moments ticked by, I became aware of a hardening within me. It felt as though my innards were forming a layer of something, like a callous, only stronger. Thoughts of volcanic rock came to mind, once hot and flowing, it soon becomes still and hard. I threw the cover back and exposed my left leg, pulling my foot up close to myself. I looked at the magus mark. It too had changed. Instead of being mole-brown it was now charcoal black. I ran my thumb over it. A strong desire swept through me to find someone else, anyone else who had this mark. I needed to know more about what I was. Who had I become? How many others were there? My mind flashed back to what Elda had said about there being scrolls from Alexandria about fire magi, but that the scrolls had likely been destroyed in the great fire. What if they hadn't been destroyed? My musings were interrupted when the door to my bedroom opened and Raf poked his head in. I covered my leg with the sheet.

"You're awake." He examined me as he approached. "You look..." he paused. "You look really good. You made quite a recovery." He sat on the side of my bed. "Gave me quite a scare."

Federica poked her head in next. "You're awake," she said, parroting Raf. She entered the room, looking hesitant. "How are you feeling?"

Suspicion whispered at the edge of my mind. I still didn't fully know the part Fed had played in all of this. "I suppose I should thank you?"

She crossed her arms over her stomach like she was cold. "I snuck my phone into the bathroom and called Raf."

"He was never going to burn you, was he," I said, my smoky voice flat.

"Well, aside from this." She held up a lock of singed hair. "No."

Anger roiled in my belly, but I was grimly satisfied to see that the fire did not leap to life at the barest emotion.

"How did you get me out of there without him noticing?"

"Raf confronted him."

I looked at Raf. "That's it? You just called him a bully and he stood aside?"

"Well, not exactly," he said.

It was then that I noticed the shadow of a bruise on his cheekbone. My heart melted as our eyes connected. I reached up and put a hand on his cheek, my throat tight.

He put a hand over mine and gave me a lopsided grin. "You should see the other guy."

My lips twisted in a smile and my vision blurred a little.

"But I'm more interested in talking about you," Raf said. "When we found you, you were too hot to touch and you were smoking like a chimney fire. I'm shocked you survived. What did he do to you?"

"She didn't tell you?" I looked from Raf to Fed.

Fed shook her head. "It's not my secret to tell."

"Please, put me out of my misery," Raf said. "I didn't sleep a wink last night. I'm not sure I'll ever sleep well again."

I looked at his questioning face. The room went quiet and a few moments ticked by as I thought about how to explain it.

"You remember Nic?" I finally asked.

"I always thought he was one of a kind," Fed said, quietly.

"You thought Nic was a one of a kind what?" Raf asked.

"He was a fire magus," I said. "And so am I."

A few heartbeats passed.

"Sounds like something from Dungeons & Dragons," Raf said.

"Show him the mark. I assume you have one?" Fed suggested.

I nodded and pulled the blanket back from my left leg. I pointed to the tiny mark on my toe.

"Huh, so they don't always appear in the same place. Nic's was here." She touched the outside of her wrist. "Dante got a tattoo there because he thought it was so cool, and he wanted to be just like Uncle Nic." Her voice was laced with derision.

Raf took my foot in his hand and turned it so the mark was exposed to the light. "Looks like a little fireball. I didn't know you had a tattoo."

"It's not a tattoo," Fed explained. "It's a natural phenomenon. A fire magus is a supernatural, someone who can control fire."

"I wouldn't have put it that way, since most times, it feels like it controls me."

I began to talk. I explained about the fire at the tabacchi and how Isaia had pushed the fire into me, how he'd only have been able to pass it on if he was dying. I explained how Dante had some crazy scheme to sic me on his enemies. And finally, how Fed had invited me to the villa and Dante had trapped me there. Fed's eyes dropped to the floor. Raf's eyes darted to Fed, but I couldn't read his expression. When I finished, we sat in silence for a long time.

"You probably shouldn't go home," Fed said, finally. "If I were you, I would leave a note for the Baseggio's and get on the first plane out of here."

"What about Elda and Isaia? He sent men to Gallipoli. He made it sound like he'd hurt them if I didn't do what he wanted. The only thing that makes me think that he might be bluffing is that Enzo has a favor to call from Elda..." I stopped myself from going further.

"For when Cristiano was kidnapped," Fed finished for me.

"You know about that, too?"

"I do. I was pretty young when it happened, but I remember the day Elda came to the villa. I didn't know who she was, but she was completely distraught so I eavesdropped on her conversation with Enzo. After she left, Enzo sent Nic to take care of it. I never saw her again after that day. I had no idea that Isaia was Nic's kid. Now it makes sense why Enzo hasn't called in his favor, yet."

"Why does it make sense?" I asked.

"Because, it means Enzo is just going to wait until Isaia gets a little older. If he's got the fire, he'll take him in and indoctrinate him."

"He'd actually take a kid from his mother?"

"Not necessarily. Enzo is smarter than that. It would be more his style to demand Isaia spend a few hours a week with him for five or eight years or something. He'd slowly gain his trust and lure him with all kinds of perks. Eventually, Isaia will *want* to work for him. He'll become part of the family, just like Nic was. Enzo has never been able to replace Nic. This is the perfect opportunity to do it. He'll bide his time. I've never known a more patient man. Elda is right to be afraid."

I shuddered. I couldn't let that happen. "Do you know if Dante told Enzo about me?"

"I have no idea," Fed said. "I didn't know you were a magus until yesterday. If I had to guess, I would say no because he wanted you for himself, maybe even to use you to overthrow his dad. Who knows with this family. We are so dysfunctional it's not funny."

"May I please see it?" Raf asked, speaking for the first time. "I feel like I can't listen anymore until I see it."

I looked from one expectant face to the other. Feeling mildly like a trick pony, I held up my right palm and lit a fire. It flickered like a little campfire; white at the center and blue on the edges. There was no pain. Holding the fire felt completely different than it used to.

Raf jumped back from the bed, the flame reflected in his eyes. He said something in Italian that I was sure wasn't gentlemanly. I closed my hand and extinguished the flame.

"It's impressive," Fed said to Raf. "But it costs her. The fire hurts its host. Dante was trying to convince me that we were actually helping Saxony by forcing her to give him the fire. Is it true?" she asked me.

"About the pain? Yes," I admitted. I threw back the covers and stood up slowly. The tenderness had already faded. The hard callous feeling had grown, and I was feeling stronger by the second. I didn't voice this new sensation. For some reason, I didn't want to give Fed the satisfaction of knowing that the torture had somehow turned out in my favor.

Fed held a hand out to me in case I needed steadying.

I ignored her hand. I still didn't know how I felt about her, the part she'd played in my torture. Her deception. She turned away, but not before I saw the hurt in her eyes.

"I washed your clothes for you. They smelled like smoke. I'll get them. Are you sure you're feeling well enough to get up?" Fed made her way toward the door, and paused with her hand on the doorknob. She kept her back to me.

"Well if being hungry enough to eat a vat of spaghetti means I'm feeling better then I'm doing just great. I'm a little sore, but I'm fine. I'm ready to get up."

Fed nodded and left the room.

Raf and I looked at each other. He spoke first. "She's torn up about what happened, Saxony. She felt like she didn't have a choice. She's made an enemy of Dante. The worst thing you can do in that family is betray your own."

The old Saxony would have made a concession for her. But the new Saxony felt harder not only physically, but emotionally, too.

"There is always a choice," I replied. The edge in my voice was foreign even to my own ears. Even though she'd done the right thing in the end, I had lost respect for Fed.

"That may be," Raf answered, "but try not to judge her too harshly. It's not been easy for her, growing up in that family."

I nodded. "I'm sure."

"What are you going to do? I can't help but think that you should just get out of here." Concern darkened his eyes.

"Trying to get rid of me so soon?" I joked.

He didn't smile. "I thought you were going to die, Saxony. I was going crazy trying to figure out what to do. I'm glad you're okay but, Madonna. A fire magus? I feel like I slipped into a different world."

He hadn't reached out to touch me since he'd seen the fire in my palm. Was it just in my head, or was he standing further back from me than usual? And why shouldn't he? I was probably terrifying to him.

Fed returned with my clothes and put them on the bed. "I made lunch. Come down when you're ready."

Raf followed her to the door and closed it behind him with one last look at me. I couldn't place his expression. Was he afraid? Mystified? Repulsed? Awed? All of the above? I shook the thoughts away. I didn't have time to worry about what he thought. Pulling on my clothing, I folded the nightshirt and left it on the bed. My thoughts turned to Isaia and my hands shook with worry. Were there men watching the Baseggios even now? How could I convince Dante to call off his dogs without giving him what he wanted?

I left the room and found the stairwell. The wide wooden steps broadened as they descended. Paintings covered the wooden paneling, and gauzy curtains blew gently from the window at the landing. I followed the sound of clanking dishes through a parlor which looked like it hadn't changed in a hundred years, and into a kitchen. Fed was spooning pasta onto three plates. Raf poured water into three glasses at the table, which was tucked into a semi-circular turret. The windows overlooked a canal. Taxi boats and gondolas floated by.

"I thought you lived on Murano?" I asked as Raf pulled out a chair for me. I sat as Fed brought plates of pasta to the table.

"This is my grandparents' place," answered Raf. "They go to Capri every summer and give me the key so I can water the plants."

"Beautiful villa," I murmured.

"Thanks." He and Fed sat down in front of their plates.

The three of us ate in somber silence. I turned things over in my mind as we ate. I was the first to speak. "Fed, do you know if Dante actually sent men to Gallipoli?"

Her face melted with real regret. "I don't know for sure. I'm sorry, I should have asked him when he still trusted me. As it is, I'm not sure I can ever show my face in Dante's presence again."

I chewed thoughtfully. Fed had her own consequences to deal with, whatever they were. My mind was full of Isaia.

The formless, smoky shape of an idea began to solidify in my mind.

NINETEEN

"I have to go back." I put down my fork.

Fed stopped talking mid-sentence. Raf looked at me over his wineglass, swallowed hard, then put his glass down.

"Where? To Dante?"

"No, not to Dante. To Enzo."

"Why would you do that?" asked Fed, her eyes widening.

"Well, I can't just run away." I pushed my chair back and stood. "The sooner I deal with this, the better. I don't see any other options better than going straight to the source, can you?"

Taking my plate to the kitchen sink, I shoveled the last of the gnocchi into my mouth, and barely chewed before I swallowed it down.

"Yes. Get on a plane and get out of here. I mean, much as I don't want to see you go, I'd rather see you safe," Raf said, his brows drawn together.

"And what happens to the Baseggios then?" I said, rinsing my plate.

The problem was clear: when Enzo came to call Elda's debt, would Elda manage to convince him that Isaia was no longer a magus? It was highly doubtful. A mother would do anything to protect her child. What might Enzo do to Isaia to determine whether or not the boy had the fire? After what I'd been through with Dante, I shivered to think of Enzo and Isaia even being in the same room together.

I turned in time to see Fed and Raf look at each other, but neither of them answered.

"Where can I find Enzo?"

Fed shook her head. "I don't think that's going to go well for you. I know you're a magus and all that, but Enzo worked with one for longer than I've been alive. He'll know how to get the upper hand."

"I'm just going to talk to him like a civilized person, that's all. You can either help me or not, but I'll find him myself if I have to."

Raf and Fed looked at each other again. Raf crossed his arms over his chest like he was hugging himself.

"I'll take you," said Fed.

FED and I stared at the wall of ivy before us. The greenery was broken only by a wide metal gate made of intricate iron curls. Somewhere within these walls, a crime boss worked and lived.

"Do you want to come in with me?" I asked.

"I don't think I'm ready for that," she said, wringing her hands. She faced me. "Saxony, I am sorry that I let Dante use me to trap you. I was very weak. I've never been strong, and I'm not too proud to admit that I'm still terrified. But, I want you to know that..." She took a juddering breath. "I want you to know that even though I'll never have the power that you have, I've been inspired by your courage. I'll think of you when I face Dante."

"Why don't you come in and talk to Enzo, too?"

She shook her head. "For you, it makes sense. For me, it would only make things worse."

"So you will face Dante? I thought maybe you were preparing to move to Hungary or something," I joked.

A shadow of a smile touched her lips. "Don't think it hasn't crossed my mind. But then, I'd always be running. For better or worse, this is my family. I have to face it."

"Good luck, Fed." I held out my hand.

She took it, knowing that this was our goodbye. "You too, Saxony."

She walked back the way we'd come as I approached the gates. A silver panel with a selection of buttons gleamed out from the leafy ivy. Each one had a label, but each label was in Italian. One of them said 'sicurezza,' which looked like it might translate as 'security.' I took a deep breath and pushed the button.

Almost immediately a male voice answered. "Prego?"

"Uh..." I began. Off to a good start. "Parla inglese?"

There was a pause and then, "Yes, go ahead please."

Wow, so polite.

"I need to speak with Enzo, please."

After another pause, the voice said, "You're early."

It took me a moment to recover after that one. "Mi scusi, I don't have an appointment."

"What is it regarding, please?"

"It is a sensitive nature. For Enzo's ears only." I winced. I sounded like a James Bond character.

There was a longer pause. "One moment."

I waited outside the gate, working on my calm and collected face. I flared the fire inside from dead to alive, just for the comfort it gave me. It was my security blanket. Time passed. Five minutes. Ten minutes. I grew antsy.

It's just a tactic, Saxony. He's letting you know who's boss.

Wait, am I overthinking this? Maybe the dude who controls the gate is just having a bad time in the bathroom.

I sat on the concrete lip in front of the gate. Another five minutes passed and I grew agitated. I got to my feet and was just reaching up toward the same button to give the sicurezza a piece of my mind when the voice returned, making me jump.

"Stand back, please."

I stepped back from the gate and the sheet metal door behind the bars swung open. A familiar man appeared.

“Karim?” I craned my neck up to look the bald hulk in his babyface.

"I thought I recognized your voice." He wasn't smiling but he looked friendly enough.

"I didn't recognize yours."

"That wasn't me, that was Luca. What's this about needing to talk to Enzo?" He hadn't opened the barred gate yet.

"It's important. Please, Karim? I need to speak to him urgently. He'll want to talk to me, I promise."

"What could Enzo possibly want with you? No offense intended, but you're not his kind of company, pretty as you are."

Something about the statement annoyed me.

"No? How about now?" I put my hand through the bars and lit five small blue flames from the ends of my fingertips. If I was going to expose myself to Enzo, what would the point be of hiding myself from Karim? He'd find out sooner or later.

Karim reacted, taking a step back, the whites of his eyes visible.

"To Enzo," I said, extinguishing the flames. "Please." I sounded more commanding than I felt, but my confidence had increased at the shock on Karim’s face.

Karim took a hand-held radio from his waistband and spoke into it. He unlocked the gate and pushed it open, then stepped aside for me to enter. He'd managed to recover his cool. "Aren't you full of surprises."

As I entered the property, I just barely stopped myself from gushing 'wowee!' We'd stepped into a massive garden. Fountains and flowered shrubs dotted a perfect lawn. Everything was shadowed by huge old trees. A gigantic yellow villa with Turkish-inspired windows and doorways peeked through the foliage. Arches ran the length of a patio and three-leafed florets topped every arch. Two large black dogs lay on the marble and they lifted their heads. I had a moment of fear until a tongue lolled out of one cute black face, and the other thumped his tail against the concrete. Karim spoke to them lovingly in Italian and bent to pat one as we passed. They got up and crowded toward him, their rear ends waggling back and forth.

I must have looked relieved because Karim said, "What, you thought they were killers? So many people have the wrong impressions about Rotties. When they behave badly, it's not the dogs fault, it's the owner. Isn't it, Dan?" he added in a baby voice. He bent his massive frame to put his forehead against the dog's face. The dog half moaned, half growled with pleasure.

"Dan?" I said, raising an eyebrow. I was starting to feel a little more relaxed. *It's just a conversation, remember?*

Karim looked at me with enthusiasm. "Yeah, like Daniel who faced the lions? From the Bible? I love that story."

I blinked at him.

"Don't you read?" he said, almost exasperated.

"I know the story, I just..." I tucked my hair behind one ear and cleared my throat. This was getting a bit weird. Was he stalling for time? "Can we go? It really is important."

"Of course." He told the dogs to stay.

I followed him down a corridor. So far, I had not seen a single individual other than Karim. We ascended an outdoor stairwell and crossed the second-floor balcony. A luxurious half-outdoor half-indoor room spread open before us. The space was wide open and had the feeling of a lounge. Several sets of furniture dotted the space, each set around their own private table and partially blocked off by gauzy curtains swaying gently in the breeze. Two men seated at one of these private tables acknowledged Karim and me. Both men made eye-contact with me but I felt neither threatened by them nor ogled. Both wore business suits.

One nodded and said, "Salve."

The other said, "Giorno."

We approached another set of curtains. Karim pulled the fabric aside.

"Saxony, meet Enzo. Enzo, this is Saxony Cagney."

"Benvenuti, piacere!" Enzo exclaimed warmly. He set his espresso on the glass table in front of his knees and stood, extending both hands to me. I took his right and he pulled me toward him to kiss each cheek. I was so surprised by this reception that I kissed him back. Enzo and Karim exchanged some friendly sounding Italian.

"What would you like?" Enzo asked. "Cafe? Espresso? Cappuccino? I know you North Americans love the cappuccino. Grappa?"

"Solo acqua," I said. "Grazie."

"Sicura?"

"Si."

Karim left us alone.

"Please, sit down." He gestured to the chair across the table from him. His accent was the strongest I had heard yet. He enunciated every consonant and spoke slowly. His voice was rough but pleasant.

I sat in the lounge chair. He pulled up the thighs of his pants to allow himself more room and settled into the cushions. The only thing that told me he was related to Dante was the confident set of his chin and the way he carried his shoulders. I didn't know what I had been expecting, but the man with the round face and warm, interested gaze was not it. Though his hair was white and thinning, his eyebrows were thick and black. The most disarming part of him was his guileless expression. His chocolate brown eyes were too big for his face.

"Where are you from?" He leaned back against the couch and crossed one knee over the other.

"I'm from the East coast of Canada. I'm here on behalf of someone who owes you something."

"And who might that be?" As he laughed genuinely, his belly shook. "A lot of people owe me things."

"Elda Baseggio."

"You are a friend of Elda's?" Enzo said, and his black eyebrows jumped like he'd been poked in the ribs. "Elda and I have not spoken in over five year."

I didn't correct his English. "But you haven't forgotten her debt to you."

"Of course not, what kind of businessman would I be if I forgot who owes me," he said, laughing again. "But, excuse me, I seem to be confused. You are not here for a job? You are a magus, are you not? You are responding to our request? Our... How do you say it... Our advertisement."

"Request?" Now I was confused, too. What was he talking about? I shook my head. "How does one advertise to hire a magus?"

"You are asking me?" He put a hairy backed hand to his chest. "You are not part of the... Again, I don't know what you call it in Inglese... the cooperativa?"

"There's a cooperative of magi?" My jaw dropped. I snapped it shut again. "Where? Here, in Venezia?"

Why hadn't Elda mentioned it? She must not have known. I couldn't imagine her hiding such a fact from me. She did say that she was afraid she might be missing some clips.

Enzo put his palms together in prayer. "Were you born yesterday, girl?"

"In terms of being a magus, yes," I cried, and my confident in-control act went up in smoke. If there were other magi—enough for a 'cooperativa' of them—then I had to meet them. If I was stuck with the fire for life then someone had to show me how to make the most of it. My heart had begun to pound.

"It's okay." Enzo put a palm out to me in a gesture of 'calm down.' "Go back. Why are you here? Something to do with Elda."

I took a deep breath. "Yes, I want you to forgive her debt to you. Leave her and her family alone."

"I'm not interested in Elda, only in her son. He is the son of someone who once meant very much to me."

"Would you still be interested in him if you knew that he was not a fire magus?"

"But he is. I have seen the boy. Only magi have eyes like that," Enzo answered.

Karim appeared, holding a small tray with a glass of water on it. Enzo and I stopped talking as Karim bent down, set the glass in front of me and then left.

"Not anymore he's not." I picked up the water and drank it all in one gulp, putting the cup down on the glass with a clack. "He gave the fire to me."

There was silence while Enzo took this in. He didn't react, beyond chewing the inside of a cheek thoughtfully.

"It must have been killing him," he said, quietly. "Nic explained that it is possible but this is the first I have heard of it done."

I nodded. "He was dying."

"This is why you don't know the cooperativa. When did this happen?"

"Only a few weeks ago. I want to take Elda's debt. That's why I'm here."

"Wait, go back. How did you come to meet Isaia? Why did he give it to you?"

"I came to Venezia as an au pair..." I began.

He whooped with laughter and slapped his knee. "You are the *nanny*?!" he bellowed. "This is beautiful. I have to tell Tab this, he needs to write a movie."

"Au pair."

"Whatever, whatever." He was still laughing. "I shall send someone to confirm that what you say is true. If the boy no longer has the fire, then you may take on her debt." A bemused expression crossed his face. "I don't know why you would do that. Once we have made an agreement it is unbreakable. I hope you know what you're getting into—"

I interrupted him, more from nerves than dominance. "This is the part where we talk terms, right?"

"Giusto." He scratched his chin, amused. Could he hear how loud my heart was beating?

"When you send someone to confirm that Isaia is no longer a magus, you must call Elda first and set a proper appointment. Don't just show up on her doorstep, you'll give her a heart attack."

"Certo," he said, looking at me like I was one brain cell from idiocy. "Do you think we are animals?"

I barreled on before I lost my guts. I held up my first two fingers. "Second, I owe you a favor, but any costs involved are covered by you, I won't do anything illegal, and you have to understand that I'm not even a legal adult yet. I have a family, parents, to answer to."

He waved this off. "I do not send children to do my work."

"Good." I held up three fingers. "And lastly, you get one debt, one favor. Do you understand? Uno."

His belly shook with silent laughter. "I like you. I am not accustomed to bargaining with a teenager. It's like un... piccolo gioco."

"This is not a game," I said, and the fire lit in my eyes.

"Well, I can see you are not lying," Enzo said, staring into my eyes, smiling and unafraid.

"This is my life. I'm not a secret agent, an assassin, or one of your mafioso—"

I was about to go on when his smile disappeared. "Mafioso? You think we are mafia?"

I blinked. "Aren't you?"

"You North Americans think you know so much just because you watch *The Godfather*, which, for the record, is a beautiful film. But no, we have no part with those devils. I am simply a businessman with long arms."

I wasn't sure what the difference was. "Okay, I stand corrected. Either way, don't send a knife to a gun-fight, okay?"

His offended expression was gone as swiftly as it had come and he laughed heartily. "A knife, or a spoon plastica?" he joked, raising an eyebrow at me.

I blushed, and the flame in my pupils sizzled out as though he'd thrown a bucket of cold water on me.

"You were making macaroni art two years ago," Enzo continued. "What can I trust you with?"

"Well..." I stumbled, "I can... light things on fire, and stuff." I cringed.

"But you won't do anything illegal..."

I wasn't sure what to say to this. What kind of task would he ask of me if I was a magus that wouldn't do anything that was against the law?

"I am not like Nic—" I began, but stopped. What if I'd put too many restrictions in place? I could lose the deal.

"Giovanni!" Enzo barked, making me jump.

Moments later, one of the men I'd seen earlier appeared. Enzo asked him for something. He nodded and disappeared.

"Tell you what," Enzo said. He leaned forward and rested his elbows on his knees. "The Baseggios can move on with their lives for now, no problema. Most likely, I will transfer her debt to you..."

Most likely? My heart sank.

Giovanni returned and handed Enzo a small black card. Enzo said, "Per lei, per lei!" pointing to me. Giovanni mechanically swung the card to me.

I took it. It had the name *Basil Chaplin* stamped on it in silver ink, and a phone number. I turned the card over. On the back was a silver symbol I recognized: the magus mark.

"But first," Enzo continued, "you call him. You spend some time with him." He swept his hands around to indicate the passage of time. "You learn things. Then you come see me. We talk then. I am a patient man. One does not get where I am without patience."

I fingered the smooth cardstock, my thumb grazing the name embossed into the soft paper. Hope filled me. To my surprise, I felt a sudden and strong bond with this person, this Basil, though I didn't know him. He was magi. He was my tribe. If I felt this connected to a stranger, how would I feel once I'd met him? I was starting to understand the connection between Isaia and Nic better as my eyes devoured the silver letters. *Basil Chaplin.* The phone number was European but I didn't recognize the country code. I was going to have to do some serious thinking about what to do next. I was facing my last year of high school, choosing a university, going back home to my family. How was I going to explain this to them? My parents were going to freak out. Should I even tell them? I didn't know how to keep a secret from them anyway, they can read my face like it's an open book. And my voice would probably never go back to normal. I crammed all these thoughts away and tucked the black card into my pocket. There was still the matter of Dante.

"Your son..." I began.

"You know Dante?" Enzo asked. Was it just my imagination or did his face darken? So Dante hadn't mentioned me.

"I don't want to get involved with your family stuff, but Dante said he sent men to Gallipoli to track the Baseggios."

If his brow had not darkened earlier, it was looking thunderous now. "What did my son do? Did you tell him you are magi?"

"He knows," I admitted.

He let out a stream of rapid Italian which sounded beautiful to my ears but it was clear that the meaning was not beautiful.

"You leave Dante to me," he growled.

"Okay." Did I really just *tattle* on Dante to his *dad*? Yup. I just did. I shoved the sheepish feeling into the same dusty corner of my brain that I shoved all the other thoughts I'd labeled 'later.'

"One last thing," he said. "Can you give me your word that you will never use your power to harm me or any of my own?"

I wasn't expecting that. Dante's face flashed in my mind. My thoughts rapidly rifled through the possible consequences of telling Enzo about what Dante had done. I finally decided that there were no downsides for me, only for Dante.

"Senior Barberini, your son locked me in a cell without water for I don't know how many hours."

Enzo's face went still. Only his pupils moved, looking at my eyes. After a moment, he said, "Go on." His voice was very different. Dangerous.

"His intention was to force me to pass my powers to him in exchange for my life."

He absorbed this, his eyes hard. "But you didn't, clearly."

"No. But I'm ashamed to say I would have. The pain was beyond anything anyone can imagine. I was rescued. By your niece Federica, and someone you knew as a boy, Rafaele Dimaro."

His eyes telegraphed surprise but he didn't say anything for a while.

Then, "You survived a burning. Do you know what that means?"

"My insides are charred beyond recognition?"

He ignored my joke. "I know it doesn't seem like it, because you were forced against your will, but Dante did you a favor. Magi who survive a burning are far more powerful than those who don't. They have superior control, can withstand more heat and expel more energy. They also don't have to live with the constant pain. Basil can tell you more about how it works when you meet him. I don't understand it fully. According to Nic, there are very few magi who survive, let alone attempt a burning. He wanted to do it but I wouldn't allow it."

My respect for Enzo grew. A burning would have made Nic more powerful, but even though Enzo could have benefited from Nic's increased power, he wouldn't let his employee take the risk.

"What happened to Nic?"

His face went flat and his eyes filled with regret. "He attempted a burning anyway. He recruited my foolhardy son to give him water at the right time. All magi are different. Some can withstand a burning for up to twenty-four hours before they die. Dante failed to give him water in time and Nic died. It only took nine hours."

I swallowed. Isaia's father had gone through the same thing that I had, only he had burned completely to death. I imagined the blond man from the video clips lying on his back, unable to speak or move. He'd been counting on Dante to administer the healing water at the right time...waiting in agony for help that never came.

"I'm truly sorry."

Enzo nodded his thanks. "I am too. Nic was much more than an employee. He was a great friend."

Raf had said that Enzo had always been disappointed in Dante, even when Dante was young. Nic's death must have been the nail in the coffin of their relationship.

"So, I guess you can understand my reticence to swear that I'll never protect myself against a member of your family?"

Enzo waved his hand. "You have nothing to fear from Dante, anymore. I still need your word. It's required from all of my men, and now... from my lady." The way he said it made me feel like he respected me.

I didn't have any intention of ever using my power against anyone, but suddenly I had another bargaining chip. "I will give you my word as long as you consider our trade complete. You won't send a man to visit Elda, in fact, you'll not visit her again on this matter."

He appeared to consider this, then he held out his hand and said, "My word also."

We shook.

He kissed both of my cheeks and then put a palm to each and squeezed my face lightly between his warm hands. "Grazie per tutto," he said, looking me straight in the eyes. "Be a good girl, eh?"

He curled his fingers around the back of my neck and planted a kiss solidly in the middle of my forehead. For a second, I felt like a pre-schooler.

"Oh," he said. "Tell Rafaele to come visit an old friend once in a while? I miss that boy."

I smiled. "I will. Although, I think you'll find he's become a man."

"And a good one, I should think." He tipped his index finger toward his forehead.

As though by magic, Karim appeared from behind the curtain.

Karim and I didn't speak until we were at the front gate.

"Well, Saxony Cagney of Saltford on the East coast of Canada. Did you get what you came for?" He held the gate open for me with one hand.

I stepped onto the street, feeling the little black card in my pocket. "I think... more, actually."

He gave a nod and a small smile.

"Good," he said, and closed the gate.

TWENTY

As soon as the gate closed behind me, I turned toward the Baseggio's villa. I froze in place and my brain skipped a cog.

Dante was leaning against the stone wall across from the villa. He had his arms crossed, and those wicked brown eyes were boring into me from across the calle.

"What have you done?" He dropped his arms and straightened.

I lifted my chin and steeled my expression. Curiously, instead of speeding up, my heart slowed down. My thinking sharpened. We circled each other in the small piazza, our hands at our sides, like gunfighters. I had just promised Enzo I wouldn't use my powers to harm him, or any of his own. As bad as their relationship might be, I was sure Dante still amply qualified as 'Enzo's own.' I swallowed and cursed inwardly.

"Coward," he spat. "I should have known. A girl can't handle the power of fire. You don't deserve it. You're an embarrassment to your kind. A failure."

The fire blossomed in my belly, but instead of rage, I felt a soothing calm. "Well, you should know what that feels like."

He froze. "What do you mean?"

"I just had a nice chat with your padre."

He bared his teeth and lunged for me.

I spat an ember at the stones in front of his feet and it ricocheted through his legs. He halted, up on his toes. He looked at the smoking gouge in the ground and back up at me, his eyes wide and fearful. Before he could gather his thoughts, I dropped my jaw and breathed a blast of hot air at him.

It was the first time I'd done such a thing. I was fully aware that I could have belched a powerful stream of fire into his face. Just like a blowtorch. What other abilities had the burning given me...had Dante given me? Oh, the irony.

His hair blew back and his eyes squinted shut. He put up an arm to defend himself and staggered backward, away from the blast of my furnace. I was amazed at how I could regulate the temperature so accurately. The wind emanating from me was quite hot and strong enough to push him back, but not hot enough to seriously burn him. Best of all, I felt no pain, and no anger. The fire and I were finally friends. I let my eyes glow. I was a fire magus, after all.

He hit the wall behind him and I let the stream of hot air fade. I closed my mouth. He peered over his forearm and tears leaked from the corners of his eyes. His face looked pink and sunburned. Harmed? Not so much. Scared? I looked at his eyes. Yup.

I fished in my bag for my travel sized bottle of aloe-vera and threw it at his chest. He gave a startled cry of surprise and caught the bottle, then looked down at it in confusion. When he read the label, he started laughing, albeit without humor. The maniacal sound made the hair on the back of my neck stand up.

I walked past him and didn't look back as the laughter faded behind me.

I WAS PLEASANTLY SURPRISED to see Raf waiting on a bench near the Baseggio's villa by the time I got home. He got up and walked toward me as soon as he saw me, his eyes worried. He opened his arms and instinctively, I stepped into the circle.

"Finally, the pretty Italian man I actually wanted to see."

He was too tense to laugh at my comment. "Everything okay?" he asked against my hair.

"Yes. Visiting Enzo was a good call."

"I'm glad."

"Speaking of visiting Enzo. He'd like to see you sometime," I said as we turned and walked toward the door.

I told Raf about our conversation. He listened with quiet concern. He took my hand and he held it until we got to my doorway. Everything came spilling out of me; my concerns about what to tell my family when I got home, my voice—which was never going to be the same, my promise to Enzo and wondering what he might make me do one day.

"I wish I could answer all your questions." He looked down at me. "But I have a feeling that you're going to figure everything out." He brushed hair away from my forehead. "We're going to stay in touch, right? You are definitely someone I don't want to lose track of."

"Absolutely," I said, kissing his cheek.

"Will you call me? After you get back to Canada. I just want to know how things go for you. You know, with your family and stuff."

"Sure, I will. But you know what I really want?" I said, looking up at him.

"What's that?"

"I want to pretend I'm just a normal girl for a while. You still owe me a night of *The Godfather*." I unlocked the door.

"Sounds great," he said, "but no kissing during the scene at the beginning where Marlon Brando has the cat on his lap. That's the best part." He pulled the corners of his mouth down and made an impressive Don Corleone impression. "You come into my house on the day my daughter is to be married, and you ask me to murder for money."

I laughed. "Whatever. I'm so giving you the sloppiest kiss, right in your ear."

He cracked a smile, and closed the door behind us.

"GOOD BYE, ISAIA." I crouched down and held out my arms to him.

The noise and bustle of the airport melted away as his warm body stepped into the circle of my arms. I was amazed at how much he had changed since the beginning of the summer. He'd been a tiny, malnourished-looking boy with pale skin and haunted black eyes. Now he was wiry with new muscle, and at least half an inch taller. His skin was brown from the sun and his black eyes glittered with mischief. He gave me a kiss on the cheek and stepped back.

"I like your voice," he said.

I laughed. "I like yours, too. I'm glad you found it."

I smiled and felt my throat constrict as I stood up and put a hand on the top of his head. I had been hoping to meet a special boy in Venice. Raf was sweet and I liked him, but I could admit that Isaia was the boy who had claimed my heart this summer.

"Where's Pietro? He was just here," I asked Elda.

"He took Cristiano to the toilet. Which is perfect because I haven't had a chance to tell you, since we haven't had two minutes alone since we got back."

"What's that?"

She took a deep breath. "I told Pietro. Not about the fire, just... about Nic."

I forgot to breathe for a second. "So he knows that Isaia... What did he say? I mean..." I glanced toward the bathrooms. "You guys seem okay. How did he take it?"

"Well, our vacation certainly wasn't the most relaxing we've ever had, but... he admitted that he'd had his suspicions. I won't lie. He's very hurt." She watched as Isaia ran to meet Pietro as he and Cristiano left the washroom. "But, he's determined not to let it destroy us, and so am I. I have a good man."

My throat tightened as I watched Pietro pick Isaia up and machine-gun kisses on his cheek. "You do. Do you feel better for telling him?"

She let out a big breath. "Like a thousand pounds have been lifted from my shoulders. I have to atone, nothing changes that. But, at least now I won't be living in fear anymore."

"Speaking of which." I had to get it out quickly since Pietro was already walking over. "You don't have to live in fear of Enzo anymore, either."

Her eyes widened. "What did you..." She abandoned the question when Pietro arrived.

Her eyes shone at me as I hugged Cristiano goodbye. She knew what I'd done. Elda kissed my cheeks and squeezed me hard, the way I had taught her Canadians hug. I wasn't sure if she didn't want Pietro to hear her, but she said quietly in my ear, "I can't thank you enough, Saxony. For everything. You're an angel, and you've changed our lives."

"Well, you've changed mine too," I rasped with my now permanently smoky voice. "That might be the understatement of the century."

"Keep in touch with us, please. If there is ever anything we can do. Anything." Elda stepped back. She looked more at peace than I'd ever seen her.

Pietro and I kissed goodbye. "Come back for a visit anytime you wish, Saxony. Your family is welcome, too."

"Thank you, Pietro." I smiled.

The Baseggios waved goodbye and made their way to the exit. Isaia gave me a last look with those shining obsidian eyes. I winked at him and he smiled, showing his dimples, before the family disappeared through the airport doors.

I stepped into the security line, double-checking that I had my passport and boarding pass. My skin prickled with a sensation that I was being watched, and I scanned the room. I tilted my head back to look up at the second level as I stepped up to the screening station. Karim and Giovanni, the man who had handed me Basil's card, leaned against the railing and looked down at me. They both nodded solemnly. The hair on my forearms stood up momentarily. I didn't know what they were doing there but I didn't doubt for a moment that it had to do with me. I made my way through security. When I looked up again, they were gone.

I rolled my carry-on to my gate and sat down to wait for boarding. I was early, and the only passenger waiting. I sent a text to my friends letting them know I was on my way home. We had all agreed to meet up when everyone was back, and I couldn't stop my knees from jittering in anticipation. Emotionally, I was doing the equivalent of rubbing my hands together.

A matronly stewardess looked up at me from behind the check-in desk. She looked a lot like the kind lady I had met on the plane at the beginning of the summer and I blinked, having a twilight zone moment.

"Tutto posto?" she asked. *Everything in place?*

With effort, I stilled my jumping legs. I subconsciously put a hand against the breast pocket of my button-up shirt. The business card pressed against my palm.

I smiled at her. "Tutto posto."

PART THREE

TWENTY-ONE

"Saxony!"

I turned toward the sound of my mother's voice, my face splitting into a grin. I was engulfed by a lilac-scented cloud as my mom wrapped me up in a hug and squeezed me tight.

"Welcome home, sweetheart. How was your flight? Did you sleep?"

She released me, and my father swooped in. I reached up on tiptoe to hug my dad.

"We missed you," he said. "Even Yuri missed you."

I laughed. Yuri was Jack's Siamese fighting fish.

"I slept. Flight was good," I rasped in my now permanently smoky voice.

My mom's smile dissolved. "You're sick! Why didn't you tell me you weren't well?" Her warm hands flew to my forehead and face. A line appeared between her brows. "You're feverish."

After the one time I had spoken with them (post tabacchi-shop fire incident that changed my life forever) I had kept our communication to texts and emails. I knew my mom was going to make a big deal out of my voice.

"I feel okay, Mom."

Annette Cagney was a mom's mom. She could mother up there with the best of them. There wasn't much I could do about it except reassure her that I was fine. The thought of actually telling my family the whole story of what had happened to me in Venice made my palms sweat. I wasn't ready for that. I wasn't sure I'd ever be ready for that.

"She's probably just jet-lagged, Annette." My dad put a dry hand to my forehead. "Oh, you are a bit warm. Let's get you home to bed."

Dad waited for the luggage while Mom got me bundled into our van. She rummaged in her purse and pulled out a package of cough drops. "Here, take one of these. I'll be right back with some tea."

"I'm okay, Mom. I promise—" The van door slid shut and she jogged across the parking lot as my dad was coming the other way with my luggage piled on a trolley. I heard the two exchange words, and the worry in my mother's voice. I sighed. I felt bad for Mom. There was nothing that could be done to fix my condition. I'd already been down that road. The rear hatch lifted and my dad put my luggage in the back.

"Thanks Dad." I smiled at him.

"We'll have you home in a jiffy, Saxony. You can go straight to bed."

"I'm really—" The rear hatched closed. "Okay," I finished to no one.

Dad opened the driver's side, got in and started the van. "So? Was Venice everything you thought it would be?"

He drove us through the parking lot and waited outside the sliding doors leading to arrivals.

"It was more, Dad," I said. "I'd like to go back someday."

In fact, I *had* to go back. I had made a promise to Enzo that I couldn't break. May as well prep my dad for the fact that I'd be heading back to Italy sometime in the future. I didn't know when that call would come. Barely conscious that I was doing it, my hand went to my shirt pocket, feeling for the business card of Basil Chaplin. Whoever he was, he was my connection to the world of fire magi.

The sliding doors opened and Mom appeared carrying a hot tea from the Tim Hortons kiosk in the airport.

"It's twenty-nine degrees outside," I said. The last thing I felt like was a hot drink.

"I know honey," said Dad. "Let your mother mother you. She hasn't been able to all summer."

"I know." My heart swelled as Mom got in and handed me the travel cup. It was nice to be home. I had been too busy and preoccupied to miss my parents much while I was gone, but now that I was back, I missed them terribly. Funny how that worked. "Thanks, Mom."

"Careful, Tim's always pours their water too hot."

97 degrees, to be precise, I thought, sensing the temperature as my palms pressed against the paper cup.

As we drove home, my parents asked questions about Venice and the Baseggios. I showed them photos on my phone of Piazza San Marco, the Grande Canal, water taxis and yachts, the beaches on Lido, and the canals at night with the moon high above lines of crisscrossing laundry. As my mom flipped through my photos, I watched the suburbs of Saltford go by. My neighborhood hadn't changed yet somehow it looked completely different. The manicured lawns, similar two-story houses painted in shades of pastels and grays, kids running through a sprinkler with a dog yapping at their heels. It all felt so safe and domestic in comparison to Venice.

"Which one is this, honey?" Mom held my phone up so I could see the image of Isaia I'd taken near the beginning of the summer. "Is this Christian?"

"No, Cristiano is the older one. That's Isaia."

My heart gave a happy little ache at the image of the pale, black-eyed little boy. Early on, I'd taken a shot of him building a plane out of Lego on the floor in his room. He wasn't smiling, and he had those awful purple smudges under his eyes. Tears pricked behind my eyelids at the thought of how much he'd been suffering at that point in time.

"Goodness, he doesn't look well," Mom said, zooming in on his face. "How old did you say he was?"

"Six."

She gave a little gasp and made a tsk sound. "He doesn't look a day over four."

"He wasn't feeling all that well when I first got there, but..." I took the phone and flipped forward to the shot I'd taken of all of the Baseggios at the airport in Venice. "He was much better by the end of the summer. See?"

While still small for his age, in this image Isaia was grinning, tanned, and noticeably healthier. His eyes had lost the haunted look.

She took the phone. "Wow, he doesn't even look like the same child." The van swerved a little and Mom said, "Keep your eyes on the road, James."

My dad grunted and quit trying to peer over her shoulder.

"What was wrong with him?" she asked.

"They weren't too sure," I said.

It wasn't a lie. *What was wrong with him is now wrong with me,* I thought. And yet, the thought didn't make me as unhappy as it used to. Probably because I didn't feel like the fire inside was roasting me alive anymore.

"Hm." Mom handed my phone back to me. "Are you going to see the girls this week? Are they all back?"

"Not yet. Georjie has been back for a while. Her mom got sick so she came home early. But her mom's a lot better now. We're going to have a sleepover at Georjie's soon, if that's okay."

"Of course. As long as you're well. You'll have a lot of catching up to do with your friends." Mom gave me one of those 'we'll see' looks from between the seats.

My stomach dropped. My voice was never going to go back to normal and my temperature would always run a bit higher than it should. I hoped Mom would get accustomed to my new normal by the time the sleepover came around.

We pulled into the driveway of our gray two-story and parked in front of the garage. Dad wouldn't let me carry any of my luggage in.

"Go on, go on," he said. "The boys can't wait to see you. RJ has soccer practice so you'd better say hi before he leaves."

"And then straight to bed," Mom called as I opened the front door to my home. The smell of freshly baked banana bread hit me in the face and made my mouth water.

"RJ?" I called, kicking off my sneakers.

"Sax?" His voice came from the garage.

My older brother knew I hated being called Sax. I pursed my lips and didn't answer. I heard him laughing.

"Saxony?" he called again. The door to the garage opened and the smell of banana bread was ruined with the smell of oil.

"You're taller!" I said when he stepped up into our foyer. "How is that possible?"

My older brother had been six feet tall already. Now he had to be pushing six-one or six-two.

"Yeah? Maybe."

He didn't even notice my voice, but I had guessed he wouldn't. RJ was blind to details like that. If it wasn't a detail on his car, it wasn't a detail he paid attention to. If RJ had even ever had a girlfriend, he'd kept it on the down low. RJ and I used to bicker a lot, but we'd grown out of it and a friendship had formed. One day, I might broach the subject of girls with him, if I thought he might answer me seriously. He was wearing a blue mechanics jumpsuit with the arms tied at the waist and a stained white tank-top. He pulled me into a hug, which was more like a hard chest-bounce accompanied by a loud back slap. RJ had started lifting weights a couple years ago and he'd grown in every direction since then. He already outweighed my dad and he wasn't quite nineteen yet.

"Watch the threads," I teased, looking down at myself for oil stains. I wrinkled my nose at the scent of vehicle fluids and sweat. "You stink. What are you doing?"

"Installing nitrous." He grinned and ran a hand through his dark brown hair. RJ was difficult to offend, unlike Jack, who was the most sensitive of all of us. RJ hit me on the shoulder with the back of a dirty hand, a brotherly love-tap. "Hey, how was Italy?" He peeled off the jumpsuit. "Game changer?"

This was how RJ talked. Sports analogies and slang he picked up who knew where. Maybe the salt mine. I laughed at his choice of words. He had no idea just how much of a game changer it was. "It was awesome. You should go."

"Yeah, the Ferrari factory isn't far from Venice, actually." He wiggled his dark brows. "That'd be worth a visit."

I shook my head at him. "Still a one-track mind. You've got practice right now?"

"In a half-hour. Game against the Vikings in two days. It's been a helluva season. You gonna come?"

He threw the jumpsuit into the garage, where it landed on a spare tire near his Corvette. He shut the garage door. RJ had taken over the garage when he bought his first car two years ago. I think my dad didn't know whether to feel annoyed or proud. RJ got a job at the salt mine just outside of town when he was in tenth grade and he'd worked there ever since. He saved part of his earnings for Uni and spent the rest on his car. The mine paid well, and his smarts got him promoted to a cushy job in the admin office.

"Course," I said. "Where's Jack?"

RJ shrugged a muscled shoulder. "Probably in his room playing video games. I'll catch you after practice."

He headed down into the basement where his man-cave was.

Mom and Dad came into the foyer laden with bags, just as Jack appeared at the top of the stairs.

"Hey, Saxony!" Jack's face brightened. "You're home."

My younger brother's voice caught me up in a pause. It was completely different from the last time I'd heard it. It was deeper, more resonant.

"Yep. Dude, you sound like a man or something." I smiled up at him. "How was your summer?"

Jack came down the stairs. His blond hair was messy and shaggy, and he looked like he'd grown at least a full inch. Unlike RJ, Jack was all elbows and legs. "Your voice sounds weird. Are you sick?"

"Naw, I'm fine," I said. "Just a bit tired."

Jack's face went through a startling transformation by the time he reached the bottom of the stairs. His blue eyes locked on mine and his smile disappeared. His chin jerked back just a little, as though someone had taken a swipe at his face. He stopped at the bottom, but came no closer.

"What, no hug?" I teased, but I suddenly felt uncomfortable, like he'd just looked right through me and saw something he didn't like. My forearms prickled.

Jack gave me a swift, stiff hug and pulled away fast. I got the mental image of a porcupine as he turned and headed back upstairs. He shot me an unpleasant look over his shoulder, one I couldn't define. Like all siblings, Jack and I had had our differences, but he'd never given me a look like that. Not even after I'd hurt him in the spring. I had thought he was over that, after all he was the one who fessed up that he'd been torturing me, and he convinced my parents to let me go to Venice when they were ready to cancel the whole thing.

"That was weird," I muttered, watching Jack retreat.

"He's probably just picking up on you not feeling well," Mom said. "You know how good he is at sensing other people's feelings and emotions."

"Is he?" I looked at my mom with surprise. It wasn't something I'd ever noticed, specifically about Jack.

"He seems to be lately," murmured my father. He squeezed by me with my biggest piece of luggage. I grabbed my carry on and my purse and followed him up the steps.

"I'll be up shortly with the thermometer," my mom called up the stairs.

"Great," I said under my breath.

"Let her mother you," Dad said again. "She's missed you. Here we are," he grunted as he set my luggage down on my cream colored carpet. "Just as you left it. Welcome home, sweetheart." He kissed my cheek. "Mom's got a turkey for dinner tonight. Try and get some rest."

"Thanks, Dad." I gave him a hug and he left me alone with my unpacking.

Nothing in my room had changed but everything looked different. The blue walls and gray trim looked terribly wrong, not like me at all. They were the old Saxony. I had just painted my walls one year ago, I wondered what my parents would think of me painting again. Maybe orange, or burgundy.

I took a black business card with the red foil out of my pocket and looked at it, chewing my lip. My stomach did a little dip at the thought of calling the number. Enzo had suggested I 'spend a little time with Basil' before he would allow me to fulfil my debt. How much time? Doing what? Presumably he was going to teach me all about being a fire magus. But, where was he? I guessed that 'a little time' didn't mean a weekend.

I pulled out my cell phone and connected it to our WIFI, then looked up the country code on the front of the phone number. +44. England. Well, at least we spoke the same language. I put the card up on my bulletin board, which was full of photos of me and my friends. Akiko, Georjie, and Targa goofing off at the beach; sleepovers at Georjie's house; making watermelon slushes and exploding pink melon all over the kitchen. I smiled wistfully. These were the times of a kid. I didn't feel so much like a kid anymore. The black card stood out starkly against my pastel photo frames and sparkly stickers. I really needed to redecorate.

My ears perked at the sound of footsteps on the stairs. I could tell my mom from my dad in a dead sleep. That was my mom, and she was coming armed with a thermometer. I panicked, snatched the black card off the bulletin board and stuffed it into the top drawer of my dresser. Plastering what I hoped was a normal looking expression on my face, I turned to face my mom as she came in.

Later.

Later, when I was alone in the house, and had screwed up enough courage—I would call him. I couldn't afford to have anyone interrupt or overhear this particular conversation.

TWENTY-TWO

I was still rubbing sleep out of my eyes when I came down the stairs the next morning. The smell of bacon, cinnamon and maple syrup filled the kitchen. Mom was standing at our picture window and looking out at the huge park behind our house, Dad was flipping the French toast.

"How did you sleep?" asked Dad. "Still on Italian time?"

He bent to check the tray of bacon sizzling in the oven. My mouth began to water and my stomach growled so loud I could feel it.

"I slept hard," I croaked, "like I was getting paid for it."

My jaw cracked as I yawned. I had fallen into a deep and dreamless stupor fueled by jet lag and turkey. Mom had made a feast to celebrate my coming home. Dinner was nice, but it would have been nicer if Jack hadn't kept glaring at me from across the table. I hoped today he'd be over whatever funk he was in.

"Good, you needed it." Mom turned back to the view.

I poured myself a coffee and went to stand beside her. The view behind our house was of Swallowtail Park, a large stretch of land that had once been owned by a farmer named Rudolph MacLeitch. When MacLeitch died, the land passed to his only daughter and she'd sold it to the city. By that time the green space was beloved by Saltford. It was never developed. MacLeitch's old farmhouse and barn were now boarded up, and the forest continued to grow in around them. The crooked weathervane on the old barn could still be seen from our picture window, poking up through the canopy of trees. It was more the sight of that old weathervane than anything else that made me feel like I was home.

Mom put a hand to my forehead, frowning. "Your temperature is only a little above normal, but it's clear you're fighting something." She shook her head. "It's that recycled plane air. Nothing will make you sick as fast as breathing the vermin of a hundred and twenty other people for eight hours or more."

"Ew. Gross." I made a face. "I'm fine. I promise."

"You sound terrible," she said. "I might make an appointment with Dr. Jacques for you."

"Please don't do that." My stomach did a little flip. "I feel perfect."

"Better to be on the safe side, honey." Dad pulled the sizzling bacon out of the oven and set it on the stovetop.

The idea of going to see a doctor had never been pleasant, but my stomach twisted with nerves when I thought about going now that I was a full-on fire magus. What if Dr. Jacques noticed something off about me? I pressed my mouth shut. As far as I could tell, except for my eyes (and they were under control now), my physical changes were all internal, and they were clearly of a supernatural nature. I had to hope that there was nothing so different about me that I could never see a health care professional ever again. I could deal with cuts and abrasions easily by cauterizing them from the inside, but what if I broke a bone? Maybe it was better to face the music and see what the doc said, because at least then I'd know sooner rather than later.

Our small kitchen television was on and my dad was watching the stock report as he made juice. He worked as an investor at one of the bigger banks in town.

"Tune in to the news please, honey," Mom said. "It's nine o'clock."

My dad picked up the remote and flicked it to our local channel.

Jack came down the stairs, mumbled a good morning to no one in particular, sat down at the table and started playing on his phone. His hair stuck up in every direction like a yellow aloe vera plant.

"Morning, Jack," I said pointedly.

He grunted.

"Where's RJ?" I asked.

"We're letting him sleep in a bit these days," explained Mom. "He's been playing hours of soccer every day after work. He's more tired than usual."

"A wooden play structure in Centennial Park was lit on fire last night, along with a section of nearby trees," said the news anchor from the television. "We go now to Knots Landing community where Daniel McGregor is on site."

We all turned to watch the report. The image showed a smoldering bunch of blackened logs and melted plastic goo. Smoke lay in a dark haze over the wreckage behind the reporter. McGregor had a grim expression on his face, like he was reporting a homicide. These kinds of things didn't often happen in Saltford.

"The Fire Department has determined the incident was arson and the police have already begun an investigation to find those responsible."

My mom set the platter of French toast on the table and turned toward the screen with her fists on her hips. "Who would do such a thing?" The indignation on her face made me bite my cheeks to keep from smiling.

"Shhh," Dad said, putting a hand out, his brows drawn together.

I started to laugh, but Dad gave me a look that silenced me. Someone lit some jungle gym on fire and the adults in Saltford didn't know what to do with themselves. Before Venice, I might have been just as horrified, but after being locked in a cell to burn to death at the hands of a megalomaniac, arson that didn't actually hurt anyone seemed mild and petty. I was going to have to readjust my world view back to a small-town level.

I caught Jack's glare and my thoughts skittered to a halt. He was drilling me with his eyes from across the table like I'd shot someone's dog.

"What?" I asked, genuinely confused. Maybe I shouldn't make light of a burnt swing set, but the nasty look he was giving me was overkill. Jack just shook his head and dropped his gaze back to his phone.

"We've never had anything like this happen in our neighborhood before," said a community woman with the microphone in her face. "Whoever is responsible needs to be stopped before they hurt someone."

"It's probably the rugby team from Hudson's Senior High," I suggested. One of the high schools across town, rivals of Saltford High, had sports teams which were notorious for acts of vandalism. Things like sheds and doghouses turned up destroyed sometimes, particularly after a losing streak. I caught Jack rolling his eyes as he forked three pieces of French toast onto his plate.

"What's your problem?" I snapped at him.

"Guys. Guys," said Dad, palms up. "Saxony's been back for one day, can we try and get along for at least twenty-four hours before we start biting each other's heads off?"

"Sorry," I mumbled.

Dad poured the juice and set a cup in front of each plate. He looked at my mom. "I thought we were past this. Don't the books say teenagers are supposed to get easier?"

Mom gave him an intense side-eye that said she didn't know which books he was reading. "Saxony's not feeling well. We're all grumpy when we're sick."

"Honestly, I feel totally fine." I felt like a broken record.

The news broadcast about the fire was still going on in the background. "This type of behavior is just simply not acceptable in a town like Saltford," another neighbor was saying.

"Everybody knows everybody, and I hope that whoever did this doesn't think they can get away with it."

"Sweetheart, would you mind turning that off?" Mom said.

Dad leaned back to snap off the TV.

I paused with my orange juice halfway to my lips as I watched Jack shove a whole piece of French toast into his mouth and chew, cheeks bulging like a tuba player.

"Wow, did they not feed you while I was away? You know that no one is going to take it away from you, right?" I said lightly, trying to ease the tension between us.

Jack pushed his empty plate away and stood up abruptly. "I'm done here," he said with his mouth full and with another glare at me. He swallowed the barely chewed food; it must have hurt. "Can I go?"

His lip curled with disgust. His expression was more than simple annoyance with a sibling. I blinked, stung, as he vacated the table without waiting for a response from anyone. I set down my orange juice, locked my jaw, and went after him. Sprinting up the stairs, I caught him in the hallway between our two bedrooms. Jack and I were the only ones with bedrooms on the upper floor. I grabbed his elbow and turned him toward me, trying to keep my voice steady. My temper was far more under control since my experience in Venice, but I still had my limits.

"What did I do to you, Jack? I don't get it."

His eyes flashed as he faced me and I took a step back. "I know you lit that fire last night," he hissed so our parents couldn't hear. "I don't know what happened to you in Venice, but I don't even recognize you anymore."

A rat began to gnaw through my insides. My heart began its powerful thud, but this was not like facing Dante. This was my family, not some bully I would never see again. Surprise froze my tongue into place. Everyone who knew I was a fire magus wasn't even on the same continent as me. There was no way Jack could know anything. I shook off the spell and opened my mouth to protest, but I took too long.

"See, you can't even deny it," Jack said.

"Jack, I—I don't know what you're talking about." I stumbled through the words, sounding guilty even to myself, but only because he'd taken me so off guard. "I was in bed, sleeping like the dead all night last night. Why do you think I set that stupid little fire? I would never—"

"Save it," he seethed.

Jack's boyish face had been transformed by righteous fury. *He* didn't recognize *me*? Who was this guy? He disappeared into his bedroom and shut the door in my face.

I felt like he'd gutted me with a fish-knife. I knocked. "Jack, I had nothing to do with that fire. I promise you."

"What's going on up there?" Dad said from the bottom of the stairs. "Are you going to come finish breakfast?"

"I've lost my appetite," I said, loud enough so that Jack could hear it though his door, then headed to my bedroom.

"Let them go," I heard Mom say from the table. "Saxony isn't well and Jack's just in a funk because RJ is getting all the attention lately. They'll sort themselves out."

"Ugh," my dad groaned. "Teenagers."

"ANOTHER ONE?" I heard my mom cry from the kitchen the next morning, a Monday. Mom and Dad both had work today.

"Another what?" I asked as I turned the corner into the kitchen.

My parents were huddled in front of the television. Dad looked over his shoulder at me. "Another fire last night. This one was in the harbor."

"Not the Sea Dog, I hope." I peered in between their shoulders. "It wouldn't be fair for something like that to happen to Phil, not after he already lost everything in the flood." Phil was the owner of a restaurant that looked like a pirate ship. Targa's dad helped to build it way back before we'd been born. It was beloved by the locals as much as it was by the tourists.

"It wasn't the Sea Dog," said Mom. "But it wasn't some cheap little dinghy, either."

She moved away from the screen to let me see. The same reporter as the day before was standing on the beach. Behind him, the smoking wreckage of a small yacht lay half out of the water, encircled by caution tape.

"Police are unsure if the perpetrator or perpetrators are the same as the ones who lit the jungle gym yesterday," the reporter was saying. "Police urge anyone who might know something to contact them."

Mom took a swig of her coffee and put her mug into the sink. "Saltford is getting too big. We should think about moving to Devon." Devon was a nearby town of six-thousand people. It was backwater compared to Salford's one-hundred-eighty-thousand.

"Got to run," Dad said, kissing her cheek. "And I know you don't mean that." He looked at me. "Feeling better?"

"I never felt bad," I intoned.

Just then Jack came down the stairs. His eyes fell on the screen and widened.

"You have an appointment with Dr. Jacques this afternoon at three," my mom said as she went to the foyer and toed her way into a pair of black ballet flats. "Don't forget. Are you okay going alone or do you want me come with you? I could meet you there."

"No, it's fine," I said. "He's just going to tell me to drink liquids and sleep it off."

"There is something going on or you wouldn't sound like Leonard Cohen," Mom said, dropping her chin. There was no point in arguing with her.

My parents said goodbye and left in the van. The real estate office where Mom worked was on the way to Dad's bank, so he always dropped her off and picked her up. Jack mumbled something from the kitchen and I went to find him, bracing myself for more freaky accusations.

"What did you say, Jack?"

"I said—" He turned to face me, his face a storm cloud. "—how did you do it?"

"How did I do what?" My eyes fell on the television screen just as the image of the burning yacht disappeared and they cut to a commercial. A stone of dread dropped into my gut. "You don't think that I had anything to do with that?"

"I *know* you did," he said. The certainty on his face made even *my* blood feel cold.

"How do you know?" I cried, my hands out in surrender. "Why are you so convinced that I've been running around late at night setting fire to things that aren't mine? It's crazy."

"I agree, it is crazy," he said. "Consider yourself caught, Saxony. I can't prove it, but I know it was you. You need to stop this," he pointed at the television screen, "and you need to get help."

"Whoa," I said. The kitchen seemed to spin and blur in my periphery. It was giving me vertigo to hear these things come out of my little brother's mouth. "You're messing with me, right? You're still mad about what happened before I left for Venice, and you're having some fun screwing with me."

But even as I was looking into his eyes, I knew that it wasn't the case. There were no cracks in his conviction. I knew my little brother, I could recognize the signs of a practical joke. There was something else going on here, something Jack needed to explain.

He stormed past me. "I can't even look at you," he said under his breath.

A panicked bird flapped in my chest and I grabbed at his elbow as he left the kitchen. "Jack," I said, my voice cracking. "I don't understand. Just stay and talk to me."

He yanked his elbow out of my grasp. "I can't talk to a liar. I can't believe a word you say anymore." He shoved his feet into his skateboard shoes in the foyer and without a last look, he was gone.

I sat down hard into a chair at the dining room table, confused, stung.

LIKE MOST SERVICES in our community, Dr. Jacques's office was not far away. In the afternoon, I retrieved my town bike from the garage, strapped my purse across my body, and headed out for my appointment. Summer was still evident in the green leaves on the trees and freshly cut grass, but there was a coolness in the air, a warning that snow was not all that far away. But it wasn't the weather that was on my mind. For the first time since my transformation, I was going to be examined by a health professional. What would he find? Besides a temperature that ran slightly too high, what else might give me away? Would he notice something strange about my eyes? When he looked down my throat, would he see flickering flames?

Visions of a balding man in a white coat with a stethoscope around his neck running screaming from an examination room scampered through my imagination. I wondered if I could get away with skipping this appointment and my mother not finding out. But Annette Cagney was a sleuth, especially when it came to her children. I had no choice but to go through with it, and I had to admit that I was a bit curious, myself.

I jammed the front tire into the bike rack and crossed the parking lot toward the clinic. I got myself checked in and the nurse showed me to a private examination room. I sat in one of the chairs, wrapping and unwrapping my headphone cord around my phone, inner tension mounting. The wait seemed to stretch out for hours and just as I had convinced myself that this was a terrible idea and got up to sneak out, the door opened and Dr. Jacques came in. He was a slender, balding man with glasses. He'd been my doctor since I was born.

"How is my favorite redhead?" Dr. Jacques said as he closed the door. "Your mom said you haven't been feeling well?"

"Actually, I feel completely fine," I said. "My voice has just gone a bit scratchy, and that has my mom's alarm bells going off."

"Yes, you do sound like you have something going on with your throat or chest," he said. "Pop up on the bench and let's take a look."

I sat down on the examination table and the paper they covered it with crinkled under my butt. Beetles of worry crawled up and down my spine. I took a deep breath.

"Open wide for me, please?" Dr. Jacques said, with a small penlight in hand.

My jaw creaked as I opened. He looked for a long time. I watched his brow for signs of concern for alarm.

"Huh," he said. "Is your throat sore?"

"Uh-uh," I grunted.

Dr. Jacques pulled back and I closed my mouth. He hadn't run from the room screaming, so that was good... at least, he hadn't run away *yet*. He turned and picked up a thermometer and stuck the silver end into my ear. I heard it click and a moment later it beeped and he pulled it back and looked at the digital reading.

"Well, you are running a touch above normal," he observed. "But it's nothing to get too worked up about."

He went about listening to my heart and my lungs, asking me to breathe deeply in and out. The routine was familiar and helped to calm me. He asked me if I had noticed any changes in weight, how I was sleeping, how I was eating and digesting, and if anything had changed suddenly in my life. I told him I'd spent the summer in Venice and my diet had changed, but that was it. I kept my eyes on the floor while I downplayed my answers. He felt my glands with warm fingertips and inspected my eyes with a light.

"What's the diagnosis, doc?" I finally asked, lightly.

"Well," he said, peering at me from over his glasses. "If your throat isn't actually hurting you, then I'm a bit mystified as to why your voice sounds so scratchy. And the fact that you're running a low-level fever is a sign that your body is fighting something. I'm hesitant to prescribe antibiotics at this stage, though I would consider it if your fever went up. Nothing else seems to be abnormal, although looking down your throat proved to be more difficult than it might be for most."

"Why is that?" I asked, twisting my hair into a rope just to give my hands something to do.

"Well, it's very dark in there. Perhaps you have a narrower esophagus than most. Funny, it's not something I remember about you," he murmured, pushing his glasses up his nose.

His comment triggered something I'd imagined after my burning—that my insides were now like volcanic rock, black and hard. I didn't think that was actually what I looked like on the inside, but it sort of felt that way.

"I recommend you get plenty of fluids, and plenty of rest. Don't do anything to excite yourself and we'll just keep an eye on that fever, shall we?"

"Okay." I hopped down. "Are we finished?"

Dr. Jacques picked up his clipboard and put a hand on the door handle. "For now. I'll give your mother a call this afternoon and tell her not to fret."

I breathed an enormous sigh of relief. "Thank you."

As I biked home, I mulled the physical over. A trained professional couldn't see anything much different other than small things about me, even a trained professional who had known me since I was born. So why was it that Jack was reacting so strongly to me?

TWENTY-THREE

The smell of fresh-cut grass, popcorn, and hot dogs filled the air as we entered the soccer stadium and found our way to our seats. It was already the second half of the game and my brother's team had the championship all locked up. The stands were buzzing with students and parents, and the Archers' supporters were easy to recognize—they were in high spirits. The sounds of whistles and screams filled the air. Spectators had taken to foot pounding on the aluminum stands whenever a goal was scored, which filled the space with a sound of metallic thunder.

Jack refused to sit by me and chose instead to sit on the other side of my parents. It was difficult to enjoy the game with his words and behavior weighing so heavily on my mind. Was it just a coincidence that I had transformed into a fire magus and suddenly my little brother was accusing me of arson? What did he know? And why was he so unwilling to talk to me about it?

"You're going to break those if you don't give it a rest," my mom said, tilting her eyes down to where I was wrapping and unwrapping my headphone cord around my phone. "Something bothering you?"

I sighed. It was so difficult for me to hide anything from my family. Akiko always said I was like an open book and had recommended that I never lie about anything really important.

"No, all good here," I said to my mom as I stuffed the headphone cord into my pocket.

Everyone in the stands leapt to their feet and began screaming and clapping and stomping as RJ's team, the Archers, scored another goal. My dad leaned toward my mom and said, "It's embarrassing. I feel sorry for the other team."

My mom smiled and said over the din, "Life is competition. It's good for them to lose."

"Isn't it important for our own son to have that experience, too?" Dad replied.

Mom tossed her auburn hair. "It's a soccer game, honey. Let's not get too philosophical."

In my periphery, I caught a face off to the right which seemed to be watching me. I turned my head to spot a guy with dirty blond hair and high cheekbones. We made eye contact and I expected him to glance away, but he didn't. I held his gaze. I was never the first to look away in a stare-down with a cute guy. His face broke out in a broad grin and he still didn't look away. My heart beat a little faster. I didn't recognize him from Saltford High, but he couldn't have been that much older than me. He must have been from one of the other high schools in town. Throughout the rest of the soccer match, he and I played the eye contact game. I'd catch him looking at me, and he'd catch me looking at him, until finally we both started laughing at the obvious. He couldn't have made it clearer that he was interested, and I couldn't have made it clearer that I was open to his interest.

A memory of the first time I'd met Dante rose to mind, and I frowned. I'd been so taken with him, and he had proven to be a jerk. It was a lesson I had needed to learn, and I could admit that now. Cute boys were great, I was all about them, but maybe I wouldn't be so eager to rush headlong into dating without weighing the guy a little more carefully.

The game wrapped up just as the sun was going down, with a score of six to two. We shuffled out of the stadium along with the crowd and stood in the parking lot to wait for RJ so we could congratulate him before he left to celebrate with his team. I stepped into the ladies' washroom, telling my family I'd be along in a minute.

As I came out of the washroom, the blond guy was standing near the white brick walls, clearly waiting for me. My face flushed as soon as I saw him. It was easy to be brave and hold eye contact with someone when you're stuck in the middle of a crowd, but when you come face-to-face, things get a little more awkward. He was even cuter close up, with a broad mouth and naturally red lips. He gave me that same grin, and propped a shoulder against the wall.

"My guess is that you've got a boyfriend in the game," he said, cocking an eyebrow. "Please tell me I'm wrong."

"A brother, not a boyfriend," I said, smiling.

"A *protective* brother?" He made a show of glancing around with fake nervousness.

I laughed. "Why? Do you have wicked intentions?"

"If taking a gorgeous redhead out for a coffee is wicked—" He put his hands up, "then guilty as charged."

My tummy warmed with pleasure, and I hated myself for being so vulnerable to flattery.

"Why don't we start with, 'Hi, my name is Saxony.'"

"Gage," he replied. "Pleased to meet you. I hope I wasn't creeping you out by staring. That wasn't my intention, there's just—" His eyelids lowered as he murmured, "something so attractive about you."

This guy was laying it on thick. I cleared my throat. "Do you have a friend in the game?"

"Several." He cocked his head to the side. "My guess is you're a senior at Saltford High? Half of the Archers are from that school. I'm friends with Danny Fair and Jordan Bell."

"Oh yeah? Jordan was in my Poli-Sci class last year." I relaxed as I identified the links between us. I didn't know them well, but Danny and Jordan were on RJ's soccer team. "You must be in your last year, too?"

He shook his head. "I graduated this past year. I'm going to do some traveling this year."

"I just got back from spending the summer in Italy. I highly recommend it."

He took a step closer. "Really? I'd like to hear more about that. When can I take you out?"

I opened my mouth to respond when I felt a tap on my shoulder. Jack was there, with his now customary black look. "Mom and Dad are looking for you," he said flatly.

"I better not keep you," Gage said. "Maybe I could be lucky enough to get your number?"

"Oh, you'll want to steer clear of this one," Jack said while examining his fingernails. "It's for your own good. No one likes to date a liar."

And with that, my little brother spun around and stalked away.

"Jack," I cried, horrified. I turned back to Gage, my face flushed with heat. "I'm sorry, I don't know what's gotten into him. Ever since I got back from Venice, he's been acting weird."

"It's okay, I have a brother, too. I know what it's like." He shifted from one foot to the other and stuffed his hands in his pockets. "So, do I have an answer?"

"Coffee would be nice," I said retrieving my phone from my bag.

We exchanged numbers and he flashed me that breathtaking grin. "Awesome. I'll give you a call later. Nice to meet you, Saxony." He turned and walked away, and I watched him for a few seconds, admiring his confident stride.

I frowned as Jack's words came back to me. I scanned the parking lot for my parents, who were standing by our van along with RJ and Jack, celebrating the Archers' victory. I didn't want to ruin this moment for RJ, but I felt like I'd been slapped. I stared at Jack until he finally looked at me. I beckoned to him to meet me on the grass behind all the cars. At first, he shook his head, and I put my palms together in a pleading gesture. He rolled his eyes and ambled toward the grass. I stalked in his direction, my jaw set.

"YOU HAVE to talk to me, Jack," I said, my voice serious. "Why would you humiliate me like that?"

"You've already humiliated yourself," he answered, crossing long skinny arms over his chest and shaking his head. "If Mom and Dad knew... What happened to you in Venice?"

My stomach dropped into my bowels. "What makes you think something happened to me in Venice?"

Why was my voice so squeaky?

"Because, I don't recognize you as my sister anymore," he said. "You used to have such a good heart, always helping people." His face was a mask of disgust. "Now you hurt people."

"I'm not hurting anybody, Jack," I said, incredulous. "I wouldn't—"

"You already have. I'm going to give you a day to fess up to Mom and Dad before I go to them myself."

"Jack." I took a calming breath. "You have absolutely no proof that I had anything to do with those fires. I have done nothing since I got home but sleep and eat pancakes and turkey. I have absolutely no reason, no motive whatsoever, to go running around town setting fire to things."

"No," he admitted. "I don't have any actual proof. But I know it was you all the same."

My fists clenched. "Do you have any idea what it feels like to be falsely accused? Especially by someone who knows you, who has grown up alongside you?"

My voice hardened. We stared each other down. He narrowed his eyes, not giving me any quarter.

"Saxony! Jack!" Dad called across the parking lot. "Come and say congratulations to RJ before he heads off."

"One day," Jack warned, and turned away.

I followed him, my insides writhing. I felt mute in the presence of such injustice. The width and breadth of it hit me like an anvil to the chest. We reached the rest of our family, clustered around the van. I arranged my face into an expression of happiness and pride, for RJ's sake.

"Awesome job, bro," I said.

"Thanks, Sax," he said, grinning. His hair was freshly washed and curly, his clothing already damp with sweat.

"You going to get into all kinds of trouble tonight?" I teased.

"I certainly hope not," said Mom. "They're going to celebrate their win like fine upstanding young citizens and be home in bed by one, right, sweetie?" She gave my brother a saccharine smile.

RJ puffed his cheeks out with an exhale, like her ask was a steep one. I noticed he didn't directly answer her, though. Instead, he gave me a curious look. "Hey, is your friend Georjayna back in town yet?"

My eyebrows shot up. RJ had never shown interest in any of my friends before. "I think so, but her mom's been sick lately, so I haven't seen her yet." A sly smile crossed my face. "Why?"

RJ shrugged and gave a sheepish grin. Even I could admit, when he smiled, my older brother was charming enough to stop a striking clock.

"She's cute." He grabbed a baseball cap from his bag in the back of the open van and placed it over his damp curls.

I grimaced. Noooo, I didn't want to know about my brother thinking about my friend like that.

"Gotta go, my man." RJ put out a fist to Jack and bumped his knuckles. "Don't strain on her." With these words, RJ tilted his head slightly in my direction.

I couldn't have been more surprised if RJ had started levitating. Even my oblivious older brother had noticed that Jack was clashing with me. I watched Jack's reaction to this request. His expression became stone cold at the suggestion of giving me a break.

"Come on, Jack." RJ sighed. "You bland out when you don't punch back."

My dad looked at my mom. "Do you have any idea what's going on here?"

She shook her head, bemused.

"They'll sort it out," said RJ. "Thanks for coming to my game, guys. Catch you later." He took off toward a crowd of his teammates loitering near the stadium entrance.

"Who will sort what out?" asked Dad.

Jack refused to meet my gaze. We piled into the van and headed for home just as the sky transformed from bright blue to gunmetal gray. On the way home, my gaze traveled up to the distant hilltop community of Bella Vista, where my friend Georjayna lived. I pulled out my phone and pounded out a text.

Me: *Hey Georjie, how's your mom doing? Everything okay?*

Georjie: *Hey! Thanks for checking in. She'll be fine. Funny, but her illness has actually brought us closer together.*

I smiled, and typed, *I think they call that a silver lining. That's awesome, Georjie.*

Georjie: *Yeah, it is. We're not best chums or anything, but things are definitely better. I'll tell you more when we're all together.*

Me: *Can't wait.*

AS WE ENTERED the foyer to our house, my phone chirped again. I dug it out of my bag and was pleasantly surprised to find a text from Raf.

Buongiorno, Bella. How are things going with your family? Care to talk?

My heart melted with appreciation. I needed a sympathetic ear, and one who understood my situation. That left only Elda, or Raf. Elda was busy raising her family and fixing her marriage. Raf's text felt like a godsend. I sprinted up the steps to my bedroom, closed the door, and dialed him. I took several gulps of water from my water bottle as the long dashes of an overseas call sounded off in my ear.

"That was fast," answered Raf in his rich Italian accent. "I guess that's a yes. Lucky me. How was your flight home? How are you?"

To my brief horror, my lower lip wobbled. I sucked in a deep breath and blew it out slowly through pursed lips. A sympathetic ear always brought emotions rushing to the forefront. I could go along pretending everything was okay for a long time, but if someone asked 'Hey are you okay?' in a sincerely concerned tone, I had to fight not to fall to pieces. I sat on my bed and pulled my feet up.

"My mom is convinced I have the plague," I said with a laugh.

"Because of your voice?"

"Yeah, she thinks I'm sick. I knew she would." I scooted backward so my back was against the wall and crossed my legs out in front of me. "I had an appointment with my doctor,"

"Oh Dio, could he tell?"

"Nope. I was sweating bullets, but he just said that my esophagus seemed narrower than usual and I have a slight fever. Nothing more."

Raf gave an audible sigh of relief. "Any pain?"

"None, thank goodness." I said. "My days of constant agony appear to be over." My lips twisted in a wry smile. "I still haven't gotten to the point where I'm thanking Dante. I don't think I ever will."

Raf laughed. "What's bothering you, then?"

I smiled. Raf was so astute. At least I didn't have to hide my real self with him. "Somebody has been lighting fires in Saltford," I said, "and my little brother is convinced that it's me."

There was a pause. Then, "But he doesn't know, right? So, why would he think that?"

"That's what I'm trying to figure out," I answered. "He has no proof, and yet he's fully convinced that I'm guilty. As if I have any interest in starting random fires in my own home town, or anywhere for that matter." My face heated with indignation.

Raf was quiet for a moment and then said, "How did he react to you when you first got home?"

"Not good—it was fishy from the start." I remembered the strange transformation on Jack's face as he came down the stairs. "It's like he knows something happened to me, but I don't know why he's linking it to the fires. Don't you find that colossally weird?"

Raf took a breath. "You know, I have an aunt that can sense things about people. If I'm feeling upset for some reason and she's around, she can pick up on my emotion, even if I'm trying to hide it. There is a word for it, but I can't think of what it would be in English."

"Are you suggesting that Jack is like that?" I thought about this. "My little brother has always been sensitive, but not in a psychic way."

"An empath," said Raf. "That's what it's called. Maybe you should just confront him, ask him if he can sense something strange that he never noticed before you went to Venice."

"I feel like I've already done that, but he won't answer me. Not directly, anyway." Feeling like a conversation hog, I added, "But, enough about me, how are you?"

Raf laughed. "My life is not nearly as interesting as yours, Saxony. I make glass plates and bowls, I hang out with my friends, I sleep, I repeat."

"Have you seen Dante?"

"Not even his shadow. But that's normal for me."

"And Federica?"

"She's around, but it's like she's afraid of everything now. It's kind of sad."

I frowned. Federica needed to get away from the Barberini family, at least for a time. But it wasn't my business.

"So, are you going to talk to your brother?" Raf asked.

"I'll try," I promised.

"Do you trust your family, Saxony?"

Surprise at this question lifted my brows. "Yes, of course I do."

"Then maybe you should just tell them."

And there it was. It was the option that I was not willing to face. Was I ready to freak my parents out beyond measure? Was I ready to put my family in danger? Though I couldn't put voice to how, I instinctively felt that if they knew what I was, it could expose them somehow. The things Dante had done to convince me to work for him had been terrifying. Telling my family would change everything, and they'd be charged with keeping my secret, too.

"I don't think I should." My armpits felt damp as the imagined shock on my parents' faces filled my mind's eye. "In Nicodemo's videos, he stressed secrecy. Most of the world doesn't know we exist. It might put them in danger if they knew."

"Or keep them out of it," Raf said. "It's your call, but I would tell them if it were me. Let me know if you change your mind and want to talk it through, okay? I know I'm far away, but I care."

"Thanks, Raf."

We said goodbye. I didn't get up off my bed for a long time after that. I sat there imagining the possible outcomes and reactions if I told my family what I was. All of them were terrifying.

TWENTY-FOUR

The next day I woke up in a quiet house for the first time since I'd arrived home. My parents were at work, RJ was sleeping off his celebrations in the basement and Jack was out with friends. Immediately my mind jumped to the black business card with the red foil. I made myself breakfast, including a double-espresso for courage. I cleaned the kitchen, something that calmed me, and then went upstairs to my bedroom. I stood in front of my bulletin board, phone in hand, heart pounding. Holding the black card between my fingertips, I rubbed the red foil fireball with the pad of my thumb. The mark of a magus. My mark. Finally, I got sick of hesitating, hit the call button, and waited while the phone did its thing.

"Yes?" answered a nasal female voice. A one-word answer to my call was not what I had been expecting, but I didn't know what I *had* been expecting so...

"I'm looking for Basil Chaplin, please?"

"He's rather busy at the moment, may I take a number and ring you back?" Upper-class British accent.

"Sure. Tell him Saxony Cagney called from Canada, a fire magus who was given his business card by Enzo Barberini."

I rattled off my phone number, which she took in silence. She then hung up without saying anything else. I made a face. All that build-up for nothing. I switched apps to check my emails and a few moments later, my phone rang. The number had the English country code, but it was different from the one I had dialed.

"Hello?"

"Mrs. Cagney?" British. Male. Resonant and serious.

I laughed. "Mrs. Cagney is my mother. Call me Saxony. Is this Basil?"

"Mr. Chaplin, yes."

Uptight much? I cleared my throat. "Sorry, Mr. Chaplin."

"I feel I must inform you that we can track a cell phone call all the way across the world, and we don't take kindly to prank calls."

My head snapped up and I blinked. "Why would I prank call you? Do you not know Enzo Barberini?"

"We've spoken briefly over the phone, when he was looking to hire—" he cleared his throat. "You say you are a fire mage?"

Fire mage? "We're not called magi? Magus for singular?"

He laughed, sounding a touch more relaxed. "They are one and the same. Magus is the Italian word for mage."

"Oh, of course," I said, feeling dumb. I could have figured that out. "Enzo recommended that I come and see you, for—" I paused. "Training?"

"How old are you, Saxony?"

"I'll be seventeen in a month."

Basil sighed audibly. The random image of Sherlock Holmes pinching the bridge of his nose in annoyance came to my mind.

"I see. Would you mind if I called you back?"

"No, I guess not. Are you going to call Enzo and verify that I am what I say I am?"

"Precisely."

We said goodbye and hung up. I sat down in the wooden chair I used to do my homework in when I was younger. It seemed to have shrunk. My knees bounced while I waited. My phone rang less than five minutes later. I snapped it up.

"Yes?"

"Saxony?" Totally different voice. Not Basil.

"Uh, yes?"

"It's Gage."

I blanked out.

"From the soccer game?"

"Oh, hey." I kicked myself for answering. The guy was cute but I didn't want Basil's call to go to voicemail.

"About that coffee—"

"Listen, would you mind if I called you back? I'm just expecting a call right now and don't want to tie up my line."

"That sounds like a brush off," he said, his voice casual.

"It's not. What about this afternoon? At Flagg's? Do you know it?"

"Yeah, Flagg's is great. That would be nice!" Gage sounded genuinely pleased.

"Three-thirty?"

"I'll be there." I could hear the smile in his voice.

My phone buzzed and the screen reported another call coming in. +44.

"I gotta go, sorry!"

"No worries. See you this afternoon."

"See you." I switched lines, hanging up on Gage and picking up the other call. "Hello?"

"Miss Cagney?" It was Basil's voice again, but he sounded different than before, almost excited. "Enzo has informed me that you are indeed a fire mage, and not only that, but that you have endured a forceful burning. Is this true?"

"It's true," I said, my voice sounding extra rough. I cleared my throat.

"This is highly unusual. Highly. Quite unprecedented. Do you have any idea how lucky you are to have survived? Well, never mind that right now. We would be very interested in working with you, but we don't deal with minors who haven't been previously vetted."

"What does that mean?"

"Simply, it means we know their families. It also means they have received the fire genetically. Enzo has informed me that you were given the fire. This is not something we see often." He finally took a breath. "Do your parents know what you are?"

My pulse ratcheted a notch at the thought. "No," I rasped.

"Do you trust your family?"

I blinked at the question I'd heard only yesterday from Raf. "Of course."

"Then you'd better tell them," he said with finality.

"That won't put them in some sort of danger?"

"Miss Cagney, they would be in much greater danger if they *didn't* know."

I stood up from the rickety chair and began to pace. "What do you mean?"

It was silent on the other end of the phone for too long. My heart rate increased.

"Are you still there?"

"I don't mean to frighten you, but there are organizations whose sole purpose it is to find supernaturals." He paused, and I knew he was trying to find a suitable word for a teenager's ears. "And apprehend them."

This wasn't news to me. It was exactly what Dante had done. "What do they have to do with my family?"

"Some of these organizations use less than ethical methods to enlist their supernaturals. If your family isn't aware, then they aren't forewarned. Should one of these organizations find you and determine you are a good recruit—and mark my words they would, because a mage who has lived through a burning is rare and extremely valuable—then they may have no qualms about using your family to get to you."

The blood drained from my face and my vision fuzzed out at the edges. My mouth opened but I didn't know what to say. I closed my eyes. This was my worst fear.

"Now I have frightened you, which is exactly what I had wanted not to do. Try to relax," he said. "Of all the supernaturals out there, you are most likely not on their radar at the moment, considering where you live and how new you are. My recommendation at this time is to tell your family. Give them a small demonstration of your power. Tell them that Arcturus exists to help, that you aren't alone. We can help prepare you for life as a supernatural. We have been doing so for others like you since before you were born."

"Arcturus?"

"It's the name of our organizations. Don't look them up. You won't find anything. My next recommendation is to keep a low profile. In all likelihood, there won't be eyes on you right now, but the more active you are with your fire, the easier you make it for them to find you. When you turn eighteen, you can make a decision about coming to join us here for a time."

My heart sank. Eighteen. More than a year away.

"We have much we can teach you—at least, I think we do. We don't work with many like you. We would be happy to have you as a guest before you turn eighteen, but you would need to be accompanied by a parent, and I presume that you are still in school?"

My mind was whirling. "I am."

A rush of possibilities ran through my head. I had to get my parents from complete ignorance to accompanying me on a flash trip to England. Curiosity about Arcturus was overwhelming, and I was beyond curious about Basil.

"You sound so reasonable."

"I assure you, many of my students think I'm not," he said brusquely. "But as I said, you are a minor. Why don't you have a discussion with your family. Take as much time as you need, then call me back when you're ready."

"Okay. Any recommendations on how to break the news to them?"

"Gently," he said.

My lips twisted. How helpful. "Where are you? London?"

"I am at present, for business. We have an office here. But Arcturus is actually headquartered in another location. One I'll share with you when we make arrangements for you to come visit for the first time."

"Is it far from London, then?" I pried.

"Later, Miss Cagney. In time," he said, not unkindly.

"Okay. Um. Thank you."

"You're welcome. The most important thing for you right now is to know that you're not alone. You can live a good life with the fire."

My heart warmed at his words. "That's good to know. I'll call you back soon."

"I'll be here. Goodbye, Miss Cagney."

I HADN'T YET PARKED my bike in the rack just down the street from Flagg's Café when my phone buzzed. I jammed the front tire between the metal bars and took out my phone.

Gage: *I'm here. What can I get you.*

Me: *Peach iced tea, thanks. I'm less than a block away.*

Air-conditioning cooled the sweat at my brow as I entered the old café. Flagg's was a favorite hangout for me and my friends. It almost seemed weird to be here without them. A hand flashed at me from the cluster of old couches at the back. I smiled at Gage and went to join him.

"Thanks," I said, plopping down across from him. "So thirsty."

"You're welcome." Gage smiled.

I took the iced tea and took a big slurp from the straw, the cold liquid soothing my throat. We smiled at each other awkwardly for a second.

"So, I'll start then," I said. "You a born and raised Saltfordite, like me?"

Gage laughed and shook his head. "Nope. I was born in Britain, but raised in Saltford." He opened his mouth to say more, when a buzzing sound came from his hip.

"Your pants are vibrating," I said, biting my straw and taking another sip.

"Sorry." Gage pulled out his phone and looked down at the screen. A deep line appeared between his brows.

"Everything okay?"

He sighed. "Sort of not, actually." He caught my eye. "You've been watching the news?"

"I catch it here and there. These fires are pretty weird."

He frowned. "They're more than weird." He lowered his voice. "That yacht she lit up in the harbor two nights ago, that was my family's boat."

I jerked upright in shock. "Whoa. Back up. *She*? You know who it is?"

He cocked his head from side to side. "I'm pretty sure."

"Have you gone to the police?"

He shook his head and raked a hand through his hair, mussing it. "No. My brother asked me to stay out of it."

"Your brother? I'm confused."

He scanned the café again. "This stays between us, right?"

"Of course." I was about to ask him why he was going to trust me because we'd only just met, but then he spoke again.

"She's my brother's ex. He broke it off with her about two weeks ago." He tilted his chin down and gave me a look filled with meaning. "She's not taking it very well."

"Why is he trying to protect her, then?"

"He's not, that's what I'm worried about."

"Okaaaaaay, that didn't really clear things up for me."

Gage took a deep breath. "Calista, my brother's ex. She's...not right. I suspected something was off about her when they first started dating. Short fuse, these weird crazy eyes." He gave me a wide-eyed look to show what he meant. "My brother said they just had a lot of passion, you know?"

My cheeks colored, my red-headed genes betraying my discomfort. "Sure, sure," I murmured, as though I knew what he was talking about. Passion, right.

"But when you've got crazy passion like that, you get the other side of it, too. And after he broke up with her, that's what he got." He raised his brows. "Her *other* side."

"But, fires?" I whispered. "She could hurt somebody. Don't you have an obligation to go to the police?"

"That's what I told him, but my brother..." Gage spread his palms against one another, long fingers splaying outward. "He's got his own ideas about how to stop her."

"I'm not gonna lie, this is sounding worse and worse the more you say."

He eyed me. "Haven't you ever been asked a favor from one of your brothers or one of your friends? A favor you thought was a bad idea, but you did it anyway because you love them?"

"Sure, but I don't think covering for my brother so he can run out and buy ice cream from the street-truck and eat it before dinner falls into the same category."

Gage snorted. "No," he agreed. He raked a hand through his hair again. "What should I do?"

I put down my iced tea. "Let me ask you this: how would you feel if the next time she lights a fire—"

"If it is her," he interjected.

"—someone dies?"

He paled. "I'd never forgive myself."

"Then, I think you've answered your own question," I said.

Gage's phone buzzed again and he looked down. He cursed under his breath and looked up at me. "I'm so sorry, Saxony. I have to go. It's my brother. Seems like the gods are against us hanging out or something." He got to his feet.

"I hope not," I said, looking up at him. "Go. Don't worry. Sounds like you've got a lot on your plate."

"Yeah." He tucked his phone away. "Can I call you later?"

"You'd better," I said. "Even if it's only to fill me in on how things turn out."

He gave a grim nod. "I will. Sorry again. Bye, Saxony."

I watched him rush from the café, his back tense. I pulled out my own phone while I sipped the rest of my iced tea. I tapped out a text to Targa.

Me: *Did the Bluejackets get called to the harbor for that burnt yacht?*

I finished my tea while I waited for her response. It wasn't until I was about to mount my bike and go back home when my phone chirped with a reply.

Targa: *What burnt yacht?*

Me: *Don't you watch the news?*

Targa: *Not since I got home. I've been busy.*

Me: *Someone's been lighting fires in Saltford. I thought maybe your mom might know something about it.*

Targa: *Did the yacht sink somewhere off the coast?*

Me: *No, it was in the harbor. Police must have pulled it up onto the beach. That's where it was when I saw it on the news.*

Targa: *The Bluejackets would only get called if there was an underwater wreck.*

Me: *Right. Just thought I'd ask. What's been keeping you so busy?*

Targa: *You wouldn't believe me if I told you.*

I smiled grimly. She wouldn't believe me if I'd told her what was going on in my life, either.

Me: *Try me.*

Targa: *How about I save it til the sleepover? I'd rather tell the story once. It's... involved.*

Me: *Such a tease.*

Targa: **smile**

I threw my leg over my bike, tucked my phone into my purse and pedaled for home. As trees and houses drifted past, my mind went back to my conversation with Basil. Around and around our conversation went, and his directive to tell my family about what I was. No matter which way I looked at it, a gentle way of breaking it to them wasn't coming to mind.

THAT EVENING, my family had finished dinner before I had screwed up enough courage to say anything. I hadn't eaten much and my napkin sat in shreds on my lap. Mom had just put a steaming casserole dish of strawberry-rhubarb crumble on the table when Dad said, "You're awful quiet this evening, Saxony. Everything okay?"

"You've also barely eaten anything," Mom said. "Honestly, Saxony. I'm concerned. Dr. Jacques says there's no cause for worry, but for the first time, I'm wondering if we need a second opinion." She sat and began to dish out the dessert. "Fellow might be losing his touch."

Jack's hostile eyes flashed to my face and back down to his plate.

"I feel fine. For the millionth time, I promise. But there is something that I have to tell you all." I cleared my throat. My stomach was nothing but a bundle of snapping nerves.

Jack's eyes darted back up to my face, brows raised expectantly.

I took a deep breath. "Something did happen to me in Venice."

"Oh no." Mom put her spoon down and immediately her brow furrowed.

"I'm all right, Mom. Just let me talk through this without interrupting me. When I'm finished, you can ask me all the questions you want, okay?"

Her mouth went into a flat line and she looked at my dad, who shared her apprehension. The two of them grasped hands.

I laughed. "I'm not pregnant, and I haven't developed any addictions."

Jack sat back and crossed his arms. "Both of those might actually be better than what is going on, though."

My parents' eyes flashed to Jack and then back to me.

"You know? *He knows*?" Mom said. "Why would you have told Jack and not us?"

RJ, who had said nothing so far, finally said, "The suspense is killing me, here. Can we please let the woman talk?"

"Thank you, RJ. And no." I shot Jack a glare. "Jack doesn't know; he's been misjudging me since I got home."

Jack snorted. "Here we go. And I thought we were going to get the truth."

"You are," I said, my face flushing with anger.

"Oh really?" Jack shot back, his voice rising.

"What is going on here?" Mom said.

"Saxony is the arsonist," Jack blurted, his hostile gaze not leaving mine.

I closed my eyes and slumped in my seat. So much for avoiding drama.

"What?!" Dad yelled, his horrified expression turning on me.

"No, I'm not," I said, slowly and deliberately. "I would never do that."

"Saxony," Mom whispered, eyes wide and frightened.

RJ leaned his elbows on the table and put his chin in his hands. His gaze moved around the table from face to face.

"Would you all just listen to me for a min—"

"To whatever lies you're about to tell?" Jack got up from the table, knocking over his chair. "I don't want dessert. Sorry, Mom."

Frustration finally boiled over. I stood up, thrust my hand out, palm up. A red flame flared up from my hand, illuminating everyone's faces.

"Sit down, *Jack*," I said, biting off the words.

Mom gasped and leaned back away from the fire, eyes wide, face white. Dad let out a few choice curse-words which I'd never before in my life heard him utter. RJ stared at the fire, body frozen. Jack stepped back, knocking over his chair. It was the fear in my family's faces that put the flame out, not my choice.

"I'm sorry," I said, immediately regretful. "I'm sorry, please." I put my hands out to Jack. "Please, sit down. Let me explain everything. I am not the arsonist." Each beloved face was staring and fearful. They were afraid. Of me. "Jack," I whispered, my eyes pleading. "Please sit down."

At first, he didn't move. But slowly, he picked up his chair and sat down.

"I beg you to let me get through this. And I'm sorry that I've butchered the job so far," I began, sitting down. I took a drink of water, hoping to snub the headache threatening in my temples. "It all began when I met Isaia..."

No one said a thing as I told the story. I didn't leave anything out, not even the forced burning, or my debt to Enzo. I had to give away Elda's secret affair, but under the circumstances I felt it had to be included or the whole story wouldn't make any sense. I concluded with my call to Basil Chaplin and his school for mages.

“Mr. Chaplin said that I could live a good life with the fire, and that Arcturus was there to help," I finished.

My voice was even more hoarse than usual. I stopped talking for the first time in nearly an hour. The looks of shock, fear, concern, and incredulity on my family’s faces had only grown. I cleared my throat and downed the rest of the water in my glass. My hands trembled so I put the glass down.

"Please, say something," I said, looking at my parents.

My mom put her face in her hands, her elbows on the table.

Dad put an arm around her. His face was completely white around his mouth. Mom gave a sob, and her shoulders heaved.

"Mom?" I put a hand on her shoulder. My own eyes filled with tears. I hated to see my mother cry.

She sat up, face anguished. She wrapped an arm around my shoulders and pulled me into her, kissing my hair. "My poor baby," she said. "We could have lost you."

Dad wrapped his arms around my mother and me. I inhaled her lilac scent, tears rolling down my own cheeks, but now with relief. They believed me. My story was unbelievable, really. But when someone produces a flame from their hand in front of your face, what choice do you have but to believe what they say?

The sound of chair legs scraping against the floor made me open my eyes and I caught RJ getting up from the table and coming around to join the huddle. He wrapped his arms around my dad, and his big warm hand fell on my arm and squeezed it. I peeked out to find Jack, but I couldn't see him through the tangle of arms around me. The tears flowed freely then, but from pure gratitude for my amazing, loving family. We stayed huddled like that until the only sounds were hiccups and sniffs. Then everyone broke and found their seats again.

That was when I realized Jack was gone. I frowned at his empty seat, heart pounding. What had he thought? Why had he just gotten up and left without saying anything?

Mom grabbed a tissue box from the counter and put it on the table. She blew her nose and wiped her face. "That certainly explains your fever," she said through the tissue.

"And her voice," said Dad.

"I wouldn't have believed it if you hadn't already shown us," said RJ, shaking his head. "I mean, who knew? Fire magi?"

"Where did Jack go?" I asked. Surely, he didn't still think I was the arsonist.

"He's just in shock," said Dad. "Give him time."

"Aren't we all," added Mom. "Why didn't you tell us about this when it happened, Saxony?" She turned hurt eyes on me and they raked my heart.

"I didn't know how to," I explained. "And I knew you'd make me come home right away, and I didn't want to."

"Of course we would have!" she cried. "I can't believe you weren't honest with us."

"I was trying to protect you," I said.

"It's *our* job to protect *you*," said Dad, his face hard. The color had returned to his cheeks but there was an angry slash between his brows that hadn't been there before. "We need to talk with Elda about this."

"Why? It wasn't her fault! It's not even Isaia's fault—he's just a little kid." After a long pause, where nobody else spoke, I whispered, "I think I was supposed to get the fire."

My parents stopped talking and both stared at me. The reality of what I had just admitted sank in, and I grew still inside.

"It's my destiny," I said.

Fresh tears trickled down Mom's face and she brushed them away. "Your destiny? Saxony, you were sabotaged. A normal life was stolen from you."

"Aren't you overreacting a bit?" RJ said. "I mean, she's a miracle. She can make fire. She's like a superhero or something."

"Actually, I think I'm more like an elemental," I said.

"Right," he said, and his eyebrows shot up. He nodded and gave me a fist-bump. "That makes way more sense, actually."

Mom skewered my brother with a look. "RJ, could you leave us alone to talk with your sister?"

RJ shrugged his heavy shoulders and got up. "It's rad you didn't die, Sax."

I smiled at my goofy, kind brother. "Thanks, RJ."

"Talk later," he said as he left the kitchen.

"So, this Mr. Chaplin," Dad began.

"Yeah." I turned back to my parents. This was the point of the conversation and the whole reason I had chosen to tell them. The goal was to get to Arcturus as soon as possible.

"What is it he's going to teach you?"

"Don't be ridiculous, James," my mother interrupted. "We're not going to send our daughter to England to go to fire school. We're going to consult a specialist and find a way to cure her of this."

"What?" I cried. "You have to let me go to England! There is no way to get rid of it, trust me. I already looked into it. I'm not going to learn how to be a proper mage anywhere else. And besides—" I snapped my mouth shut. I hadn't yet told them everything Basil had said.

"Besides, what?" Mom narrowed her eyes.

I took a breath. No point in leaving anything out now. "He said that there are organizations who look to recruit people like me. Supernaturals. The way Dante wanted to."

Her eyes went so wide, I could see the whites of them. "Recruit them to do what?" She grabbed Dad's hand and they both squeezed so hard their knuckles turned white.

"I don't know, jobs that only someone with fire can do, I guess. Same reason Enzo had hired Nicodemo." My voice trailed off.

"You want a job as a fire thug for a corporation?" Mom looked horrified.

"No, of course not. I didn't say that." I twisted my hair, nervously. "Mr. Chaplin said that sometimes these corporations are not the most ethical..."

"They would blackmail you?" My mom's voice had gone up an octave and my dad was looking ill. This was a lot for a couple of Saltford parents.

I spread my hands. "I don't know exactly, but maybe, yes. At Arcturus, I can learn how to protect myself from these corporations, stay off their radar."

My mom flashed terrified eyes at my dad. "How did this happen?" She ran both hands through the hair at her temples and pulled it back from her brow in frustration. "I feel like I've gone insane. James!"

"It's all right," my dad said. His expression said it was anything but. One of the things that cut me deeply was his look of helplessness. My dad was always in control. Always. But right now, that control had slipped and he didn't know what this meant for his daughter, for his family.

"We should never have let you go to Venice," Mom said. She covered her face. Through her fingers, she said, "We're the worst parents in the world."

"No, Mom." I let out a sound of frustration. "None of this had anything to do with you. I'm glad you let me go. Maybe I wasn't when I was burning up in that cell..."

"Oh, God," she moaned. She slid her chair back and put her head between her knees.

"But I'm glad now," I added hastily. "I feel more like me than I ever have."

Mom sat up, hair frazzled, face red. She put a hand out. "I need some time. Saxony, would you mind giving your dad and me some privacy?" She held up a piece of shredded tissue to her nose and a clump of it broke off and fell into her lap.

"But—"

"It's a lot to take in, Saxony," Dad said softly. "It's all right. We're not angry. Thank you for telling us. Your mom and I just need to talk, and I think we all need a good night's rest to gain some perspective. We'll discuss this again tomorrow."

I looked from one stressed out, anxious expression to another and nodded. "Okay. But please, just consider the benefits that Arcturus could offer me. I need it. I—"

Mom put a hand on my arm. "Tomorrow, Saxony. I can barely think." Her eyes misted up and she grabbed another tissue.

I sighed, resigned. "Tomorrow." I got up and was halfway through the kitchen when the sound of chair legs scraping against the floor made me turn around. My mom's arms swallowed me up in a bear hug and she squeezed me so hard the breath wheezed right out of me.

"I love you, Saxony," she whispered.

"I love you too, Mom." I squeezed her back.

TWENTY-FIVE

Dinner the next evening began as a tense, quiet affair. Jack's seat was noticeably empty.

"Where's Jack?" I asked as I poured a round of waters for my parents, RJ and me. "I haven't seen him all day."

He hadn't answered any of my texts either, but I left that part out.

Mom and Dad shared a look. "He went to Zack's for the evening."

I frowned. "Does he still think I'm the arsonist? Even after I explained everything?"

"Give him time," said RJ before shoveling a forkful of mashed potato into his mouth. "Dude's freaked out."

My mom looked pale and drawn, and it seemed as though the lines on the sides of my father's mouth were deeper. My heart ached for them and a twang of guilt went through me. They sure hadn't asked for this, but neither had I. And it wasn't like I had contracted cancer or some other horrible disease. There were families dealing with much worse things than we were.

As we were cleaning up our dessert dishes, Dad finally spoke. "RJ, would you let your mom and me have a bit of time with Saxony, please?"

"You got it, Pops," said RJ, giving a nod and an enigmatic close-mouthed smile.

"Take your plate, please," my mom added.

RJ took his dish and even grabbed the leftover food from the table. Then he came back for the rest of the dishes.

My mom mouthed, "Wow," at my dad. It was normally agony for either of my brothers to have to clean up after a meal, but here RJ was doing it without being asked. It was a testament that he realized how stressed my parents were and how serious the situation was. I smiled my appreciation at him. As RJ disappeared into the basement, my dad threaded his fingers and rubbed his palms together. This gesture was classic James Cagney preparing himself for a difficult conversation.

"We were up all night, Saxony," he began. "Your mother and I."

"I'm sorry," I said.

"It's all right. This isn't your fault," he replied. "But we spent hours researching online and we couldn't find anything about your condition. Nothing that wasn't part of gaming or fantasy stories, anyway." His mouth turned down. "It seems that pyrokinesis has never been proven to be a real thing, but you"—he scratched his head absently—"can easily prove that it is. Unless that flame you made in your palm was some sleight-of-hand you perfected while you were away in order to play some kind of joke on us." He looked at me hopefully. "We won't be angry if it was—just be honest."

"It's not a joke, Dad."

I wanted to explain that what I had wasn't as simple as pyrokinesis either, the fire inside me seemed at times to be its own entity. At least, it had in Venice before I'd been trapped in a cell with no water. After that, it felt more like a part of me and not a potential enemy.

He nodded and cleared his throat. "No, I suspected not. We were just hoping. Anyway, your mom and I would like to arrange a conference call with this Basil fellow over in England. Seems he might be our only source of information."

My heart gave a thud of hope. This was heading in the right direction.

"Okay." I took out my phone. "Want me to call him right now?"

"It's ten-thirty in the evening in England right now, sweetheart," Mom said.

"Maybe it's best we get this over with," Dad said at the same time. My parents looked at each other. "This is what he does," Dad said to Mom, softly. He looked at me. "It's worth a try. If he doesn't answer, we'll try again tomorrow."

I nodded and hit dial on my phone and put it to my ear. The long dash of an international call sounded once and the phone clicked.

"Miss Cagney?" It was Basil.

"That was quick. Did I wake you?"

"Not at all. I'm pleased that you called back so soon. Have you spoken with your family?" His voice was hopeful, expectant.

"I have, and actually I have both of my parents here with me. We're hoping you have time to speak with us. Is that possible?" I smiled at my parents, hoping I looked reassuring. A lot was riding on this conversation.

"Yes, yes!" His voice perked up even more. "I would welcome the opportunity."

"Okay, I'm going to put you on speaker phone." I gave my parents a thumbs up.

A complicated look flashed between my parents: anxious, concerned, hopeful.

I pressed the speakerphone button and said, "Okay, you are live, sir." I put the phone down in the middle of the table.

No one said anything.

After a prolonged pause, Basil's voice came from the phone. "Hello?"

My dad cleared his throat. "Mr. Chaplin? It's James Cagney. Saxony's father."

"Yes, Basil Chaplin here. Pleased to meet you."

"Thanks. My wife, Annette, and I are both here and..." Dad took Mom's hand. "We're not doing very well with what we've learned about our daughter."

My heart sank.

"Understandable," said Basil.

"Saxony has told us a little bit about what you do, but not very much. And I guess—" Dad paused.

"You'd like to know more about how I can help your daughter," offered Basil.

"Yes, exactly."

"And you, Mrs. Cagney? How are you doing?"

My parents shared a look of appreciative surprise that he'd asked after my mom specifically. It was like he'd been through this before or something. The butterflies in my stomach began to settle. Basil's voice emitted confidence and empathy. It felt like we were dealing with a professional.

"To be honest, I'm upset and I'm frightened," came my mom's response. "And I'd like to know if there is a way to cure my daughter of whatever this is." She took a breath as she reached over and squeezed my shoulder. I kept my face carefully neutral. I had already explained that there was no cure, but if I didn't have enough credibility in her eyes, maybe Basil would.

"Mr. and Mrs. Cagney," said Basil, not unkindly, "I understand you're in shock and you're upset. That is all perfectly understandable. I am here to help, and I believe the best way I can do that is by not mincing words. As far as we are aware, there are only two ways for the fire inside your daughter to go out." I could almost picture him holding up a finger as he spoke. "When she dies." I pictured a second finger joining the first and I knew exactly what words would accompany it. "Or it can be passed on to another individual if she is dying. That's it. Other than those two events, neither of which are desirable, there is no cure."

After several long seconds, my father answered. "That's what our daughter told us."

"She's correct."

"So, what's next then?" asked Mom. Her voice was heavy. Defeated. Her eyes had misted up and the corners of her mouth turned down. My heart gave a painful ache at the look on her face.

"This is where I come in. Before I explain any more though, I'd like to see Saxony light a small flame. It's the final step before I'll talk about Arcturus any further."

My parents both looked at me. I picked up the phone and switched on the video. A clean-shaven face in black spectacles appeared. Basil was an attractive older gentleman, with a wide mouth bracketed by deep smile lines.

"Hello, Mr. Chaplin." I smiled into the camera.

Basil nodded and smiled back. "Hello, Saxony." He gave a nod and his wave of brown hair flopped elegantly onto his forehead. "Go ahead, please."

I lifted my hand in front of the camera so my fingers were visible, and pushed a small flame out the tip of my finger.

"Thank you," said Basil. "Good enough. You can turn off the video if you like."

"No, please." Mom got up and grabbed a mug from the cupboard. "Leave it on. I'd rather see your face."

"If you prefer." Basil smiled.

I felt that same feeling of a bond forming as I looked at his face. I had felt it when I'd first seen his name printed in foil on the business card, again when I had spoken to him for the first time, and I felt it growing now just talking with him. I propped the phone against the mug and set it in front of my parents. Mom and Dad slid their chairs closer together and I pulled mine next to Mom's. The three of us huddled our faces close so that Basil could see all of us.

"Oh, that's lovely," said Basil. "It's nice to see all of you." He took off his glasses and they disappeared from the screen while he cleaned them. "I founded Arcturus in 1991. I had the means and the property to fortify a kind of private school, a safe place." He put his glasses back on and pushed them up the bridge of his nose. "The objective of the school has always been to train mages for the kind of life a supernatural can face."

"Do you have the fire?" Mom asked.

Basil nodded. "I do. I was born with it."

"What kind of life does a supernatural face?" asked Dad.

"That's up to the individual, but what's important is that they are aware of their options and can make an educated decision. They need coping strategies, and camouflaging techniques to protect their identities. I know you have a lot of questions," said Basil. "My suggestion and preference is that you visit me here at your earliest convenience. You could see the kind of environment I've set up here for young people like Saxony. We can discuss Saxony's future at length and I would better be able to assess your daughter."

My parents shared a look. My heart began to pound in earnest and I shot Basil a grateful smile. He couldn't have said things any more perfectly to put my parents at ease. The more he talked, the more I wanted this. I folded my hands in my lap and deliberately tried to keep my body and face calm, but inside I was thrumming with excitement.

"Consider yourself formally invited," added Basil.

"I have another two weeks until school starts," I said to my parents. Every cell in my body was now vibrating with hope.

My mother shushed me and put an arm around my shoulders. "This is all very sudden, Mr. Chaplin," she said to Basil. "We'll take the school year to think things through. When Saxony graduates, maybe—"

The school year? My heart dropped like a stone and I stared at my mom in horror.

"Annette," my dad said gently. I gave my dad the most pleading look I had ever given him in my life. My father turned to the phone. "We'll discuss things and call you back, if that's all right?"

"Of course," said Basil. "Anytime, day or night. People like Saxony are why I exist. I'm here for her, and for you."

"Thank you for everything," said my dad.

"Yes, thanks, Mr. Chaplin," I added.

"You're welcome."

I pressed the button to end the call and closed my eyes so my mom wouldn't receive the glare I wanted to shoot at her. I knew her. We'd had enough clashes where I had let my temper fly at her. It had never turned out in my favor.

"Mom," I began, my voice trembling with emotion. "Please don't make me wait a whole year." I opened my eyes and looked at her. "I need to go. I have never wanted anything more than I have wanted this. Do you remember how much I wanted to go to Italy?"

My mom took my hand, her lips parted.

"Italy was nothing compared to this. Mr. Chaplin is the only person in the world who can help me. Can't you see that?"

My dad spoke up. "I have vacation days I haven't used up, I could take her tomorrow and be back by—" he paused to think.

I perked up with excitement. This would be perfect.

"Mom," I put a hand on her shoulder. "If you want to keep me safe, send me to Arcturus. Otherwise, I have no idea what I'm up against."

"Or what we're dealing with as a family," added my father, putting a hand on her other shoulder.

Mom's mouth was a flat line. She looked at my father. "You'd better get on the flights. They'll be very expensive at the last minute."

I wanted to leap up from the table and dance around the kitchen. My dad and I shared a look of relief. My heart pounded with excitement and my tummy was full of tremors.

"I'll call Basil and let him know," I said. "How many days?"

"I'd better take no more than two," said my dad. He got up and grabbed his laptop case from where it was propped against the island.

I grabbed my phone and got up from the table as my dad sat down and booted up his laptop. I redialed Basil's number with trembling fingers and waited.

"That was quick," answered Basil.

"We're coming. My dad and I." I couldn't have wiped the grin off my face if someone had paid me.

"Excellent!" He sounded almost as enthusiastic as I felt.

"Two days is okay?" I asked.

"Plenty. Book your tickets for Gatwick. I'll have a car pick you up. My valet's name is Pete."

"Okay." I turned and made a wow face at my parents, who were both watching me. "I'll text you our landing time then?"

"Perfect. I'll wait on you."

"Thanks, Mr. Chaplin."

"Not at all."

I hung up the phone. "He'll have a car pick us up." My whole body felt wired with energy. Sleep would be impossible tonight. "Just have to tell him when we land."

My parents glanced at each other.

"That's awfully nice of him," said my father. He turned to his laptop and pulled his glasses out of his pocket. He tilted his head back and peered at the screen through his lenses. "Looks like there's a flight tomorrow night," he added, scrolling with his ergonomic mouse.

I couldn't help the sound of joy that squeaked out of me as I bounced in place.

Mom skewered me with a stern look. "Don't get too excited, Saxony. This is just a fact-finding mission. We're not leaving you there."

"I know," I said.

"Then you'd better go pack."

"Yes, ma'am." I bolted from the kitchen and took the stairs two at a time up to my room to do just that.

TWENTY-SIX

Dad and I had barely rolled our carry-on luggage out through the one-way sliding doors at Gatwick and into arrivals, when I spotted a portly man in a black suit holding up an iPad with 'Cagney Family' on the screen.

"You must be Pete," I said with a grin as we rolled up to him.

"Yes, miss," he said, smiling. His face was soft and jowly, and he reminded me of a St. Bernard dog. "How was your flight?"

"I slept the whole way because I didn't sleep a wink the night before we left," I said, shaking his hand. "This is my dad, James Cagney." I stepped aside and Pete shook hands with him.

"Pleased to meet you," Pete said. His accent was thicker than Basil's. "Have other luggage, do you?"

"No, this is it," said Dad. "We packed light."

"Excellent, excellent. I'll take this, miss," Pete said as he reached for my carry-on. "Anyone need anything before we take-off?

Toilet's that way. Coffee, water, and nibbles that other way." He pointed in the two directions. "What's your pleasure?"

We said we were ready to go.

"Very well," he said. "This way to the car then."

The humidity in the air reminded me of Italy, but the temperature was cooler. I pulled my cardigan close around me and closed the tie at the waist, more for looks than any feeling of being cold.

"I didn't think I'd be back in Europe so soon," I said to my father.

He gave me a tense nod. "Or for such a strange reason."

"Yeah." I gave him my most reassuring smile. "Thank you, Dad."

He wrapped an arm around my shoulders and kissed my temple as we walked through the parking lot.

The car Pete led us to was a larger version of a black London cab; longer and more luxurious, but with the same curves and glossy black paint. Pete chattered away as he loaded our luggage into the 'boot' and held the back door open. Dad and I piled into the roomy back seat. There was enough legroom for a Great Dane to lie down in front of our feet and still not rub up against the back seat. The seats were cushy black leather and there was a tinted window between the front seat and the back. Pete got into the driver's side. The car shook and growled like a diesel as he turned the engine over. The glass between the back seat and the front slid back.

Pete said, "We're little more than an hour to the manor, just knock on the glass if you need anything. Remember that we drive on the other side of the road here in jolly ol' England, so don't be alarmed. I've been driving nigh on forty years. You're in good hands."

"Thank you, Pete," I said, fiddling with the seatbelt.

"Not at all." The glass slid closed.

The car made its way out of Gatwick airport parking and we soon found ourselves on a narrow freeway and in the middle of fast moving traffic. As Pete drove us through various round-abouts and turns I began to notice a consistent destination listed on the signage.

"I think we might be headed to Dover," I said. "It's been on all the signs every time we've taken a turn."

My dad peered out the window. "As in the White Cliffs of? Always wanted to see those."

Soon the road became less busy and the scenery much prettier. Everything was green and lush but the sky was overcast with thick gray clouds. For the first time, we passed an exit pointing to Dover without taking it, and the road became a single-lane road. Trees arched over from one side and a stone fence lined the other. I could see the ocean in the distance. We took another turn toward the water, trees closed in as we began to descend. Pete downshifted and the car slowed as the downhill became steep, and forested land closed in on both sides. The road traversed the hillside and Pete guided the car around the steep switchback and headed back the other way. We passed three more switchbacks before the ground leveled off. Around the last bend, we pulled up in front of a gate which was already sliding open. There were no identifying signs to tell us where we were.

"Saxony, look," said Dad.

"I am," I said, in a voice just as awed as his.

The whole property was closed in by a tall stone wall laced with ivy. The driveway was a large circle, the center of which was bursting with rose bushes. A tiered water feature in the center towered high above the blossoms and water cascaded into to a pond where the lazy shadows of koi were drifting. The car pulled up in front of an old stone manor. This time, I did spot a plaque to the right of the door reading *Chaplin Manor, Est 1814*. The place even shared Basil's last name. The car came to a halt in front of the wide double doors and we spilled out into the humid sea air. I could hear seagulls screaming in the distance and waves crashing onto shore.

"Welcome to Chaplin Manor," said Pete as he got out and opened the boot. The car was still running as he took out our baggage.

Our eyes roamed the steep roof, stained glass windows, and castle-like turrets. The front door opened and Basil stepped out into the overcast light. He was finely dressed in a suit jacket and bow-tie. He had a cane in one hand but I was pretty sure he didn't need it. He stood straight, wide shoulders back and spine erect. His brown hair was perfectly coiffed and sprinkled with gray above the ears. I thought he was quite handsome for an older gentleman.

"You must be Mr. Chaplin," Dad said, holding out his hand. “Thank you for having us on such short notice.”

Basil gave a nod as they shook hands. "My pleasure, Mr. Cagney."

Our host turned to me. The moment our eyes met, I had a strange feeling rock through me. It was as though we were already connected by some invisible tether. It was difficult to describe. I had bonds with my parents, of course; no one could replace them in my heart. But Basil was different. This man was a mage, just like me, and that made us family. I could feel it.

"Saxony," he said, looking down into my face, searching my eyes. He held out his hand and I took it.

As if the link I had felt only moments ago wasn't enough, the heat that shot up my arm from his hand gripping mine was startling. It zinged like a live wire straight into my heart. It felt like our hands had become molten metal and were now welded together. My brows shot up with surprise at the unexpected sensation.

"It's a mage bond," he murmured. "Try not to be alarmed by it."

I opened my mouth but no words came out. As he released my hand, my arm continued to throb. It wasn't unpleasant, just unexpected and distinct. I looked down at my palm, but it appeared normal.

"Saxony?" I looked up at my father's voice. He and Basil were already on the doorstep, ready to head inside. Dad raised his eyebrows. "Are you coming?"

I grabbed my carry-on and took it up the steps. "Sorry. Yep."

We stepped into the house and Basil closed the door behind us. The foyer was large and carpeted, with multiple arched doorways leading off in different directions. A huge empty fireplace with soot darkening the chimney stood off to the right. The ceiling went up and up, showing another three floors of balconied halls above us.

"It's eerily quiet these days," said Basil. "I'm sorry about that. My students are on summer break. It's a good time for you to visit, though."

Dad and I gaped in wonderment.

"So," Basil continued. He stepped back from us and spread his hands, his cane dangling from his right fingers. "Welcome to Arcturus Academy."

BASIL SHOWED us the main floor, which included three large sitting rooms full of comfy furniture and decorated with very English-looking wallpaper and paintings. He said they were common rooms and could be used anytime by anyone. Two of the rooms had sprawling windows facing out into a large back yard and the ocean was visible just beyond the green space. He showed us the kitchens and dining room, a library that smelled musty, and pointed out the direction of his office. He led us out into a courtyard. Across the flagstones stood another building, which looked much newer than the rest of the manor.

"This building is fire-proof," said Basil, "for obvious reasons." He unlocked the big metal door with a key he took from inside his coat. "This is where we do our practical classes and coaching."

We stepped into one of the strangest spaces I had ever been in. The air was cool, the ceiling was high, and there were a lot of metallic surfaces, strange looking instruments, and a couple of closed off rooms with black-tinted glass windows.

"Everything done in here has to do directly with our fire-power; utilizing it, controlling it, perfecting and honing skills," explained Basil. "Not all students are interested in learning these things."

"Why is that?" My dad's eyes jumped from oddity to oddity; the metal beams, the glittering black floor, the contraptions with digital screens and panels.

"Being a fire mage hurts, as Saxony will know." Basil nodded at me.

"Yes, I told them," I said. "But I don't have any pain anymore."

"I imagine it ceased not long after your burning?" Basil asked.

I nodded.

Basil faced my father. "As a supernatural, your daughter would have been unusual had she not passed through a burning. But now that she has, well..." A look passed over his face that I couldn't define. "She is exceedingly rare."

"Have any of your other students done it?" my father asked, putting his hands in his pockets like he was tempted to touch things.

"Heavens no!" cried Basil. "We actively discourage it. It's far too dangerous. It is better to learn to manage the pain than to risk a burning." He turned away and walked through the space. We followed him. "As I was saying, once my students pass the first-level exam, many of them quit the practical training. They don't have any interest in utilizing the fire, only in being able to live with it."

Looking around at the training space, I could admit it freely to myself: I was fascinated. What *could* I learn to do with the fire? Basil had said I was extremely rare, so wouldn't I be doing myself a disservice if I didn't at least try and see what I was capable of? The idea of training with Basil made my heart speed up. "What kinds of things do you teach in the first-level?"

"I'm glad you asked." Basil stopped beside what looked like a big square, flat panel covered in vinyl. There was a strange digital meter attached to it. "With your father's permission, I would like to put you through a few basic tests. It would help us have a clearer picture of where you're at." He looked from me to my dad. "Knowing this would help me make a recommendation for Saxony; how long she might expect to be here and such."

Dad said, "Makes sense. It's okay by me."

Basil reached into his breast pocket and pulled out a folded sheet of paper. "I'll need you to sign this form. And then I'll have to ask you to watch from there." He pointed up to a metal room that looked like it had been bolted to the ceiling. It was completely encased in glass and could only be reached by a long metal staircase along the wall. "It's just a precaution," Basil added. "We are overzealous with safety here."

"That's appreciated," Dad said, taking the paper from Basil and opening it. He skimmed it, took the pen Basil offered, and bent to sign it against the low metal railing.

"Thank you," said Basil, taking the page and tucking it inside his coat. "I'll file it when we're done here. If you wouldn't mind?" He nodded up at the high room.

Dad climbed the stairs, his footsteps sending out a metallic echo. He entered the small glass room and closed the door. He appeared at the glass, watching.

I turned to Basil. "Can he hear us?"

"Yes," he answered. "There's a speaker that picks up what's going on down on floor level." He took off his jacket and tucked it into a metal drawer. "Would you like a drink of water before we begin?"

"Please." My stomach unleashed a horde of dragonflies. This was it. I was going to be tested by someone who could actually tell me something about myself.

Basil took a metal cup from a stack on a nearby shelf and poured me some water from a dispenser. I drank every last drop and handed it back to him. I took off my cardigan and he tucked it into the same drawer as his jacket. We faced each other and I was reminded once again of the bond between him and me. He was relaxed, so I relaxed.

"Do you mind if I ask you a few questions first?" Basil leaned against the desk and worked on rolling up his shirtsleeves.

"Ask away."

"During your burning, do you have any idea how many hours you went without water?"

I frowned, trying to remember. "I'm not sure. I was unconscious for some of it." My eyes flicked to the cage. Hearing the details might upset my dad.

"More than eight hours?"

"I would think more than twelve," I answered.

Something crossed Basil's face. A shadow of emotion. Surprise? Horror? I wasn't sure.

"And what did you experience after you'd had water, I mean within the next day or so. Emotionally speaking." He finished with his shirt sleeves and crossed his arms.

I hesitated as a realization struck. "You've been through this, haven't you?"

"I have," he said. "I had to. I wouldn't be able to run Arcturus if I hadn't."

I felt a dart of shock. Basil had endured a burning just so he could start this school? He must have been very driven to make it happen.

"I felt harder," I said, truthfully. "Stronger, I guess. Emotionally speaking." I thought about how I'd felt toward Federica and her betrayal. "Not without forgiveness, but..." I paused. Basil waited, not prompting me with suggestions. "I think my judgement got a bit harsher, but it's weird."

"Why weird?"

"Because my temper is actually easier to control now. I used to be more of a hothead."

Basil's eyebrows flicked at this. "Interesting. And your body, how did that change?"

"On the outside, only my mark changed," I answered. "On the inside, I couldn't tell you if I changed physically but I definitely felt different. Almost like, uh—" Self-consciousness washed over me. It sounded so dumb.

"Go on." His voice was gentle.

"Volcanic rock," I finished, feeling lame.

He didn't seem surprised at that. "If it doesn't make you uncomfortable, could I see your mark?"

"Sure," I answered, toeing off my left shoe. I peeled off my sock and rolled my foot inward so the mark on the middle toe was visible.

Basil knelt down. He took my toe in his fingers and turned it gently. The mark was buried in between my middle toe and fourth toe. It was shaped like a tiny fireball, no larger than a mole, and black as pitch. I couldn't see Basil's face as he inspected it. When he stood, he looked pale.

"Could I see yours?" I asked, feeling a touch awkward.

In answer, Basil pulled aside his collar. His mark was just under his collarbone. It looked almost identical to mine, so black that it looked like ink.

"I assume your mark changed color after your burning?" Basil asked. He really did seem more affected by the look of my mark than anything else so far, or maybe he'd just stood up too fast.

"Yes, it used to be brown. Like a freckle."

He nodded. His upper lip looked damp and he ran a hand over his mouth. "Do you mind if I take a photo of it?"

"I guess not," I said. "What for?"

I waited while he took out a cell phone and snapped a couple of close up pictures of my toe. "It will go into your student dossier," Basil said while he captured my mark. "Because you're so rare, you're of particular interest. Working with another mage like you will be a first for me." He stood up and shut off his phone. "There is very little formal scientific study of our kind. What there is, would be secret. I do my own but I'm not a scientist. I do it for my own knowledge and to have something valuable to pass on to the next generation. You would be of great help to me in that."

"Oh." I smiled but I wasn't sure what to say. I had come here for Basil to help me; it hadn't occurred to me that I could be of some help to him too. I liked the idea.

"Can you feel the fire right now?" he asked.

"No. If I didn't already know I was a magus, sorry, a mage, I wouldn't suspect anything. I feel normal."

"Can you light it for me, and look into my eyes as you do so. Don't try and affect how they look in any way."

"Okay." I lifted my gaze to his and he stepped closer. I called the fire to life in my belly and felt its heat lick up my insides at my request.

"Is it lit?" Basil asked, brows up.

"Yes."

"Remarkable," he murmured. "Can you illuminate your eyes for me please?"

I drew the heat upward through my neck and pushed it through the thin stems of my eyes. They grew hard and hot. My vision sharpened. The stubble of Basil's shadow became more pronounced.

"Can you make them orange instead of red?" Basil stared into my eyes, unblinking. He reminded me of my doctor, looking from pupil to pupil, probing at the secrets there.

I pushed more heat upward and outward.

"Now yellow?"

I pushed further. The heat in my eyes increased, but there was no pain. I had never made them this bright on purpose before.

My vision sharpened again, almost startling me with all the distinct edges and contrasts that I hadn't noticed until now. I had thought Basil's eyes were a brown, but now I could distinguish flecks of olive in them. I could make out paler threads of rust around his left pupil. His pupils took on a strange cast, like there was a glow of dark red far inside them.

"Are you able to make them blue?" he asked.

I cranked up the heat. A low frequency vibration began in my core and radiated outward. The little muscles around my spine quivered and my brain felt like it was pulsing softly. Then something very strange happened. Basil's face looked for a moment like it had become translucent. I thought I could detect the vertical shadows where the roots of his teeth were, the dark hollows of his orbital cavities. His skull seemed to waver in and out of detection, like a faulty x-ray.

"All right?" he asked. "If anything feels bad, you can stop at any time."

I pressed my lips closed and the shadows of Basil's skin faded to opacity, and his skull disappeared. I wasn't sure I had even seen it. Maybe I had imagined it?

"I'm fine," I said, and held the heat in my eyes steady.

"May I touch your hands?"

I held them out and Basil took them and held my fingers gently. His eyes closed for a moment as though he was thinking, the shadow of a line appeared between his brows. He was properly sweating now; a sheen of moisture beaded on his brow and upper lip.

"That's enough," he said softly, letting my hands go. "Thank you."

I loosened the heat from my skull and it slipped quietly back down my spine and went to sleep. My insides cooled instantly, and I once again felt like a normal teenage girl and not a walking furnace.

Basil studied my face. "How was that? Did you notice anything particular about your vision?"

I hesitated.

"Be honest, please—it's the only way I can do you any service, Saxony."

"I thought for a second that I could see the bones in your face."

Basil nodded like this was normal, but his shirt was growing dark at the armpits. "Anything else?"

"Just that my vision got sharper the hotter my eyes got."

He nodded again. "All right." He leaned back against the desk behind him and took a handkerchief out of his breast pocket. He wiped his brow with it and stuffed it back, making a crumpled lump in his shirt. He crossed his arms. "Have you ever felt the fire detonate in your joints before?"

My mind flashed back to Dante beating me up in the back yard of his villa. I frowned. "Yes."

"Do you remember if light came through your skin?"

"I didn't let it. You're talking about internalizing and externalizing."

"You know about it?" He looked surprised. "How?"

I nodded. "Uh, well, did Enzo tell you where I got my fire from?"

"He mentioned that it was passed to you from a dying boy. Is that right?"

"Yes, but that boy's father recorded some video clips before he died, and I got to see them. He talked about controlling the eye-glow thing, and also how a magus can detonate the fire in their joints to make them stronger."

"Have you experimented with that?"

"Not really. I can internalize, I guess. But I've only been a mage for a little over a month." I laughed. "I'm still getting used to the idea."

Basil smiled. "Are you willing to throw a few punches for me?"

I shot him a side-eye. "Did you just ask me to hit you? Like some frat boy at a house party?"

He laughed. "Not me." He jerked his chin toward the contraption with the padded panel behind me. "The bag."

"Oh." I turned to face the bag and laughed, relieved. "Sure."

Basil bent down beside the machine and flicked a switch at the back. The digital panel beside the punching bag flashed with multiple glowing zeros. He came to stand in front of me. "Make a fist for me."

I curled my right hand.

"Put your thumb here," he said, moving my digit off my first knuckle. "And hit with your first two knuckles right here." He tapped a finger on my knuckles. "Keep your wrist straight and try not to send your fist in an arch. Come straight at the stuffing from the shoulder, okay? Keep the bones in your first two knuckles aligned with your forearm so you don't hurt yourself."

"Okay." I nodded. "With the fire?"

"Without for the first throw." He stepped back. "Whenever you're ready."

I brought my fists up, went onto my toes and bounced for a second, then threw a punch with everything I had, but without using the fire.

The digital screen flashed the number 45.

"What does that mean? Is that good?"

"It's expected for a girl of your age, weight, fitness level and inexperience," Basil answered. "The number is in psi, pounds per square inch. Your fist is roughly four inches square so you've delivered a peak punching force of 180 pounds. It's average for a woman." He reset the digital screen. "This machine is accurate within half a pound, so it's not perfect. However, it's good enough for our purpose." He turned to face me. "I'd like you to try it with the fire, but I won't coach you. And then we'll try it a second time, and I'll give you some tips."

"All right." The fire flared up inside me, ready to accommodate.

Basil stepped back. "Give it your best shot."

I bounced on the balls of my feet and then sent another shot at the bag, at the same time the fire went off in my right shoulder, elbow and wrist.

The digital screen flashed again. The number read 382.5.

"Whoa!" My hand flew to my mouth and I glanced at Basil in shock. "That's a crazy difference!"

Basil blew out a breath. It was the first time he'd given any kind of obvious emotional reaction. He ran a hand over his mouth and chin. "That was 1,530 pounds of punching force." He lowered his chin and looked over his glasses at me. "You just broke the world record by 110lbs."

My jaw dropped. I looked up at my dad. He looked dazed and somewhat amused.

I let out a guffaw of surprise. "I'm a freaking Marine!"

Basil gave a bemused, lopsided grin, but the sides of his mouth were tight. "I'm not sure a Marine would know what to do with you. Let's try it again and this time I'll coach you."

Basil explained how to place my feet and how to use my whole body to throw a punch. He explained how he wanted me to use the fire in almost every joint in my body. "The explosions need to be microseconds apart," he explained as he was crouched down beside me. "Do you understand? To follow the flow of energy. If you mix up the detonations and fire one moment sooner than you should, you'll dampen your efforts instead of optimizing them." He lowered his voice, and his forehead wrinkled with concern. "You could even hurt yourself and we don't want that. Do I need to worry about you externalizing accidentally?"

I shook my head. "I internalize without even thinking about it now. I've just never tried to make so many detonations at once before."

"You don't have to do this. It's your choice."

"I want to." I narrowed my eyes at the soft surface of the bag, preparing.

Basil stepped back. "Anytime, Saxony."

I went through the motion in my mind first, and the fire flickered in response to my mental dress rehearsal. I felt heat flare up in my joints in reaction to my mind. When I threw the punch, it seemed time slowed down. I could feel the heat as it traveled through my body, hitting every joint involved and going off like successive bombs inside me. The square surface of the punching bag, which was more like a vertical platform with a metal arm bracing it, made a strange sound upon impact, almost like a drum. The digital meter beeped and the number appeared.

Basil and I stared at the meter.

"That can't be right," I said, looking at him finally. "Can that be right?"

Basil sort of drooped back against the desk. "It's right," he said quietly. "You just produced more than four tons of force. 8,900 pounds, give or take."

I looked back at the reading. *2243psi*. My whole body was tingling, but the fire had gone quiet. My punching hand throbbed a little and my heart was pounding, but otherwise I felt normal.

"Have you done this test?" I asked.

Basil's mouth quirked and a bit of color returned to his cheeks. "Want to know if you can out-punch your superior?"

I grinned. "Can I?"

He blinked and put a hand to his heart. "A bloke has to have some secrets."

I laughed. "Fair enough. What else can we do?" My blood was up and I liked this game. I looked around the room at the other contraptions and curiosities, wondering what they were all for.

"That's quite enough," said Basil, taking off his glasses and rubbing his eyes. He looked up at my dad and gestured for him to come down. "I'll show you to your rooms and give you some time to freshen up. We'll talk more over lunch."

TWENTY-SEVEN

Basil showed us up the grand staircase from the foyer to two rooms across the hall from each other. The rooms weren't unlike a hotel, each with an ensuite bathroom and a writing desk stocked with paper and pens. He told us he would have lunch ready at one and to take a rest and meet him in the dining room. Once he'd left us, my dad and I faced each other in the hallway.

"How did that feel?" my dad asked.

"The tests?" I opened the door to my room and rolled my carry-on inside and then came back to join my dad in the hall. "It was good actually. I mean—" I laughed. "A bit weird, I guess, to be tested on my power, or whatever you want to call it. But it was amazing to meet another person like me. I could learn so much from him." I looked up at my father. "Can you understand why I need to come to this school?"

He nodded. "What do you think of Basil?"

"I like him," I said truthfully.

My dad sighed. "I do, too."

We made our way down for lunch together. A single table among many in the dining room had been dressed for a meal. Basil stood near one of the tall windows talking quietly with a woman in an apron. She had dark glossy hair swept up into a high bun on her head. She was petite but strong looking, with square hands. Her skin was olive but lightly freckled. They looked up and smiled as we entered.

"I hope you're hungry." Basil gestured to the lady beside him. "This is Susan Palmer, our resident chef during the school year. She was kind enough to come take care of us on short notice." He turned to Susan. "This is James Cagney and his daughter, Saxony.'

Hands were shaken all around.

"Nice to meet you," said Susan. She grasped my hand firmly and when we shook, she deliberately looked me in the eye. The subtlest telltale glow reflected in her pupils.

My calves swept with gooseflesh as heat shot up my arm. "You're a mage, too!"

Susan laughed. "I am."

"But, you're the cook here?" My father sounded surprised.

"Yes. Food has always been my passion."

"Susan teaches an elective here called *Food and Fire*," said Basil, rocking back on his heels. "It was her idea, and a jolly good one at that."

Susan smiled up at him. At the glance that passed between the two of them, I had immediate suspicions that Basil and Susan might be more to each other than just colleagues.

"I hope you join us, Saxony," said Susan. "Right now, enjoy the meal. I'll leave you to it." With a nod, she left the room through a swinging door.

We sat down and Basil lifted the silver lids from the food. The scents of steamed trout, braised vegetables and mushroom risotto made my mouth water. A thought occurred to me as we began to fill our plates. "Did Susan use her fire to cook this food?"

Basil chuckled. "She could have, but no. She doesn't do that anymore, except when she teaches. She's a second-degree mage."

"Is that a popular class?" my dad asked, looking skeptical. "Cooking?"

Basil shook his head. "Not very, but the ones who take it seem to enjoy it." He bent to take a bite of risotto.

But my mind caught on something else. "You have degrees?"

I took a bite of the trout and it melted in my mouth. My stomach gurgled and I realized then how hungry I was. I followed the trout with a forkful of broccolini.

"We do, but it's an internal thing. It helps Arcturus to classify the mages who pass through our school. White wine?" Basil put a hand on the neck of a bottle in a bucket of ice and poured white wine for himself and my dad.

"Tell me more about these degrees?" I asked.

"We have five classifications. Simply—first, second, and third-degree mages are those who have not passed through a burning. The first is untrained, the second has some training, and the third has mastered some kind of specialty."

"What's the difference between fourth and fifth?" I asked.

Basil put the wine back in its ice-bath. "Fourth-degrees have passed through a burning and so have the benefits of heightened power. The fifth is the highest classification we have, reserved for mages who have passed through a burning and are trained." Basil cleared his throat. "I should make it clear that at Arcturus, we don't talk about anything above the third degree with our students."

"Why not?" asked my father.

"We don't want to encourage mages to attempt burnings, so it's not something we want to glorify." At a questioning look from my dad, he added, "Too many mages die that way."

I glanced at my father but he appeared stoic. I was grateful, not for the first time in the day, that my mother hadn't come with us.

"So, how would Saxony fit in at Arcturus then?" my dad asked, looking confused. "If you don't talk about anything over third-degree, and she's been through a burning..."

"Saxony would be a special case," said Basil.

"Wait." My dad sat back in his chair. "How many students have you trained that have passed through a burning?"

"None," said Basil simply, picking up his wine glass. He took a sip and set it down. "Saxony would be the first student ever at Arcturus to be at this level."

"You're a fifth-degree?" my father guessed.

"That's right," Basil replied. "But please remember that this classification is something I had to give myself. There's no third-party who does this, that I know of. I don't mean to sound arrogant, but I am the most powerful mage I know." He shrugged. "There may be other mages out there who are more powerful than I am; in fact, I would bet on it. But where Saxony is concerned, there is no one better to coach your daughter than myself, and other staff members I have here who are both third-degree."

"So, Saxony is higher than your instructors, according to the way you rate them," Dad observed. "How would they be able to train her, then?"

"They have some specialties that they could teach Saxony, but for the most part," he looked at me, "I would train you personally."

My dad asked, "How will the other students feel about having her here?"

"It's hard to say, as I've never taken a student like Saxony. She would require one-on-one coaching, so she wouldn't be in so many classes with other students." Basil frowned. "It might require some sensitivity but I'm confident we can make Saxony and the other students comfortable in spite of the gap between them. They may even look up to Saxony, see her has a prodigy to respect."

I wasn't sure if Basil believed these words, and my tummy did a little flip at the idea of being with a bunch of other mages my age. It followed with a tumble at the thought of leaving my friends behind for my last year of high school. I frowned. It was a steep price to pay, but maybe I could go home for Christmas.

"How many students do you have?" I asked.

"I'm afraid I won't say for now. Confidentiality." He gave me an apologetic look. "But you'll meet them all if you join us."

Dad's back straightened. "I thought you didn't take minors. Are we talking about this year, or next year?"

"Ah, yes." Basil set his fork down, then patted his mouth with his napkin. "That brings me to my proposition. I have never taken anyone under eighteen before, but Saxony is such an exception that I would be willing to bend the rules. Mr. Cagney, I sincerely believe that Arcturus Academy is the right place for your daughter at this point in her life. I realize she is young, but she seems very mature for her age, and I can tell you that as a mage"—he leaned forward with a look of emphasis—"she is exceptional."

My dad's spine straightened a little. Warmth filled me upon seeing this, as I recognized it as pride in me.

Basil continued, "If you are willing, and you agree with me that the sooner she gets her mage education the better, I would like to invite her to join Arcturus this year. I would not charge any tuition, only living expenses. Consider it a 'full-ride' as they say in North America." He held up a hand. "You don't need to decide right this minute. Take your time to think about it. Please also take into consideration that I have tutors on staff who will follow any syllabus you require, so that Saxony can finish her high school credits without interruption."

A torrent of conflicting emotions and observations went through me. One was the sinking in of the very real possibility that I would have to say goodbye to my friends before I was quite ready to. The other was the feeling that I should have the right to make this decision for myself, in spite of being legally underage. What did the law know about my state? Did governments even know that supernaturals like me existed? I had no idea, but I most certainly felt that this particular legal restriction shouldn't apply to me. If we couldn't convince my mom to let me go, then she and I would go head to head, and that might make for a permanent rift. I deeply hoped that that wouldn't be the outcome here, but I was braced for it.

"There is something else you should consider," Basil added.

"What's that?" Dad leaned forward on one elbow.

"Saxony may prove to be so advanced that she learns everything I can teach her in a matter of half a year. Who knows. This commitment doesn't have to be years long."

"Do you have any documentation about what you plan to teach my daughter?" Dad asked. "Any certifications you have, that say you can do what you're doing?"

Basil was unruffled. "I would be happy to give you course descriptions, though they'll seem awfully strange to you, I'm sure. As for accreditation, well, we are a top-secret branch of SIS."

"British intelligence." Dad ran a hand over his mouth. "You answer to MI6?"

Basil shook his head. "We don't answer to them, but they know about Arcturus. The only reason they don't try to dismantle my program is because they like to recruit from among our students, and they are unqualified to do what I do." He frowned. "We have a tenuous relationship that has held for years."

My dad was quiet for a while. "Do you have children, Mr. Chaplin?" he asked finally.

"Not anymore," Basil said.

My dad blinked and sat back, his mouth grim.

"I had a daughter," Basil went on. "Dara. I started Arcturus for lots of reasons, but Dara is chief among them." He spoke without self-pity, and my admiration for him went up another couple of notches. "She would be twenty-seven today had she survived," he added. "The fire took her when she was seven. And I couldn't do the only thing that would have saved her."

"I'm so sorry," said my father. "What would have saved her?"

"Having her pass on the fire to someone else near the moment of death. Anyway." Basil put up his hands to signal he didn't want to say more. "I do understand what it's like to have a child with the fire, better than you think. I'll respect any decision you make." He put his hands flat on the table on either side of his plate. "Perhaps it's time to let you rest and I know you might wish to call Mrs. Cagney. It's been a long journey and this has been quite a paradigm shift for you. I do have some business to attend to this afternoon. Please feel free to roam the grounds, explore the manor as you wish. Sleep. Talk. Make a list of questions. Do whatever you like." He smiled reassuringly at both of us. "We can meet again for supper."

AFTER LUNCH, my dad and I went upstairs.

"Are you going to call Mom?" I asked at the top of the stairs. "What do you think?"

"What do *you* think, Saxony? Are you ready for this?"

"More than ready," I said.

"What about leaving the girls behind? Your friends? You won't know anyone here."

"It will suck to say goodbye," I answered, truthfully. "But this is too important to pass up. Don't you think?"

He nodded. "I do."

"What do you think Mom is going to say?"

He put a hand on my shoulder. "Leave your mother to me."

I let out a long, pent-up breath, and went into my room. I lay on my bed for a time, tossing and turning. I finally got up and made my way downstairs and out into the back yard.

There were multiple dirt paths crisscrossing the hilly property and leading down to the ocean. Listening to the waves in the distance and the gulls crying out soothed me. If I closed my eyes, I could almost pretend I was home. I followed a trail all the way down to the rocky shoreline and stood where the grasses met the pebbly shore. In the distance, I could make out a line on the horizon. I squinted at it, but it was mostly lost in cloud. I called on my fire to sharpen my vision, the way I had earlier, and as my eyes grew hot, the land across the water came into better focus.

"That's France," said a voice.

I turned to see Susan, Basil's chef, approaching from along the grass line.

"Yeah?"

"Yes, a port town called Calais." She came to stand near me. "This is the narrowest part of the English Channel and on a clear day, the French can see the White Cliffs of Dover. It was a particularly welcoming sight during the war. The soldiers coming home from Dunkirk wrote songs about seeing those cliffs and knowing they were almost home."

The wind blew the hair off my shoulders. It smelled of salt. "What makes them white?"

"They're made of chalk," she said. "It's sort of amazing that they haven't all crumbled into the sea by now. Every once in a while, a piece breaks off, so I guess it's only a matter of time. Are you going to see them while you're here?"

“Dad is going to ask Pete if he can take us by the cliffs on our way back to the airport. We're so close that it would be silly not to," I said. "Have you lived here your whole life?"

"Ha!" She shook her head. "I grew up in London. The Whitechapel area. I was on a downward spiral when I met Basil. Not sure what I would have done without that man. I probably wouldn't be alive."

She tucked a stray lock of hair behind her ear and looked out to sea. I noticed a network of scars on the side of her neck that I hadn’t seen the first time I met her.

I was screwing up the courage to ask her what had happened and if she was in a relationship with Basil, when she asked, "What was it like?"

The question was so soft, almost lost on the wind. But I knew exactly what she was asking about. My forced burning.

"It's okay if you don't want to talk about it," she added when my answer didn't come right away.

"No, that's okay," I said. "I'm not sensitive about it. It was awful. Truly, truly awful. I wouldn't wish that pain on my worst enemy." The wind blew my own thick curls into my face and I pulled them to the side and held them there. "It's the only time in my life I wished for death. Imagine being a roast pig, cooking for a full day, but without dying."

She looked appropriately horrified, but she also narrowed her eyes a little, like she wasn't sure she believed me fully. "Was it worth it?"

I hesitated again. I began to get a sense of what a slippery slope this could be. If I said yes, it might encourage Susan to attempt her own burning. I also sensed how an unburned mage might suspect that the burned ones would be motivated to keep the truth hidden, to give themselves a leg up, make themselves more powerful. There was no way this type of difference wouldn't cause some kind of divide between mages. Truthfully, it had been worth it because I no longer had to deal with the pain on a daily basis, but it was only worth it now that it was over.

"No," I said, finally. "I'll just say that if I had to do it over again, knowing what I know now, I would never choose it. The everyday pain wasn't so bad that I couldn't live with it."

"Hmmm," she said, and shoved her hands into the pockets of her jeans.

Feeling like I hadn't convinced her, and suddenly nervous that Basil might hear about this conversation, I added, "If I had gone into the burning knowingly, aware of the change that would occur, and there had been water nearby, I would not have cared. I would have drunk the water to stop the agony. I don't think there is a person on earth who could withstand that kind of torture willingly."

"Well, of course not," she huffed. "That's why mages get themselves locked up, so that they can't thwart the process. They would just have to start it all over again."

"There's more to it than that. From what I understand, there is only a tiny window of time to give water. A few minutes this or that side of it and you'll fail."

She nodded. "Yes. Basil says the window can be less than fifteen minutes."

"He's told you a lot about this?"

She gave a humorless laugh. "Not because he wanted to, but because I asked. It's natural for a mage to need to know more about it. It's one of the hardest parts of his job; educating the mages who come here and discouraging them from wanting to take their skills to the next level. Arcturus is the strangest academy you'll ever come across."

We fell silent and stood there in the wind for a time, watching the waves.

"Don't waste it, Saxony," Susan said abruptly.

"What do you mean?"

"I mean that you survived for a reason. Basil says that the percentage of mages who survive a burning is less than two." She turned her shoulders square to me, took her hands out of her pockets and crossed her arms. "Basil is the best man I know, mage or no mage, and he's offering to give you his personal time to make you the best you can be. If you say no to that, you're an idiot. He's never done that for anyone before. He's a busy man." She looked down at her feet. "I kind of can't believe he's even offering you this. Just"—she brushed away the hair blowing in her face—"don't throw it away."

I frowned. "I don't intend to, Susan."

She nodded once, then walked back up the bluff and around the corner of the manor, disappearing from my sight. On my own way back up to the manor, my phone rang. I pulled it out of my pocket and saw Jack's name on the screen.

"Jack?" I answered, breathless. "Is it really you? I thought you might have run away and joined the circus or something, just to avoid me."

"Ha ha," Jack said. "It's me."

"You sound normal," I answered, head perking up. "Like you don't think I'm the devil anymore." I walked up over the sandy bank and onto the grass behind the manor.

There was an audible sigh. "I owe you an apology."

"Excusez-moi?" My heart felt instantly lighter.

"I'm sorry. I was wrong about you."

"You don't think I'm the arsonist anymore?"

"I know you're not."

"How do you know?"

"Because there was another fire last night."

I stopped walking. "No. Where?"

"You know that little antique shop down on the corner of Pepper and 7th?"

"Radar Antiques? It's been there since before we were born."

"Yeah, that one. Radar. It was burned to the ground last night. Police are saying it's the same arsonist as the playground and the yacht."

My mind immediately went to Gage. Was this Calista, his brother's ex, at work? Why would she burn the antique shop? "Was anyone hurt?"

"The house behind the shop, across the alley. Their roof caught fire, but the fire department managed to put it out before the damage got too bad. It's fixable. The little old lady who lives there went to the hospital for smoke inhalation, but no one was seriously hurt."

I frowned. "It's only a matter of time, though."

"Yeah," he agreed. "Seems like whoever is doing it is lighting bigger and bigger stuff. How long before they burn down a house with people inside?" I heard him breathing into the mouthpiece and it sounded like wind. "Is there..."

I waited but when he didn't continue, I said, "What, Jack?"

"Something we could do about it?"

"*We*?" I had already been considering whether I should involve myself, against what I knew would be Basil's directive. "You mean me? Because I'm a fire mage?"

"Yeah. I guess."

"Maybe." I closed my eyes. Was I really thinking of taking this situation into my own hands? I knew what Basil would say. I knew what my parents would say, and I knew what the police would say. But what did my conscience say? "I don't know, Jack. But thanks for telling me about it. Dad and I will be home soon."

"Okay. Sorry again, Saxony. I was wrong."

I smiled. "Thanks. Let's just put it behind us."

"Sounds good to me. See you tomorrow."

I hung up the phone and looked at it, chewing my lip. I pounded out a text to Gage.

Me: *Are you connected with Radar Antiques?*

Several seconds later, my phone rang.

"Hey," I answered.

"Yes," came Gage's voice. It was rough. Stressed. "Radar was my mom's business, and my grandfather's before her. That store was in our family for forty years."

"I'm so sorry, Gage." I squeezed my eyes shut. Gage's family had lost their livelihood. I could only hope the store wasn't their only source of income. "Was this her? Calista?"

"I think so." His voice trembled with anger.

"Have you talked to the police?"

"We had to. They've been asking us questions all day. My dad is livid. He's got a temper at the best of times but I've never seen him like this. And my brother..." He cleared his throat. "He had to tell them about Calista, but as soon as he was finished making his statement, he left. Just vanished. He hasn't been answering my calls." His voice went soft. "I know what he's doing."

"What's he doing?"

"He wants to catch her before they do."

"And do what?" But the gooseflesh was already rising on my body.

"I don't know." His words whooshed out on a breath. "But it won't be good. It's not good."

"Do you have any idea where she is?"

"None. Wherever she is, she'll be hiding where there aren't a lot of people. She's got to know the police are on to her now. Along with Ryan, my brother."

"I'm so sorry, Gage. Please let me know if there is anything I can do." I could lay it out there that I was prepared to help, but Gage didn't know that fire was in my wheelhouse. The more I thought about it, the more I felt that it might be my responsibility to do something. But what?

"Thanks, Saxony. I'll look forward to hanging out with you when all this blows over," he said.

"Yeah." But if I got my way, I wouldn't be in Saltford much longer. Gage was just another cute guy who would pass through my life like a summer breeze through an open window. "Your family—are you going to be okay?"

"Yeah, we'll pick up the pieces. Mom had a huge insurance policy on the store, because it was full of expensive stuff. She's a scrapper. She's already scoping for real estate and planning buying trips."

I smiled. "That's good. It'll give her something to focus on. In the meantime, let the police do their job. They're bound to catch Calista."

He chuckled but his words were bitter. "If my brother doesn't catch her first and do something stupid."

TWENTY-EIGHT

The exhaustion of two international flights within three days caught up to me in the van on the way home. I fell asleep in the back seat within minutes of pulling out of the airport parking lot. Once we reached the house, it was all I could do to drag myself up to my room and collapse on my bed. But the downside of falling into bed before dinnertime was waking up bright-eyed and bushy-tailed at four in the morning.

I opened my eyes in a dark room, on top of my covers and still wearing my clothes. I rolled off my bed, stood up, and stretched. My room was stuffy and hot. I went to open my window, tripping over my suitcase. I cranked the metal handle on my window and the hinges creaked as it opened. The smell of smoke came in on the breeze and I inhaled more deeply, growing alarmed. The sky was dark. There was no sign of flickering light anywhere, but there was definitely fire somewhere outside. I took another sniff. It didn't have the scent of burning leaves or bonfire; it had the more acrid and rank smell of burning garbage.

I grabbed my phone and stuffed it in my shirt pocket. Taking an elastic from my bedside table, I raked my hair up into a ponytail as I padded silently down the stairs. The house was quiet, everyone asleep. I went into the kitchen to look out the large picture window. The back yard and beyond were also in darkness. I went to the foyer and jammed my feet in my sneakers, then went out onto the porch.

The night air was alternately sweet and humid, then stinking of smoke as the wind shifted. I scanned the street as I went down our front walk to the sidewalk. There was still no sign of light or life anywhere—all the houses were dark. *Where there is smoke, there's fire. So where's the fire?*

I wandered down the sidewalk. There was no moon in the sky, and the only light came from the streetlamps along our street, illuminating circles of pavement, grass and parked cars. I passed the narrow alley that led to the park, and beyond that, a large patch of forest where the old MacLeitch farmhouse stood. That's when I finally caught the sight of flickering light. It was faint, and a smudge of smoke above it blocked out some of the stars. I chewed my lip, weighing my options. Finally, I began to jog down the alleyway. I passed through the park and into the bush.

The smell of smoke grew stronger. I took out my phone and dialed 911. When the voice on the other end of the phone asked what my emergency was, I said, "One of the abandoned buildings in Swallowtail Park is on fire."

"Is there anyone inside the building?" asked the woman on the other end.

"I don't know, but I doubt it," I said. "Those buildings have been boarded up for years."

"Where are you?"

"I'm in the park. I woke to the smell of smoke. I live in the suburb of Swallowtail."

"Are you anywhere near the building?"

"No, but I can see that it's burning from the light and the smoke."

"Okay, good." She took my name and phone number and told me to go home, and that the police and fire department were on their way.

I ended the call and stood on the path leading toward the old MacLeitch farmhouse, hesitating. What was my responsibility here? Did I have any at all? I was a fire elemental, so what did that mean when I was faced with an actual fire?

I was standing there deliberating when I heard the high sound of female laughter. Or was it crying? My ears perked. It was coming from the same direction as the farmhouse. Was there someone in the building after all? My feet moved of their own accord, down the path and toward the rear of the old farmhouse. The fire was in full view now, licking up through the gaping windows of the top floor. That strange keening sound came again and my hair stood on end all over my scalp. I had never heard a sound like it.

My heart throbbed as I approached the back yard of the house. An old, falling-down wooden fence half wrapped itself around the yard. I stepped over the rails lying in the undergrowth. Long stalks of grass brushed against my shins.

I stopped when I heard the sound again. This time I thought for sure it was not laughter. Someone was crying, and it was coming through the windows, from inside the house. My mouth went dry as powder at the thought of someone inside. How had they even gotten in there?

The boards covering one of the upper windows caught fire, and the crying sound stopped.

I ran toward the house and skidded to a halt just outside the back deck. I looked down at myself. If I went inside, my clothing would almost definitely go up in flames, and then what? The fire department would catch an un-singed, naked redhead scampering away from a no-longer burning building? Perhaps dragging a person out of the building? For a breath, I felt completely paralyzed. What to do? There *was* someone inside. I was the only person here. I was a fire mage. Time was running out. Was this fire also lit by Calista? Was that her voice?

I glanced around, my nerves screaming at me to *do something!* I stopped thinking and just moved. It felt like I would imagine bungee jumping might feel; at a certain point, you have to stop deliberating and jump. I stripped off my clothes and stuffed them under a bush.

I called my inner fire to life. The familiar liquid heat rolled up and down my spine, promising power. My mage thoughts concluded that the best way to walk into a burning building naked was to become part of the fire, so I lifted my right hand and ignited a blue ball of flame, then allowed it to dwindle and become red. My eyes trailed up my forearm and the flames followed my vision, up to the crook of my elbow and beyond. When the fire hit my shoulder, I closed my eyes. With a sound like hot dry wind, I ignited my entire frame. I became a human torch, blazing with flames shooting skyward from the top of my head and shoulders. Pulling off the boards covering the back door of the house, I stepped through the gap, scanning for signs of life.

The heat that greeted me inside was intense. The air was full of cinders as dirty flames licked up the doorposts, across the lintels, and along floorboards. Furniture blazed in smaller bonfires, crackling and snapping. Though the heat around me would have cooked another human, yet it was nothing compared to the heat inside me. It was a new feeling, to have every inch of my flesh, every limb ignited. My fire crackled happily and seemed to want to elevate itself, become even hotter. I held it steady, my abdominal walls trembling slightly.

I crossed what used to be the living room and entered the kitchen, peering around. An exposed beam dropped partially from the ceiling with a loud creak. When I passed from the kitchen to the front foyer of the house, I saw her. The sound of sirens in the distance barely penetrated my consciousness as I stared at the woman.

She was kneeling just inside the open front door. Her hair was so short that it looked like it had been shorn only a few weeks earlier. Her palms were up and her head was tilted back, and she was looking up the stairs at the flames that could be seen through the stairwell, licking along the spindles. She was sweating and her eyes were glassy and wide.

I was so shocked by the sight of her that I froze at the end of the hall. I received a double dose of shock when my eyes zoned in on the mage tattoo on the soft part of her shoulder. It was obviously not real; it was too big and too stylized to be a real mage mark. Where had she come across the symbol of my kind?

The flames of my own body made a fiery wall of heat in front of my vision as I stared at the kneeling woman who had to be

Calista. The strangest sight came through to me. Overlaid against her face and head was black and white fuzzy static, like the snow on an old TV that wasn't working. I took a step back and squeezed my eyes shut, but when I opened them, the static was still there.

That strange keening sound came from her throat and jolted me back to life. We both had to get out of here.

"Hey! Calista!" I walked toward her, half forgetting that I was a flaming apparition. "You have to get out of here! What are you doing?"

Her strange eyes fell from the upper floor to me, and widened. Her mouth opened in a huge O and her hands flew to the sides of her face. The static overlaying her head hadn't gone away. It was then that I saw the can of fuel and the lighter on the floorboards beside her.

Despite her shock at seeing me, she wasn't moving, wasn't getting up.

"Please, get up," I said.

When she didn't respond, I closed the gap between us and reached for her, dousing my fire from my hands and arms.

“Calista,” my voice sounded strange even to me, breathy, and hissing on the ‘s.’

At the sound of my voice saying her name and the sight of fleshy arms reaching from a flaming body, Calista screamed and jerked to her feet. Then she stumbled backward through the open farmhouse door, screaming all the while.

The lights of trucks and cars, sirens wailing and lights spinning, came flashing through the trees down the fire road that led through the park. Calista had fallen onto her back on the lawn and was propped up on her elbows, staring at me, terrified. My body was still ignited, and I couldn't even imagine what I must have looked like to her. A burning body? A walking inferno?

As the police and fire vehicles halted just beyond the trees in the front yard and the voices of people shouting commands reached my ears, I turned and bolted back through the house.

My rescue mission had gone in a very unexpected direction, but at least Calista was out of the house and safe. She'd clearly lit the fire, and there was nowhere for her to go.

I flew out the back door and made a mad dash for my clothes. I hadn't any fear about walking into a burning building, but the fear of the police or fire department catching me made my knees feel week. I put my flames out and yanked on my clothes, breathless and feeling more than a little ridiculous.

I WAS CRAWLING through the evergreen trees at the back of the overgrown yard, pulling my t-shirt down over my hips, when a voice surprised voice said: "What are you doing here?"

I stood up so fast that I smacked my head on a tree branch and a bunch of dry needles showered down on me. A shadowy figure materialized just past the post of the old fence. I narrowed my eyes and took a few steps closer, rubbing the top of my head.

He had his arms crossed over his chest and his short hair was combed back. He wore a black zip-up hoody with black jeans. I probably wouldn't have even seen him if he hadn't spoken, the way he was camouflaged in the shadows.

Something about his face was familiar. The wind blew the cloud cover away from the moon and its cool blue light helped bring his features into focus. My eyes widened. "Gage? What are you doing here? You scared the crap out of me!"

I walked closer to him, my heart pounding—not just from the startle but from the fact that I didn't know how much he'd seen.

He dropped his crossed arms and the gesture struck me as surprised. At first, he didn't answer.

I thought for a second that maybe I'd remembered his name wrong, but no, I hadn't. It was too unique a name to forget.

"Where did you meet my brother?" His voice seemed heavy with suspicion. Of what, I didn't know.

I blinked as the puzzle fell into place. "At the soccer game less than a week ago. You must be Ryan. Gage didn't mention that you were twins." I stopped a few paces away and observed him in the moonlight. His features really were identical to Gage's, but there was something a little bit different. In the poor light, I couldn't put my finger on what it was.

He frowned and his eyes flashed to the burning building behind us. "You're not the arsonist, so what were you doing inside that dump?" He jerked his chin toward the burning house. The flashing lights of the sirens and the sounds of firemen working could be heard on the other side. His eyes widened. "Did you see her?"

"Your ex, you mean?" I said. "Yes."

He gave a quick intake of breath and then bolted toward me. I had a mere moment to react when I realized he was heading for the house, and for Calista. I shot out an arm. My inner fire ignited inside my shoulder, elbow, and wrist, and I caught him across the chest, arresting his spring.

“What the—” Ryan snapped. “What are you doing?” He tried to tear away from me, but I locked my fingers around his wrist, my grip as firm as iron, my arm hot. His eyes found mine. Shocked. “Let go!”

“The police have already caught her, Ryan,” I said. “You hear those sirens?”

A frustrated frown crossed his face, making him ugly in the moonlight, but he relaxed.

I released him. "Get out of here before someone sees you and thinks you had something to do with this."

I started jogging down the narrow trail. Ryan fell into step behind me. My heart had slowed its thunderous pounding, but something about Ryan made me feel on edge. “I’m sorry for what she put your family through,” I said over my shoulder. “But it’s better to let the police handle it.”

Ryan didn’t answer, but I could hear his breath catch. In a hard voice, he asked, “What did my brother tell you?”

“Not much,” I replied. “Just that you broke up with her and she didn’t handle it well.”

"It's better for her that the police caught her," he said, his voice as cold as ice.

The hair on my forearms stood up as I caught his expression. We slowed to a walk.

"Why? What were you going to do with her?" I fought to keep my voice calm, but the desire to get away from this guy was mounting by the second. He gave off a completely different vibe from his twin.

He shrugged. "Doesn't matter now." He turned back and his cool eyes fell on me. "You still haven't said what you were doing in there." He slowed down his words and lowered his voice. "Without your clothes. And how did you...stop me like that?"

My mind skittered for an excuse until I realized that I didn't have to tell this guy anything. "It's none of your business," I said, coolly. "I'm going to head home. Have a nice night."

He put a hand on my shoulder and stopped me from walking, then he pulled me toward him.

"Take your hand off me," I said through clenched teeth, stepping back. The intent behind his touch reminded me so much of Dante that I shuddered. The idea of someone making my body do something I didn't want it to do just because he was bigger than me lit off anger inside me. I'd had my fill of forceful boys already in my life.

"Okay, okay, just chill," he said, holding his palms up. That's when I saw it. A mage mark, on the heel of his right hand where the skin of his palm met his wrist. It was a medium-brown, dark enough to see in the moonlight.

"You're a mage!" I blurted without thinking. "That's where Calista knows the symbol from." My heart had started pounding again. "She's not a mage, but you are, and you gave up your secret. That's why you were so intent on catching her before the police did. Is she going to give you away?"

His eyes went so big, I could see the whites of them. He took a step back and a flash of fear passed over his face. I watched him wrestle his shock under control.

He hissed, "How do you know what I am?"

I gave a sharp intake of breath, and my brain skittered over multiple things at once. Did I tell him I was one, too? How could there be another mage in Saltford? Basil had said we were rare, so what were the odds of there being two of us in the same town. No, wait...*three*?

"Does Gage have the fire, too?" I asked, rocked to my very core. Another thought crashed into my brain on the heels of the first few. "Are you students at Arcturus?"

His jaw dropped and when the shock of being identified hadn't even yet passed, he looked even more astonished. He raked a hand through his hair, messing up its neat lines. "I—how do you—"

"Your mark gave you away," I said, almost feeling sorry for him. His complexion had lightened a few shades, and in the moonlight, he looked nearly vampiric. I probably didn't look far from it myself. "Do we have to worry about Calista spilling all kinds of mage secrets to the police?"

He looked down at his wrist, and then back up at me. Understanding began to dawn, finally, passing over his features like a sunrise. He looked at me with an entirely new expression; respect, even delight.

"You're a mage," he said. He shook his head, staring at me, eyes wide.

"Keep up," I snapped. "Calista? Is she a danger?"

"No, all right? No," he barked back. "She won't spill. I wanted revenge more than anything." His voice softened and he shook his head. "I can't believe it. A fourth mage in Saltford," he crinkled up his face in disbelief. "This has to be some kind of a record."

"Four?" I said. "You know of two more?"

"We got it from our dad," he explained. "Actually five, right? One of your parents, also. Which parent did you get it from?"

"Neither," I said.

He cocked his head to the side, looking at me in disbelief. "You had to."

"No, I didn't. The fire was imposed on me." A chill wind blew over us just then, and as sure as I felt the hair lifting from my forehead, I felt a warning. I didn't want to tell Ryan my story. I couldn't explain why, but I shut my mouth and said nothing more.

"How is that possible?"

I turned away and began to walk toward home again. "It just is."

"Can I see your mark?" He began to follow me, then caught up and walked beside me.

"I'd rather not," I said. "It's late. I'm exhausted. You should go home."

"You saw mine. Turnabout is fair play," his voice took on a wheedling tone.

"I saw yours by accident, and I don't really care about what's fair," I replied, keeping my tone as neutral as I could manage it.

"What were you doing in that house? Were you trying to put out the fire? Because it takes a lot of skill to do that." His words took on a slightly holier than thou tone. "How old were you when you got the fire, then? I was born with it."

"Good for you." I kept walking, but as my street got closer, I realized that I didn't really want to lead Ryan to my home, so I crossed over my intersection and kept walking farther from home instead of closer. Now I had a different problem. Ryan showed no signs of leaving me alone.

"How do you know Basil?" he continued.

The more he pried, the less I wanted to answer his questions. I kept my mouth shut.

"So, you're the redhead that Gage was talking about," he said after I didn't answer. "Can't imagine what he saw in you. You're stuck up."

Before the summer, those words would have riled me up. I would have shot something hurtful and witty back at him. But thanks to my transformation, his words had no effect on me whatsoever.

"Good night, Ryan," I said, calmly.

"Come on," he said, his voice getting a notch louder. "It's the first time I've ever met a mage other than my dad and my brother, and you don't want to talk about it? What, are you some kind of hero? Some kind of lone wolf?" He sneered. "Fighting crime at night with your superpowers, thinking you're better than everyone else."

"Keep your voice down, we're in a suburb. People are trying to sleep." My voice was calm, but my brain was whirring. He'd become a yappy dog nipping at my heels, and he wasn't showing signs of losing interest. "When are you heading to Arcturus?" I asked, giving myself a bit of time to think.

"Next week," he answered. "Are *you* going to be there?"

"I'll be there," I said softly. "I guess we'll be schoolmates." I looked over at him with a warning in my expression. "You don't seem to know how important secrecy is to our kind."

"But not *between* our kind," he shot back. "Your story is going to come out, Saxony. If I don't hear it from you, I'll hear it from Basil."

I laughed. "No you won't. Student files are confidential. He'll never talk to you about me, just like he'd never talk to me about you."

He smirked at me, and for the first time in this encounter I wanted to slap it off his face. "Yes he will. Basil and my dad are old friends. He's my godfather."

That was interesting news, but I didn't give him the satisfaction of showing surprise. "Can you hear yourself? What is this, second grade? You basically just told me your godfather can't be trusted." I raised my eyebrows. "Is that what you're telling me?"

Ryan frowned and jammed his fists in his pockets like a petulant child.

"Didn't think so," I said. "Like I said, good night, Ryan. Go home."

He stayed in step, matching me stride for stride. "And if I don't?"

I stopped dead. He stopped, too. I turned to face him. He looked me in the eye and cocked an eyebrow as if to say 'what are you going to do about it?'

I gave him a little smile, lit the flame in my gut and let my eyes light up only briefly. "See you in Dover, Ryan." Then I bolted down the street.

"Hey!" he yelled behind me, and I heard him take off running.

It sounded as if he was sprinting with real effort, trying to match me. I let him think he was catching up and I heard him laugh, his breath coming faster now.

"That's so immature," he said. "Really? You're going to try to run away? You might as well just spill your secrets now. It would be easier than tiring yourself out. Or don't you know that boys can run faster than girls? I would have thought you learned that little lesson on the playground years ago."

That was my cue. I let the fire go off. Explosions of hot power went off in my joints in a natural sequence that I didn't even have to think about. Toe joints, ankles, knees, hips, shoulders, elbows. I accelerated so fast I felt the weight of my head on my neck as it resisted. My arms pumped and my legs moved like pistons, my strides became unnaturally long.

Ryan fell behind rapidly. I turned the corner up ahead and kept running. The blocks flew by in a blur and I turned again, falling out of sight of my pursuer.

I finally slowed to a walk when I arrived back at my block. I watched the end of the street ahead of me in case Ryan came back the way we'd gone, but there was no sign of him.

I smiled as I let myself into the house. So Gage had an identical twin. They might be identical on the outside, but Ryan seemed absolutely nothing like Gage on the inside.

TWENTY-NINE

Instead of going back to sleep, I took a shower to wash the smell of smoke off my body and mull over the events of the morning in my mind. The strange static I had seen in Calista's head while my body was lit, the fact that there were three more mages in Saltford alone. It all seemed too strange to be coincidental. After I got out of the shower and dressed and toweled off, I checked the clock on my bedside table. 5:26 a.m. I grabbed my phone and dialed Basil. It was after nine there.

"Saxony?" came the familiar voice I liked so much.

"Hi, Mr. Chaplin. Do you have a minute?"

"Certainly, Saxony. Everything okay? Did you have a good flight home?"

"Yes, the flight was fine. I've just had a strange night and I have a couple questions for you."

"Fire away." He paused. "Pun intended."

"Cheesy," I said with a smile.

"Just wait till I get going," he replied, his voice full of mirth. "What's on your mind?"

"I never told you that we've had some problems in Saltford with an arsonist," I began.

"Really? How curious."

"Yes. Not anymore, because she was caught tonight."

"Did you have anything to do with that?"

"Only a little," I lied. "But I did happen to get a look at her."

"Mm-hmm." He was starting to sound mildly apprehensive.

"I happened to be"—I took a breath, and my heart had begun its pounding again—"alight, when I saw her."

"Alight!" He sounded full-on alarmed, now. "All of you? Entirely?"

"Yes."

"Good heavens. Did she see you in this state?"

"Um, yes, but I'm not sure she'll remember me as human." More like a pair of hands reaching out from a flaming body.

I heard a sound like skin slapping on skin.

I asked, "Did you just do an actual face-palm?"

"Yes. Yes, I did." He sighed. "I don't even know quite what to say to this recklessness, Saxony. Why did you do that? We talked about keeping your identity a secret."

"She would never be able to pick me out of a lineup," I protested. "And there won't be any more property going up in flames because of her."

"That is not the point." He sounded ruffled. "How the blast am I supposed to help you if you don't—"

"Have you ever lit yourself fully on fire before?" I cut off his now very heavily accented rant. I guessed he sounded even more English when he was angry.

He paused. "Yes. I have."

"Did it change how you saw things?"

He paused again. "Why? What did you see?"

I launched into the description of Calista, the look on her face before she saw me, the strange glassy eyes, the ecstasy. And the strange static that overlaid her expression. "It was like the snow that a TV screen shows when it's not receiving a signal," I said. "Moving and flickering, just like that."

"And it was only in her head? You didn't see it anywhere else in her?" The chastisement had passed out of his voice. Now he sounded like someone taking a statement from a witness.

"No, just her head and face. What was it—do you know?"

"I have a suspicion," he said after a moment's thought. "Obviously, I didn't see it, but based on your description, I'd suggest you were seeing some kind of mania."

I frowned. "Mania? What do you mean?"

"I have reason to believe, although I haven't done any thorough experimentation with it, that when you ignite fully like that, it gives you a kind of vision. An understanding of what lies under the surface."

I thought of how I'd seen the bones in Basil's face when my eyes had been at their hottest. "Like x-ray?"

"Yes, like x-ray. But not of material particle. Instead, it reveals emotional and spiritual makeup."

I let those words sink in. "Um—"

"Let me see if I can explain better. Arson is a criminal act, yes?"

"Yes."

"It's a deliberate undertaking. To destroy property in that way for the purposes of looting or simple carnage takes a certain kind of immorality. If this girl you saw had that strange static over her heart, I might have suggested she was simply nefarious. A psychopath, even. But you didn't see it over her heart, you saw it in her mind. Pyromania is a compulsive behavior. Individuals who suffer from it fail time and time again to resist the urge to deliberately set fire to things."

"The result is the same. Loss of property, even life," I replied.

"Yes. I'm not excusing her behavior, simply pointing out the difference to you. It's just my best guess to explain what it is that you saw, based on my limited knowledge."

I thought about this. "So, she's a pyromaniac. She can't control herself. It's an illness."

"If I'm right," Basil answered, "yes."

"Why could I see it?"

He sighed. "I'm afraid I don't have all the answers, Saxony. We are supernaturals."

"Not everything we do can be explained," I added.

He surprised me by saying, "I disagree, actually. I think we can explain everything that we are capable of. Or rather, we *will* be able to when we have the right technology. We still have to operate within certain laws. We're just trying to figure out what those laws are because clearly, they aren't the same ones that apply to naturals. As far as I'm aware, no one has done the work yet, aside from Arcturus. And we've only just scratched the surface."

The line went silent for a short time. I asked, "Do you think the police will take her mania into account?"

"I have no idea, Saxony. I suppose if they have a therapist assess her, they will discover it, and it could have some bearing on her case."

"Is it curable?"

"Maybe. I've had occasion to study it a little. Given the nature of our own abilities, I thought it would be a good thing to know something about. Lighting fires induces euphoria in pyromaniacs, so I suppose it might not be dissimilar to breaking a drug addiction. Like any disorder, it will have a root cause, usually stemming from something in early childhood. A good therapist should be able to pinpoint that cause and prescribe treatment for it."

"Maybe I should write a letter," I mused.

"Excuse me?"

"Anonymously, to the police. Just to ask them to get her tested."

He was quiet for a moment. "I'm not sure that's a good idea, even anonymously."

"Why not? They'd never link it to me."

"Did anyone see you there?"

Crap. I closed my eyes. "Yes."

"Bloody hell, Saxony," he said, passionately. Then, "Sorry. But why didn't you mention that little fact sooner? It didn't strike you as important?"

"I was going to tell you, I just hadn't got that far yet." I took a quick breath. "You weren't able to tell me that the two new students you have joining Arcturus this year are from Saltford."

Silence. Then: "You've got to be joking."

"I'm not. Ryan saw me."

"What on earth was *he* doing there?" Basil's voice was full of frustration. I could only imagine what he was thinking about what kind of trouble all of us irresponsible teenagers were going to be when we arrived on his doorstep.

"He said you're his godfather."

"I am," he answered without any hesitation. "His father and I have a long history."

"And you're Gage's godfather too?"

"Gage was there also?" His voice was now laced with incredulity.

"No, he wasn't there. I met Gage at a soccer game before I ever talked to you for the first time. Pretty weird coincidence."

"I suppose the three of you have commiserated now," he said wryly.

"Actually, no. I haven't seen Gage since before I met you in England, and Ryan and I, well, we didn't exactly *commiserate.* Dude is kind of a jerk."

I expected a smackdown but what I got instead was, "Yes, I know. He takes after his father."

I spluttered a delighted laugh. "Just when I thought I couldn't like you any more—"

"Don't be obsequious," he said with a sniff. "I'm going to be your professor, and I don't play favorites."

I closed my mouth and pressed my lips together, still with a smile. I wasn't even sure what *obsequious* meant, but I could probably take a stab in the dark.

"Yes, sir." I didn't buy the favorites line, because I could *feel* Basil's affinity for me. But I wanted to show him respect. "Don't you think it's strange, though? That there are four mages in my small city alone?"

"Yes," he admitted. "Yes, it is strange. And I can guarantee you, it's not a coincidence. I no longer believe anything about the supernatural world is coincidental."

"Me, either," I said.

"But that's enough for now," Basil said. "You need to focus on getting yourself here and then on your studies."

"Yes sir," I said again.

"Have I at least helped to put your mind at rest about what you saw?"

"I think so," I said. "Thank you."

"You're welcome."

"Goodbye, Basil."

"Talk to you soon," he replied. "And Saxony?"

"Yeah?"

"Please, for the love of Pete, don't go around igniting yourself on fire or getting involved in petty crime. Don't write letters to the police, they can handle things. Please," he beseeched me. "Just, don't do things."

I couldn't help but smile. "I won't."

AN HOUR later found me drinking coffee at the breakfast table, looking out over the smoky cloud hanging over the old barn in the park. The sound of footsteps on the stair made me turn. Jack came into the room, his hair spiking up all over the place.

I smiled. “Morning, Jack.”

"Hey." He gave me a shy smile. His eyes widened as they fell on the spindle of smoke in the park. His lips parted in surprise.

“She's been caught,” I said. “There won't be any more fires lit in Saltford. At least, not from her.”

His brows shot up. “You helped? What did you do?”

“Long story,” I said. “I'll tell you later. Let's talk about you instead. This morning is the first time you've smiled at me since the day I got home from Venice.”

"Yeah." He wrapped his fingers around one wrist and twisted it, nervously. "Do you wanna go for a walk?”

"Absolutely," I said. I got up and put my coffee cup in the sink.

"So, I guess your trip to England was good." Jack said as we entered the foyer.

“Yeah, did Dad tell you anything about it? I’m sorry I didn’t see you, I fell into bed as soon as I got home.” I slid my feet into a pair of flats.

"That's fair," he murmured, bending to pull on a pair of sneakers.

Jack and I went out the front door and closed it behind us. Jack scuffed his shoes along the pavement. Birds chirped in nearby trees and a light breeze tugged at my hair. The soft light of dawn had graced the neighborhood and the street lamps were flickering off.

“So, what’s been going on with you?” I asked, softly.

Jack took a breath and jammed his hands into his pockets. "I didn't have anything nearly so crazy happen to me as you did over the summer, but I kind of had my own weird development."

I thought back to what Raf had said about his aunt. "You can sense things about other people?"

He laughed. "That's a mild way of putting it. All I can feel whenever I get within ten feet of you is fire, fire, fire. Super-hot, super bright, and noisy." He rocked his head side to side. "And I could feel that you were hiding something, but I couldn't tell more than that. The fires started as soon as you got home. It just made so much sense to me. You had to be the arsonist."

My mind caught on the most peculiar part of this admission. "Wow, really? It's noisy?"

"Yeah, standing near you sounds like a wind tunnel. It's as distracting as the heat. I was sure you had to be the arsonist. The sense of fire, and the feeling that you were hiding something from everyone pretty much clinched it for me." He shrugged. "I never would have guessed that you're a..."

"Fire mage?"

"Yeah, that. Whatever that is."

"When did you first start noticing that you could feel things from other people?" We crossed the grass toward the swing set.

"Actually, it was just before you left for Venice."

He sat on a swing and I took the one beside him. The hinges squeaked as we swung back and forth, scraping our feet against the dirt.

"It wasn't as strong then," he continued. "But one of the reasons I convinced Mom and Dad to let you go to Venice was because I could feel how sorry you were about hurting me. It made me take pity on you."

I looked down at the hard-packed earth between my feet. An arrow of regret and shame sliced through me at the memory of what I had done. I had been so angry at Jack that night that I had thrown him out of his room. I hadn't meant for him to slip and hit the doorjamb, but that's what happened. He'd cut his face and chipped a tooth. I'd never forgive myself for it.

"Don't feel that way," Jack said, quietly.

I gaped at him. "What, you can read thoughts now?"

"No, I can't read thoughts. But I can feel what you're feeling. You're still punishing yourself for it. I don't want that." He shifted on his swing like he was sitting on a thistle. "I might have wanted it if I couldn't feel what's in your heart. We want people to feel sorry when they've hurt us. But it's..." he struggled for the right words. His face looked so young under the park lights and I was reminded that he was only fifteen.

"Out of proportion?" I offered.

He nodded enthusiastically. "Yes, you get it. And how you feel makes me feel even worse."

"But you're the one who was hurt—you shouldn't feel worse."

"I know. It doesn't really make sense. But I could feel how much you're punishing yourself, how mad you are at yourself. I don't like it."

I considered this. "This new ability of yours, is it hard to live with?"

"It's annoying as hell," he said, with passion. He rubbed his face vigorously, making his cheeks pink.

"Don't you think it's weird that we both have these strange abilities now?" I said. "I mean, as a ratio of supernatural person to normal person in the world, you'd think the odds of two supernatural types ending up in one family were nil to zero."

"You think my ability is supernatural?" He blinked at me as though the thought had never occurred to him before.

"Of course it is. How many people do you know who can actually *feel* someone else's emotions?" There were those who were more empathetic than others, but far as I knew, the fact that Jack could feel my heat and hear my fire sent him rocketing way outside of normal.

"Yeah, but what good is it? I can't make flames, like you." He gave me a lopsided grin.

I laughed. "I think your ability will turn out to be much more useful than mine in the long run."

"I doubt it," he mumbled. He wrapped his arms around the chains and clasped his hands in front of them. "It's hard to tell where my own feelings end and the other person's starts. That's why I had to leave the table that night that you told us what happened to you. I could feel Mom's heartbreak, RJ's amazement. He thinks it's really cool, by the way." He shot me a side-eye. "And he's kind of jealous."

"Really?" But my mind had caught on something else. "Mom is heartbroken?"

"Yeah, of course!" He looked surprised that I didn't know this already. "You're not her little girl anymore. She feels like your future has been stolen from you. In a way, she feels like she's experiencing a death. Dad's really angry, or at least he was before you went to England. He came back feeling way better. He had some really violent feelings about what he would have done to Dante if he had been there." He stopped suddenly, catching the horror on my face. "Sorry, Saxony."

My heart was pounding and I was gripping the cold chains tightly. My breathing had gone shallow. I closed my eyes and took a deep breath.

"I shouldn't have said all of that, I'm sorry."

"No, it's okay," I said. "Better to know the reality. Do you think Mom will agree to let me go to England?"

He nodded. “Dad’s already convinced her. They were up late last night. I could feel the conflict go like a heat wave through the house. I couldn’t sleep until they came to an agreement.”

“But they did come to an agreement?”

We got up and began to head back towards home.

Jack peered over at me. “They did. Looks like we have to say goodbye again.”

I nodded. “Yeah. I guess we do.” I threw an arm over my brother’s neck and kissed his forehead. “I’m glad you’re not mad at me anymore.”

When I released him, he rubbed his temple, looking pink and embarrassed. “Do that again and I will be.”

“Oh, whatever,” I said and shoved him sideways into a bush.

The Beginning.

AFTERWORD

I hope you enjoyed Saxony's origin story. She came to me as a character fully formed while I was living in—you guessed it—Venice. I've lived in many magical places, the Dolomites, the Canadian Rockies, the coast of the Mediterranean in Asia Minor, but I have to say that Venice is special in a way that nowhere else can possibly match. I knew that I had to use it as a setting for a story, and I knew that I wanted my main character to be a spitfire with a heart of gold.

Every main character in this series is a favourite of a subset of readers, but Saxony and Targa seem to have pulled ahead of the rest. I couldn't let Saxony go after writing her origin story, and she ended up having five more book which follow her through her *Arcturus Academy* experience.

The next main character in our group of girlfriends to have an adventure that changes her life forever is Georjayna Sutherland. Follow her as she travels to Ireland expecting to have a pleasant summer vacation and finds a dangerous family secret and strange cocoons growing in her aunt's greenhouse.

Turn the page and read the excerpt for a taste of Georjie's story, and if you feel so compelled to post a review for this story, I'd sure appreciate it. Thanks for reading from the bottom of my heart.

Love

Abby

Asia Minor, 2023

EXCERPT FROM BORN OF EARTH

PROLOGUE

I have never been a diary kind of girl. Yet here I sit, laptop open, fingers flying. I'm imagining you are my future child or grandchild, it helps to think we're related and that maybe these words will help you.

It's the end of the most mind-blowing, amazing, disruptive, life-changing summer of my life. I am not sure how I could have understood the happenings and changes I faced these past two months without the scribblings of an ancestor. And with that, I have become... a diary girl.

In a few days, I'll see my best friends - friends who have become my family. I haven't decided how to tell them what happened to me, who I've become, what I am. I'm still trying to figure that out myself. I don't want to spook them, especially with what I've learned about Saltford, our hometown. I guess I'll worry about that when time comes. For now, I'm going back. Back to the evening I last saw them, and back to a place of blissful ignorance.

ONE

I closed the front door and leaned against it, sighing. Alone again. Our gigantic foyer echoed with the sound of my footsteps as I crossed the marble expanse in my Jimmy Choo flip flops, past our restaurant-sized but mostly un-used kitchen, through our quadruple sliding patio doors and into our perfectly-kept-by-complete-strangers back yard.

I dumped the melted ice from four used iced-tea glasses, stacked them, and folded the blankets, still warm from the bodies of my best friends - Targa, Saxony, and Akiko. My friends were gone for the summer. Our goodbyes had been said.

These are the girls who know that all it takes to make me cry is a video of a horse running in slow motion - I'm not kidding - the waterworks just start. These are the girls who know how to get me laughing so hard I get cramps. These are the girls who know that I left anonymous love-notes inside Gregory Handler's shoe in Grade 4.

A hollow feeling buckled my knees. The familiar metallic glint of loneliness soured in my mouth and I plopped down in one of the deck chairs. The dark sky, so beautiful in its star-speckled glory while my friends were here, now looked like it was going to swallow me in its cold gaping maw. I stared into the dying embers. The insects had stopped singing and the fire had run out of heat. Silence stuffed my ears in one of those moments where you wonder if you've actually gone deaf. The dwindling fire gave a snap and confirmed I hadn't lost my hearing, just my besties for the summer.

The grinding hum of our garage door alerted me that Liz was home. Liz was about to get some happy news. Targa's last-minute opportunity to go to Poland with her mom meant that I'd be leaving, too. Decision made. Ireland, here I come. I hadn't been planning on leaving. It had been twelve years since I'd been to visit my Aunt Faith, she's practically a stranger. Then again, so is Liz. So what's the difference? Stay home in Saltford with my laptop? Or get on a plane and visit the Emerald Isle for the summer?

I loaded my arms with the blankets and took them inside. "Liz?" I closed the patio door behind me with my toes.

"In here, Poppet," she answered from her home office, in her manufactured aristocratic English accent. *Poppet.* Why is it that when a term of endearment isn't delivered with any actual affection it sounds like you're calling over a barnyard animal? Perhaps a piglet?

Liz should have an Irish accent, like my Aunt Faith does, but not long after she made partner she took classes to train herself to sound British. Why? No idea. Maybe she thinks legalese comes out better in an English accent.

I dumped the smoky blankets in the laundry hamper and padded down our plushly-carpeted hallway, silent as a panther. I swear you could drop a dead body down our stairs and you wouldn't hear a thing. Targa takes off her socks just so she can feel the thick softness of our carpet with her toes. I can't bring myself to do the same, I hate the feeling of bare feet. My soles are too sensitive. Every little piece of dirt, pokey bit of carpet, or blade of grass feels magnified.

"Hey," I poked my head into Liz's office. She was already pecking away rapid-fire on her laptop, a stack of file folders at her right hand, her Prada bifocals perched on the end of her nose. Her hair looked like it hadn't budged since she left at 5:45 on the nose this morning. "Got a minute?"

"Just. What is it?" She didn't look up from the keyboard, and her fingers flew faster if that was possible. Any moment now, they could start smoking.

"I'm going to go to Ireland for the summer. Like you wanted."

That got her attention. She looked up. Lines creased her forehead as she peered over her glasses, her bionic fingers momentarily paused. "You are? What happened, I thought you and Targa were going to hang out, camp, that sort of thing. Isn't that what you said last week? I'm sure that's what you said."

Camp? I hate camping. Seriously?

She took off her glasses and put the end bit in her mouth. I could see the gears turning, the drawers of files opening and closing in her mind as she searched for the most up to date information. "Did you and Targa have a falling out?"

Targa and I never fight. If Liz had ever observed us together or ever asked me anything about my best friend, she'd know that.

"No. Targa is going to Poland, last minute decision. No point in me hanging about the house by myself all summer. I thought you'd be happy." I stepped inside and sat in one of the two matching leather chairs facing her desk, like a client. I crossed my ankles and folded my hands in my lap. Might as well play the part, make her feel at home. My physical sarcasm was lost on her.

"I am happy, Poppet. That's great. Call Denise on Monday and she'll set you up with flights. She's updated your passport already, so you're good to go." She put her glasses on and attacked her keyboard again. Denise is Liz's secretary. She makes sure I don't miss a dental cleaning, a haircut or a manicure (I don't do pedicures. Ugh). They all happen like clockwork. Thanks, Denise.

"Are you going to talk to Aunt Faith? I mean, she already said I can come, right?"

Liz didn't look up. "Yes, Poppet. She's good with it. Denise will settle everything with her next week. She'll even pick you up from the train station. Faith, not Denise, obviously." Liz was especially adept at clarity-to-go. I think it's a lawyer thing.

"I have to take a train?"

"Fly to Dublin, train to Anacullough. You don't remember?" *Type. Type. Type.*

"I was five."

"Denise will explain, it's easy. Ireland's public transport is excellent."

"Excellent." I watched her type. I cleared my throat.

She blinked up at me, then back down. "You'll have fun. Jasher will be there too, your cousin. You'll have a friend to play with."

Wow. Did she really just say that I'd have a friend to play with? What was I, three?

"What's he like?"

She frowned. "I don't know, never met him. You know that. I'm sure he's lovely."

"Well, how old is he? I know he's older than me but by how much? What does he do? Is he a baseball kind of guy, or a movie-buff?"

She blinked. I'd bewildered her with these questions about her adopted nephew. She wasn't prepared. She hated not being prepared. "Ah," she said, holding up a finger. She opened one of her many desk drawers. Rummaged. Closed the drawer. Opened another one. Rummaged. She pulled out a stack of envelopes wrapped with an elastic band. She plopped them on the edge of her desk with a thwack and set her shoulders back triumphantly. "There you are."

"What are these?" I crossed the expanse to her desk and picked up the stack of letters. Elegant handwritten scrawl. Postmarked from Ireland.

"Letters from your Aunt Faith. Once you've read those you'll know everything I know about Jasher, and you'll be all caught up on the goings on over there." She waved her fingers as though doing a spell. Embarrassment over her lack of information, magically averted.

"Looks like I'll know *more* than you, Liz. Half of these aren't even open." I thumbed through the stack.

"Good!" She looked up and flashed me one last winning smile.

"Good," I echoed. I stood there for a moment, bathing in the sound of typing. In her mind, I was gone already. "Okay, I'm going to go numb myself with technology now."

She glanced up as briefly as blinking. "Okay, Poppet. Have fun."

I left, the carpet muffling the sound of my exit.

BOOKS BY A.L. KNORR

Elemental Origins Series

Born of Water (Targa)

Born of Fire (Saxony)

Born of Earth (Georjayna)

Born of Æther (akiko)

Born of Air (petra)

The Elementals (The ensemble story)

The Elemental Origins Boxed Set (the Completed Series)

Mermaid's Return (Mira's story)

Returning

FALLING

Surfacing

Mermaid's Return, the complete box set

The Siren's Curse (Targa)

Salt & Stone

Salt & the Sovereign

Salt & the Sisters

Earth Magic Rises (Georjie)

Bones of the Witch

Ashes of the Wise

Heart of the Fae

Arcturus Academy (Saxony)

Firecracker

Fire Trap

Fire Games

Legends of Fire

Source Fire

The Scented Court

A Blossom At midnight

A memory of nightshade

A Daughter of Winter

A Prince of Autumn

The Rings of the Inconquo (Ibby's story)

Born of Metal

Metal Guardian

Metal Angel

Elemental Novellas

Heat, A Fire Novella

The Kacy Chronicles

Descendant

Ascendant

Combatant

Transcendent

Visit www.alknorrbooks.com to sign up for A.L. Knorr's newsletter.
Get notifications for new releases and free stories.

ABOUT THE AUTHOR

A.L. Knorr is a USA Today bestselling author and award-winning fantasy writer. She is Abby or even Abs to friends and family. She's Canadian but lives on the Mediterranean coast with her husband, a talented chef—which is handy because she struggles with toast. Since leaving Canada she has traded in her snowboard and mountain bike for bottles of sunscreen and a snorkel. Why not hang out where the mermaids are? They love the Mediterranean too.

Visit www.alknorrbooks.com to learn more or to connect with Abby.